DEADLOCK

Quintin Jardine
DEADLOCK

HEADLINE

First published in 2021 by
HEADLINE PUBLISHING GROUP

1

Cataloguing in Publication Data is available from the British Library

978 1 4722 8281 1 (Hardback)
978 1 4722 8282 8 (Trade paperback)

Elf Illustration © Sebastian ignacio coll/Shutterstock

Typeset in Electra by Avon DataSet Ltd, Arden Court, Alcester, Warwickshire

Printed and bound in Great Britain by Clays Ltd, Elcograf S.p.A.

HEADLINE PUBLISHING GROUP
An Hachette UK Company
Carmelite House
50 Victoria Embankment
London EC4Y 0DZ

www.headline.co.uk
www.hachette.co.uk

This work is dedicated to Fiona Purves, and to Sunny the Second. Without them I would never have got through the last year and it would never have been written.

One

'What the fuck is that?' Sarah asked, staring at the screen of her husband's laptop.

'It's my Mental Elf,' Sir Robert Morgan Skinner replied. 'I'm very aware of him and protective of him too, all things considered. The virus can get you in all sorts of ways, even without your being infected. I have to say, Professor Grace,' he added, 'that your language has taken a turn for the worse over the last couple of weeks.'

'Can you blame it?' his wife protested. 'Two weeks of confinement with you would have sent Saint Teresa of Calcutta into industrial paroxysms. I've been looking back over our eventful years, and I don't think we've spent this length of time together, exclusively, since our honeymoon . . . our first one, that is.'

He gazed at her. 'Are we all right after it? Apart from your vocabulary.'

'Which is still less colourful than yours.' She reached across and grabbed a lock of his thick steel-grey hair, which was longer

1

than she had ever seen it. 'Yeah, we're good. Never better in fact, now that we've come through on the other side of fucking Covid.' She brandished a print-out of the email that confirmed their negative test results.

His frown was sudden, and deep. 'Not everybody has.'

'No,' she sighed. 'Poor Xavi, losing Sheila to the monster; that is tragic. Will he get over it?'

'Who knows?' Bob sighed. 'Xavi internalises everything. My guess is that he'll work even harder, for their daughter's sake. Paloma might be his salvation.'

'You're probably his best friend. Do you want to go over to Girona, spend some time with the two of them?'

'I'm over there regularly on business,' he pointed out. 'But maybe I could stay longer next time, knowing that I have antibodies in my bloodstream. Meanwhile, we have our own family to catch up with. I've never missed the kids, all of them, as much as I do now. Talking to them through the window isn't the same, and,' he added, 'God knows how the home schooling's been going, unsupervised.'

'I know,' she admitted. 'I've missed Dawn especially. If we hadn't had Alex to look after them, I don't know what we'd have done. Even so, it's really been tough not being able to hold my baby.'

Bob Skinner had contracted Covid-19 on a January business visit to Spain, for a board meeting of Intermedia, the Spanish company owned by his friend Xavier Aislado: he had become a director after leaving the police service. He had opted to fly to Girona in the recently acquired corporate Gulfstream jet, rather than take scheduled flights to Barcelona via London, in the expectation that the risk of second-wave infection would be less. He had taken Sarah along for what was for her a short vacation, a break from her duties as a pathologist, which had become stressful almost beyond endurance in pandemic conditions.

The trip had been a disaster. On the third day, Sheila Craig, Xavi's Scottish wife, had been hit by severe coronavirus symptoms. The Skinners had flown home immediately, and had gone into quarantine, only for Bob to test positive two days later. Sarah had been vaccinated in late December because of her profession, but she had been required to self-isolate with him. Bob's symptoms had been mild, limited to a cough and bizarre changes to his sense of smell, but he knew that he had been one of the lucky ones, a fact underlined on the twelfth day of their isolation, when Xavi had called them through FaceTime. 'Your daughter Alex told me that you've recovered, Bob. Sadly, I have to tell you that my lovely Sheila did not. She passed away last night.'

'Are you ready to go?' Sarah asked.

'What? Yes. Sorry,' he replied. Not for the first time over the last few days, he had been lost in contemplation of how he would have felt had things gone another way and he had been in his friend's shoes. He stood and picked up the small case that held their clothing. He smiled lightly. 'Let's make the long journey home. We'll still be locked down, but it'll be nice to have a bit more room.'

Sarah led the way out of the small apartment that had been built above their garage block as accommodation for Ignacio, Bob's son from a relationship in the dying days of the last century. He was absent from the household; at university when lockdown was called, he had opted to shelter with Pilar, his girlfriend, in Perthshire with his mother, Mia, and his stepfather, Cameron McCullough. Bob had been irked by his choice, not least because he had been keeping Grandpa McCullough at a distance, after a situation a year before. They walked across the turning area at the end of their driveway, but before they reached the front door it was opened from inside and their younger sons emerged from the main house. Trish, the children's live-in carer, had been stranded in Barbados since December, having visited her parents for Christmas. The boys and their younger sisters had been looked after during their parents' isolation by Alexis, Bob's daughter from his first marriage. She had been able to combine the role with her professional life, which had become largely virtual. She had left for Edinburgh that morning as soon as their test results had been confirmed, pleading a need to catch up with her correspondence.

'Are you two not schooling?' Bob exclaimed.

'It's Saturday, Dad,' James Andrew exclaimed, in a deeper voice than either of his parents had heard before. To his mother, Jazz seemed a little taller, a little wider in the shoulders.

Skinner laughed. 'So it is. In there, every day was like the one before. Hey,' he added, 'remember that chat we had about puberty a year or so back? Seems to me you've dropped an octave in a fortnight.'

'He's got zits too,' Mark volunteered. 'And his—'

'Nobody's exempt from those,' his adoptive father reminded him, raising an eyebrow as he cut him off in mid-sentence. The teenage Mark looked different too; Bob realised that the down on his top lip was missing. *Christ, he's started shaving,* Bob thought. *Even in a couple of weeks I've missed part of their lives.*

'You guys had breakfast?' he asked.

'Dad, it's half past ten,' Jazz pointed out. 'We're thinking about lunch. Haven't you and Mum been eating over there?'

'Time's been a little fluid,' Sarah confessed. 'Your father's been watching Australian cricket from God knows what hour. He's tended to forget about mundane things like mealtimes. I've been reading medical articles about Covid, so I wasn't best placed to remind him.'

'What I need most is exercise,' Bob confessed. 'I'm going for a run. Do you guys want to come with me?' Mark stared at him. 'Okay son, I know that was a rhetorical question for you. Jazz, you up for it?'

'Can we do that? Go out for a run?'

'As long as we don't mix with other households, I believe we can.'

'Okay. I'll take it easy on you, Dad. I mean, you have been locked up for a fortnight.'

He nodded. 'Tell you what, pal, you be the hare, I'll be the tortoise. That way you don't have to take anything easy.'

'Oh dear,' Sarah murmured. 'I've been dreading the day when it becomes really competitive between you two. It seems that it's here. But Bob, are you sure? I mean—'

'I had no symptoms. I'll be fine.'

Two

'Well, how's the tortoise?' Sarah asked as her husband stepped into the kitchen, carrying his muddy trainers. She was leaning against the work surface, with the toddler Dawn on her hip.

'Thoroughly knackered,' Skinner admitted, breathing heavily. His tracksuit top was sodden with sweat. 'The hare put on a sprint at the end and won by a couple of hundred yards. I tell you, I might have been mostly asymptomatic, love, but it's had an effect. That was far more than just being out of shape.'

'In that case, I'd better keep an eye on you for a couple of days. We don't know nearly enough about the longer-term effects of the virus.' Sarah paused. 'Speaking of tortoises, Neil called.'

Neil McIlhenney had acquired the tortoise nickname after his appointment to the top job in the Scottish police service, after the resignation of Margaret Rose Steele, overtaking his closest friend and virtual twin, Mario McGuire, in the process. All three had been protégés of Skinner during his time as chief of the former Edinburgh police service, before its replacement by the national force, but McIlhenney had lagged behind the others in rank, until a move to London and the Metropolitan Police had given new impetus to his career. In fact, there had been no contest for the post between the former Glimmer Twins, because McGuire had not applied.

'The chief constable?' Bob exclaimed. 'What did he want?'

'To congratulate us on our recovery,' she replied.

'How the hell did he know we were . . . ?'

'Alex posted the good news on her Facebook page. "Now it can be revealed that my parents have emerged safe and sound from the viral nightmare," she wrote.'

'I'll be having words with my oldest daughter about that,' he declared. 'I'm sure I said to keep quiet about it when I told her we had tested negative.'

'Don't do that,' Sarah advised. 'The danger's over and now we're a good news story. I've had calls myself. By the way, Neil said he couldn't get through on your mobile.'

'That's because it's upstairs. I didn't bother taking it. Didn't you notice? Oh thanks, darling, just what I needed,' he added, as Seonaid, his middle daughter, twenty-three years younger than her half-sister Alexis, handed him an energy drink. He glanced at her mother. 'Can I talk about lunch now?'

'There's a big pasta salad in the fridge,' Seonaid told him. 'Alex made it, after she took Dawn and me for a walk down to the beach.'

Bob grinned. 'I suppose that makes up for her Facebook indiscretion. I'm off to shower.' He headed for the stairs, removing the sodden top as he walked, awkwardly switching his drink from hand to hand. He peeled off the rest of his clothing in the bedroom, dumping it in a basket before heading for the shower in the en-suite, whistling a Runrig tune that had been in his head all morning.

It was still nagging away at him as he dressed. His post-run fatigue had faded, but a heaviness unlike anything he could remember remained in his legs. He went to his bedside and unplugged his phone from its charger. The screen lit up showing that he had seven missed calls. He checked the list; the first was from Ignacio, the second from an unidentified mobile number, the third from Mia McCullough, the next from McIlhenney, followed by Maggie Steele, then Mario McGuire, and finally June Crampsey, the editor of the *Saltire*, Intermedia's flagship Scottish newspaper. She was one of only four people outside the household who had known of his Covid diagnosis, the others being Alex, Xavi Aislado and Sarah's deputy in the pathology department.

Four of the callers had left voicemail. He listened to the messages; Ignacio managed to sound both relieved and angry at the same time, his accent even more Spanish than usual. 'You keep this secret from me, Padre. Am I not entitled to worry about my father and his wife? I tell my sister this too: Alex had no business keeping it from me.'

He sent a text in reply. 'Sorry, Nacho. I should have told you, but I didn't feel ill, so I didn't see the need.'

The other messages were from Mia, Maggie, and Mario, all saying much the same thing, 'Happy to hear you and Sarah are okay.' He resolved to call them all, but gave priority to the editor. Crampsey reported to him and with her it was always business first. She had emailed him several times during the isolation, mostly updating him on the newspaper and on the online edition that had been launched the summer before.

'What's up?' Skinner asked as she picked up his call, mimicking her abrupt style.

'You are,' she replied. 'I've had calls from most of the rivals, asking about Alex's Facebook post. They wanted to know if you really have recovered. I think a couple were hoping you hadn't.'

'I could almost tell you who they were,' he grunted.

'You have, haven't you? Recovered, that is.'

'I thought I had until Jazz showed me different. Covid leaves its mark on everybody, I reckon, symptoms or not.'

'And Sarah?'

'She's good. Yes, she's had both doses of the Pfizer vaccine, but nothing's a hundred per cent effective, so it was a worrying few days for me.'

'Can I publish the fact that you had it?'

'If the rest are going to,' he agreed, 'of course you can . . . as long as you don't downplay the seriousness of it. I didn't recognise any of the common symptoms in myself, but there is anxiety involved. Who wouldn't be scared by the prospect of ending their days dry-drowning in an intensive care ward full of strangers, cut off from their loved ones? I don't mind admitting that I was, until our negative tests came through this morning.'

'I don't suppose I can use all that as a quote?' Crampsey ventured.

'Why shouldn't you?'

'Because it's not like you. You always downplay things.'

'Not this. That would be irresponsible.' He frowned. 'Have we reported Sheila's death?'

'Sheila?'

'Xavi didn't tell you?' he exclaimed. 'She died two days ago.

We should report it, with an obituary; she was an Edinburgh woman, and she was an important part of the *Saltire* family. We shouldn't do it without Xavi's consent, though. Leave it with me. I'll talk to him this afternoon. As for Sarah and me, please report that as I described it. The virus affects you in all sorts of ways; all the vaccine sceptics need to know. Agreed?'

'Of course. Would you say all that in a feature?'

'If I can write it myself.'

'Deal.'

'It'll be with you by four.'

Next, Skinner turned his attention to Neil McIlhenney, summoning his mobile number from his contact list. 'Chief Constable,' he said as his call was answered. The thought of his friend at the top of the mountain still gave him a surge of satisfaction. It was an outcome no one would have predicted twenty years earlier, but the man had possessed a storehouse of unsuspected potential that had been uncovered, piece by piece. 'How's the family?'

'Great, and very happy to be back up north. I would not fancy London right now.'

'Scotland's no barrel of laughs, mate,' he pointed out. 'I guess you're busy with lockdown breakers.'

'Across the country,' McIlhenney admitted. 'Brian Mackie's coordinating our responses to infractions, making sure that we're being even-handed, that Dingwall, Dundee and Drumchapel are being treated in exactly the same way. So,' he continued, 'you and Sarah had a brush with the bug. Handy for you, being isolated with a doctor.'

'Aye,' Bob chuckled. 'If it had come to it, she could have done my autopsy without ever leaving the flat. As it turned out that wasn't necessary; I had a few uncomfortable days but not bad. I have some recovering to do, though. How's Lauren? Has she had any long-term effects?'

The chief constable's daughter had contracted the virus a few months earlier when it had swept through her student accommodation. 'Not that she's told me, although she did say that it took her a few weeks to shake off the residual tiredness. I suppose you've got a vested interest in asking that.'

'I suppose I have, but that wasn't why I did. Is she back in Glasgow?'

'Yes.' Skinner thought he heard a chuckle. 'I tell you, Bob, I'll be astonished if there isn't a population surge this year, among late teens and early twenties. I don't mind telling you, I had a word with her before she went back.'

'I don't agree with that guess,' he countered. 'I suspect that most of the young females are on the pill. I'm sure you're right about the birth rate overall, but my forecast is that it'll be more noticeable among the older age groups, unexpected additions to existing families and so on.'

'You got any evidence to back that up?'

'Personally, no,' Skinner laughed, 'but it's the way I'd bet. There will be all sorts of spin-off from this. Social media's going crazy, globally and locally. You can use it to start a revolution, or you can use it to tell your brother to get out of the bathroom, like my middle daughter did the other day.'

'Seonaid?' McIlhenney exclaimed.

'Yup; I gave in and got her a phone for her last birthday. We have a family WhatsApp group, believe it or not, and she's a major player. Mark set it up; Mark sets everything up. He's doing coding classes online, teaching I mean; he has his own website, and it makes him money. The boy is something of a genius. I doubt that there's anything he can't do on a computer.'

'That could be worrying, could it not?'

'Tell me about it, Neil. I had a talk with him a while back about setting limits for himself, about where not to go exploring. Fortunately, he's more interested in maintaining our security than in breaching other people's. The nuclear deterrent is safe.'

'Our kids are getting away from us, Bob,' McIlhenney sighed.

'Not that far. Alex left home about fifteen years ago, but we're still close.'

'How is she? Is she still with our friend Doctor Jackson?'

'She never was with him, not in that way. He saw her through a crisis, got her back in emotional shape. They're close, yes, but it's a friendship, no more, of that I'm sure.'

'She got a mention in the papers the other day, after her latest successful prosecution. What made her become an Advocate Depute? Last I heard she was committed to being a defence counsel.'

'Two words. Griff Montell. When he was murdered, and the truth came out about him, the last of her idealism disappeared and she accepted the Lord Advocate's offer. Mind you, we were all naïve when it came to Montell. He fooled us all, big time, me most of all. Now,' Skinner said, abruptly. 'What can I do for you?'

'What makes you ask that?'

'You didn't leave a message, and you called the landline as well as my mobile. You're after something.'

The chief constable sighed. 'God, you're cynical. You're also right, damn you. I want my people vaccinated, Bob. I've just seen the sickness figures. Police officers are front line and need to be given priority. I don't care what fucking Westminster says, Holyrood can take a different line.'

'Why tell me?' Skinner asked. 'What can I do about it?'

'Two things. The first is to get the *Saltire* to back it. The second, I know that you're pally with Clive Graham, the First Minister. Put some backbone into him, and bring him on board.'

'What if I don't agree with you about police priority?'

McIlhenney gasped. 'You're kidding me.'

'Yes, I am,' he chuckled, 'but you're not alone in pushing the priority case. June Crampsey was lobbied by the teaching unions a couple of days ago. She didn't give them an editorial commitment, but she did give them front-page treatment. She'll do the same for you, I'm sure.'

'Aren't you her boss?'

'I'm chair of the Intermedia UK subsidiary company and a main board director, but that doesn't make me June's boss. I may suggest, but I don't instruct. Call her, and she'll listen to you, but are you sure that's the way to play it?'

'What would you do?'

'I'd put on my best uniform, and I'd get the media department to call a press briefing, where I'd sound off to everybody about the need to vaccinate police officers now that the elderly are pretty much done. Then I'd tell the First Minister to grow a pair and do the right thing for Scotland rather than following Westminster's lead. You do that and I will talk to Clive behind the scenes. I'm not saying he'll bite, but obviously he has no love for the Prime Minister.'

'Okay,' McIlhenney agreed. 'I'll play it that way. Hopefully, Graham will have an attack of common sense. I'll do it on Monday.'

'No, tomorrow. Nothing happens on a Sunday. You'll get better coverage.'

'If you say so.'

'My recommendation,' Skinner said. 'Your choice.' He paused for a second. 'Apart from your sick-leave figures, what else is the virus affecting?'

'On the positive side,' the chief constable replied, 'petty crime is down significantly. Bad times for housebreakers, with everybody at home. Then there's sport; football being behind closed doors, therefore not needing to be policed, that frees up a hell of a lot of uniform time. The pubs being shut, we're seeing the same effect, especially in the city centres. Then there's traffic; fewer cars on the road equates to fewer RTAs. I've got somebody doing the sums to see what the savings are. On the negative side,' he continued, 'there's more domestic violence . . . although maybe not as much as you'd think. Then there are the suicide figures. When the stats are published there'll be a spike in those, for sure. I don't know what we can do about that.'

'I do. We need to encourage more self-help groups.'

'We? You mean the police?'

Skinner laughed. 'No, I don't. That was the media mogul speaking. We need groups of volunteers in every community, identifying the vulnerable and the lonely, and bringing them inside the sheltering bubble. Social media can help too: yes, it may be a menace, but it's also positive when it's used properly. Its purpose is, or should be, to bring people together, not drive them apart.'

'I'm glad that you're moving on, Bob,' McIlhenney remarked quietly.

'What do you mean?'

'That you're starting to cut the cords that tied you to the police service. You must have noticed that you haven't heard from Mario in a while. Not about police business, at any rate.'

'Maybe,' he admitted. 'I assumed that meant things were quiet, as they are.'

'Yeah but . . . Look, Bob, I know you've been mentoring young officers, the likes of Sauce Haddock, and I know how hands-on you've been in a few major investigations. But the thing is, Maggie was always more committed to your continuing role than Mario. Everything you've done, well, it's appreciated, but the view now, Mario's and mine, is that we'd prefer to keep you at arm's length from now on. Not least because if you have insider knowledge of stuff that's going on, there could be a conflict of interest with your media role.'

'I've always been aware of that,' Skinner countered, 'and I've made sure that no conflicts have ever arisen. My media role's potentially beneficial too. Christ, man, this call began with you asking me for a favour through the *Saltire*.'

'I know,' McIlhenney agreed, 'and I'd like to keep that relationship.'

'But you want me to hand in my Special Constable warrant card?'

'No, but I'd like you to frame it and hang it over the fireplace, so to speak.'

'Okay, I will . . . figuratively. But,' he warned, 'if Sauce, or Lottie Mann, or Jack McGurk, or anybody else from my old team ever want to call me for advice, in confidence, I won't be hanging up on them.'

'I don't expect you to, and I won't prevent them from doing that either . . . not least because I'm sure I'll be calling you myself from time to time. Okay?'

'Aye, okay. You can fuck off now.' He chuckled. 'You've got to set up your press event, and I've got a feature to write for June.'

As he ended the call, Skinner reflected on McIlhenney's awkwardness. He could have made it easier for him by telling him at the outset that he had decided for himself that the cords that bound him to his former career would have to be loosened, and if necessary, cut. Almost a year before, in the wake of Maggie Steele's unexpected burn-out and resignation, he had been invited to lunch in the Honours by Steven Lennon. He respected the recently appointed Lord Advocate, but the man was famously intense; for that reason he had doubted that the invitation was purely social, but the agenda had remained hidden until the coffee stage.

'Bob,' his host had begun. 'Some of us have been considering the situation with the police force. After the blip caused by the unfortunate first appointment, the general view was that Chief Constable Steele had done a good job in securing public acceptance of the new system. She even seemed to have brought you on-side, one of the most vocal opponents of a national police service.'

'I live in the real world,' he had retorted. 'That means, when politicians fuck it up, I have to accept it and live with it along with everyone else.'

'Fair enough, but you are doing that, and it's appreciated. It's known to insiders that you've been helping the police leadership informally, looking after detectives with potential. You were very much hands-on in the Montell investigation.'

'I knew the guy, or thought I did. I was cleaning up my own mess.'

'And clean it up you did. Look, Bob, let me cut to the chase.

We are about to advertise the vacancy created by Mrs Steele's departure, and I want to point out to you that applications will not be restricted to serving officers.'

Skinner's stare had shown real astonishment. 'You're asking me if I want my old job back?'

'I suppose I am. You're not wedded to your media work, after all.'

'That's where you're wrong, Steve. I am. Yes, I was brought on to the board by a friend. We both took a chance that I'd be any good at it, but as it's transpired, I am. The business is expanding in the UK, a subsidiary board has been created and I'm its chair. I couldn't walk away now, even if I wanted to . . . which I don't. Besides, you can't afford me.'

'The salary is nearly a quarter of a million, Bob.'

'Exactly. I'd be taking a fifty per cent pay cut; nearer eighty per cent if you work it out on a daily basis. Sorry, Steve, you're not on. The fact is, I know I could apply, you didn't have to tell me. Yes, I have considered it but no, it is not something I want to do. So, thanks for lunch, but no thanks. Now, you're new in your job. I've worked with half a dozen like you, so is there any advice I can give you?'

He had left the restaurant more focused on his new life than ever and more determined to back off from the old one. McIlhenney's appointment had pleased him; indeed, he had provided a reference, something he had declined to do for two other candidates. His decision to distance himself had been made easier by the onset of the pandemic, but he had noticed a lessening of the regular phone calls from the Command Corridor, as he still thought of it, a hangover from the Edinburgh days. The only surprise about McIlhenney's formal intimation was that it had taken so long.

Skinner moved downstairs, heading for his office but looking into the kitchen as he passed. His eyebrows rose as he saw James Andrew at the work surface, plugging in a blender. 'What the . . . ?' he exclaimed.

'Starting dinner, Dad,' Jazz said. 'Carrot and coriander soup. You don't think Alex has been cooking everything for us, do you? She's been in court most days, virtually, in your office.'

'Are you telling me that Mark's been cooking?' he asked, sceptically.

'Hell no! He's been food shopping . . . with a list, before you ask . . . but I'm too fond of my sisters to let him in here.'

'Er . . . he's too young to buy beer, and you've been leaving Corona for me at the door.'

'Don't worry, you've got plenty,' his son promised. 'Alex did a Tesco run for that, and for her own supplies.'

'So what's the main course?'

'Chicken cacciatore with orzo.'

'You what!' Bob gasped.

'Mark sourced the recipe. He's good for that.'

'I guess. A word of advice, Jazz. Curb your enthusiasm or you may have a job for life.'

'Fine, but I don't come cheap.'

He left his son to concentrate on his blender, stepping across the hall and into his office. As he switched on his computer, he saw that several software updates were due but scheduled them to be done overnight. His first priority was his business email, which had heavy traffic seven days a week. The working language of Intermedia was Castilian Spanish, in which he had made himself fluent. In the office in Girona, Catalan was spoken; he had a working knowledge of that also but did not regard himself as literate. He had cleared five messages when his ringtone sounded. Checking the screen, he saw the unknown number that had registered earlier. Frowning, he clicked 'Accept'.

'Bob.'

Skinner recognised the voice instantly, and felt himself tense.

'What the fuck do you want?' he snapped.

Three

'The thing I miss most about CID is being able to wear my own clothes,' Inspector Noele McClair said.

'You don't like the uniform, ma'am?' Constable Tiggy Benjamin asked.

'Honestly, I hate it; comfort counts for nothing alongside functionality and political correctness. The buzz phrase is "non-gender specific", Tigs. Within this vehicle, I think that's bollocks, even though that's a gender specific description. In the immortal words of Tammy Wynette, "Sometimes it's hard to be a woman." In the police service it's not bloody allowed! Our first chief constable signed off on it, one of his many mistakes. When Maggie Steele became chief, quite a few of us women hoped she might review it, but she never did, and now she's gone.'

'Maybe the new chief will reconsider it.'

'He's had six months to do that, but don't hold your breath. Diversity is a *sine qua non* as far as racial and social backgrounds are concerned; nobody's going to argue about that. But a non-gender-specific uniform as a matter of policy; to me it flies in the face of diversity. If ever a tail wagged a bloody dog, that's it.'

'Speaking of which,' PC Benjamin murmured, as she

20

turned the vehicle into the road that led to Gullane beach car park, 'what about that lot, ma'am? Is that within the regulations?'

McClair followed her gaze; four adults, five children and three dogs were heading across the bents towards the pathway that led down to the beach. Even from a distance she could see that none of the children appeared to be older than ten, and that none of the adults were masked. 'Park up, and check them,' she said. 'I'll stay here; one of those kids is in my Harry's class at the primary, although I don't know the parents other than by sight. If it needs action, I'd rather not be involved.'

Benjamin drove down the access road and parked on the grass, close to an array of bins. She donned her regulation bowler hat as she stepped out. Self-conscious, McClair slumped down in her seat as the constable approached the group. One of the four adults glanced at the police vehicle, but only briefly before turning his attention back to Benjamin. He appeared to be the spokesman; he held up a hand as if to stop her in mid-sentence. He was animated, but as far as she could judge, controlled. The constable nodded as he finished, a few more words were exchanged, amiably, as far as the inspector could see, before the party split into two and moved on, in different directions, the one including Harry's classmate towards the nearest beach path, the other heading for the picnic area and possibly beyond.

'Sorted,' the young officer declared as she stepped back behind the wheel. 'They're next-door neighbours, but they claimed they just happened to leave for their exercise at the same time and to be heading in the same direction. They promised me the adults maintained social distancing all the time.'

21

'And you believed all that?' McClair asked.

'No, ma'am, not a word,' Benjamin replied. 'The guy who did the talking gave me the impression it was more than my job's worth to argue with him. I would have,' she said, 'but there was no way of disproving anything, so I just nodded and wished them a nice day. Was that your son's pal's dad?'

'The very one. He's a civil servant, I believe.' She sighed. 'I have to say this is not why I joined the police force. Covid's a bastard and there have to be restrictions but we're talking about civil liberty. Instead of maintaining it, we're enforcing constraints. You handled that fine, Tiggy. I doubt that I would have been as tolerant of a would-be Sir Humphrey.'

'Who?'

She laughed. 'Before your time. Come to think of it, it's almost before mine. Come on then; we've shown the flag here, let's get along to Yellowcraigs and see what mischief's afoot there.' She glanced around the sparsely occupied car park. 'I guarantee you it'll be busier than here.'

Before Benjamin could turn on the engine, McClair's radio commanded her attention. 'Ma'am,' a male voice intoned. Immediately she recognised Hugh Jackson, the grizzled sergeant who was part of her team. 'We've had a request passed on from comms for a car to attend in Gullane. You being in the vicinity, can you take it in?'

'Attend what?' she asked.

'It's not clear. The only detail I've got is that it's a female who's having difficulty accessing a property. The address is Twelve Redway Court. It's in the new houses, according to Maps. The caller's a Mrs Granton.'

'Okay Shuggie, leave it with us. We're two minutes away.' She glanced at her driver as the radio went dead. 'Let's get moving. Just go to the Main Street and turn left and I'll find it on my phone. Redway Court,' she repeated. 'New Gullane indeed.' The expansion of the village in the recent past had been controversial, opposed by a significant number of long-term residents anxious about the impact of more family housing on the primary school and other local infrastructure. McClair, who lived on a steading development on the edge of the village, had been concerned herself, but the bonus of a massive and long-awaited extension to the school had won her over.

As Benjamin drove away from the beach, the inspector pointed to their right towards the substantial houses that overlooked the bents. Most were built of stone, and were over a hundred years old, but one was rendered in modern materials. 'Bob Skinner lives up there,' she murmured. 'Sir Robert.'

'Who's Bob Skinner?' the constable asked.

McClair smiled. *'Sic transit gloria mundi,'* she murmured.

'Who's Gloria?'

'I don't really know but she was sick in a van on Monday.'

'Why was it reported to us?'

'Never mind, Tiggy,' the inspector sighed. 'Head down Sandy Loan; it's the quickest way.'

Four

'I'm still on your shit list, then,' Sir Andrew Martin said.

'I don't have one, Andy,' Sir Robert Skinner replied, less tersely than before. 'I never had. If I have an issue with someone, either I confront it and sort it, or I decide it's not worth bothering with and forget about it.'

'I guess I'm in the second category.'

'No, you're not,' he sighed, softening. 'Granted, when you and my daughter started a relationship behind my back, that was an issue between us. When you restarted it, not so much. She was older and second time around she was in control. Truth is, Andy, when I look back on you and Alex, I feel a shade guilty.'

'You?' Martin exclaimed. 'Guilty?'

'Yes, for not telling you the truth, either time.'

'That being?'

'That you bored her, Andy,' Skinner told him. 'That's the truth of it. Oh, back then you were the great ladies' man, before Alex, and before your wife. But before them, you never had a long-term relationship, and you had no idea how to run one. After the first couple of dates with a woman, you didn't know what to do, other than the obvious, and it takes a bit more than

24

that. I could see that, I could see it while it was happening, but I never said anything.'

'I never read you as a relationship counsellor.'

'I don't pretend to be one, but over the years I've acquired a degree of self-awareness. I could see you making exactly the same mistakes as I did with Alex's mother, but I never said anything. I took Myra for granted; I was more focused on the job than on her. She craved attention and when she didn't get it from me, she went looking elsewhere. So did her daughter, with you, first time around.'

'You were happy when Alex and I split, though.'

For the first time since he had taken the call, Skinner felt himself smile. 'Of course I was fucking happy. It would have been an expensive wedding.'

'If it's not Alex, what is your issue with me?' Martin persisted. 'And don't tell me you don't have one.'

'I don't. I did, but it fell into category two, not worth bothering my arse about. I was more than annoyed by the bollocks you made of it when you finally got into the chief constable's chair. It was as if you asked yourself at every turn, "What would Skinner have done here?", then did exactly the opposite. When you got behind that desk you must have deleted my number, for I never heard a word from you. You were still involved with Alex at the time, yet you never called me.'

'Did you call Jimmy Proud when you took over from him?'

'Of course I fucking did!' Skinner exclaimed. 'At least twice a week. In the beginning I hadn't a clue what I was doing with much of the non-CID stuff that makes up the bulk of a chief constable's workload. But I learned, and it was Jimmy that helped me. You never thought to ask.' He paused. 'That, of course, is petty and egotistic on my part, but it's how I felt.

25

Legacy's an over-used word, but most of us like to think we've left something behind us when we move on. The feeling I got was that in your eyes my legacy wasn't worth having.'

'I'm sorry,' Martin said quietly. 'You're probably right. I admit I was determined to do it my way, not least because I knew that some people saw me as Bob Skinner's bag man, even after I headed the Crime Agency. I wanted to prove them wrong, didn't I? When I got into difficulties, I should have reached out to you, but I didn't. Instead I jumped into a lifeboat, rowed all the way to America, and left Maggie to pick up the bits. How is she, by the way?'

'She was burned out in the end,' Skinner told him. 'She did pick up your pieces and got the force running properly, but it took its toll on her. Cancer survivor, widowed, single parent, it was inevitable. She got out at the right time, though, and she's got it together again. I see her often and she's happier than she's been since Stevie died on duty. Pre-lockdown she visited us quite often. She took her Stephanie and our girls to the beach. She has a couple of non-executive directorships to keep the wolf at bay, and she hopes to find herself a part-time job, lecturing, like you did in the US.'

He sighed. 'It's my turn to apologise, Andy. I shouldn't have taken the hump at you keeping your distance. Neil's just told me, very gently, that he intends to do the same.'

'Has he now?' Martin murmured. 'I confess I'm still amazed by McIlhenney going all the way to the chief's office. I still think of him as a big lumbering plod, always in McGuire's shadow.'

'Then maybe that's another reason why the job wasn't for you, Andy. You can have the best admin skills in the world, but if your people management isn't up to scratch, you'll never succeed. I understand what you're saying about Neil, but you need to reject first impressions and look beneath the surface of everyone, and everything. Mario's a great detective, and always was. Neil's made himself a great all-round police officer. If anyone can make something of the misbegotten national force, he's the man.' Skinner paused. 'Now,' he boomed, 'as I asked you earlier, what the fuck do you want? If it's just to congratulate me on getting over Covid, you could have messaged me.'

'You've had Covid?'

'Just finished isolation, both Sarah and me. I was exposed visiting Spain on business. The fact you didn't know about it tells me that you don't follow Alex on Facebook. She told the world this morning.'

'I don't follow anyone on Facebook. I don't have a presence there. You don't, do you?'

'No, but I don't need one. I can keep an eye on everything through the Intermedia presence.'

'Of course,' Martin said, 'you're a newspaper magnate. I was forgetting.'

'I'm an employee,' Skinner corrected him. 'Xavi Aislado owns the show, and he runs it. That said, he has other things on his mind now. He just lost his wife. God knows how that will affect him. Come on, though,' he continued, 'back to the question. What's up?'

'I think I'm being stalked.'

'Stalked? You?'

'I can't explain it, but that's how it feels. Things have been happening to me, and around me. I first noticed it when I put an envelope of shredded mail in my recycling box, and saw that it had been disturbed.'

'What do you mean? How could you possibly tell that?'

'I'm neat, Bob, to the point of being OCD. I don't just put stuff away, I do it very carefully, and I consider what should go where. Once I've done it, I don't forget.'

'I'll grant you that, Andy,' Skinner admitted. 'That photographic memory of yours. I used to lean on it from time to time. Go on.'

'There's that, then there's the stuff that's been arriving through the post, things addressed to me that I never ordered. Shoes for a wee girl. A kid's book, *Charlie and the Chocolate Factory*. A Black Sabbath CD, for Christ's sake; I hate them. I tried to return them all but I couldn't because they don't show on my account. Then I had a mailshot from an undertaker the other day, not an email, a brochure through the letter box. I called the number and asked them what the hell they were playing at; they said it had been sent in response to a website enquiry. See what I mean, Bob?'

'That last one could be a simple system screw-up.'

'Could be but it's not.'

Skinner frowned. 'Which Black Sabbath CD?'

'Can't remember. Hold on. It's in the living room.' There was a short silence, then Martin came back online. 'It's called *Paranoid*. Second studio album, it says.'

'Had to be that,' he grunted, 'if your fear's justified. Okay, I'll buy into your stalker. How can I help?'

'I'm not afraid, Bob, I'm fucking angry. I need advice, I suppose; just to talk it through with me. Tell me what you'd do in my place.'

'I'd probably rage for a couple of days, then I'd do the sensible thing and call the police. Where are you living now, Andy?' he asked. 'You're on a UK mobile number, but that doesn't even tell me what country you're in. Are you still in America?'

'No,' Martin replied. 'I gave that job up last summer, and moved back to Scotland to be near Karen and the kids. They're in Hamilton; I've got a place in Motherwell.'

'Sounds cosy. Are you getting back together, you and Karen?'

'No; not yet, at any rate, but we're getting on. I haven't got anyone else in my life.'

'Has she?'

'I don't ask; she doesn't say.'

'Like me with Sarah when we were getting close again,' he said. 'Is it on the cards? You and she?'

'We've never discussed it head on. I've told her that I miss being a family man. She tells me I always will be, but she knows what I mean.'

'And let me guess, you've got a toothbrush at hers.'

'Yes,' Martin admitted. 'But only because I stay over sometimes to look after the kids, if Karen's working late.'

'Is she still in uniform? I've lost touch with her career.'

'No, she's a detective chief inspector; promoted last year. She works in Lowell Payne's operation now, counter-terrorism, intelligence and the like. Okay, she's a spook of sorts but it's remote surveillance, mostly. For a lot of the time that the kids have been off school, she's been able to work from home.'

'So tell her about your problem,' Skinner suggested. 'Surely that's the thing to do?'

'I don't want to do that. If I did she might be nervous about letting me near the kids.'

'If the situation was reversed, wouldn't you feel that way?' Skinner asked.

'I suppose I would,' Martin admitted, 'but there's no risk to them, so I'd prefer it if Karen didn't know.'

'Your choice, but I'd be telling her. Regardless of that, the first thing you should do is beef up your own surveillance. If somebody's going through your bins, it tells me you don't have cameras.'

'I'm ahead of you on that one. I called in the guy who installed my alarm system; I'm having him fit six of them all around the house. I'll get alerts every time someone comes on to the property.'

'Have you pissed off anybody lately?'

'Not since I've been back, not that I know of. My profile's low, Bob. I'm not like you.'

Skinner felt his hackles stir. 'What's that supposed to mean?'

'You've never backed away from the limelight. You've always been media friendly. You can't deny it.'

'I suppose not,' he admitted. 'Once I reached senior rank, I always believed in speaking for myself rather than through spokesmen. It left less room for misunderstanding.'

'Nothing's changed, from what I've seen. You still have a high profile.'

'You seem to know a lot about me for a guy who was out of the country for a while.'

'I kept an eye on you.'

'And on Alex?'

'Yes, I admit that too. I took an interest in her career; it's still there.'

'Andy.' Skinner's tone carried a warning.

Martin read it and reassured him. 'Only from a distance.'

'Keep it that way. You focus on Karen. She's a lovely girl and if you want my advice, if she'll take you back, don't waste a second. It's worked for Sarah and me. We've never been as happy: I've never been as happy. As for Alex, don't worry about her. The Montell business hit her very hard, but she got over that with the help of family and friends; well, friend really, Dominic. She's back on form and God help the guilty. Which brings us back to your stalker. Do you have the faintest idea who it might be? Have you gone back over your CID years? Has anybody been released that might be carrying a grudge? Have you made any enemies since you've been back?'

'None. I've hardly met anyone since I've been home. As for the old days, you and I never left anyone feeling better for having met us, but there's nobody who comes to mind with the subtlety to enact what's been happening.'

'I'll do some thinking too,' Skinner promised. 'If any names come to mind, I'll reach out and see what I can find out about them. Mind you, most of them are either dead or have no wish to cross either of us again. Keep in touch . . . and Andy,' he added, 'it's good to have the old you back.'

Five

The Maps feature on McClair's phone led the officers directly to Redway Court, a cul-de-sac on the small estate that had been developed on the site of the former Scottish Fire Service Training School. As PC Benjamin drew up in a parking bay beside an apartment building, a middle-aged woman, dressed in a waxed jacket, jeans and boots, strode briskly towards them. The inspector recognised her as a familiar face around the village but struggled to recall her name.

The problem was solved at once. 'Thanks for coming so quickly,' she said, as they emerged from the vehicle. 'I'm Prue Granton; I'm a carer. I look after a gentleman in Number Twelve, Mr Stevens. I look in on him every day, but this morning I can't get a response. I've got a key and usually I let myself in, but this morning the door's on the chain, so I can't open it beyond a few inches. I've called to him but I'm getting no response. He's very deaf, so the chances are he's fallen asleep in his chair and just hasn't heard me, although that's not like him.'

'How old is Mr Stevens?' McClair asked.

'He's eighty-six. He has arthritis, and vascular dementia was diagnosed nine months ago. Poor old chap: his wife died last September, but he doesn't really understand she's gone. He

32

really shouldn't be living alone, but his daughter's against having him admitted to a care home. Between you and me, I think her concerns are more about cost than Covid.'

'I don't blame her,' Benjamin said. 'My granny died in one of those last year. A man was discharged from the Royal with Covid, and it just went through the place. Poor wee soul.' Her lips pursed, and for a second, the inspector thought that she would cry.

'Do you want to force entry?' she asked.

'I think so,' Granton replied. 'I could have, the chain's only held in place by a couple of screws but I didn't want to put my shoulder to it until you arrived.'

'There's no need for that,' McClair told her. 'We've got a bolt cutter in the car. Go get it, Tiggy,' she ordered.

'That's handy,' the carer said. She peered at her. 'Do I know you?'

'Possibly. Noele McClair. I live at West Fenton; my son Harry's at Gullane Primary.'

'I knew it. My granddaughter Kim's there too. There's a Harry in her class, but his name's Coats. That's right,' she frowned, 'his dad was . . .'

McClair finished the sentence. 'Murdered. That's right. He was my ex.'

'Oh God, sorry,' Granton murmured. 'See my big mouth.'

'Not at all.'

The awkwardness passed as the PC arrived with the cutter. The carer led the officers towards the four-storey building. They were about to step on to the pathway to the entrance door when a young male cyclist sped in front of them, all but running over the constable's toes. 'Hoi!' she called after the jacket-clad youth. 'Careful, you little —'

''Tiggy,' McClair warned, 'you be careful.'

'Sorry, ma'am,' Benjamin said, 'but really; little shits like that shouldn't be allowed on bikes.'

'Little shits like that should be doing home schooling under lockdown, but we don't have time to go chasing after him to tell him. If I knew who he was I'd be calling on his parents, but unfortunately I do not.'

They carried on into the apartment block and into a lift that took them up to the top floor. The door to Number Twelve faced them as they stepped out. Granton turned the handle and opened it, stretching the restraining chain and making room for Benjamin to use the bolt cutter from the police car. It took little or no pressure to slice through a link, giving them access.

'Mr Stevens, it's Prue,' the carer called out. 'Are you awake yet? I couldn't get in and I was worried about you, so I've got the police with me.' She stepped towards a door on the left, but McClair stopped her with a gentle touch on her sleeve.

'Me first,' the inspector murmured, switching on her body camera. 'Is that his bedroom?'

'Yes.'

She moved forward. The door was slightly ajar; as soon as she opened it further she could see that the room was undisturbed. 'Do you make his bed?'

'Every morning.'

'Then it hasn't been slept in. Living room?'

'Straight ahead.'

The door had two vertical glass panels; they were opaque, but McClair could see that a ceiling light was on. Even as she stepped into the room, she knew what she would find. A white head lolled against the back of an old-fashioned armchair, and

34

a walking stick with four small balancing legs lay on the floor beside it. The curtains were drawn, even though it was mid-morning.

Mr Stevens' skin had a pale yellow hue. His mouth sagged open and his cheeks seemed to have collapsed inwards. His eyes were not completely closed; they were slits of blue in his head. McClair sniffed and took in the faint odour of urine. She took off her right glove and touched his forehead, feeling its coldness.

There was no need to state the obvious. 'What was his evening routine?' she asked.

'Another carer was supposed to check on him at nine,' Granton replied.

'Do you know who that is?'

'Not for sure. He's got a care package in place, three visits a day. I'm his getter-upper six days a week, tomorrow, Sunday, being my day off. Somebody else looks in on him at one, to give him his lunch and have his evening meal ready so he just has to put it in the microwave. Then there's the evening carer, to give him his medication and help him get ready for bed if he needs it . . . needed it, poor old man. We work for a company, and there's a rota for the other two visits, so last night could have been one of two or three people.'

'You said he had arthritis, but he could put himself to bed. How handicapped was he?'

'He could get his outer clothes off. He slept in his vest and pants,' the carer explained. 'Sometimes he'd let himself be helped, sometimes not. It was his choice; it probably depended on how tired he was, or what was on the telly.'

'If last night's visit hadn't happened, would you have been told about it?'

'I would if the company knew. The other carer might have called in sick, but if that had happened, I'm sure the company would have sent another, or even called me. If she just didn't turn up, we'd only know if Mr Stevens told us.'

'She?'

'More than likely,' Granton said. 'We only have one man on the staff.' She smiled, sadly, and pointed to a round table on the right of the chair, on which a crystal tumbler stood. 'At least the poor old chap had his whisky for the journey.'

'Where's the bottle?' Benjamin asked her.

'Good question; it must be back in the sideboard, where he kept it. That tells me the carer must have been in. His hands were affected by the arthritis, and there were some things it was difficult for him to do. Screwing the top off a whisky bottle was one of them.' The carer smiled, with a look of sadness. 'That's why he always drank a good malt, with a cork.'

'And yet he managed to set the chain on the front door,' McClair pointed out.

'Good point,' she conceded. 'That's the first time I've ever found it like that. I suppose he must have been able to do it and undo it. He'd have been up before I got here, maybe more than once through the night. An eighty-six-year-old man usually needs to. What do you do now?' she asked. 'Do you even need to be here? Mind you, I need to be going myself. I've got another client to see.'

'He died alone, so you'd have needed to call us anyway. I'll arrange for a medical examiner to attend, and then for the removal of the body to the mortuary at the Royal Infirmary. You'll need to advise your employer, and Mr Stevens' next of kin will have to be involved. If you can give me contact details, we can let them know.'

'Good luck with finding a doctor to attend,' Granton murmured. 'It's like they're under siege just now.'

The inspector smiled. 'I've got someone in mind who might be all too keen to attend.' She took out her phone and scrolled through her contacts until she reached 'G', then hit on a saved number.

'Sarah,' her companions heard her exclaim as her call was answered, 'it's Noele. How are you?' They saw her eyebrows rise as she listened and heard her gasp. 'Bloody hell! You're okay though? Look I won't bother you in that case.' She paused again. 'Well, if you're sure. I've got a situation here, a sudden death in Gullane, and I need medical attendance. There are no suspicious circumstances, but it needs a pathologist rather than a GP. It's not exactly your weight, I appreciate, but if you could . . . That's great. The address, Twelve Redway Court, on the old Fire School site. You'll see our car outside.'

She ended the call and pocketed her phone. 'Taken care of,' she announced. 'Mrs Granton, you make your call now and get me the next-of-kin details, please. Then I think you can go. The cavalry's on its way.'

Six

'I appreciate the thought, Pops,' Alex Skinner said, 'but you needn't have bothered. Andy Martin's whereabouts are of no interest to me. He could move in next door, far less to Motherwell, and he still wouldn't get over my threshold. Not that we parted on bad terms second time around, but it was for good nevertheless.'

'How would you feel about him going back to his wife?' her father asked.

Her sudden smile seemed to light up his phone screen. 'Smug, to be honest,' she retorted. 'If Paddy Power had been laying odds on it, I'd have taken them. There was a period after he and I restarted when I felt guilty about breaking up a marriage. Word got to me that someone in the Edinburgh force, a woman officer who'd been a friend of Karen's, had described me as a disgrace to my gender.'

'You should have told me,' Skinner growled. 'I'd have marked her card, and posted her to fucking Hawick.'

'That's why I didn't tell you. That guilt trip didn't last long anyway, only until I realised that it wasn't me that broke them up. Andy would have left home anyway, Pops. The thought of being middle-aged was giving him anxiety attacks and he rebelled against it. His problem was that indeed he was fucking middle-aged, no longer the guy in the leather jacket who attracted me the first time.' She winked at him. 'At least you fitted another wife in between your marriages to Sarah. Andy came back to me because he was afraid he couldn't hack it in the single's world any longer. If he goes back to the wife and kids now it'll be for the same reason. And you know what? The whole cycle will repeat itself. If you can pass Karen a message from me, tell her not to do it. Shag him if she feels like it, but don't be his emotional crutch.'

He chuckled. 'I don't think I'll be doing that, somehow. If the subject comes up again when I talk to Andy I might feed the thought in, in reverse so to speak. Speaking of emotional crutches, are you seeing much of Dominic?' he asked.

'Not under lockdown conditions, Pops. We WhatsApp like everybody else, like you and I are doing now, but that's it. If that's your way of finally asking if I'm sleeping with him, the answer is no. I think we both know that would be a bad idea.'

'Probably,' he agreed. 'How's the work situation?'

'It's good,' she said. 'I'm in the High Court again on Tuesday, prosecuting a forty-year-old man from Glasgow who put his fifty-two-year-old partner in a critical care ward after a domestic assault, where she contracted Covid-19 and died. I wish I could do him for culpable homicide, but attempted murder is the most we can go to.'

'Will the fact that you don't have a live victim to put in the witness box damage your case?'

'No, if anything it'll help, because defence counsel will have nobody to intimidate in the witness box. We have very specific photographic evidence of the injuries he inflicted and we have forensic evidence to back them up. The jury'll be in a cinema, so they'll see everything on the big screen. There was a boot print on the victim's back, we have her blood spattered on his clothing, and there was skin, hers, under his fingernails. She was violently sodomised as well. We can't actually prove that wasn't consensual, so he isn't charged with rape, but I can make sure the jury knows about it. Defence can object all he likes but once it's out there it won't be forgotten by them whatever the judge directs. My expectation is that on Monday I'll hear from the defence, wanting a deal for a guilty plea to assault. The deal I'll give him will be that I ask for a minimum twelve years instead of life. When she sees the evidence, I'll be surprised if the judge gives him less than fifteen.'

'Me too, from what you've said. Good luck with it.'

'Luck is what the accused will need,' she replied. 'So long, Pops.'

The image on his screen froze for less than a second, then vanished. As it did, Skinner remembered that he had forgotten to chide his daughter for outing his Covid on Facebook. He smiled, while going to his contacts list and clicking on a number.

'Bob,' Assistant Chief Constable Lowell Payne greeted him as he took the audio call. 'Welcome back to the world. I saw Alex's post. You and Sarah really are okay, yes?'

'Yeah, Lowell, we're good. So good that Sarah's just gone out on a job. Local though, here in Gullane.'

'What, a suspicious death?'

'No, I don't think so. An old man found dead in his chair, as they are sometimes. She's doing a favour for a friend really, to save her waiting at the scene all day for an ME from Edinburgh.

How are you? How's Jean?' Payne's wife was the sister of Alex's long-dead mother, Myra.

'We're both fine; waiting for the vaccine. Jean's stir crazy, but otherwise okay. You two won't need the jag now, I guess,' Payne said. 'You'll have antibodies.'

'I will,' Skinner agreed. 'But for how long? I'll be having the jag, as soon as it's offered. Sarah's been vaccinated already, because of her job, but she still had to isolate with me when I showed positive and be tested as well, all the way through.'

'Lucky Sarah. There's ill feeling in the service about us not being prioritised.'

'Watch this space. The *Saltire*'s being lobbied about that, and I expect we'll support it.'

'Let's hope you get results. Is that what you called to tell me?'

'No, it isn't; something else. I hear you've got Karen Neville on your team now.'

'That's right,' the ACC confirmed. 'She's very good.'

'I take it you looked at her background before you took her on.'

'I didn't have to. Mario was up front with me when he put her forward for the vacancy. I know she's Sir Andrew Martin's ex-wife.'

'Did you know he was back in Scotland?' Skinner asked.

'No,' Payne exclaimed. 'I did not. Since when?'

'For a few months now; he left his US job last year. I didn't know either until he called me this morning.'

'That's a surprise. Alex told me that you and he weren't on the best of terms. She assumes it's because of her.'

'We weren't, but it wasn't. We've had a chat and it's fixed now.'

'Is he looking for a job with Intermedia?'

Skinner laughed. 'If he is he didn't say so. No, he called me because he thinks he's got a problem. He reckons that someone's got him under surveillance; someone's stalking him. From what he told me,' Skinner said, 'he could be right.'

'That's concerning,' the ACC agreed, 'but why's it one for me?'

'You're the guy he should have called in the first place, Lowell. He's in touch with Karen, does his bit with the kids. If someone's watching him, it's possible they're looking at her as well. That's something that should interest you, is it not?'

'Yes, it is . . . but what do you suggest I do about it?'

'What I would do if I was in your chair. Discreetly have someone look at their service records, both of them, to see if anyone jumps out at you from their time in CID. Off the top of my head, I can't come up with a name, and neither can Andy, but he saw plenty of action in his career. So did Karen before she took time out to have the family. I don't have access to those records any more, and neither does Andy, but you do.'

'Okay, Bob,' Payne said, 'but if I do this, I'll need to report it up the ladder, to the new hierarchy, McIlhenney and McGuire.'

'Absolutely,' Skinner agreed. 'When you do, though, keep my name out of it. They wouldn't be happy if they knew I was involved. They're big boys now, and they need to be seen to be standing on their own four feet.'

'I can see that,' the ACC admitted. 'As far as I'm concerned, I'll always be grateful for all the advice you can give me. Also, given that you have a continuing connection with MI5 that nobody talks about, there's a valid reason for us to keep in touch, professionally as well as personally. And that,' he added, 'brings another thought to mind. If this character isn't a figment of Sir Andrew's vivid imagination, and he's watching Karen as well, given their long associations, shouldn't we consider the possibility that he might have an interest in Alex too?'

'Jesus,' Skinner hissed, 'you're right. In that case, Lowell, keep me in the loop. I will look after my daughter, whatever the new high heid yins think about it.'

Seven

'Thanks for doing this,' Noele McClair said, as she greeted the new arrival at the door. 'I could have got a GP to handle it, if only I'd the patience.'

'It's all right,' Sarah Grace assured her. 'I know how much pressure the practices are under, and I wasn't doing anything else. Where is the deceased?'

'Through here. Follow me.' She led the pathologist to the living room, standing aside as they reached the doorway.

Grace put her bag on the sideboard, opened it and slipped on a pair of disposable gloves. She stepped up to the armchair, and leaned over its occupant, put two fingers against his neck, then shone a light into the slitted eyes. 'The formalities,' she murmured, as she raised the arm that lay on his lap then replaced it gently. 'He's been dead overnight for sure; rigor's worn off. When was he found?'

The inspector recounted the events leading to the discovery.

'You let the carer go?'

'I had to. She was due somewhere else, with another vulnerable client. Her company's getting me the name of the next of kin.'

'Fine, she wouldn't have known his medical history, anyway.

I need that in determining a cause of death. If I can do that without cutting the old fellow open, it'll be better.'

'She did say that he'd been diagnosed with vascular dementia, if that helps.'

Grace nodded. 'It does. My first thought is that there's been a cerebral accident, a major stroke. It's a common cause of death among patients with that condition; maybe even the most common. Did she say what medication he was on?'

'No,' Benjamin said from the doorway, 'but I found this in the bathroom.' She held up a long flat box, with compartments.

The pathologist took it from her. 'It's a dosette box. It holds his daily medication.' She opened the section marked 'Sat', and peered inside, at a white pill and two capsules. 'Yeah,' she murmured, 'they're what you'd expect in a dementia patient. That looks like Ramipril, for blood pressure, the white one, I guess will be a statin for cholesterol, and the third is Dabigatran, that's a blood thinner. Preventative, all of them. You can't cure dementia, you can only keep it at bay, and then only for so long.' She turned to McClair. 'Noele, do you see anything here that gives you cause for concern? I'm looking at a sudden death, no more.'

'Me too.'

'In that case I'll issue a death certificate. I don't see any need for a post-mortem. When you advise the next of kin, you can tell them that Mr Stevens can go straight to the funeral parlour.'

Eight

Skinner stood in his garden, gazing northwards across the Firth of Forth, towards the Fife coast, which was bathed in pale winter sunshine. In his hands he cradled a mug of his son's carrot and coriander soup, which he had to admit was pretty damn good; Jazz might find himself extending his kitchen duty, he decided. The thought lifted his spirits but did not erase his funk completely. During his isolation he had cut himself off from all but family, close friends and necessary business contacts. In the days following his positive test, as he was riding out his symptoms, and fighting off visions of being ventilated in an intensive care ward, he had come to realise what depression really was. He had made light to Sarah of his Mental Elf emoji, but it was serious to him, a symbol of the secondary peril of the pandemic, its dangers to individuals and to society as a whole. The most immediate threat, as he saw it, was a downward spiral of resigned pessimism, and the smile on the tiny hair-braided figure's face was his shield against that. Of course, he worried about the longer-term effects of the mutating virus on society, in ways that the majority had yet to confront. There would not, that he could contemplate, be a benchmark date in the history that was yet to be written when the world would say, 'It's over,' and life would return to what it had been. On day six in their confinement quarters, the face of Professor Brian Cox had appeared on the TV screen that he and his wife were barely watching. 'That's all you know, mate,' he had grunted. His wife had cast a bewildered stare in his direction, but he had declined to elaborate. The academic's role in the banal and over-optimistic anthem 'Things can only get better', would always outweigh in Skinner's mind his contribution to popular understanding of the cosmos.

He had barely finished his soup when his ringtone sounded in the pocket of his jacket. Laying his mug on the stone garden table he dug it out and peered at the screen. The caller ID 'M Reid' was displayed. With a faint grin he took the call. 'Hi, Matthew,' he said. 'How are you doing?'

Matthew Reid was a member of what Skinner referred to as his village circle, a small group who had risen to the status of friends rather than simple acquaintances. When society was free and unrestricted, half a dozen of them had been in the habit of gathering in the Mallard Hotel late on Friday evenings. Most were retired; Reid was still working, although his age was a mystery, even within the circle. He was an author, the creator of a series of crime novels, a second career that had begun by accident thirty years before and which showed no sign of reaching a conclusion. His protagonist was an Edinburgh man with the unlikely name of Septimus Armour . . . 'My granny was an Armour, one of a family of seven,' he would explain . . . who had risen from an under-privileged background, running away from a life of petty crime in the capital and, as Reid put it, 'blagging his way into Strathclyde Police as what he saw as a temporary hiding place from his former associates, and staying on when he realised it was a hell of a lot more lucrative than crime.' At the turn of the century the series had come close to being commissioned by a television channel, only to fail at the last hurdle. Reid maintained that while it might have cost him a lot of money it had saved him even more grief.

'More to the point, Bob,' he countered, 'how are you? I saw your daughter's Facebook announcement.'

He and Skinner had met in the early years of the series when the author had approached the cop, tentatively, for background information on police practice. He had been happy to help, on condition that it was not acknowledged publicly. 'Otherwise I'll have every bugger ringing my doorbell,' he had said.

'I've been better,' Skinner admitted, 'but others have suffered worse than I did. My friend Xavi's lost his wife to the thing. Are you vaccinated yet?'

'Ten days ago. No side effects, I'm pleased to say.'

'I'll have to wait my turn for mine, although I suppose that Sarah and I will have antibodies for a while. It'll possibly be this month, if not, early April they say. Maybe by that time we'll be able to meet up in the pub again, although the virtual Friday nights you've been running are a good substitute.'

'They've been cheaper too,' Reid grunted. 'It'll be a while before we're back in the Mallard, and even then, it won't be the Mallard. Have you heard that the new owners are changing the name?'

'Yeah, we'll see how long it takes the village to catch up. Are you busy, Matthew? Will there be a new Armour yarn out this year?'

'Yes,' the author replied, 'it's taking shape in my brain even as we speak. All I need to do is keep making the time to write it.'

'I thought the current situation would be perfect for guys like you.'

'It should be, but I have other interests. That's why I'm calling. Bob, would you have the time or the inclination to join the resilience group?'

'What the fuck is that?' Skinner asked, chuckling. 'It makes me think of the Maquis, the French resistance.'

'In a way it's much the same. It's a bunch of us offering our time to look after people who need it and who've been over-looked by the system, the elderly, disabled, people shielding. Checking they're all right, running errands, getting prescriptions, doorstep chats, whatever helps.'

'Does it get you out of the house, legitimately?'

'We believe so,' Reid replied. 'The real question is whether it allows you to enter other people's. We're advised that it does, but only if there's a need.'

'In that case, I'm up for it. How does it work?'

'Through Facebook, for starters. People who need help can post on the group's page, but mostly we're working through word of mouth. We've established a list of people needing assistance, and we keep in touch with them, by phone mostly, checking they're all right and whether they have anything that needs taking care of. The responses are wide and varied. One old lady couldn't flush her toilet and was panicking about the . . . the backlog, so to speak.'

'Nice choice of words, Matthew.'

'It's what I do,' Reid retorted, cheerfully. 'That one was easy to fix. Our friend Joe's son-in-law took care of it. As you know, he's a plumber.'

'I thought he was a golfer, the time he spends on the course.'

'No comment. Thanks for agreeing, Bob. I'll email you a list of people, and you can get going. You'll probably know most of them.'

'Don't count on that,' Skinner warned. 'It doesn't matter, though. I spent much of my career knocking on the doors of people I didn't know . . . sometimes knocking quite hard!'

Nine

The nameplate on the door of the modern suburban villa read 'Martin'; initially Lowell Payne was surprised but understood after a little thought that while Detective Chief Inspector Karen Neville might use her maiden name at work, with two children of school age from her marriage, it would be generally confusing if she carried this into her private life.

He was about to press the button on the bell when the door opened.

'Boss.' Neville's eyes registered curiosity rather than surprise. 'Clever things, these video doorbells. My watch told me there was someone there, then my phone told me it was you. Mind you, with that mask on, I had to take a second look.'

'I wish we could hack into these systems,' the assistant chief constable remarked, as he removed his face covering. 'It would make parts of our job a hell of a lot easier.'

'Tell me about it,' she said. 'This thing records video and stores it on the Cloud. I have a camera in the back garden that does the same thing. My ex was here earlier on, picking up the kids; he told me he's invested in a similar system. But enough of that,' she exclaimed. 'What brings you here on a fine Sunday morning? Don't tell me you were just passing on your way home from church, for I won't buy that one.' She paused. 'By the way, I would invite you in, sir, but as things stand, I'm not allowed to.'

'I know,' he conceded. 'I have to admit that I forget about lockdown conditions from time to time. However, we're both essential services; maybe that would cut us some slack, and also, the fact that you're working from home most of the time. We can talk on the doorstep though.'

'So it is work related, this visit?'

'Yes and no.'

'In that case, let's compromise and talk in the garden.' She picked up a black device from a table by the door and pressed it. There was a buzz and the door of the garage, to his left, began to rise. 'Go through that way. There's a door at the back that lets you in.'

Most of the neighbours had their cars in their driveways but he had to squeeze between Neville's blue Volkswagen and two children's bicycles. The space into which he emerged was a mix of paving and grass, with leafless trees and shrubs. Its maturity surprised him; he lived in the same town and knew that the estate had been developed only recently.

She seemed to read his mind as she emerged from a double glass doorway. 'Do you like it? I got a real bargain; I bought the showhouse, and the garden had been laid out. Mostly you're lucky if you get grass. Coffee?' she asked. As he nodded, she pointed towards a square green plastic waterproof covering. 'The outside table's under that thing; it's where it lives in the winter. Peel it off, please. I'll only be a minute. I'm in the middle of making myself some lunch, but I can set that aside for now.'

Payne did as she said, folding the covering and laying it

beside the doorway. Looking inside, he saw a spacious modern fitted kitchen, all blinding white units and stainless steel handles. Glancing at it, he saw chopped vegetables on a board, eggs, flour and milk unmixed in a blender, and dishes in a rack beside the sink, two cereal bowls. *The leavings of breakfast,* he surmised. *I wonder whose the second was.*

'No kids?' he asked as she emerged with a tray, laden with two mugs and a plate of KitKat biscuits. He pulled out two of the four seats that were stored under the table, maintaining an appropriate social distance between them.

'They're with their dad for the weekend. Did you know he's back from America?' Neville added.

'Yes, I'd heard. For good?'

'We'll see.' She looked into her mug. 'Whisper it, but there's talk of a big job in the Met, Deputy Commissioner, no less. That would be ironic, wouldn't it? We get McIlhenney, they get Andy. Who'd get the best of that trade, do you think, boss?'

The ACC grinned. 'No comment.' *Bob Skinner never told me that,* he thought. *I wonder if he knows.*

'Me neither,' she murmured. 'Are you going to tell me now?' she continued. 'What you're doing here?'

'Call it a job satisfaction interview,' he replied, grateful for the time he had been given to come up with a plausible story. 'In normal times, I'd be doing this in the office. Serious organised crime and counter-terrorism: the work might be low profile, but the stress is disproportionate. As its leader I have a duty to ensure that all my people are coping.'

The DCI peered at him. 'As do we all, sir, don't we?'

'I suppose,' he agreed. 'Do you have any concerns within your team?'

'Mine's a widespread crew as you know,' she said, 'given

that my job is oversight of possible terrorist activity across our three divisions. I'm happy with all my officers. They all report on time and flag up situations as soon as they arise. Liaison with the Security Service in Westminster might be a bit sticky from time to time – whenever London deigns to ask us for help, that is – but when it's channelled through Clyde Houseman, their Scotland watcher, that's okay too.'

'Do your paths cross often?' Payne asked.

'We're doing the same job,' Neville pointed out. 'For different masters answerable to different governments, but essentially the same job, spotting possible terrorist activity at an early stage and shutting it down if it turns out to be real.'

'What do you know about Houseman?'

'What's to know?' she countered casually. 'As spooks go, he's less spooky than most.'

'He's an interesting guy,' the ACC told her. 'Most of these Security Service people are recruited from university, but not Houseman, he followed another pathway. He was a gangbanger in Edinburgh as a kid, but he straightened himself out in time and instead of becoming an enforcer for some drugs gang, he joined the Royal Marines and got himself a commission. Then he transferred to special forces, the Special Boat Service . . . the waterborne SAS. He came out as a captain, or maybe even a major, can't remember. I don't know whether he was headhunted by the Security Service or he applied, but they're a good fit. Bob Skinner reckons he'll be moving up the Millbank ladder soon, and he knows these things. Bob's still connected there and will be as long as Dame Amanda Dennis is in charge.'

The DCI frowned. 'I hope it doesn't happen too soon,' she said. 'Clyde would be hard to replace.'

'Agreed,' Payne said, 'but I can think of a very good candidate.'

She looked at him, curious. 'Are you going to share?'

He raised his mug. 'No, but she makes a damn good cup of coffee.'

Her eyebrows rose, and then she laughed. 'You can forget that. Andy wouldn't allow it.'

'Would he have a veto?'

'He can be persuasive. We haven't discussed it, but if the London thing materialised, I'm pretty certain he would ask me to relocate too. For the kids' sake, you know.'

'I'm sure you'd have no trouble getting a transfer.' The ACC's eyes found hers. 'But if it happened, would you want one?'

'Would I stay in Scotland? Would I go down there as a cop, or would I go down there as a wife and mother? Is that what you're asking?'

'I suppose so. Sorry, Karen, it's none of my business.'

'Of course it's your business.' She smiled. 'I'm on your team, sir. The short answer is, I don't know. It's never really been discussed, but Andy's been throwing out hints. The London thing isn't certain. As for Andy and me, that isn't necessarily connected to it anyway. He hasn't flat out asked me about the chances of a reconciliation, and I am sure as hell not going to ask him. But . . . If he did, I would have to be satisfied that he's over a certain Ms Alexis Skinner . . .' She paused, her hand going fleetingly to her mouth. 'Oh God, of course, she's your niece.'

Payne nodded. 'She is, but I understand what you're saying. I can tell you that Alex is very definitely over him.'

'That's good to hear, but it would have to be mutual.'

'There's been no recent contact between them; I can tell you that too. She'd have told her aunt, and Jean would have told me.'

'Also reassuring, but . . .' Neville sighed. 'Look, boss, I haven't closed my mind to the idea of us getting together again. If it happened, it would be good for Danielle and Robert. Put it this way, I'm not being pulled in any other direction; I am not looking for commitment. I was vetted before I joined our department, so you will know that since I've been divorced I've had two relationships, neither of which lasted longer than a couple of months, and a few encounters through a dating site, which I left before I was transferred to counter-terrorism. I'm not a nun, never was, but I liked it when I had stability in my life. If Andy can offer me that and convince me that he'll deliver, well, we'll see. Mind you, that's assuming he has any such intention. As I say, we're just dancing around it so far.'

'You will let me know if you wind up as *Strictly* contestants, won't you?'

'I promise I will, boss.'

'That's good,' Payne said. 'Meanwhile, you're okay in yourself, are you? Not feeling constrained by the pandemic circumstances?'

She laughed. 'Boss, I've felt constrained since my first child was born. I'm well used to that, believe me. This lockdown is business as usual as far as I'm concerned.'

Payne finished his coffee and left, via the garage. He still wondered about that second cereal bowl, but he had decided that to ask the question would have been an invasion of what little right to privacy their secretive, sensitive jobs allowed them. *If it's Andy's,* he thought, *fine.*

Neville closed the garage door as soon as he had gone, then

picked up the cover for the outdoor furniture. As she finished securing the set in its waterproof cocoon she glanced up at a first-floor bedroom window that overlooked the garden. She smiled at the man who gazed down at her. He was dark-haired, mixed race, and in his mid-thirties. He wore a white T-shirt which revealed an elaborate tattoo on his right deltoid; a crowned lion above a globe encircled by a laurel wreath, with a motto beneath that she knew read, *'Per mare, per terram.'*

He opened the window and called to her. 'Can I come down,' he asked, 'now that your mystery caller's gone? I feel like a prisoner up here.'

She shook her head. 'I don't think so, Clyde,' she replied. 'You stay there, and I'll come to you. Lunch can wait for a while.'

Ten

Every weekday morning, when she arrived at her office, Inspector Noele McClair reflected on her good fortune in having a mother who had been a teacher. Yes, without her, her son Harry would have been found a place in a school hub for the children of key workers, but she suspected that would have damaged his educational progress. He had been assessed as borderline dyslexic; with his grandmother taking charge of his home schooling, she had seen steady improvement in his reading, writing and general comprehension. Although he was missing his classmates, Harry was enjoying the change too. Granny was more patient than his teacher, and her lessons were shorter, naturally, as they were one on one. That meant longer playtimes, in the small garden of the steading where they lived, and sometimes in the play park near the school, if the weather was fine. A return to normality was weeks away, and stresses might develop in that time, but for the moment Noele was content.

'How was the rest of the weekend, Shuggie?' she asked Sergeant Jackson, who was coming to the end of a five-day-duty stint.

'The night shift had it quiet,' he replied, 'from what they

said at handover. North Berwick was bulging yesterday though, and Yellowcraigs. The traffic folk were there, checking addresses through the number plates of parked cars. They handed out a fair few fixed penalty notices.' He grinned. 'Some of them got parking fines as well; that really ruined their day, ken. Oh aye, and that car you said we should station at the top of the Aberlady straight, that was very busy yesterday afternoon stoppin' cyclists and checkin' their addresses. Everybody from outside East Lothian got told to get straight back home again.' He paused. 'I know all of it's national policy, Noele, but do you no' think that's a wee bit heavy-handed?'

She shook her head, firmly. 'No way. There's a great big beach in Portobello, so no need for the Edinburghers to cross council boundaries to go to Yellowcraigs or Gullane. Rules is rules, Shuggie. This isn't a game, it's about containing a deadly virus, and people have to be made to take it seriously, if necessary. It cuts both ways. I can't go to Marks and Spencer!'

'You wait till Rangers win the league,' he said, portentously, 'and see how seriously it gets taken through in Glasgow.'

She smiled. 'Do you think Edinburgh should worry about Hearts winning their league?'

'Speakin' as a lifelong Hibs fan, that would be a no.'

Grinning still, she moved into her office, where a few incident reports waited for her in a tray on her desk. She was working her way through them, when her landline phone rang. 'There's a caller here, Inspector,' Jackson said as she answered, 'a Mrs Langham. She asked for you by name. She said she wants to speak to you about her father, Michael Stevens.'

'Stevens? The sudden death Tiggy and I attended on Saturday?'

'I guess so.'

'Okay, put her through.'

She waited for a few seconds, until a deep female voice boomed in her ear. 'Is that Inspector McClair?'

'Yes,' she confirmed, sensing a possible confrontation. 'How can I help you?'

'My name is Lynn Langham. I'm the daughter of Michael Stevens. I'm told that you attended his death on Saturday.'

'That's correct, and I am very sorry for your loss. What is it you'd like to know?'

'I'd like to know why the police aren't taking it seriously,' the woman snapped.

McClair felt her eyes widen in surprise. 'I'm not sure how to react to that,' she said. 'My colleague and I were asked to effect an entrance to your father's flat by his carer, after she couldn't get a response from him. We did, and sadly found that he'd passed away in his armchair. I can assure you that we treated him and his property with the utmost respect. If you're concerned that we didn't involve his GP, doctors are under special pressure just now, so I found someone else to certify his death.'

'Just like that?' Langham exclaimed.

The inspector felt her patience approaching breaking point. 'Let me explain something to you, Mrs Langham. Your father died alone, which meant that whoever found him would have been required to call the police. In those circumstances I'm required to submit a report to the procurator fiscal.'

'Without a post-mortem?'

'Not my call. The fiscal isn't obliged to ask for one, and in most sudden death cases he doesn't. In most the cause of death is self-evident, as it was with your father. He had a stroke history and against that background the pathologist was clear that's what killed him. Does that make it clearer for you?'

'Although I live in England now, I have a Scottish law degree,' the bereaved daughter told her. 'You're not telling me stuff I don't know. But what you don't realise is that you are describing to me, almost exactly, the circumstances of my mother's death a year ago. I find that extraordinary, don't you?'

'I find it unusual,' McClair admitted, 'but I know nothing of your mother's case, so I can't comment on it.'

'Dad came in from golf,' she said, her tone noticeably calmer and less aggressive. 'They lived in Whim Road then. He'd had an early tee time, and so he'd given Mum a cup of tea and left her in bed. When he came back she was still there, but she was dead. If you check your incident book, you'll find that you were called then too.'

'Was an autopsy required after your mother's death?'

'No. She'd had a heart procedure, a minimally invasive aortic valve repair, but it hadn't been a hundred per cent successful. She was on the waiting list for a valve replacement. The GP consulted her cardiologist, he had a look at her most recent scan and decided that the balance of probability was that the wonky valve had caused her heart to fail, suddenly and fatally. I was okay with that at the time, but now, for my father to go in much the same way, I'm not.'

'Are you telling me you regard your father's death as suspicious?'

'No,' Langham conceded, 'but I would regard it as unexplained. I believe that it needs to be investigated.'

'Almost certainly that would involve a post-mortem examination. Are you prepared for that?'

'More than prepared,' she retorted. 'I'm insisting on it.'

'Okay,' McClair agreed. 'I will take that on board, but as I

61

told you, I can't order it myself. I will have to speak to the procurator fiscal. It's his decision, and he may balk at it, given that there will be cost implications.'

'Sod that,' the woman snorted. 'I'll fund it myself if I have to. I don't want some first-year pathology student doing it either; I want the best.'

'It was the best who certified your father's death in the first place. Not because I felt it necessary to call in someone at that level, but because she's a friend and attended as a favour to me.'

'Then ask her if she's prepared to risk proving herself wrong.'

Eleven

'He didn't tell you?'

'No, he bloody didn't,' Bob Skinner complained. 'Did Karen say where these whispers were coming from?'

'No,' Lowell Payne replied. 'But Karen seemed to regard them as substantial. She's weighing up the possibility for moving south herself if it happens.'

'I can find out,' Skinner said. 'Dame Amanda will know, and I'm sure she'll share it. If it's true, I would guess he's been sounded out about it either by someone in the Home Office, or by one of the Mayor of London's people.' He chuckled softly. 'And if that's the case, it probably explains his feeling of being stalked. If he is being considered as the new Deputy Commissioner, they're bound to do a positive vetting job on him, not least since he's been out of the service and working overseas for a while. I'm surprised Andy hasn't worked that out for himself.'

'Do you think he's up to the Deputy Commissioner job?' the ACC asked. 'After all, he did fuck up in Scotland.'

'Actually, I'd question that, Lowell,' he countered. 'I know that's the perspective within the service, but my view is that once his ambition had taken him there, Andy was frustrated by the nature of the job and by the structure he was saddled with by the politicians. I can empathise with that; I was dead against the national force from the start, as everyone knows. However, and I've never said this publicly, he was the wrong choice to head it. I'll take the blame for that, because I never taught him to delegate, never having learned to do that properly myself. I'd have been as bad at the job as he was if I'd gone for it.' He paused. 'The Met, though, that's a completely different service. It's a city force, albeit an enormous city, and it's got a well-established management structure. The Commissioner's more of a chief executive than a copper, and the same goes for the deputy. The structure is there and everyone knows what it is. It's oversight that's required not delegation or micro-management.'

'Do you think he'll get it?'

'He'll be a strong candidate, no doubt about that. If he's been sounded out about it, I'd say he's more than halfway there.'

'I might be looking for a new DCI if it happens.'

'Are you telling me that Karen will go with him?'

'For the children's sake, I suspect she will.'

'I hope it works out for them both. Cheers, mate,' he said. 'Got to go. I have some calls to make.'

Ending the conversation, Skinner turned to his computer and studied the list that Matthew Reid had sent him, six women and two men. Three of the eight names he recognised; the others were strangers to him. The first fell into the latter category. Mrs Wendy Alexander lived in a terrace on the Main Street; a note against her name suggested that she had difficulty with stairs. He took a breath, and dialled her number.

His call was answered within five seconds. 'Yes?'

'Mrs Alexander?' he ventured. 'My name is Bob Skinner.'

'Sir Robert Skinner?'

'Yes,' he confirmed, 'but I don't go by it, not usually.'

'I read your article in the *Saltire* Sunday edition this morning. Very interesting; it made me happy I've had the vaccine. The doctors are very good, you know. They arranged for me to be done at home by a district nurse. That was a blessing, I have arthritis and it's very difficult for me to get out. Now, what can I do for you, Sir Robert?'

'It's more, what can I do for you?' he replied. 'I've been asked to join a group that's looking after vulnerable folk like yourself, to see if we can help with anything.'

'Really?' Mrs Alexander exclaimed. 'When he called on me, Mr Reid said someone would be in touch with me, but I never thought it would be you. You could get my papers for a start. Today was one of my good days, I managed to get down the stairs and along to the Co-op. Mostly though, the steps are too much for me and I'm stuck in the house.'

'That will be no problem. What's your favourite paper?'

'The *Saltire*, of course, every day, and the *Daily Star*, then there's the *People's Friend*, and *Hello* magazine . . . for the photos, you understand. They're once a week.'

It occurred to Skinner that he had never knowingly met a *Daily Star* reader, but he kept that to himself. 'Okay,' he said, 'I, or someone else from the resilience group, will bring those to you every day.'

'Could you get me money from the cash machine, Sir Robert? I do mean you,' she added, 'and nobody else. Although we've never met I know that you were a policeman, so I can trust you.'

'Sure, I can do that for you. Anything else we can help you with?'

'You couldn't do my Tesco shopping, could you? I've been getting by on the Co-op, but it doesn't have all the things I like. Wine, for example; there's more choice in Tesco.'

He laughed. 'I'm with you there, Mrs Alexander. I'll visit you myself, this afternoon. I'll go to the cash machine for you, assuming it hasn't run out. You can give me a shopping list too, and I'll get that done tomorrow morning. I'll see you soon.'

'Whenever you like,' the veteran said. 'I'm not going any-where.'

Half an hour later, he had worked his way through the list. Both of the men were Golf Club members. One was offended to find himself on a list of the potentially vulnerable and made that very clear. The other had laughed, and told Skinner that if he could arrange for the clubhouse bar to reopen, that would be help enough. 'Otherwise, Bob, I'm okay, thanks.'

The other five ladies had been more pragmatic. Only three had specific needs, but the others had been grateful, for the show of community concern, he sensed, as much as for the offer of help.

Before heading out to keep his promise to Mrs Alexander, he called Matthew Reid. 'Thanks for including me in the group, mate,' he said, sincerely. 'It occurs to me that I haven't put enough into the village over the years. So it's good to have the chance. By the way,' he added, 'given your age, should you not be on the vulnerable list yourself?'

'Fuck off,' the author said, cheerfully.

Twelve

'Let's be clear, Inspector,' Maria Mullen exclaimed. 'You're asking me to overrule Professor Sarah Grace and order an autopsy on what she's certified as a straightforward sudden death?'

'No,' Noele McClair countered. 'I'm asking you to respect the wishes of the dead man's daughter. Put yourself in her shoes. If your parents had died alone, each in exactly the same way, wouldn't you be concerned about it?'

'Suppose I was,' the deputy procurator fiscal countered, 'I'd still be obliged to consider the cost of what will almost certainly be a pointless exercise. If Professor Grace is satisfied that the old fella died of natural causes, you should be too.'

'Professor Grace is happy to do the post-mortem herself if it makes the daughter happy. I've spoken to her.'

'Without consulting me?' Her tone was arch.

'Sarah's a friend,' McClair said, combatively. 'I'm the reason she attended in the first place. Plus, I had no obligation to consult you.'

Mullen sighed. 'Look, if I authorise this, shouldn't I be ordering the exhumation of the mother as well?'

'That would be a trick beyond even the Procurator Fiscal

Service. Lynn Langham told me that her mother was cremated and her ashes scattered in the rough on the fourth hole of Gullane Number Three.'

'Why, in God's name?' the prosecutor gasped.

'It was her wish, apparently. It was because she spent half her life there looking for her ball.'

'What about the father? What are they going to do with him?'

'Bunker on the eighteenth fairway, for the same reason. They'll ask a greenkeeper to rake him in with the sand.'

'What will the golf club committee have to say about that?' she murmured.

'Mr Stevens was a past captain, so they'll probably allow it.'

'Jesus, these Gullane members!' Mullen sighed. 'It would never happen at Newbattle, where I play. Okay,' she declared, 'you can go ahead with the post-mortem. If it turns up anything suspicious, we'll even pay for it.'

Thirteen

Skinner suspected that Mrs Alexander would have been less than pleased to hear her home described as a tenement flat, but that was the phrase that his Lanarkshire upbringing brought to mind as he opened the green door on the Main Street and stepped into the stairway that in his home town would have been called a close.

Many of his school mates in Motherwell had lived in closes. In the more deprived areas of Glasgow, that might have carried a certain social stigma. He frowned suddenly as he remembered a man he had met in his twenties, a politician who had been brought up in the Gorbals between the wars, the days before antibiotics when tuberculosis was rife. 'Son,' he had sighed, 'there was not a close where the undertaker was a stranger.' TB was known in Lanarkshire too . . . one of Skinner's maternal uncles had spent a year, as a young man, in a sanatorium in Aberdeenshire . . . but his town was made prosperous by its steelworks, and its closes were occupied by healthy families whose children went to school well clothed and well fed.

The steps that led up to the first floor flat were stone. They were made more secure by adhesive non-slip rubber tiles, but the handrails were too far apart for a vulnerable person to hold both of them. He understood why Mrs Alexander found them perilous.

There were two doors on the landing. He guessed left, peered at the nameplate and went to the other, pressing a bell that sounded so shrilly that he thought it might have stopped a passing bus. It took the old lady some time to answer; when she did, he recognised her as someone he had seen around the village for years, without ever learning her name. He felt a flush of guilt asking himself, 'Am I a stranger in my own home town?'

'Sir Robert.' As she greeted him, Mrs Alexander looked him up and down, not without difficulty as her spine was severely curved, by ankylosing spondylitis, he guessed, remembering a long-dead cousin of his father. 'A pleasure to meet you. I'd have known you from your photo in the paper, even though you're wearing your mask. It's so good of you to help out in this way. Would you like to come in for a cup of tea?'

'That would be nice,' he replied, 'but maybe not right now.' He handed her the newspapers that he had picked up in the Co-op. 'No *Daily Star*, I'm afraid. The Sunday edition sells out fast.'

'Never mind,' she said. 'You got *Hello*.' From a table beside the door, she picked up a bank card and a folded sheet of paper. 'The PIN number is on there,' she told him, 'along with my shopping list. It says sausages, but they have to be best beef, not pork, and no more than two of them. It says yoghurt too, but only Tesco own brand. Toilet rolls too, but definitely not Tesco own brand, only Andrex. Is that all right? If you draw out a hundred and fifty pounds from the machine, that should cover it all and leave me enough for my daily needs for a while.'

'That's all perfectly fine, Mrs Alexander, and I'm sure it'll be enough. Is your wine choice on there too?' he asked.

'La Ina sherry, if they have it. And perhaps a bottle of a nice German Riesling, if it's not too dear.'

'I'll look out for that. I'll go along for eight tomorrow morning. It shouldn't take long, but it'll depend on how busy the place is, with the social distancing procedures and everything. I must confess that my wife and I do most of our food shopping online these days.'

She laughed, a tinkling sound. 'That's all right for you young folks. The internet's far too modern for the likes of me.'

As he stepped out on to the street, closing the door behind him, Skinner was still beaming behind his mask at his inclusion by Mrs Alexander among the 'young folks'. The grin was wiped off his face as a cycle whizzed past him, so close that he withdrew his left foot in a reflex action. He noted, as the young rider pedalled furiously away, that he had flowing shoulder-length hair and wore a green puffer jacket. 'Hey!' he bellowed after him. 'Not on the pavement!' The youth held up his right hand, middle finger extended. *That was a mistake, son,* he thought.

Scowling, Skinner slid into his car, a Tesla that Xavi Aislado had insisted he take as a company vehicle. 'Every executive director in Spain and Italy has one, Bob. You must too. Besides, there's a great tax deal in the UK on electric company cars.' He had accepted, although his beloved Mercedes still sat in the garage.

The offending cyclist had crossed the road and was passing the golf pro shop, his speed unabated, hair still streaming out behind him. The Tesla would have caught him in seconds, but he decided to let it go. Instead, he turned into Sandy Loan, meaning to head for home, only to have a change of mind. *No reason to wait until tomorrow,* he thought. *I might as well do the shopping now.*

There was still traffic during lockdown, but much less than in normal times. Happily, very little of it was heading for Tesco. When he arrived there, he found that the car park was no more than a quarter full and that the queue was short. Before joining it, he drew out Mrs Alexander's cash from the ATM. Looking at the PIN number he hazarded a guess that she had been born on the third of March, nineteen thirty-four.

The old lady's shopping list was short and simple. She had good taste in sherry, he thought, but she was welcome to the Riesling as far as he was concerned. There was room to spare in the trolley, and so he loaded on three bottles of a Spanish verdejo, Sarah's favourite drinking white, and a box of eighteen Corona beers to replenish further the stock that Alex had topped up during his confinement. He paid for his purchases first, with a card, then packed Mrs Alexander's provisions into a reusable bag. Her list used up just over forty-three pounds of her hundred and fifty.

When he stepped out of the stairway entrance after completing his mission, he paused, glancing in either direction for speeding young cyclists, hoping that he would find one in particular. 'Long hair, green jacket,' he murmured, as a reminder to himself for the report he intended to make to Noele McClair. 'If that had been Mrs Alexander stepping out of her doorway, it could have been fatal. An eighty-something-year journey isn't going to end like that, not on my watch.'

Fourteen

'Do you think the gaffer will take the huff?' Chief Constable Neil McIlhenney asked his friend and deputy.

Mario McGuire grinned. 'That's an absolute certainty,' he replied. 'But what's equally certain is that he'll never let us know. Look, I've been there before with him, after Maggie took over as chief and I became her designated deputy. She went to him for advice at the beginning of her tenure. I was a bit miffed that she didn't rely entirely on me, and I let it be known.'

'How did he react?'

'As I recall he just fucking ignored me. Before long I realised that I was leaning on him just as heavily as Maggie was. It's the old story; Bob taught us everything we know, but he didn't teach us everything he knows. He didn't have time.'

'So you're saying I was wrong to be so blunt with him?' McIlhenney suggested.

'Not at all. You have to make your presence felt, to stake out your territory. You were right to do that.' McGuire frowned. 'Not just to him,' he murmured. 'You were staking it out to me as well. I was happy to use Bob as a mentor for rising stars like Sauce Haddock and Lottie Mann. You take a different view on that. You're the chief constable and that view needs to be seen to prevail.'

'Even over you?'

'Absolutely over me; especially over me. Look, Neil; look, sir, there are still a lot of people in this force who know about you and me, even though you were away for a few years. We've been best mates all through our careers, even though I was a rank above for some of the time. Man, we were fucking legends for a while. But now you're back from your wee sojourn in London and you've jumped over me on the ladder.'

'That was your choice, by not applying for the chief constable job,' McIlhenney pointed out.

'Never. That choice wasn't mine to make,' McGuire countered. 'You're selling yourself short, mate. If I had gone for it . . . and that was something I never intended to do at any time, by the way . . . and we'd both had interviews, any selection board would have been crazy to pick me over you. I'm a detective, pure and simple, with the emphasis on the simple. I was a small-city cop who never thought about leaving there. You did; you went off to the Met, and you picked up experience that makes you much better qualified than me to be chief constable. Jesus, if Bob himself had applied for it . . . and there was nothing stopping him from doing that, even though he'd retired. I know he was lobbied . . . you'd have been a better choice than him. Bottom line, you are right to be doing things your way and to be seen to. If that includes moving me out of the criminal investigation reporting chain, so be it.'

McIlhenney looked at his friend, and gasped. 'Why would I do that?' he asked. 'As you've just said, you're bugger all good at anything else. You're a strength, so why make you a weakness? That's the one thing that made me hesitate before telling Bob I didn't want him to be a mentor any more. Am I cutting off my own nose by doing that? Will the officers he was mentoring suffer as a result?'

'I don't think so. We're talking about Lottie Mann in Glasgow, Sauce Haddock in Edinburgh and Lesley Gray in Inverness. All three are now heading up major incident teams; they can stand on their own feet.'

'The only one of them that I know at all is young Haddock.'

'Gray's the oldest,' McGuire told him, 'and she's been in post longest. She's very efficient, popular and she has a good clear-up rate. Currently her only open investigations are historic, going back well before her time. She's probably plateaued, but that's fine, she can stay there until retirement. Lottie Mann, now she's a formidable officer, in her mid-thirties. She's known adversity in her time, maybe even career-threatening. But she overcame it. Her ex-husband, Scott Mann, was a cop, but a bad lot with links to criminals. He got found out and did some time as a result. In the old days she'd have been tarred with his brush, and at the very least stuck behind a desk until she died of boredom, but Bob was her chief then and he stood by her. She had it tough for a while in her private life too. When he got out, Scott, the cheeky bastard, tried to get custody of their son, Jakey. His father's minted and turned out to be as big a shit as his son. He set some very expensive lawyers on her. They might have pulled it off, but big Bob got Alex to represent her at the Children's Hearing, and she wiped the floor with them all. Lottie's in a new relationship now, with Dan Provan, who was her DS until he retired. He's twenty years older than her, but they fit together like a semmit and drawers. Lottie's ACC material in the future, no question.'

'And young Sauce,' McIlhenney asked, 'how's he shaping up?'

'He's a DCI even though he's still short of thirty. Okay, his progress was accelerated by poor old Sammy Pye being hit by career-ending illness, but the boy was always on the fast track. Five years from now, Sauce'll be ACC Harold Haddock, in the job Becky Stallings has now, overseeing criminal investigation and reporting to me, or my successor. After that, whenever you decide to retire, he'll move into this office. That's the future I predict for him.'

'Thanks to big Bob's mentoring? Is that what you're saying?'

The DCC shook his head. 'Not at all, Sauce was a flier from the moment he walked in the door. Yes, the gaffer's done a lot for his career development, but it was actually Maggie who spotted him first, when she was a divisional head and he was a still-wet plod.'

'And yet he's done all that in spite of him being married to Cameron McCullough's namesake granddaughter? Isn't it surprising that didn't hold him back?'

McGuire frowned. 'Look, Neil, there is actually no proof that Grandpa McCullough has ever been involved in organised crime. Sure, there was lots of intelligence saying that he was, but the fact remains the only members of the family who were ever nailed for anything were his sister, Goldie, and his daughter, Inez, young Cameron's mother. Further to that, since Goldie died, Dundee's gone quiet.'

'On the other hand, could McCullough have cleaned up his act because he's now got a connection to Bob Skinner?' McIlhenney asked. 'With him being married to the mother of Bob's boy, Ignacio?'

'It could, I'll grant you,' McGuire admitted. 'I know that Bob keeps McCullough at arm's length, particularly since those murders a year back, Montell and Coats. You won't know this, but there was a piece of evidence linking Inez to them. It was uncorroborated though, and the Crown Office decided not to pursue it. I don't think Bob believes Grandpa had anything to do with the killings, but there's something niggling at him that he's never spelled out to me.'

'Have you ever asked him about it?'

'No.'

'Should you?' the chief constable asked quietly.

'Not unless you give me a direct order.' He smiled, grimly. 'Even then, I'd probably tell you to do it your fucking self . . . sir.'

Fifteen

'It's funny you should call right now,' Noele McClair remarked. 'I've just had your husband on the phone.'

'Christ,' Sarah Grace laughed. 'Can he not keep his hands off? What did he want?'

'He was being a concerned citizen,' the inspector replied, 'reporting a kid on a bike who nearly knocked him over on the pavement on Gullane Main Street. I said I'd advise patrol officers to keep an eye out for that sort of behaviour . . . not that there's a hell of a lot we can do about it, in truth.'

'Lucky kid. I wouldn't put it past Bob to have clotheslined him clean out of the saddle. We're not great cycling parents,' she confessed. 'Jazz has a bike, and Bob did go out with him when he was younger. He also sent him to a police safe-cycling school. Now he goes out on his own pretty much all the time, knowing what's right and what's wrong.'

'I'm not at that stage yet with Harry. The West Fenton road is too narrow and twisty; I wouldn't feel safe on it myself on a bike.'

'We'll need to start with Seonaid soon,' Sarah said. 'When I say "we", of course I mean Bob. I'll ask him if he'll take Harry under his wing at the same time.'

'If he would, that would be great. He wants a bike for his birthday and I've run out of reasons why he can't have one.'

'When you go shopping for it,' she warned, 'make sure it's a good off-roader. That's where they'll be going most of the time. The cycle shop in North Berwick is very good.'

'That's where I was thinking of going.' McClair paused. 'Now, why are you calling? I'm assuming there's a work reason.'

'There is,' she confirmed. 'I've just completed the post-mortem examination of Mr Michael Stevens. As I expected, he died of a cerebrovascular accident, in other words a major brain haemorrhage. From the size of the bleed, he'd have known very little about it: a few seconds' headache and that would have been that. There were no contributory factors that I could see. The brain showed significant volume loss, the kind that I'd associate with Alzheimer's. That suggests the vascular dementia diagnosis could have been wrong. He had a knee replacement when he was seventy-five . . . funnily enough, I remember that, because Bob played him in a golf tie when he was recovering. He was allowed to use a buggy, but he wouldn't let Bob get in it, even though it was raining. His excuse was that it would be giving Bob an unfair advantage. Bob was livid when he got back home, not least because he lost three and two.'

The inspector laughed. 'Just as well we're not talking about a suspicious death,' she chuckled, 'otherwise Bob would be a person of interest.'

'He would indeed. I think he's forgiven him by now, but you never know. Between you and me, Sir Robert is no stranger to a long-held grudge. Mind you, neither am I. That was one of the reasons we split up for a while.' She paused. 'But I digress,' she continued. 'Mr Stevens: his knee repair worked out fine, although he did have osteoarthritis, affecting his hands quite badly. Also, he had a minimally invasive aortic valve procedure, three years ago. Because of that he was on Dabigatran, a blood-thinning medication, and a mild dose of Ramipril to keep his blood pressure in check.'

'I thought most people were on Warfarin as a blood thinner,' McClair commented.

'Most people are,' Grace agreed, 'mainly because it's as cheap as chips, but it's a bit of a bugger to monitor. If patients complain, GPs are able to prescribe alternatives. Mostly it would be Apixaban, though; Dabigatran isn't common.'

'Are there any known side-effects from it that could lead to sudden death?'

'None that have been identified. If you stop taking it for an extended period you could be in trouble, but with carers involved that wasn't going to happen to Mr Stevens.'

'Covid? Could that have been a factor?'

'According to his medical records, which I accessed, he had his first dose of the AstraZeneca vaccine four weeks ago.' She sighed. 'Look Noele, I understand the concerns of the family. Coming to terms with the sudden death of a parent can be difficult. Coming to terms with the sudden deaths of both can threaten to overwhelm a person. Jesus, I know that from personal experience.'

McClair was taken aback by her sudden vehemence. 'What happened to yours?' she asked.

'They were murdered, sitting on their own front porch. I saw the police photos. The place was gothic, idyllic, but they were as far from the Grant Wood painting as you can get. So you see, I empathise with the daughter to an extent, but the vision she's conjuring up, it's fantasy, a wildest dream, no more than that. Her father died a natural death, peacefully, in the fullness of his years. She should be happy about it; you can tell her that from me.'

Sixteen

June Crampsey looked up in surprise at the person who stood in her office doorway. 'Bob,' she exclaimed. 'I didn't expect to see you here in person.'

'To be honest, this morning I didn't expect to be here.' He grinned. 'One of the things that puts me firmly on the side of law and order is my dislike of confinement: I could never hack it in jail. Even at home I'm restless, and come coffee time I'd had enough. I've been doing what I can about the village for the last couple of days but I still had to break free. Ours is an essential industry and I'm in charge of the British end of the company. I can't do my job properly from home, June, any more than Huw Edwards could read the news from his garden shed. I've decided that I'm coming in for at least two days a week, and this is one of them.'

'I have to confess I'm glad to see you,' she said. 'There's been a strange atmosphere among the senior staff for the last few days, ever since we heard about Sheila passing away. We all knew her from the occasional visits she paid us when she was over for her Marks and Spencer fixes, and we know how important she was to Xavi. How's he going to react to her death? Will he lose interest in the business? Since his dad,

Joe, died . . . and Roca, the editorial director, retired, it's been driven by him one hundred per cent. What if he's had enough? Will he float the company? Will he sell off the non-Spanish elements? Could the *Saltire* have a new owner? Whatever, it's good for you to be here, to damp down that sort of speculation.'

'How can I damp it down,' Skinner countered, 'if I don't know the answers to those questions myself? Any one of those things could happen, June. I'll tell you one thing, if Xavi does decide to sell this up, I won't be up for leading a management buy-out. That'll be down to you young guys, like Hector Sureda, the CEO . . . a lad not to be underestimated, by the way.'

'God,' she gasped, 'I hadn't even thought of that.' She shook her head. 'If it came to it, we don't have the expertise in-house to attempt that. But I'd hate to see the *Saltire* fall into the hands of a media tycoon, the likes of . . . you know who I'm talking about.'

'Me neither,' he admitted. 'Maybe I do have the contacts who could interest potential investors, but . . .' He paused, frowning. 'Let's not anticipate crises. When the time's right, I'll have a conversation with Xavi and find out what his thinking is. We've never discussed it, but my assumption has always been that he expects Paloma to succeed him in the fullness of time. She starts university this year; she's going to LSE to study accountancy and finance. Further down the road he wants her to do an MBA at Edinburgh.'

'How's she handling the loss of her mother?' Crampsey asked. 'Did Xavi say, when he called you?'

'No, but my guess is she's holding him together. She's a special kid.'

'What about the funeral?'

'It's happened already. Spanish law requires that it happens very quickly, within a couple of days normally. There's a burial ground on the Aislado estate, and Sheila's there, beside his grandmother and Joe.'

The editor's severe face softened. 'Aw, that's nice.' Then she frowned. 'But is it healthy for Xavi? Won't it be a permanent reminder of his loss?'

'He'll see it as a permanent reminder of their good life together. You know,' he said, 'I've never asked you, but have you read Xavi's book, the autobiography he commissioned? He must have given you a copy.'

'No, he didn't; indeed, I've never heard of it. Xavi might be my half-brother, but he rarely acknowledges the fact. Paloma's my niece, but we don't know each other. Xavi really hates our mum, but I have no idea why. She never spoke about it.'

'It's all in the book,' Skinner said. 'I was going to let you see my copy, but on second thoughts, no. If Xavi's never told you, it's not my place.' He straightened his back, pushing himself from the door jamb against which he had been leaning. 'But enough. I came here to work, not blether, and you've got a paper to get out. What's tomorrow's lead? Do we know yet?'

'Not for sure. The new Scottish Tory leader's having a press conference this afternoon. We've been briefed that he's going to call for the Health Minister's resignation.'

'Are we going to back that editorially?'

'Certainly not! The view of the *Saltire* is that she's done a decent job over the last year, under immense pressure.'

'Agreed,' Skinner said, with equal firmness. 'Same as the guy at Westminster. When you consider the situation they've faced some might argue that they're heroes.'

'That's not a view we'll be sharing, unless you order it . . . and if you do, I'll resign! I'm fairly sure that the majority of our readers wouldn't go that far.'

He grinned. 'I'm as sure as you are about that. Either of them could have clay feet that we know nothing about. Who's covering the Tory thing?'

'Jack Darke.'

'Will he ask them if the Scottish party want the Westminster Health Secretary to go as well?'

'I don't know,' Crampsey admitted, 'but I can make sure that he does.' She smiled. 'Are you sure you weren't a journalist in another life, Bob?' she called after him as he left.

He felt buoyant as he settled into his chair and switched on his computer. His conscience was slightly pricked by his decision to delegate home-schooling duties to Mark, but he had confidence in his teenage son, who knew as much, he reckoned, as most of his own teachers, and was competent to look after Jazz and Seonaid.

He had two email inboxes, business and personal; each was open only to those on his contact lists, which were restricted. He had been able to manage both while sitting out the coronavirus, but his work folder replenished itself on a daily basis, most of the messages and documents in Spanish. The last message caught his eye. It was timed ninety minutes earlier, at midday, and was from Xavi Aislado. He opened it immediately.

'Bob,' he read, 'when would it be convenient for us to have a Zoom meeting? One on one, nobody else in the room.'

He keyed in a one-word reply, 'Now,' then turned to the rest of his business mail. The lunch break in Spain ran well into the afternoon, catering for the siesta that many people still took, therefore he was surprised when an invitation to join a meeting in progress appeared in his box. He clicked on it at once and Xavi's solemn face filled his computer screen. His friend looked awful; there were circles of tiredness under his eyes, his face was pale, thinner than Skinner had ever seen it, and his chin was grey with a two-day stubble.

'Hey,' he murmured. 'How are you doing?'

'I don't know for sure yet, Bob,' Aislado confessed, 'truth be told. But this I do know. I spend an hour every morning sitting beside Sheila's tomb, talking to her; sometimes longer than that. It's all I really want to do.'

'How's Paloma taking it?'

'Stoically,' he replied. His accent had evolved, but under stress his Scottish origins seemed to be reasserting themselves. 'She insists that she'll still go into Girona every day, to her job as a gofer on the paper . . .' A faint sad smile flickered on his face, without reaching his eyes. 'Intern, that is. She'd kill me if she heard me call her that. I wish she could start LSE right away, but then I don't for that would mean she'd be in London.' He sighed, and for a moment, Skinner thought that he would cry, but he shuddered and with an effort seemed to pull himself together. 'What I do know, Bob,' he continued, 'is that I'm not fit to run the business, nor will I be for a while. That's not good, for it's bound to lead to uncertainty for our employees, and we have hundreds of them. Because of that, I'm going to step back as executive chairman of the Intermedia group, indefinitely, until I feel fit to return. That means,' he continued, 'I need a replacement who's up to the job, who thinks the same way as I do, and most important someone that I can trust. I need you, Bob. I want you to run Intermedia for me.'

Skinner felt his eyes widen. 'Xavi,' he exclaimed, 'I don't

have the background for this. I'm the wrong nationality for a start. It's one thing having me oversee the UK elements of the business, but to expect me to exercise authority over what's a largely European team, that's a big step. I don't know that I could do it.'

'Bob,' Xavi rumbled, 'if aliens landed in Edinburgh this afternoon, you'd exercise authority over them. As for nationality, I had a British passport until last year, when I changed it because of fucking Brexit. Look, man, I don't run the whole company hands-on. People report to me, you among them, and I take the strategic decisions. I don't tell our editors what to report and I don't tell our broadcast outlets how to present their programmes. This is my family's business; we don't have investors, we're not geared up to our armpits, and I don't have to kiss bankers' arses. If I did, we wouldn't be having this meeting, for I'm well aware that wouldn't be your strong suit. I want you to help me here, I need you to help me. Will you?'

'Have you asked the other board members?'

'Hell no! I'm the boss. I don't need to. But suppose I did, I've seen the way my senior people, board level people, react to you, and that makes me confident you'll be able to step in, seamlessly.'

'Would you want me full-time in Girona?' Skinner asked. 'I don't think I could do that.'

Aislado shook his massive head. 'We live in the age of remote management. It'll be your choice when to be in Spain. You could even commute, using the company jet. Come on, man, just say yes.'

He sighed. 'Yes.'

'Thank you. It'll be a twelve-month rolling contract. You'll find it in your email inside half an hour.'

'I don't want a contract,' Skinner protested, 'rolling or stationary.'

'Then don't sign it,' Aislado countered. 'The terms will apply regardless. Go on, read it. Call me back if you need to.' His hand moved, and a second later his image vanished.

Skinner went back to his business email inbox and found an email from 'Iceland@intermedia.com', with an attached Word document. He opened it and saw that it was bi-lingual, written in Spanish and English. He went straight to his own language and read through it, slowly and carefully. It had been drafted by the company's legal adviser, and appointed him as group executive chairman for a period of twelve months with effect from that day. All levels of management would report to him, directly or indirectly, and the only obligation on him was to keep Xavi updated on performance and profits every three months. Acquisition of new businesses within Intermedia's area of operations, or disposal of corporate assets, would be debated at board level, but he would have the power of veto, subject to the owner's endorsement. The last section covered remuneration. His eyes stood out as he read his proposed salary. It was in Euros, payable in Spain; the stated amount staggered him, and there was a performance bonus clause. The contract had been signed, by Aislado, and witnessed by the lawyer who had drawn it up.

He reopened the secure Zoom app and sent a meeting invitation. Xavi accepted immediately; he was smiling as he appeared on screen.

'Fucking hell, man!' Skinner exclaimed. 'I'll do the job, but you can't pay me that much.'

'Why not?' his friend asked. 'It's the rate for such a job in an international media company. It's what I pay myself;

the only difference is that as a shareholder ... the only active shareholder now; Paloma's holding is still in trust ... I take my bonus in dividend. I'm sorry that it has to be paid in Spain, but the Madrid tax authorities are real bastards about anything that's sent offshore. In fact they're bastards in every respect. If you really don't want to sign the contract, I'll respect that, but I'd be happier if you did. I know that the lawyer would too.'

He sighed. 'The last thing the world needs is another unhappy lawyer. Okay, I'll sign it, and bring it with me when I come over for the board meeting that I want him to call.'

'When do you want it?'

'This is Wednesday, so let's say Friday, if the aircraft can be ready in time.'

'I'll make it so; it'll be an early flight and the board meeting will be a working lunch. That way we'll get you home on the same day. Does that suit you?'

'Yeah, that's fine.'

'Thanks, Bob, neither of us will regret it.'

Skinner stared at the screen as Xavi's image faded. 'What the hell have I taken on here?' he murmured, frowning. For a few moments he considered calling back and withdrawing his acceptance of the post, until it dawned on him that he actually felt excited by the prospect. Instead, he called his wife using WhatsApp video and told her what had happened.

'They're paying you how much?' she exclaimed. He smiled at her amazement.

'I know, to us it's ridiculous,' he conceded, 'but the big fella says it's the rate for the job. We don't need the money: we're already well off by most people's standards, wealthy by some. I'll accept the salary and have the Intermedia accountant sort out the tax but then I'll probably put most of the balance in trust for the kids.'

'Including Alex?'

'No, just the younger ones. Alex had an inheritance from her mother and grandfather, so she's mortgage free, and Cameron McCullough told me that he's provided for Ignacio in his will. They're both covered in mine anyway.'

'How do you feel about that?'

'Why should it bother me? Nobody's ever proved Cameron is or was bent, and I'm past caring about it.'

'And yet you're keeping your distance from him,' Sarah pointed out.

"That's different,' he said abruptly. 'To hell with it, the important thing about my new job is that I do it properly and get the results that Xavi expects. The more I think about it, love, the more confident I become. In my police service I was the Chief Executive Officer of complex organisations with bigger payrolls than this one. They were in a different sector, I will grant you, but I've come to know the modern media industry in the time I've been with the company.'

She smiled. 'When you were chief constable, both in Edinburgh and in Strathclyde, even the dogs in the street knew that your big weakness was an inability to stand back from the action. How's it going to be different in this job?'

'In this job,' he replied, 'I don't know as much as the guys on the ground, so I won't presume to intervene. If I tried it here, June Crampsey would put me in my place in no time, and it will be just the same in Spain. Plus, there's the language issue. My Spanish is good these days, but my Catalan is still hesitant, and that's the working language in Girona.'

He paused, as his computer screen showed an incoming

FaceTime call. 'What the hell?' he murmured. 'Sarah, Andy Martin's trying to reach me. I'd better find out what he wants. Speak later.'

He discontinued the conversation and clicked to accept the incoming call. Without preamble, as Martin appeared on screen he launched into him. 'You were a bit fucking coy when we spoke,' he barked. 'Not as much as a whisper about the Met job. Did you think I wouldn't find out about it?'

'It never occurred to me to mention it,' his friend replied, 'seeing as I'd already asked for my name to be taken off the list. I was approached, Bob, that's true, but I never said yes. I didn't say no either, not until I heard that my name had been put to the Mayor of London by the Home Office. Once that filtered back to me I told the person who approached me and said I wasn't interested. How did you hear about it?'

'Not saying, but maybe you should drop the word to whoever does know about it within your loop.'

'That would be only one person,' Martin said. 'Who the hell else has she told? When did you speak to her, Bob?'

'I didn't.'

'Then let me guess; she's told her boss, Payne, Alex's uncle, and he's been speaking to you.'

'No comment.' Skinner smiled, momentarily. 'However, if you have taken yourself off the short list for London, you really should tell Karen.'

'I don't think I'm telling her anything at the moment. I've just discovered she's got a bit on the side.'

'Isn't that her business, not yours? You're divorced, remember.'

'Yes, but I thought . . .'

He gazed at the tired and solemn face on his screen. The

man was in his mid-forties but looked older. During his police career he had neither had nor made room for much of a life outside work. For most of that time, Martin had been Skinner's closest friend, as well as his protégé. The first crack had appeared when he had begun a relationship with his daughter, one that had been on-off and, ultimately, doomed. The initial breach had been repaired, but in truth, Skinner recognised, things had never been the same between them. Seeing Martin for the first time in almost three years, he felt an unexpected pang of pity and it shocked him.

'Andy,' he sighed, 'she's a single woman. She's entitled to a sex life. How did you find out anyway?'

'I saw him when I took the kids back to hers on Sunday. He was in the street by that time, but I saw him coming out of her drive as I turned the street corner. I'm sure of it, Bob; I'm not being paranoid here. I only had a quick look at him as I passed him in the car; he's tall but not huge, thirty-something, mixed race, well-dressed, and well-groomed too. Make me guess, I'd say he's ex-military, maybe even still serving. But the damnedest thing is, for all I only caught a glimpse of him, I feel that I've seen him somewhere before. I'm sure of it, and yet I can't remember where or when. You know what my memory's like. I have almost total fucking recall, and yet I can't place this guy.'

'Nobody's memory's a hundred per cent, son, but . . . why's it bothering you? You're divorced and have been for a while. You've had relationships. Why shouldn't Karen meet her own needs, so to speak? "A bit on the side", you said. That's not what it is, Andy. There is no side; she's entitled.'

'If he's around my kids, I'm entitled to take an interest in him. I remember when you were with Aileen de Marco and

Sarah was living in the US, you were still interested in what she was up to. Don't deny it.'

'I won't,' Skinner conceded. 'Look, can I make a suggestion?' he ventured.

'Could I stop you?' Martin countered.

'Probably not, I'll grant you. So, if you're that bothered, why don't you ask Karen about it?'

'It may come to that. I suppose I want to give her the chance to tell me.'

'Andy, this is getting to you. You really do want her back, don't you?'

He saw his friend's hesitation. 'Yes and no,' Martin admitted. 'Part of me would like to give it another try, but the other part's afraid of fucking it up again. I had a second chance with Alex and I did exactly that.'

Skinner grinned. 'If you've become that insecure, pal, I'm glad you opted out of the London job. Listen, is this why you FaceTimed me, to see if I can put a name to Karen's bloke?'

'Can you?' Martin challenged.

He was almost certain that he could, but he shook his head, frowning. 'If I could, I wouldn't tell you. You have to ask Karen.' He paused. 'So, was that it, or is there another reason for the call? Do you still think you're being stalked?'

Skinner could have sworn that his friend blushed. 'Squirrels,' he replied. 'I installed a security camera and caught the culprits straight away. Waste food recycling is not the greatest Green idea. The other stuff, probably some disgruntled plod who found out where I live and decided to take the piss. It wouldn't be the first time that's happened. Remember that ACC somewhere who had a ton of horse manure dumped on his front garden? No, Bob, there is another reason. I'm looking for a new career, one that's different from anything I've done in the past.'

'But definitely not in London?'

'Definitely no, that's out.'

He paused, considering a possibility. 'Not with the *Saltire*, surely,' he said.

'Not unless there's one going that fits my skill set and will pay the sort of money I'm used to.' Martin smiled, faintly. 'Bob, you're going to tell me I'm crazy, I know, but I'd like to go into politics.'

Skinner gasped. 'Politics? You?'

'Yes, me,' he retorted, defensively, but still with a grin. 'Why not?'

'No, no, no. Why yes? What's your motivation?'

'Simple, I want to make things better. Not for myself, like too many of them, for people in general.'

'So go and work for a charity. You've got a "Sir" before your name, that'll open most doors.'

'That might help individuals, but it wouldn't change anything, and you know it. I want to be an influencer, Bob, not an administrator. That's all I was as a chief constable, a gamekeeper for humans. You know that, you were one yourself and that's why you walked away.'

'I can't deny that,' Skinner admitted, 'even if don't care for the analogy. I always thought of myself as a public servant, first and foremost. I still do, to be honest.'

'And that's what I want to be too, but I want to be the kind who initiates, rather than implements. I have experience that none of the people in the Holyrood Parliament can match; I could shake the place up if I got in there, but I don't have the contacts to take the first steps. You have. Can you help me?'

'Are you having a mid-life crisis, mate? Is this the sort of thing that a good shag would put right?' He paused. 'Sorry,' he said, 'cynicism must be an after-effect of Covid-19. But Andy, do you even know the party you want to represent?'

'Of course,' Martin insisted. 'I'm pro-independence, so it would be the Nationalists.'

'Not necessarily,' Skinner countered. 'I know a few Tories who voted Yes in the referendum. Mind you,' he admitted, 'they keep their heads down. Nevertheless . . . you are an SNP member, yes?'

'Not yet.'

'Fuck!' he gasped. 'So you want me to go to Clive Graham, the First Minister, and tell him that I have the answer to all of his prayers, a potential SNP front-bencher that someone outside the Scottish Parliament has actually heard of, and that he'd even join the Party if it gave him a leg up?' He grinned, suddenly. 'Actually, that might work. Clive's been in the job for years, and one of the things that keeps him there is the private belief that none of his colleagues come close to being up to it. If I do this, Andy, you're not going to let me down, are you? This isn't a whim, is it?'

'No,' he promised. 'I'm serious.'

'Then we'd better move fast. The election is looming and most of the candidates will be in place. I'll call Clive and if he's up for it, I'll arrange a private meeting between the two of you. Any days you can't do?'

'I have the kids at the weekend, but I suppose Karen would take them . . . if she isn't otherwise engaged. Will you be there, Bob? It might be helpful. I've never met the man, not even when I was chief constable. I dealt with the Justice Minister and the chair of the Police Authority.'

'Hell no! You'll be on your own, mate. I have a new job myself, and I can't be seen to be involved in that sort of manoeuvre. Plus, you may be a man of leisure, I certainly am not. When I'm not running an international operation, I'm delivering groceries to old dears in Gullane.'

Seventeen

The day began earlier than Sarah Grace had anticipated. Her husband had tried not to waken her as he showered and shaved in preparation for his early morning flight to Spain, but inevitably she had stirred. Once she was awake, there would be no return to sleep, she knew, and so she went downstairs and made him coffee. Breakfast could wait, she decided, knowing that there would be catering on the company aircraft.

'You'll let me know if your flight time slips?' she asked, in the kitchen.

'Yes,' Bob promised, 'but it won't. There'll be hardly any air traffic out of Girona today.'

'This is weird,' she said, smiling, 'this whole thing, you as chairman of the board, company jet, the whole works.'

'Isn't it just?' he agreed. 'But it's an adventure too, and I'm ready for it. One thing I learned in isolation was how low my boredom threshold is.'

'Low? It's non-existent.' She glanced out of the window. 'Go on, get out of here. That's Campbell arriving in his taxi, your lift to the airport.'

Bob finished his coffee; she walked with him as he headed for the door. 'What have you got on today?' he asked.

'A Zoom lecture at ten o'clock, at the infirmary. I could have done it from here, but I have a couple of autopsies scheduled, on Covid victims, plus whatever emergencies the day might throw at me.'

He kissed her on the cheek. 'Knock 'em dead,' he murmured, opening the front door.

'No need,' she replied. 'They come that way.'

She returned to their suite and readied herself for the day, aware of stirring noises from the children's rooms. The boys and Seonaid were all self-starters, but Dawn had to be taken care of, and in Trish's continuing absence the task fell to her, mostly. In theory her sons could have helped, and even Seonaid, but she found that she still enjoyed the basic tasks of motherhood. Knowing that she would never have another chance, she relished them.

Grateful that none of her brood needed to be taken to school, she was able to leave for the Royal Infirmary by nine, arriving well in time for her remote lecture, even after dropping Dawn off at the hospital creche. Most of her students logged in on time, although some of their questions were affected by inadequate broadband connections.

Her scheduled post-mortem examinations were part of a national study into the effects of the coronavirus. The great majority of Covid-19 victims were not autopsied, only a few, selected because of underlying conditions and other factors, and always with the approval of their families. When she read the notes that accompanied her first subject, she was shocked, even before her assistant removed the sheet from the body on the examination table. It was a twenty-three-year-old woman who had succumbed to the disease within three days of displaying the first symptoms. Her medical history was minimal;

she had not seen a doctor since contracting chickenpox as a primary school child. 'God help us all,' she whispered, 'if it can do this.' The memory of Sheila Craig, Xavi Aislado's wife, sprang into her mind, laughing and joking over the dinner table in her Spanish home, and dead two weeks later. She had been middle aged, with a history of asthma in her youth, but no recent episodes, not in a high-risk group, and yet she was gone, leaving grief and bewilderment behind her.

The woman on the table was less than half Sheila's age. She had the body of someone who was used to regular exercise, a gymnast, perhaps. No, a rower, Sarah decided, when she noticed crossed oars tattooed on her right forearm. She made the Y incision herself, as she always did. Some pathologists left that to their assistants, but she did so only rarely. Her instinct had always told her that it was disrespectful to the patient . . . always 'patient' in her mind, another of her idiosyncrasies. She went straight to the lungs; the cause of death had been certified as multiple organ failure, but its origin was self-evident. They were spongy, almost solid. She opened them, dictating as she worked, and found the answer straight away, an undetected tumour attached to the left primary bronchus. If the woman had been a rower as her body art suggested she must have been exceptionally fit when the virus struck, or more likely, to have been in denial. She checked the other organs for metastases, finding two in the lymph nodes and one in the brain.

She was in the final stages of dictating her summarised findings, when her phone sounded, its screen advising that the caller was Adrian Spott, the head of the lab where autopsy samples were analysed. She had known him since her earliest days in the pathology department and liked him immensely.

'Good afternoon, Lady Skinner,' he began, jovially.

'Piss off, Adrian,' she replied, in the same spirit. 'Do you have anything for me or are you just plain bored?'

'Bit of both, truth be told. Me and my fella, we're sick of the sight of each other. I imagine you and Sir Robert are the same.'

'We were after a couple of weeks of self-isolation.'

'That said we're still rushed off our feet here, as you can imagine.'

'That's too bad,' Grace said. 'I'm about to send you some more tissue samples from a Covid victim with an undetected underlying condition. Somebody, somewhere will want to know whether the coronavirus affects tumour growth and if so how. Imagine if it turned out to be a cure for cancer.'

'Aye, right,' Spott said, dryly. 'Send them across, but you're not jumping the queue. Meanwhile . . .' he drew a breath, 'the blood sample you sent me from your elderly stroke victim, that was interesting. I don't think I've ever seen anything like that before. How much do you know about the subject?'

'Personally, not a lot. I'd met him, in the village and through the golf club. I did certify his death, though, for no other reason than I was the easiest option for the police. I only did the autopsy to satisfy his family. As straightforward a cerebrovascular accident as I have ever seen.'

'You could certainly be forgiven for thinking that,' the scientist agreed. 'How was his mental state? Did he have dementia?'

'Yes, probably Alzheimer's. Early stages, I was told.'

'What was his medication?'

'Ramipril and Dabigatran.'

'Did he live alone?'

'He had carers coming in, but yes.'

'Then he shouldn't have been; he certainly shouldn't have

had access to his own medication. He must have been popping the Dabigatran capsules like they were jelly babies. I've never seen such high levels as there were in that sample. I'm not saying that they killed him, that's your department, but they could easily have been a contributory factor.'

'There's no doubt about this? Sarah asked.

'You wound me, Lady Skinner, you wound me. None whatsoever. I think you'd better change your report to the fiscal and make it accidental death.'

'As you well know I won't be writing that report. But still, I'd better pass your findings on to the person who will.'

She ended the call, then found McClair's mobile. 'Noele,' she said as they were connected, 'have I got news for you!'

Eighteen

'So, DCI Neville, tell me about yourself.'

'There isn't a lot to tell, Captain Houseman,' she replied. 'People see me as boring, really: divorced mother of two, very much a plodder as a police officer. Half my colleagues think I only got where I am because I used to be married to the founding chief constable of our glorious service, the other half don't know that but would think the same if they did. And you know what? They might be right.' She raised an eyebrow. 'That's not to say I haven't had my moments. I once got drunk at a police do and made a pass at the new chief constable. I was even accused of sexual harassment in a cupboard by a brother officer. Fortunately Bob Skinner didn't believe it. Mind you, I did shag someone else in the same cupboard.'

He laughed. 'Don't tell me any more. But I wasn't asking about your job, I really did mean yourself. You have very nice stretch marks, but I don't know anything else about you.'

'That really is boring,' Karen sighed. 'I'm an only child. My parents were mid-ranking civil servants who played bridge, did the *Scotsman* crossword on alternate days and listened to Radio Four. When I was allowed the telly I saw it through a fog. They both smoked too much and as a consequence died when I was in my twenties, Dad first, from heart disease, Mum two years later from lung cancer. I have one brother, Gareth. He's ten years older, inherited the family home and most of the rest of Mum's estate, never gave me a penny of the proceeds, fucked off to a job as an assistant golf pro in Dubai, and never keeps in touch. I have one uncle who's a dear. He lives on the other side of the country but still I see a lot of him. We bubble together, each of us being single. I saw much less of him when I was married to Andy, because they couldn't stand each other.'

'I have met him, you know,' Houseman said, quietly, gazing across the dinner table.

Neville stared back at her lover. 'Who?'

'Your ex-husband,' he replied.

She frowned. 'When he was chief constable, I suppose?'

'Once at a meeting I can't talk about, not even to you. The other time, it was way before that. It was the day I laid eyes on Bob Skinner for the first time. I was a rough kid then, my teens, top dog my gang. He parked his car in my street, and I pulled the old "Watch it for a tenner" trick . . . or I tried to. He put me right very quickly, made me realise that however tough I thought I was, there would always be someone tougher. We didn't talk for long, but he made an impression on me. I cut myself loose from the local disorganised crime and joined the Marines as soon as I was old enough. The memory of that meeting stayed with me, crystal clear, every detail, including his gofer, a young fair-haired guy in his twenties, with green eyes. He didn't make any impression on me, but Skinner scared me, and I'm not ashamed to admit it.'

'Maybe he did,' Karen said, 'but don't confuse Andy with a softie. People have forgotten now, but he played rugby for

Scotland at B level before he chose his police career over being a full international. Did you ever play rugby?'

'I played truant more than anything else. There was a bit of football, and I used to run, but I never did anything organised until I joined the armed forces. In the Marines, I played cricket, believe it or not.' He smiled. 'I was an all-rounder, bowled a bit, batted a bit, but it was my fielding that got me into the team and kept me there. That ended when I joined the Special Boat Service; that was full on, no time for games. The training left you too knackered for any leisure activity more strenuous than chess.'

'Where did you serve?' she asked. 'Can you talk about it?'

'It's discouraged. We're not sworn to secrecy but given some of the stuff we do, we're advised against writing our memoirs. That hasn't stopped some guys, but what I was involved in, that's definitely not for publication.'

'You're not even going to tell me?' she teased.

He grinned. 'I suppose I can trust you, given that you're part of the state security network as well. Some of my SBS service was in Iraq, but most, the heavy stuff, was in Afghanistan.'

'Eh? I thought that was pretty much desert and poppy fields. Why did they need boats there?'

'We weren't exclusively water-based, we did land-based ops too.'

'Such as?'

'Occasionally there would be rendition. Intelligence would pinpoint a Taliban or AQ target, we'd go in on foot, sometimes after dark, sometimes in daylight, extract him then be picked up by choppers. Back at base he'd be handed over to the Americans.'

'What did they do with him?'

'I don't know for sure; we were never told. The popular belief was that they'd take him to one of those places that officially didn't exist, a secret base, maybe Diego Garcia, and go to work on him with so-called advanced interrogation techniques.' He raised an eyebrow. 'I'm not sure what's advanced about water-boarding, or attaching wires to somebody's balls, but who am I to judge?' He winced as he sipped a little of the Malbec that he had brought with him. 'Rendition ops were the exception though. Mostly we just killed them.'

Karen felt herself shiver in the candlelight. 'In cold blood?'

He shrugged. 'None of us ever had moral issues, if that's what you're asking. The people we were taking off the pitch were responsible for the death and maiming of hundreds, thousands, through roadside devices that blew up military vehicles, and suicide bombers in crowded areas that killed and mutilated troops and civilians alike, indiscriminately. Our targets were the leaders, people who carried Kalashnikovs for show but never got close enough to the action to use them. They thought they were safe; we showed them they were wrong.'

'How many Taliban did you kill?'

'I don't know,' he admitted. 'In the eighteen months I served there, we carried out three missions a month, on average. My unit took three casualties in that time, two of them fatal, but the enemy didn't fare so well. We left nobody alive.'

'Does that include children?' she asked quietly.

'Please, Karen,' he exclaimed. 'We didn't kill these people in their homes. We were given specific targets, in combat zones, more often than not in places where drones couldn't be used. Our intelligence was good enough for us to minimise collateral damage. I'm not saying there were no accidents, but we did our best.'

'Still, you might have shot women and kids.'

He shook his head. 'I never did, nor to my knowledge did anyone else on one of my ops. We were very well trained, we knew our targets in advance; it wasn't a case of killing anything that moved. Morally we were on the high ground,' he said firmly. 'Jesus, these people used women and kids as suicide bombers! We saved a lot of lives by killing a few fanatics. I will never apologise for it, and I will never feel guilty. I might have the odd bad dream, but only about the men I lost, not those I killed.'

'So you didn't suffer from PTSD, after it was over?'

'Not even close. Selection for special forces involves psychological fitness as well as physical. The criteria are way beyond those of the police service.' He refilled her glass.

'Andy had PTSD,' she said, taking him by surprise. 'Just before he and I got serious. A man with a gun and a grudge held him prisoner. The guy was going to shoot him, beyond a shadow of a doubt, but Andy overpowered him, and killed him. I won't say how, but he was a wreck after it. He never woke up screaming, but there were periods when he didn't sleep for days on end. Eventually I made him undergo counselling . . . he'd turned it down before . . . but it took a while. There was another incident too, way in the past. It was an anti-terrorist operation that he and Bob Skinner were involved in. He's never talked about that to me in any detail, nor has Bob, but I just know that something traumatic happened.' She frowned. 'He's been very good to me over the years, has Bob Skinner, and to the kids, but I'm under no illusions about him. He used to be a very dangerous man.'

'He still is,' Houseman murmured. 'I've seen him in action, in an armed situation.'

'But he would worry about it,' she continued. 'He would have bad dreams, or so he told Andy. He had a brother, you know. When Andy was deputy up in Tayside and we lived in Perth, he was found dead there. Bob came to our house, and he cried like a baby. Yes, he's hard as nails, but he has that in him too. Judging by what you've said to me about Afghanistan, you don't.'

'So?' he asked.

'So . . .' she paused '. . . while we may quite happily fuck each other's brains out until we get bored with it, from my perspective it won't go any further than that. I'm not going to fall in love with you, and I'll never let you get too close to my children. Understood?'

Houseman nodded. 'Understood.' He emptied his glass and smiled. 'Meantime, I'm a long way from bored.'

Nineteen

'The thing I like most about my garden,' Matthew Reid declared, 'is the complete absence of grass. It wasn't quite like this when I moved in; there were more trees and more planted areas. I've spent the last thirty years making it as low maintenance as possible.' Every part of the discreetly sited property that was not paved was filled with gravel beds in which various shrubs and trees were planted. Bright February midday sun shone as the author and his visitor sat at a glass-topped table, each clutching a tall glass coffee mug.

Bob Skinner grinned. 'That explains why you're the only bugger who never talks about tomatoes, leeks and runner beans on a Friday evening in our Zoom virtual pub.'

'I don't hear you contributing much to that area of discussion,' his host countered. 'Stop that, Sunny,' he said to the young red-coated Labrador which lay at his feet, making a determined effort to unfasten his shoe laces. The dog ignored him.

'I don't grow a hell of a lot,' Skinner conceded. 'Going to the farm shop's easier. But I do cut the grass . . . or did until I decided I could trust my youngest son to use the ride-on mower. Mark, my middle boy, he surprised me last year by planting herbs beneath the kitchen window. He linked it in some way to a computer program that he'd written. He says it's just the start, and that by the end of the summer the entire garden will be computerised, with humidity sensors, automatic watering, et cetera.'

'Who's going to do the weeding?' Reid asked.

Skinner laughed out loud. 'Mark's working on a robot for that very purpose. He's been in touch with a scientist in Heriot Watt University who's been involved in designing explorers for a possible European Mars mission, asking her for advice on construction.'

'How did that go down?'

'She's offered to swap; her design for his program. I told him to agree to nothing until the commercial possibilities have been explored. She's happy with that; now they're talking about setting up a company to develop the idea. Once that's done I'll fund the construction of a prototype.'

'Will we see you on *Dragons' Den*?'

'As far as they're concerned I am the fucking dragon.'

Reid nodded in the general direction of his garden. 'Good luck with it. When they develop a remote that power-washes concrete slabs, let me know. I'll be their first customer.' His mood changed, he became sombre. 'When do you think the handcuffs will be taken off us, Bob? When will this lockdown be eased?'

'Don't broadcast this,' Skinner warned, 'for I haven't shared it with June at the *Saltire*, but it will probably get worse before it gets better. I've taken on a new job that involves me flying to Spain every so often. I spoke to the First Minister yesterday on another matter and happened to mention it. Clive warned me it's possible that people flying into Scotland from anywhere outside the British Isles will be banged up in hotels for ten days, at their own expense.'

'In theory that would affect me,' Reid said, 'but since I can't fly to my other place anyway, it's irrelevant. We may as well buckle down and do what we can here. So thank you again for joining the resilience group.'

'Not at all. I owe this village; it's sheltered me for most of my adult life and I haven't given enough in return. Plus I'm getting to meet some real characters . . . Mrs Alexander for one. It's a pity about some of the men on the list, though; crusty old bastards.'

'You're right about that,' the writer agreed. 'They don't want to admit weakness, none of them, that's what it is. All we can do is keep an eye on them even if it has to be from a distance.'

'We missed old Michael Stevens, that's for sure,' Skinner observed. 'He's one that fell through the cracks, even though he was a foxy old bastard.'

'Was his death preventable?' Reid asked.

'I doubt it, not the way he was living. Again, this is not virtual pub talk, but effectively he died of an overdose of his blood thinner. Sarah did an autopsy at the request of the daughter. She thought he was still okay to be living on his own, with a care package, but he wasn't, not with open access to his medication. It should have been secured, but it wasn't.'

'How old was he?'

'Eighty-six.'

'Christ, man, that's no age, no age at all. Not a patch on the next person I have for you to reach out to.'

'Who's that?'

Reid disclosed the name.

'Wow!' Skinner said, grinning. 'I can see why you're passing that one down the line, but I'm not sure I'm brave enough.'

Twenty

'First Minister,' Martin began as the sound caught up with the tele-conference image, 'thanks for agreeing to talk to me.'

'Not at all, Sir Andrew,' Clive Graham said. 'When Bob Skinner told me about your plans, I was intrigued and pleased too that they included my party.' He paused. 'I have to be honest and say that from my observations of you over recent years, I have never thought of you as politically ambitious.'

'I wasn't. As I hope Bob explained to you, I've come to recognise that I've done all I can as a police officer but I don't want to sit on my hands for the rest of my life. I want to contribute my experience to the public service.'

'Have you had any experience of politics?'

'By the very nature of my job, no, I haven't,' he admitted. 'But I don't see that as a bad thing. I've always been suspicious of those people who take their honours degrees in politics and economics straight into a party research department, become special advisers then smooth their way into safe seats. Westminster's riddled with them. I have a quaint belief that those who seek to govern working people should have real experience of working themselves.'

'Do you know what my background is?'

'Yes. You were a general practitioner who allowed his name to be put on a Scottish National Party regional list for the second Holyrood election with no expectation of success. As it happened, you were wrong and you've been there ever since. You've been in the cabinet for fifteen years, half of them as Health Secretary, the rest in the top job. In your administration, every member has hands-on workplace experience, but unlike you, none of them are responsible for departments that include oversight of their own profession.'

The First Minister smiled. 'You have been doing your homework, Sir Andrew. Can you guess why that is?'

'I think so. Most of your cabinet are aged under forty, with at least half a career ahead of them. Let's say you appointed a teacher or lecturer as Education Secretary, and that person lost his or her seat at the next election. They'd find it very awkward to go back to the classroom, or the lecture theatre.'

'Got it in one. Whereas that wouldn't be a problem with you . . . although I am getting way ahead of myself there. My first question is whether you're a Party member or not. I did try to find you on our database but I couldn't.'

'I've never been a member of any political party, First Minister, but I voted Labour in my early years, when they were the dominant force in Scottish politics, until they were replaced as the left-of-centre flag-bearer by the SNP.'

'What's your position on independence? It's Clive, by the way.'

'Likewise, it's Andy. I believe in it. I fear for England in the coming decades. It's becoming more divided than ever; the north and the south are growing further and further apart and I can't see that getting better any time soon, or in the longer term. We need to cut ourselves completely adrift.'

'What about the EU? Would you support re-joining as an independent nation?'

'I'd like to consider all the options. For example, could we form a trading bloc with the Norwegians? The governance of the EU worries me; it has an unfortunate habit of appointing second-raters and nonentities to its top posts. There's still an outside chance it might disappear up its own arse. It's making a bollocks of its vaccination programme at the moment, probably creating thousands of new Brexit supporters every day.'

'Between us,' Graham admitted, 'I share some of your worries, but Scotland voted Remain; that has to be respected.'

Martin smiled. 'Scotland voted No as well, but you're hoping to re-run that one. Won't it be difficult not to put EU membership to the people?'

'Let's get independence done first, Andy,' Graham chuckled. 'For that I'm going to need the strongest team available, and your approach is welcome.' He paused, frowning. 'Before we go any further, though, let me be blunt. Is there anything you need to tell me now that might embarrass the Party if it came out at a later date?'

'Does any video exist of me singing "The Sash" at a stag do? No, I'm a Catholic; we don't have good tunes. Seriously though, I had a couple of episodes in my police career that are classified as secret, but I see no chance of either of them surfacing.'

'If they did?'

'I would deal with them.'

'And your personal life?'

'Divorced, two kids. Two failed relationships with the same woman; if you don't know who she is I'm not going to tell you. No current involvement and no, I don't use dating sites. There's nothing in my back story to worry either of us.'

'In that case, let's go for it,' the First Minister declared. 'The first thing you need to do is join the Party. There's no legal requirement for this, believe it or not, but you're high profile so we should be prepared for journos sniffing around. As for the election itself, we have candidates in place for every one of the hundred and twenty-nine seats, but we still have to finalise the lists from which the top-up MSPs are selected under our quaint system. Bob said you live in Motherwell, yes?'

'That's right.'

'In that case, Andy, you'll be the second name on the West of Scotland list; that will mean you'll most certainly get a seat.'

'As a matter of interest,' Martin ventured, 'whose is the first name?'

'Mine.'

Twenty-One

Bob Skinner frowned as an incoming-call alert sounded in his ear-pods. As he walked he had been engrossed in the latest Michael Jecks audio novel, a departure from the author's norm in that its time frame was twentieth century rather than medieval. With a silent growl, he tapped his right ear twice and accepted the intrusion.

'Pops!' his daughter exclaimed. 'You're never going to guess what I just heard as the top story on the Radio Scotland news.'

'I'll take a stab,' he replied. 'Andy Martin's running for the Scottish Parliament under the SNP banner.'

'You knew? And you never told me?'

He laughed. 'I didn't know it had gone that far. All I did was make an introduction. Andy took it from there. I'm surprised the story's broken so quickly but Monday's a slow news day. The Nats' press office probably decided to take advantage of that.'

'What's brought this about?' Alex asked.

'He says he's after a new challenge in life. London came calling, but he decided against it.'

'And you introduced him to Clive Graham?'

'That's right.'

'I can't work out whether you were doing him a favour or getting even,' she said.

'Forget the latter. Andy's made his peace with me. I don't believe he's as much as glancing in your direction anymore. I could help him, so I did.'

'Where is he glancing? Do you have any idea?'

'Nowhere new, I reckon. I believe he'd like to get his family back together, but I have no idea whether that's possible.'

'Is Karen still single? That would surprise me; she's an attractive woman.'

'As far as I'm aware,' her father replied. 'Your Uncle Lowell would know better than me. She works for him.'

'Do you think Andy will get a seat in Holyrood?'

'I'd be surprised if he doesn't. Clive wouldn't have taken him on as a candidate just to humiliate him. The way the electoral system works the leaders can make sure their top people all get seats. If they don't win a constituency, they get in through the second ballot and the top-up system.'

'And if he does, will he be a minister?'

'For sure,' he declared. 'Just be grateful he doesn't have a law degree. That means he can't become Lord Advocate and be your boss.'

'That had never even occurred to me,' Alex said. 'Justice Secretary would be bad enough.'

'That would break one of Clive Graham's rules.' He paused. 'Mind you, as Andy will never re-join the police service, it might not apply. Got to go now, kid. I've reached my destination.' He ended the call and put on his mask, a black three-filter version emblazoned with the newspaper's crest that was supplied to all *Saltire* staff and management.

In fact, Skinner had not gone far from his own front door.

He had walked to the top of Gullane Hill, then followed a path that led him into a cul-de-sac in which his destination was located. Mrs Anne Eaglesham was something of a legend in the village, and in the Ladies' Golf Club in particular. He had known her since his earliest days as a Men's Club member, and they had always been on good terms. She had been captain almost half a century before. Her name appeared seven times on the Champions board, in gold lettering, and she had won the trophy eight times in the years before those recorded. In her youth, and even into her middle age, she had played at national level. Mrs Eaglesham had been Scottish Ladies champion three times, the first as Miss Anne Worthington, and had played against the USA in the Curtis Cup, on the winning side on both occasions. She had been a widow for almost forty years; Mr Eaglesham had been very much older, and a non-golfer, thus there were very few people left in Gullane who could remember anything about him, least of all the source of his considerable wealth. They had one daughter, dead herself by the Millennium, and there were known to be two grandchildren, both American citizens, of whom she spoke rarely.

Gravel crunched beneath Skinner's feet as he walked up the long driveway that led to The Eyrie. When the house had been built, it had been christened Eagle's Nest, but that name had been changed in the nineteen forties, at the insistence of Mrs Eaglesham herself, as a condition of her acceptance of Mr Eaglesham's proposal. It was a large villa, in rattlebag sandstone with a slate roof, with bay windows on either side of an oak entrance door, on which there was a bronze knocker in the shape of an eagle. Skinner was in the act of reaching out to grasp it when the door opened, with a creak, framing a large, formidable woman.

Mrs Eaglesham's age was the subject of speculation . . . her date of birth was not recorded in the Ladies Golf Club lists . . . but Skinner knew that she was a month short of her ninety-fifth birthday. He had asked his secretary to check the *Saltire* library and she had found a record of her first Curtis Cup appearance, in which it was recorded. He had feared that isolation would be hard for her, but there was no outward sign of it as she gazed at him from her doorway.

'Bob,' she exclaimed, her voice as deep and steady as usual. 'I assume that is you behind that mask and not the Lone Ranger. I should be wearing one myself, I suppose, but to be honest I don't possess any.'

Buried in a pocket of his jacket he had half a dozen Saltire masks, each still in its sterile wrapper. He took out three and laid them on top of an umbrella rack beside the door. 'Now you do,' he said. 'How are you doing, Anne?' he asked.

'I'm bored out of my noggin, truth be told,' she admitted. 'Everywhere's closed . . . everywhere I want to go, that is. Most of all I miss the golf club. I could play, I know, but I can't grip a club properly just now.' She held up her left hand, and he saw it was twisted. 'I have a tendon that's misbehaving. It's a simple procedure but not a priority, apparently, not even in a private hospital.'

Skinner frowned. 'That's too bad,' he said. 'What about food shopping? Can we help you there?'

'I do it online,' she replied. 'Yes, Bob,' she said, smiling at his involuntary reaction. 'I joined the twenty-first century some time ago, although I doubt that I'll see it out. I have a Tesco delivery every Thursday morning. Also, John the fish man comes with his van every Tuesday, and leaves me enough for two or three meals. My freezer's still stocked too. I filled it full last November when it became obvious that we were heading for another lockdown. If I feel lazy and want a night off cooking, the Italian's doing home deliveries and so is the place in Aberlady.'

'How about cleaning?' he suggested, feeling increasingly superfluous.

'Bob, I live in four rooms in this place, most on the ground floor. The rest are all closed off. According to the Blessed Clive's rules, I can't have my cleaner in, just as I can't invite you in just now, but I can still wield a duster and one of the Dyson man's machines.'

He frowned. 'Maybe you could have your cleaner in,' he suggested. 'There are exemptions for vulnerable people.'

'Vulnerable?' She seemed to stiffen; it was an act of pure theatre. In that instant, Skinner could think of nothing other than Oscar Wilde's magnificent Lady Bracknell. 'Do I seem to you to be vulnerable, Sir Robert?'

'Not you, Anne,' he assured her, suppressing the urge to grin. 'It's a generic term for people of a certain age, living alone.'

Mrs Eaglesham's own smile broke through. 'Those who are less resilient than others, to borrow the title of the group you spoke of when you called me.'

'That would be another way of saying it.'

'Say it however you like, I don't know whether to be flattered or narked to be counted among their numbers. Who's the ringleader of your gang? I know it isn't you because your name never shows up on Facebook. Mind you,' she added, 'neither does mine. I'm there under an alias, GeeGee. I suppose people assume that I'm horsey, but actually it stands for Gullane Granny.'

119

'Nice one, Anne,' Skinner said. 'I don't think the resilience group has a leader as such, but I was brought in by Matthew Reid.'

Her augmented eyebrows rose. 'The author, no less? He called on me a few days ago, but he didn't say anything about resilience. He told me he was working on a book that involved golf in the days when we played with persimmon rather than metal woods and wanted to know how far they could reasonably be hit by the average lady golfer. He said it was relevant to the plot. I confess that I can't stand his books, but he did bring me one as a gift, a signed hardback, so I won't hold it against him. And it is good to know, I suppose, that people care. On reflection I could have been kinder to my last caller, although I doubt that he really was one of your crowd, although he claimed to be.'

'Who was that?' he asked.

'A boy on a bike. He banged my brass eagle as if he was trying to knock the door down and asked if I had any jobs that needed doing. He was quite annoyed when I told him to be on his way, but he went. Raining silent curses on my head, I have no doubt.'

That's not good, Skinner thought. 'Can you describe him?'

'He was like any other lad on a bike. Jeans, puffer jacket and attitude. Early teens, I'd say. It was well seen the barber's is closed. I know that parents have a lot on their hands . . . not that I speak from experience; Sophia had a nanny . . . but the odd trim wouldn't go amiss. If he comes back, as I'm sure he will, I might find something for him to do, as long as it's outside. The same is true of your group.' She scratched her chin. 'There's the Bentley, of course. I turn it over every so often, and back it out of the garage, to make sure there's still a charge in the battery. There's a chap in Dirleton who's desperate to buy it, but he can wait until I'm dead. In the meantime, perhaps Mr Reid would like to clean it.'

Skinner shook his head. 'I doubt that. He's never been known to clean his own.'

Twenty-Two

'They're sure about that?' Lynn Langham asked.

During her career, Noele McClair had understood the need to make allowances for the recently bereaved. She had been among their number herself when her ex-husband had been murdered. She had been summoned to the crime scene by the former chief constable, and had been barely rational in the aftermath. Nevertheless there was something about the tone of the late Michael Stevens' daughter that set her on edge.

'The pathologist's report is quite clear,' she replied. 'Your father's sample showed dangerously high levels of Dabigatran, his prescribed blood thinner. The absorption life of one tablet is between twelve to eighteen hours. Tests showed that he had at least a dozen in his system. While a cerebrovascular accident can occur at any time, there's a very strong chance that it contributed to his death.'

'What happens now?'

'It's happened already. I interviewed his carers this morning and they both assured me that they gave him only the prescribed doses of each medication. In the case of the Dabigatran that was twice daily, morning and evening, a hundred and fifty milligrams each time.'

'Did you believe them?'

'I have no reason not to. They're trained, experienced people, both of them.'

'How did you verify that?'

'With the care company that employs them,' McClair said. 'The morning carer was a nurse before she had her family. The evening person has worked in personal care for over twenty years.'

'And yet my father overdosed,' Langham persisted.

'He did, but the belief is that he did it himself. We found boxes of Tic Tacs in his kitchen and in his bedroom. They're about the same size as the Dabigatran capsules.'

'Yes, he was addicted to those things.'

'Indeed? Well, our best guess is that he was confused. His medication was kept in a bathroom cupboard. In hindsight it should have been secured, but it wasn't. The door was open and there was an empty Dabigatran box beside the basin. It looks as if he'd been taking them like sweets, literally.'

The inspector heard a faint snorting sound. 'Why did nobody think of this?' Langham demanded. 'Why wasn't the stuff under lock and key?'

McClair's patience wore out. 'You tell me,' she said, quietly. 'You're his daughter. You were obviously happy that he was still capable of independent living. The company told me that you made the care arrangements and that they reported to you every month, but his physical security was something else. Was he ever visited by an occupational therapist? Was his home ever assessed to see if he needed aids?'

'No.'

'Maybe he should have been. When did you see him last?'

'Early October, after Mum's funeral.'

'Four months ago.' McClair let the words hang in the air for a few seconds. 'Was your father on a care home waiting list?' she asked, although she knew the answer.

'After what happened a year ago?' Langham retorted. 'No, he was not!'

'He'd received his first vaccine,' the inspector pointed out. 'Things are different now. The proprietors have learned from experience and all sorts of safety protocols are in place.'

'Even so! The cost of those places! They're outrageous.'

So Prue Granton was right, McClair thought. 'That's not an issue for your father now, sadly,' she said. 'But if he had been in care,' she added, twisting the knife, 'he wouldn't have had access to his meds, would he?'

Twenty-Three

The Merchant City had been trendy for so long that nobody could say for sure when it had attained that status. Once it had been what its name suggested, in the days when Glasgow had claimed to be the Second City of the Empire. It had fallen into decline during the twentieth century, only to undergo a process of gradual gentrification as it drew to a close, with lawyers, financiers and other young professionals adopting its poshed-up pubs and pushing up prices for old tenement flats, some in dire need of renovation. Without their intervention it was conceivable that many would have been demolished.

Philomena McBride had been a post person there for ten years and knew the area better than most. In her early days her round had been early too, and she had come to know many of its residents by sight and some by name. Latterly her deliveries had become later and most had left for work long before she slid their mail through their letter boxes. She had seen changes in their design; once they had been simple, a brass-covered slit with nothing behind it and a soft sound as letters hit the lino. Replacement doors though, they were different. The City Council was very fussy about anything that showed on the outside of the precious buildings, but inside, up the closes, that was fair game for the UPVC salespeople. More often than not the letter boxes in those doors came with two layers of fur lining and a powerful spring on the closer that could break a lady's nails.

There was one of those on the second floor flat in Candleriggs, a real nail-cruncher. Philomena had never met the owner, but she could see that he took his security seriously, from the sensors that were set in the doorframe. She had been around long enough to know them as a sign of a sophisticated alarm system. As for the door itself, that was steel, not fancy plastic; to her it suggested one thing above all else: drug dealer. It was built to withstand a few whacks with the polis's big red knocker, giving those inside time to flush the product down the toilet before entry was effected. An occasional user of nose candy herself, Philomena had nothing against such precautions, other than the beast of a letter box that went with them.

Her theory about its owner was given weight by the fact that there was no nameplate in sight, and by another, even greater, oddity. The address received absolutely no junk mail, a virtual impossibility in the new era of online and mail order shopping; she could think of no one else on her round to whom that applied. Also, he or she was anonymous. The few items of mail she delivered there were all addressed to 'The Occupier'.

She had one that Tuesday afternoon, a slim envelope with something stiff inside, a replacement credit card, perhaps. She prised the letter box open and pushed it into the opening . . . and to her surprise, the door swung open. That was not uncommon in older dwellings with a Yale that had seen better days. A surprising number of householders were sloppy in the way they secured their property. For it to happen in Fortress Candleriggs, though, that was another matter.

Ignoring her training, and setting aside common sense, she stepped inside, hope rising in the back of her mind that The Occupier, if he was there, might reward her with a wee baggie of something nice.

There were four doors off the narrow lobby, but only one of them was ajar. 'Hello,' she cried out, moving forward tentatively. 'It's Phil the Postie. Your front door's wide open.' Nervousness caught up with her as she waited, her shout unanswered. Finally she summoned up the last of her courage, stepped into the open doorway and stopped.

The Occupier was male, and he was very dead.

Twenty-Four

Noele McClair checked her watch. It told her that her shift had another seventy-five minutes to run. She sighed, inwardly. The inspector had sounded off to nobody, not even her mother, but she was bored. After the shock of losing her former husband and her lover in the same violent incident she had been ready to leave the police service, but she had been persuaded to stay on by Maggie Steele, the former chief constable, with an offer of promotion, a move out of CID and a posting near to her home. At that time she had been horrified by the thought of ever visiting another crime scene, but her discovery of Michael Stevens' body, although it had been a natural death, had disturbed her not at all. She was ready to re-join the action, but detective inspector vacancies were few and far between.

She was entertaining thoughts of uploading her profile to LinkedIn when her office door swung open after the briefest of knocks and a tall man in a black tunic stepped into the room.

She had never been introduced to Deputy Chief Constable Brian Mackie, but knew him instantly from his image on the police service website. He was the third highest ranking officer on the force, after Mario McGuire and the new chief, Neil McIlhenney, all three graduates of what older cops and cynics referred to as 'The Skinner Academy'. She made to rise, in deference to his rank, but he waved her back down.

'Don't get up, Inspector McClair,' he said. 'This is an informal visit; I'm doing the rounds in the absence of your divisional commander.'

'I'd heard he was off sick, sir. Not Covid, I hope.'

Mackie shook his dome-shaped head. 'No, the poor bugger's got shingles. That's bad enough from what they tell me. All going well in your sub-division?' he asked, briskly.

'Fine,' she confirmed. 'I could do with another couple of uniforms, but we're coping.'

'That's a smart young lass outside.'

'Tiggy Benjamin? Yes, she shows promise.'

'That's good. Look, Inspector,' Mackie continued, 'a couple of things. The first is something I didn't want you to hear through official channels, or the grapevine. Chief Inspector Sammy Pye passed away this morning. You worked with him, I believe.'

A wave of sadness swept over her. 'Yes sir, I did. Not for long, but long enough for me to get to like him.' Pye had been diagnosed with motor neurone disease two years earlier; his wife had discouraged visits from colleagues, as she had feared they would upset him. Only Sauce Haddock had visited regularly, but he had never spoken about it. An unbidden thought appeared in her mind. For sure, Sauce would be confirmed as DCI in charge of the Serious Crimes Edinburgh team. Would that create a detective inspector vacancy? The notion was washed away by a wave of guilt that overwhelmed the sadness; she felt her face flush and hoped that the DCC had not been able to read her mind.

'There'll be an announcement from the Press Office at five

o'clock,' he continued, apparently oblivious. 'Ruth Pye has agreed to that. The funeral will be subject to Covid restrictions, of course, but we're going to have video links to the service in all the stations where he worked.' He smiled, sadly. 'Do you know what his nickname used to be? Luke Skywalker: because he was such a high flyer, they said. Then Sauce Haddock appeared on the scene and people started calling him Master Yoda.'

'So that's why,' McClair murmured. 'Sauce always called him Luke, but it was like a private joke. They were very close; he'll be devastated.'

'We all are. I remember Sammy as a young plod, in this very station.' He smiled. 'There was a story about him and a female officer, in the stationery cupboard, I seem to remember.'

'In flagrante?'

'Not quite, but I'm told there was substance to it. Said female officer had form in that respect.'

'Do tell, sir.'

He grinned. 'No names, Inspector, and no more detail. She's still in the service.'

She looked up at him, deciding that she liked DCC Mackie.

'There's one other thing,' he said. 'Who's Lynn Langham?'

His question took her by surprise. 'She's the daughter of a senior citizen found dead in his flat in Gullane last week. Tiggy and I had to break in, after his carer reported that he wasn't answering. He'd had a stroke and died in his chair. I asked my friend Sarah if she'd attend. She's a pathologist,' McClair added.

'I know who Sarah is,' Mackie told her. 'I was Bob Skinner's exec for a spell.'

'In that case you'll know how good she is at her job. She

certified the death and I sent the papers off to the fiscal. Next thing we knew the Langham woman was on the phone doubting Sarah's finding and demanding a post-mortem. Her mother was a sudden death last September and her head was full of wild ideas about them being suspicious. I sent her off to the fiscal. She folded, of course and Sarah did an autopsy. That found that the old man had unfortunately overdosed on his blood-thinning medication, to the point where, basically, his head exploded.' She hesitated, before adding, 'Why are you asking, sir?'

'She's been on to the chief's office, kicking up merry hell,' Mackie explained, 'demanding a criminal investigation and all sorts. He asked me to get a report from division; since your boss is off, I decided to look into it myself . . . because it gets me out of the bloody office,' he added.

'He's not going to give in to her, is he?'

'That'll depend on what I report back. What's your feeling? Put your CID hat back on and tell me.'

'CID or uniform, my feeling is the same. Based on the information we got from the autopsy, I'd expect the fiscal to classify it as an accidental death and close the file. If CID get involved, the first thing they're going to do is interview the social workers; if the media get hold of that they'll be portrayed as under suspicion. I've interviewed them already and I'm satisfied they had no involvement.'

'And Sarah? What's her view?'

'Same as mine. Mr Stevens had free access to his medication; he had dementia and in that condition he had no idea how much he was taking or, like as not, what he was taking. If you ask me, Mrs Langham is lashing out in all directions to divert attention away from her own guilt.'

'Guilt for what?'

'For buggering off back to England as soon as her mother's ashes were scattered and leaving her eighty-six-year-old father to fend for himself. Mr Stevens deserved better; I know that and so does she.' She stood, stretching her back. 'The chief isn't going to give in to her, is he? He won't take the easy option and open a suspicious death file, will he?'

The deputy chief smiled. 'You don't know Neil McIlhenney, do you?'

She shook her head. 'No, sir, he had moved to London long before I transferred to this area.'

'If you did, then you'd understand that he's never taken an easy option in his life, in any respect. Jesus, he used to play football with Bob Skinner's Thursday night mob. I never saw them in action but, from what I've heard, that was life-threatening!'

Twenty-Five

'Can I finish my round now?' Philomena McBride asked the senior of the two uniforms, as the trio stood on the landing.

'No chance,' Sergeant Malcolm Robertson declared. 'You'll wait here for CID and forensics just like us. The detectives will want a statement from you and the SOCOs will want fingerprints and DNA swabs for elimination.'

'But what about my mail?' she moaned. 'I'm letting folk down here.'

'Call your office,' PC Mary Hill suggested. 'Get them to send someone else out to take over from you.'

'Wi' our staffing levels? Fat chance of that.' She nodded towards the open door of the flat. 'What d'you reckon about him?' she asked.

'I reckon he's dead,' Robertson replied. 'The fact that his blood's splattered on the wall, that's a fair indicator. Other than that, you probably know more than us.'

'That's the thing,' Philomena said. 'I don't have a clue. It's like the place is an Airbnb; there's never a name on the mail.' She checked her watch. 'How much longer are they gonnae be?'

'God knows. The SOCOs are coming from Gartcosh, so

they'll depend on traffic. This'll be a job for Serious Crimes, obviously; they'll be pulling a team together.'

As the sergeant spoke, a tall figure appeared on the staircase in a crime-scene tunic with the hood pulled back, revealing a shock of red hair. 'Paul Dorward,' he announced. 'Who's in charge?'

'That'll be me, for now,' Robertson replied. 'We're still waiting for CID.'

'Have you been inside?'

'Obviously,' the sergeant replied, dryly, 'to verify what Ms McBride here reported.'

The young scientist looked at the officer's feet. 'Do you lot not carry overshoes in your kit?'

'We do,' Robertson said, defensively, 'but we assumed it was a sudden death from the information we were given. I didn't realise it was a crime scene until I walked in there. As soon as I did I backed out and told PC Hill not to come any further. We didn't go any further than the doorway. Okay, it'll be contaminated, but not by much. And by the way,' he added, 'I don't appreciate being told how to do my job by somebody whose university degree hasn't dried yet.'

'You'll take it from me, though,' an older voice said, firmly. The police officers and the post-person looked round at the staircase as the newcomer reached the landing. Thirty years separated the two men, but the resemblance was striking, emphasised by the colour of their hair. 'I don't care how long you've been on the job, Sergeant,' Arthur Dorward growled, 'when you're called to a fatality you assume nothing and you go in with sterile footwear and gloves, minimum. If you've still got them, put them on now.'

'The horse has bolted, surely,' PC Hill suggested.

'You've got a body in there and a suspicious death. Is the perpetrator still inside? I guess not. That means that he entered and left by this landing, so you three are walking all over his tracks. Get those overshoes on, now.' He turned to his assistant, a step behind him on the staircase. 'Lance, give the post lady a pair.' He looked back at the sergeant. 'How many dwellings are there in this close?'

'Six,' Robertson replied, 'two on each floor. I gave the next-door neighbour a knock but got no reply.'

'You should check the others. If you find anyone, ask them to stay indoors.' He raised an eyebrow. 'Not that I'm telling you how to do your job, mind.'

Twenty-Six

'What do you make of the Martin announcement?' June Crampsey asked.

'I think nothing until he's elected,' Skinner assured her. 'After that, we'll see.'

'Did you know what's behind it? How did the Nats come to recruit him? I'm assuming you'll know,' she added.

'Boredom, frustration, a sense of failure leading to a desire to restore his reputation. I don't know any of that for sure, but it's one of those, or even a combination of all three. After Andy resigned after his brief stint as chief constable, I heard someone remark that he got his knighthood for bugger all. The same thought will have occurred to him; it'll have hurt him, and will have wound him up. As for his recruitment to the ranks, he approached the First Minister, through an intermediary.'

'He's going to get a seat,' she said, 'and the way things stand the Nationalists will win the next election, possibly outright. Will Graham give him a job?'

'For sure; it'd be an obvious snub if he didn't. Which one? That will depend on whether Clive sees him as an ally or a threat. If he's wary of him he could give him a job in a poisoned chalice department, health or education, for example. If he rates him, he'll give him something with fewer landmines to step on.'

'Justice?'

'That would be my bet.'

'Can I run a leader speculating along those lines?'

Skinner grinned. 'Why are you asking me? You're the managing editor.'

'And you're the group executive chair.'

'In which case that's well below my pay grade. Manage and edit,' he chuckled. 'Get on with it. You won't hear from me unless our sales plummet. Now,' he said, 'I have to go. My real job is calling me. One of my elderly clients in Gullane asked me if I could pick her up some bananas from Marks and Spencer at Fort Kinnaird on the way home. She prefers them to Tesco bananas, apparently. Maybe they're straighter.' He frowned. 'You know, June, I haven't been in that store for a while. Ever since that awful incident in the car park, I haven't been able to go back.'

'So go to another. There's an M&S food place in Morningside. Or,' she suggested, 'you could nip into Waitrose instead. She won't know the difference.'

He laughed. 'And you don't know Mrs Alexander.'

Skinner returned to his office, cleared his desk, and took the lift down to the basement garage. That held bad memories for him also; in the recent past he had been mugged there by a Russian hoodlum. In the event, his attacker had come a bad second, but it had been a reminder that he was no more immune than anyone else to the advance of time.

He switched on the Tesla and steered it silently out of the garage. It was a senior executive model, an S Type, with a quoted ability to reach sixty from a standing start in under two seconds. It was a claim he had never tested; the cop in him felt that manufacturers should be barred from unleashing a car that fast on the public highway. His boys, on the other hand loved it, because it allowed gaming in the back seat, with an alleged ten teraflops of processing power. Skinner had no idea what a teraflop was. When he had asked Mark to explain it he had told him to stop after the word 'trillion'. 'Everything uses up brain capacity, son, and at my age there's only so much of that left. I'd rather keep it for things I need to know.'

With lockdown in place, the roads were almost deserted; for all that, the lights held him up at the five-way Holy Corner junction, as they always seemed to do. Beyond them, and past the Church Hill Theatre, he took advantage of the lack of traffic to slow as he passed Newbattle Terrace to glance along at the Dominion Cinema, the Art Deco movement's finest gift to Edinburgh. It had been a favourite of his and Myra's when Alex was a baby and they could find a sitter, and again when Sarah had moved back to Scotland and their reconciliation was in its early days. He made a silent vow to return, if it survived the burden of enforced closure.

The M&S food-store did indeed have bananas. He chose the straightest bunch he could find, and on a whim added two stalks of rhubarb. The route out of the city took him so close to Maggie Steele's house that he found himself making an unplanned stop. *Mrs Alexander isn't going anywhere,* he told himself.

The Margaret Rose Steele who answered his ring was a version he had never seen before. She wore jeans, ripped at one knee and a sweatshirt. Both were marked with paint matching the colour of the brush she was holding. Her grey-flecked red hair was long, tied back in a ponytail. 'Bob,' she exclaimed.

'This is a surprise. You should have warned me, so I could change out of this mess.' She smiled; he thought she looked as relaxed as he had ever seen her, and certainly happier than at any time since her husband, Stevie Steele, had been killed in the line of duty.

'Just passing,' he explained, 'only I couldn't.'

She raised a questioning eyebrow. 'Coffee withdrawal symptoms?'

'Something like that.'

She led him through to her large kitchen, where she dropped the paintbrush into a large jar of white spirit. 'Thankfully the DIY stores are still open,' she said. 'The longer lockdown lasts the more I'll get done.'

'Where's Stephanie?' he asked. 'Pasted behind a strip of paper? Myra did that once, with a contact lens, behind a roll of anaglypta, if you can remember what that was. By some miracle we found it and got it out with the aid of a razor blade.'

'Nothing so dramatic,' Steele replied with a smile. 'She's watching Peppa Pig. It makes a pleasant change from Iggle bloody Piggle.' She opened a cupboard, produced a jar of coffee and scooped four measures into a cafetiere. 'So, what's happening in the *Saltire* building?' she asked as she filled the kettle. 'Congrats, by the way. I saw that understated announcement on the business pages. Group chair, indeed.'

'Temporary, and I wish it didn't have to be. I do get to fly in my own plane though, and to drive a ridiculous electric car.'

She glanced out of the kitchen window. 'That one out there? What does it do?'

'Everything. It's got fucking teraflops in it.'

'What's a teraflop?'

'Christ knows. My only concern is that they're not

carnivorous. Have you heard about Sammy?' he asked, suddenly and quietly.

She nodded. 'We all knew it was coming, but it's no less of a shock, a lad his age, dying in such a God-awful way. Do you have a contact for Ruth? I want to get in touch with her, not so much as a former colleague, but widow to widow. She's had a while to get used to the idea, but you never truly believe that the worst is going to happen until it does. Sometimes,' she added, 'you never quite believe it.'

'Sure,' he promised, 'I'll give you her number. I called her myself this morning; stoic, describes her best. She's a strong girl, but she sounded wasted.'

'Of course, you know her; she used to be your secretary at Fettes.'

'That's right, the best I ever had. She'll be all right financially for the moment, but I've told her that if she wants to go back to work, I can fix her up with something, either at the *Saltire*, or somewhere else where I have influence.' He sighed. 'God, it makes me feel very old. I remember Sammy as a fresh-faced kid, working out of Haddington. He was a really bright lad, full of promise even then, the sort that stood out from the rest.'

'Me too: I can picture him as he was back then. He was a good-looking boy, no question.' Steele paused. 'Here, didn't he and Karen Neville . . . ? There was a story about the storage cupboard. I wonder if it was true?'

'Oh, it was true all right,' Skinner confirmed. 'But really they were just . . .'

'I think "friends with benefits" is the approved term these days.' She smiled. 'Listen to us. A couple of fogeys. So,' she continued, 'is this really an impulse call?' she asked. 'Or have you called in to tell me you're going to the House of Lords to be one up on Andy?'

'I turned that down,' he said, deadpan, for it was true. 'Do you fancy joining him on the hustings? I know you're not a Nat, but I know a couple of senior Tories and, believe me, they'll accept any reasonable offer.'

'It's funny you should say that,' she remarked. 'I had one of them on the phone this morning. I told him where he could pin his rosette.' She stopped the kettle just before it reached boiling point and filled the cafetiere. 'Have you been in touch with Andy?' she asked.

'The other way round. He called me last Friday, looking for a way into Clive Graham.'

'So it's your fault!'

'He'll be fine,' Skinner insisted. 'Better than fine; Andy will be a good MSP, and a good minister too, if he gets that far.'

Steele shrugged. 'I don't doubt it.' She paused. 'I've heard from him too,' she admitted. 'He called for a chat and before I knew it he said if I wanted to bring Steph through to his place one weekend she could play with his kids. I had to tell him that Clive doesn't allow that at the moment.'

'Did he suggest what you two might do?'

She shook her head, firmly, then filled two mugs with black coffee, adding a little milk to both. 'Nothing was even implied,' she said. 'You know, in the years when we were both younger and single, Andy Martin never made a move on me. I was almost huffed by that, Andy being as he was then. It would be a sign of desperation if he did it now. Mind you, if he did, he might be surprised by the outcome.' She winked. 'It's been a while, Bob. In fact, that was one of the reasons I gave up the job. It was destroying me as a social animal. I was stuck in the uniform and it scared men off.'

He laughed. 'If that was the case, Mags, they weren't worth having.'

She smiled, her eyes twinkling. 'Not worth keeping for sure, but possibly worth having, if you get my drift. In a weird way that makes me wonder how Noele McClair's getting along. Your kids are friends, right?'

'Yes, in the same primary class. Noele's okay; coming out the other side, I'd say.'

'But still alone. I guess Neil's family base will be an advantage in his position.'

'Oh it will, be sure of it. He and Lou are solid. She's virtually given up her career for him. Have you heard from him lately?'

'No,' Steele replied, 'not since he took over. Even Mario's become more distant. How about you?'

'He's distancing himself from me too,' Skinner admitted. 'Mario told me as much, and I understand why, completely. Not only does he want to be his own man he wants it to be seen.'

She laughed. 'Has he asked for your Special Constable warrant card back? The one I gave you.'

'We did talk about that. As I recall, I gave it to myself when I left the Strathclyde job. I still have it but it's in a drawer somewhere. We agreed it would stay there.'

'Alongside your MI5 credentials?'

'No,' he replied, solemnly. 'I know exactly where they are. Tell me, and this is a spur of the moment thought, would you be interested in a relationship with that organisation?'

'What? Chasing terrorists and spies?'

'Not quite. Advisory, more like. They have an operative

responsible for their interests in Scotland, but you have a background that might be useful to Amanda Dennis.'

Steele frowned, and was silent. 'Bob,' she said, when she was ready, 'I'm a cancer-surviving single mother with a couple of non-executive directorships to keep us fed. When I'm ready I'll find a full-time job or start a business myself. That's my vision of the future and Dame Amanda Dennis doesn't feature in it, nor anyone who comes after her.' She finished her coffee; he took it as a sign and did the same. 'Sorry if I'm rushing you,' she apologised. 'I have to finish my painting then take Steph up to Holyrood Park for some exercise. If I tire her out, then later on I might get some quiet time to work on my book.'

'You're writing a book?' he exclaimed. 'A memoir?'

'Hell no!' she exclaimed. 'It's a crime novel. Every other bugger's doing it, so why not me too?'

Twenty-Seven

The uniformed officers were guarding the closemouth on Candleriggs when an unmarked car drew into the kerb. Sergeant Robertson was about to move it on when a tall, solidly built woman emerged from the passenger side. 'DCI Mann,' she announced, unsmiling, although her self-identification was un-necessary. There were few officers in Glasgow who did not know, or know of, Charlotte 'Lottie' Mann, the head of the west of Scotland Serious Crimes Unit. 'Ma'am,' the sergeant said, straightening his posture but stopping short of coming to attention.

'Which floor?' she asked, as she was joined by the driver, a man several inches shorter.

'Second,' he replied. 'You'd better get the sterile kit on before you go up there, ma'am. The forensics gaffer's a right martinet.'

'Red hair?'

'Him and one of the younger ones.'

'That'll be Arthur Dorward,' Mann said. 'The younger one's probably his son. I'd heard he had graduated and was working out of the Crime Campus.'

'The older one's a grumpy bugger, whatever he is.'

'He gets away with it by being the best in the business,

144

Sarge,' she said as she slipped on a sterile overshoe. 'Maybe you should learn from him before you lecture senior officers about crime-scene procedure.' She stepped into the close, her colleague following, leaving a grim-faced Robertson to decide that it really had not been his day.

'Arthur?' Mann called out, as she and DS John Cotter reached the second floor landing.

Within a few seconds the older Dorward was on the doorway. 'It's Lottie and Tyrion,' he said, dryly as he surveyed the CID team. 'You're welcome to this one.'

Cotter shot him a heavy-browed look. 'I'm not that fucking short,' he complained, in a Tyneside accent.

'Don't take it to heart, John,' Mann said. 'Tyrion wound up at the head of the table at the end of *Game of Thrones*. One dead male, we were told, Arthur,' she said, briskly. 'Do you have any more than that?'

'Identifying him is your job, Lottie,' Dorward replied, 'but I see nothing in there that's going to help you. The postie who found the body couldn't put a name to him either.'

'Where is he?' Cotter asked. 'We only saw two uniforms outside.'

'She,' he corrected, 'was bitching about finishing her round. The PC took a statement from her and got her personal details so she can be contacted to sign it, then they let her go.'

Mann scowled, but offered no judgement on the decision. 'What can you tell us about the deceased?'

'You're best seeing for yourselves,' the scientist said. 'Mind you, it's tight in there; my people are still at work. We're still waiting for the pathologist as well, so be careful not to touch the body, not that you'll want to. You hear about these things but to see one . . .'

Twenty-Eight

There were no parking places to be seen on the main street. Rather than cruise around in vain hope, Skinner drove home and put the Tesla in the garage. After checking that Sarah was home from Edinburgh with Dawn, and that Mark still had a semblance of control over his younger siblings, he changed from his suit into chinos, a heavy shirt and boots, took his waxed jacket from its hook and set off back towards the village and Mrs Alexander.

His emotions were mixed as he walked. He was filled with sadness over the death of Sammy Pye, a friend lost rather than a former colleague. He hoped that Ruth, his widow, would approve of him sharing her number with Maggie Steele, but was confident that she would, and that in time, she would take strength from her. The women were not strangers. Ruth had been his PA during Maggie's time as his executive officer and they had worked together in efficient harmony. At the same time he was pleased by the radical change in Steele, having freed herself of the burden of an office that he had decided not to seek. Had he made a different choice and had he been appointed, would he have lasted, he asked himself, any longer than she or Andy Martin? Probably not, he conceded to himself.

And McIlhenney? How would he manage? Better than any of them, he decided. There was a stolid calmness about the man; he would make each decision logically and, having done so, he would leave it in the office rather than take it home. Bob Skinner knew that was something he had never been able to do, and it had cost him two marriages.

Arriving at the street-level door to Mrs Alexander's flat, Skinner was surprised to find it slightly ajar, but given its age and lack of maintenance he thought no more of it and headed for the stair, donning his *Saltire* mask as he went. In contrast, her front door seemed to be firmly closed. He rang her bell and waited. And waited. And waited.

He frowned as he took out his phone and found the old lady's number. Standing close to the door he heard it ring, once, twice, on and on until he cancelled the call. He tried the door, but it was secure. He assessed the situation: an ordinary citizen would be advised to call the emergency services. What was he but an ordinary citizen?

'Fuck that,' he murmured, as he raised his right foot and slammed the sole of his boot into the door, just above the handle. His first kick weakened it; the second sent it flying open.

He stepped inside, pausing for a second to consider the likely lay-out. The living room and main bedroom were on the right, overlooking the street. He checked them both. The bed was made; the central block of a nineteen-fifties vintage Gas Miser glowed in the hearth of the reception room. He crossed the small square hall, checking the bathroom before moving into the kitchen.

It was a generous size, with ground-level cupboards and shelving above an L-shaped work surface, with a porcelain sink below the window that overlooked the back green. It was big enough to accommodate a little breakfast table, beyond which Mrs Alexander lay, on her back. He knew at once that she was dead, from her pallor and the angle of her neck. A set of aluminium folding steps were on the floor alongside her, open, with the four feet pointing towards the shelves and the work surface, upon which there lay a box of custard powder, open, with some of its contents spilled out.

Skinner sighed as he knelt beside the body, feeling for a pulse that he knew he would not find, realising from its coldness that the old lady had been dead for some time. Her eyes were slightly open and if there was any expression there, it was surprise. Leaning closer, he saw a mark on her left temple, an odd right-angled wound. The skin was broken but there was very little blood. He looked at the corner of the breakfast table; the shape was a match; the picture was complete. He returned to the hallway and took out his phone again. Rather than go through the police switchboard, he called Noele McClair's mobile.

'Bob,' she said. She sounded surprised but also tired, as if she was glad that her working day was drawing to a close. 'What can I do for you?'

'Are you still in the office?' he asked.

'Yes, with one eye on the clock.'

'Do you have a car handy for Gullane?'

'Not just now,' she told him. 'There's been an accident on the A1, just past Torness.'

'In that case you might want to attend yourself, and call a medical examiner. I'm at the home of one of our resilience group's sheltered seniors, Mrs Wendy Alexander, on the main street. I called to drop off some M&S goodies and couldn't get a response. I kicked the door in and found her dead.'

'Oh dear,' the inspector sighed. 'This is turning into an epidemic.'

Twenty-Nine

Lottie Mann had been a police officer in Glasgow for fifteen years, but even she stopped in her tracks, when she stepped into the sitting room of the Candleriggs apartment. It stank of death, of human waste, and of copious blood, that metallic slaughterhouse smell that, once experienced, could never be excised from the memory. Automatically, without thinking about it, she extended an arm to keep Cotter back, as if she could protect him from what he was about to see.

A tall young technician whom she took to be Dorward Junior, from the wisps of russet hair protruding from his crime-scene hood, was working in the centre of the room, extracting samples of hair and other detritus from a white leather swivel chair, one of a pair on either side of a wall-mounted television. Another man, older, turned to face her.

'DCI Mann,' Professor Graham Scott, the city's chief pathologist, said. He appeared annoyed, uncharacteristically. 'I'm not surprised to see you here, but I don't quite know why you need me. Standard call-out practice, I suppose, but it's self-evident that this chap's dead. My work's done in the autopsy room at the mortuary. Get him there and I will tell you what I can.'

She stared back at him, hiding her embarrassment over her

momentary loss of composure. Cotter was still behind her, as her bulk was blocking the doorway.

'Are you not even going to hazard a guess at cause of death?' she growled, stone-faced.

As if in denial of the horror behind him, Scott smiled as he shook his head. 'I'll treat that as a joke. It will all be in my report, Detective Chief Inspector, as usual. Now for goodness sake, Lottie, are you going to let me get out of here?'

She nodded and stood to one side. 'Let the professor past, John. He's wanting home for his tea.' She looked back at Scott, serious once again. 'Soon as you can, Graham, please. God knows where this one's going to lead.'

'Agreed, Lottie. When you find the missing piece, let me know.'

'What?' Cotter exclaimed.

'You'll see. Or rather, you won't.' He headed out of the flat, stepping quickly along the raised walkway that the forensic team had laid down.

The two detectives stepped into the room. As Mann had done, Cotter recoiled then gathered himself. 'Fuck,' he whispered.

Dried blood stained the wall that faced them like an abstract painting. Its spray could be seen on a mounted television screen and a wood-burning stove; on the parquet flooring it formed a dark circle, a pool of horror. Its source lay at their feet. It was human and it was male. He had been exsanguinated but still it was apparent that he had been a person of colour. However, that was all the detectives could tell on first examination, for he had been decapitated.

Mann turned to call for the senior Dorward, but he was close behind her. 'Where's the head, Arthur?' she asked, her voice hoarse and not much above a whisper.

'It's not here,' he replied, 'and we've looked everywhere that it could be, short of taking up the floor. Whoever did this must have taken it away with him. To mess us about? As a trophy? Who knows why?'

'Have you found anything that'll identify him?'

'We haven't done that kind of search, Lottie. You know that; it's not what we're here for. You need to get your team in here, but not until my three are finished, please. Even in sterile suits there's always some contamination. All that I can tell you is that we've seen no personal items as we've been working. No photographs, no mail, no holiday postcards.'

'Phone?'

'No, but we haven't looked in his pockets. There's a jacket over there.' He pointed across the room to the far wall and a gateleg table with a chair on either side. On one of those hung a light tan leather jacket. 'I'll look,' Dorward said, as Cotter took a step towards it. 'John, I would rather you stayed out of here, and you too, Lottie, until we're finished. It'll save time in the long run if we don't have to eliminate either of you.'

'Go on then,' Mann agreed.

The scientist crossed the room and searched the garment, looking into each of its four pockets. He shook his head as he finished. 'Nothing at all,' he announced. 'Not only is there no phone, there's no wallet either, no keys or anything else. Also,' he added, 'we've seen no computer or laptop. There doesn't appear to be a landline phone, but there is internet, high-speed fibre to the house.'

'That doesn't tell us who the victim is, though, does it?' Cotter said. 'I spoke to the plonk downstairs, who took the postwoman's statement. According to her there's nothing on the incoming mail to identify him.'

'Somebody's paying the bills,' Dorward countered. 'Somebody's paying the council tax.' He nodded at the blood-spattered television above the stove. 'Someone's paying the TV licence.'

'But not necessarily the victim on the floor,' Mann pointed out.

'You might be able to find him, Lottie, if his prints and DNA are on a national database. Go on now,' he continued 'let us finish our work then your people can tear the place apart.'

'Okay, Arthur,' the DCI sighed. 'I won't bother asking you to hurry up. I know that's not in your DNA. We'll be outside if you do find anything useful.'

She ushered Cotter back to the landing. 'What do we do in the meantime?' he asked.

'You get a team assembled,' she replied, 'ready to do a search as soon as we can. Then you can locate the folk on the stair that aren't at home. I don't imagine that'll be too hard. When they find they're shut out of their own flats they'll come looking for you. While you're doing that, I'd better call DCC McGuire. Graham Scott was right; this one could lead anywhere and maybe right to his door. So he'd better know, soonest.'

She left the sergeant and walked downstairs, pausing on the first-floor landing to tear off her sterile garments. Outside, in Candleriggs, four people were engaging with the uniformed officers. She moved away quickly, leaving them for her sergeant to deal with, crossing the street before calling the deputy chief constable. When he answered her call, she heard road noise.

'DCI Mann,' his voice boomed in her ear, 'please don't tell me I'm going to have to turn around and head for Glasgow.'

'Head,' she repeated. 'That's not a word that sits well with me right now, sir, but when you hear what I have to tell you, I think you might want to.'

Thirty

'Poor wee soul,' PC Benjamin sighed as she looked at the body. 'That could be my granny lying there.' Mrs Alexander had been pronounced dead by one of the doctors from the village medical centre. Together, he and Skinner had carried her through to her bed, where she lay on her back with her eyes closed. The GP had folded her arms across her chest, a clear sign that *rigor mortis* had passed, and that she had been dead for some hours.

'Do we know who her next of kin are, Bob?' Noele McClair asked Skinner. 'Tiggy,' she added, 'go downstairs please and wait for the mortuary hearse.'

'I don't,' he admitted, as the constable left. 'To tell you the truth I know nothing about her other than that she was a nice old dear. I called Matthew Reid—'

'The writer?'

'Yes, he's one of the coordinators of the resilience group that I help out with. I wondered if he had a list of next of kin, and thought I should tell him anyway. He doesn't. You should say hello,' Skinner suggested. 'He likes to meet cops and ex-cops; he uses us as a resource base if he's ever concerned about a procedural point. Not that he's too bothered about procedure, he says. Don't let it get in the way of a good ending, that's his philosophy. Truth be told, it was mine too when I was a detective.' He smiled as he glanced at the inspector. 'You're missing it now, Noele, aren't you?' he said. 'The buzz of CID.'

'Is it that obvious?' she asked.

'It comes off you in waves. Let me hazard another guess,' he added. 'With Sammy, God bless and keep him, having passed away as a serving officer rather than one who was retired on health grounds, certain things will follow, among them the creation of a DI post in your old unit in Edinburgh. Sauce's promotion to DCI Serious Crimes will be confirmed, and that'll leave a gap to be filled. I don't see Tarvil Singh stepping up.'

'Why not?' she interrupted. 'Tarvil's a solid operator.'

'He is,' Skinner agreed, 'and he could do a DI job. But these days, in the brave new world, the Peter Principle's a thing of the past.'

'What's that?'

'Promotion to the level of the individual's incompetence,' he explained. 'It happened all the time in the old days. Maybe not so old; I've heard that levelled at Andy Martin, although in my opinion, his problem was never ability, it was management and temperament. Whatever, those being promoted detective inspector these days have to be perceived to be able to function competently at least two ranks higher. That's not Tarvil, capable though he is today.' He fixed her with his gaze. 'It's you, though, Noele. You wouldn't be expected to stop at DI.'

'But I chucked it, Bob,' she sighed. 'When Terry and Griff were killed, I was determined that I never wanted to see another crime scene. I'd have left the police altogether had it not been for Chief Constable Steele persuading me to stay on and fixing me up with a promotion into the Haddington job. That's not much more than a year ago. I can't stick my hand up and say that I want to come back. If the judgement's whether I'm likely to rise to detective super, there's no chance of that.'

'There's every chance,' he insisted. 'I'm not just saying this as a friend. I did fitness reports on officers for years; I'm qualified to say how qualified you are.'

'That's kind of you,' she said, gratefully, 'but how would I even go about it?'

'Stay here,' he instructed, and moved into Mrs Alexander's living room, taking out his phone. He scrolled through the contacts until he reached 'H', and called the first number.

'Gaffer,' a familiar voice exclaimed. In the background Skinner could hear the sounds of open air. 'You just caught me. I've got a golf tie; on the tee in ten minutes.'

'Is your club still doing competitions?' Skinner asked, surprised. 'Ours are Covid affected.' Without waiting for a response he pressed on. 'Quickly then. Has your DI slot been filled yet, DCI Haddock?'

'Not yet. The DCC's looking at a few names.'

'But you'll have input when the selection's made, yes?'

'I would hope so.'

'If Noele McClair was interested . . .'

'I'd take her like a shot,' Haddock retorted.

'In that case, Sauce, you should give her a call, then put her name in the frame.'

'I will do that as soon as I can, tonight if possible. But, gaffer, why don't you call DCC McGuire yourself and tell him?'

'Let's just say I'd rather not. They're big boys and girls now, they don't need their hands holding, and certainly not by me. Have you met the new chief yet, by the way? Officially, that is?'

'This morning. He called me to headquarters at Falkirk to confirm my promotion. The DCC was there too. He asked me about the DI vacancy then. He ran some candidates by me. To tell you the truth, I didn't fancy any of them, and one least of all, but we didn't discuss them.'

'You can talk about it now, Sauce, but do not, repeat not, mention my name.'

'Have you and Neil McIlhenney fallen out, gaffer?' the new DCI asked.

'No, and I want to make sure that we don't. Get it?'

'I think so. Cheers, my opponent's on the tee.'

Skinner returned to McClair, beckoning her out of the bedroom. He had seen enough of Mrs Alexander in death, and preferred to remember her as she had been, a bright chirpy personality who had cheered him up. 'You should be getting a call from Sauce,' he told the inspector. 'Not within the next three or four hours, and maybe not even until tomorrow, if it's his turn to change the baby, but it'll happen.'

'Thanks, Bob,' she said, gratefully. 'Do you think I have a chance?'

'I wouldn't bet on anyone else.' He glanced at his watch. 'Talking about babies, it'll be Dawn's bedtime soon. I have to say goodnight to her or she won't be happy. Are you all right here on your own?' His eyes widened and he laughed. 'Listen to me! I'm a bloody civilian; you're the cop.'

McClair smiled. 'Your presence is always comforting, Bob, but on you go. Dawn comes first. I have a bit of a time constraint myself,' she added. 'I can't leave Harry with my mother for ever.'

He moved towards the door, nodding towards its shattered lock. 'Have you got . . . ?'

'Yes,' she said, 'I've got a joiner coming to make the flat secure. Benjamin can stay on her to take care of that. We brought separate cars so I could go straight to Mum's.' She looked up at him. 'Can you give me a statement for my report to the fiscal?'

'Sure,' he promised. 'I'll knock something out tonight, Docusign it and email it to you.'

'You're happy with what my report will say? Accidental death?'

'Absolutely,' he frowned, 'although I blame myself to an extent. I was in Mrs Alexander's kitchen and I saw the things she had on those shelves. If I'd persuaded her to move everything within reach, she wouldn't be lying in that bedroom now.'

'You can't think that way, Bob,' the inspector countered. 'If your auntie had balls she'd be your uncle, and so on.'

'In this day and age,' he snorted, 'that's not necessarily true, but never mind. Yes, Noele, you write it up as accidental, non-suspicious. I can see nothing untoward here. The old lady's purse is in the living room. I took a look in it; her bank card's still there along with the balance of the cash I drew out for her last week. Bottom line, we can shield the vulnerable from Covid, but we can't shield them from themselves.' Skinner grinned again. 'It is good that you're asking, though. It shows that your CID instincts are still there. Question everything, that's the rule.'

'And all your questions have been answered?'

'Nearly,' Skinner replied. 'I called here twice before today. Each time Mrs Alexander had the door on its chain. When I kicked it in today, it wasn't or I'd have ripped it out along with the Yale lock keeper. But that's not enough to declare a suspicious death, and get a team of SOCOs in here. Not even at my most paranoid would I have done that. Write it up and write it off, Noele, but one thing, please,' he added. 'When you locate the next of kin, let me know. I'd like to tell them what a pleasure it was to have known the old dear, if only briefly.'

'Will do, Bob.' As she spoke they heard footsteps on the stairs.

'If that's the mortuary team,' Skinner said, 'I'm off. I'd rather not see her being carried out of here. Good luck with the transfer, Detective Inspector.'

Thirty-One

'Are you getting ahead with your investigation, Chief Inspector?' Mario McGuire asked as he emerged from his car into Candleriggs.

On the pavement, Lottie Mann stared at him.

His grin verged on Satanic, rather than merely sardonic. 'Oldest and worst CID joke in the world,' he said. 'Someone was bound to crack it eventually, so I thought I'd get it over with.'

'I'm sure I'll hear it from Dan as well when I get home . . . if I get home any time soon that is.'

'How is Mr Provan?' the DCC asked.

'In prime form,' Mann replied. 'He's started jogging, would you believe, although he insists on calling it running.' Until his retirement from the police service, her partner had been her detective sergeant, Cotter's predecessor. 'No disrespect to John, but I could do with Dan here,' she admitted. 'I'm at a dead end before I've begun. I have no idea who the victim is, and no means of identifying him. Arthur Dorward took his prints with a scanner and sent them for a search of every criminal database there is, even bloody Europol, but there are no positive matches. We'll see what results we get from his

DNA when we have a profile, but based on that I'm not hopeful.'

McGuire frowned. 'Who's paying the council tax?'

'I don't know yet. I haven't been able to dig up anyone from the City Council; even working from home they clock off at the back of four.'

'How about the utilities?'

'So far that's a blank too. We've tried all the major power companies, but this property isn't on any of their lists. Yes, there's any number of small suppliers these days, but it'll take us a while to go through them all. There's nothing upstairs to help us either, not yet. The SOCOs are finished and I have my own search team in now, but so far all they're telling me is how clean the place is.'

'What about the victim himself?' McGuire persisted. 'Does he have any distinguishing marks?'

'Nothing that's apparent from the bits of him we're left with. The rest will be for Graham Scott when he gets to work in the mortuary.' She gave a rare thin smile. 'And as for dental records . . .'

'Don't you start!' McGuire contrived to growl and chuckle simultaneously. 'Okay, Lottie,' he continued, 'let's accept that we're stuck for an ID of the victim, at least until we have a DNA profile, but that doesn't mean we can't trace the perpetrator. Glasgow's city centre CCTV coverage is pretty comprehensive. It's early, I know, but have you had time to assess that?'

'DS Cotter checked with the monitoring unit half an hour ago,' she replied. 'All he's been able to establish so far is that Candleriggs is a bit of a dead zone, no pun intended. There's a camera at the junction with Argyle Street, but nothing that covers the entrance to the crime scene.' She turned and surveyed the street. 'Looking around I don't see any private systems either. But even if the coverage was perfect, sir, we'd be hamstrung, as we are with a door-to-door canvass, until Professor Scott gives me a time of death.' She glanced back towards him. 'Do you want to take a look upstairs, sir, at the crime scene? The body's still in situ.'

'Most of it is, you mean,' he grunted. 'I'll leave it thanks, Lottie. I know you have to but I would rather not carry that image home with me tonight. Rank does have its privileges. If you've been waiting for me before you moved the victim, that's appreciated, but get him off to the morgue as quick as you can.' The DCC paused for a second. 'In the flat,' he continued, 'have your people or the SOCOs found a possible murder weapon?' he asked.

Mann considered her reply for a few seconds. 'Not obviously so,' she ventured. 'As in, there wasn't a machete with blood all over it. But I did see a knife block in the kitchen. One of them? I'm assuming that Dorward's team will have examined them. Any blood or tissue traces, they'll find them. But someone went there to commit that murder, sir. It wasn't spur of the moment, not with that level of violence. I'd be surprised if they didn't go prepared.'

'Me neither,' McGuire agreed. 'Lottie, I want you to report this to ACC Payne. This crime could fall into several categories; terrorism has to be one of them and that's his field. Brief him, please, as soon as you can.'

Thirty-Two

'He's fucking joking, isn't he?' Matthew Reid exclaimed. 'Sunny!' he called out to his dog. 'Fetch.'

Obediently the Labrador trotted after the yellow ball, which had rolled ten yards past his owner when he had released it at full gallop. 'Thank you,' Reid said, as it was dropped, more carefully, at his feet. He picked it up, fitted it into a long slinger device and with a flick of his forearm tossed it fifty yards along the beach, skirting the breaking waves of the outgoing tide. Bob Skinner watched, smiling, as Sunny tore off on his recovery mission.

'Very impressive,' he said, admiring the power of the throw. 'No, he's not fucking joking. Procurators fiscal are not given to taking the piss. In fact, I've met a few who were so dry I doubt they ever had any piss in them. Sarah had a call yesterday evening, about ninety minutes after I got home, asking if she could fit in a post-mortem examination of Mrs Alexander.'

'Even though the police said there was nothing suspicious about the death?' Reid asked.

'Even though.'

Skinner had spotted owner and dog walking across the park below his house, heading for the steps that led down to the bridle path. He had texted his friend. 'Hold on a minute, I was just going for a run. I'll change my footwear and join you.'

'Why is he overruling them?' the author asked.

'It's not a matter of overruling anyone, Matthew. All we . . . sod it . . . all the police do is report the circumstances. Subsequent action is determined by the Crown Office, usually through the local fiscal's office.'

'After fifty crime novels I should know this, but at what level?'

'Usually it would be a deputy but in this case the word came from the top man in Edinburgh. After Michael Stevens died, Maria Mullen, the depute, had her ear bent by his daughter and was more or less bullied into ordering an examination. My guess that she kicked this one straight upstairs as soon as it hit her in-tray rather than be waylaid by another next of kin.'

Reid frowned. 'Isn't . . . ?' He paused as Sunny returned with the ball, timing its release perfectly. Picking it up, he launched it again further along the shoreline. 'Isn't there an issue here?' he said. 'If the Crown Office gives in every time a relative asks for an autopsy, it would be cheaper just to make them mandatory for every sudden death, and what sort of an effect would that have on the public purse . . . not that I'm grudging Sarah her fees, mind. Or should we change everything and adopt the English system, having a coroner with judicial power?'

'In *Line of Duty* they thought we have already,' Skinner observed. 'That one would never have got past you, Matthew, would it?' he added.

'Being Scottish, no it wouldn't,' the crime writer agreed. 'That said, I'm sure there are umpteen things about the English judicial system that I'm liable to trip over. Have they traced

Mrs Alexander's next of kin?' he continued. 'Nobody I've spoken to ever heard her mention any.'

'I wouldn't know.'

'Where would they start looking, Bob? I'm interested professionally, you understand.'

'If it was me,' the ex-cop replied, 'I would begin by going through her personal papers; there might be a lead there. For instance, there might be correspondence with a lawyer. What about Mr Alexander?' he continued. 'This is assuming that he's dead and didn't run off years ago with a cocktail waitress, but assuming he is, was there a will lodged with the Sheriff Court? If so by whom and who were its beneficiaries? Or, find the lawyer who lodged it and maybe through them you'll find the old dear's will.'

'The cat and dog home doesn't count as next of kin,' Reid grunted. 'A lot of charity income comes from bequests from the likes of Mrs Alexander.'

'Granted, but before I even looked for a lawyer, I'd go through her Christmas card list. Every household, even when it's one person, has one of those. Unless the poor old lady, nice though she seemed, was completely estranged from her family . . .'

'I get it.'

'What about you, Matthew?' Skinner asked. 'Who's your next of kin? You never talk about them either, come to think about it.'

The author retrieved the ball yet again and flung it, even harder, on a low trajectory. 'I don't have any,' he replied, quietly, his eyes following Sunny as he sped along the beach in pursuit. 'No siblings, no wife, no nothing. I was divorced thirty-five years ago . . . you know what they say about divorce, Bob, it's like having your balls ripped off through your wallet . . . and unlike you I never sought to repeat the process. I had an uncle on either side, my father's brother in Lanarkshire, my mother's in Canada; neither of them was fecund. In fact, you could say that my family has proved to be fecund useless. I've left barely a footprint on the planet—'

'Other than having your name on a few million books,' Skinner pointed out.

'There is that,' Reid conceded, 'but I'm hardly Robert Louis Stevenson. I've never analysed it, but maybe I got involved in the village stuff to make a meaningful contribution to society for a change.' He grinned wryly as his dog pounded back towards him through the surf. 'And look how that's going.'

Thirty-Three

'The DNA profile of *Homo Candleriggs*, to give him a provisional name, should be on its way to you,' Professor Graham Scott said. 'I hope it helps identify him, for I can't think of another way you're going to do it quickly, not without finding the missing piece. I expect that's in the river,' he added gloomily.

'Cheers to you too, Prof.' Lottie Mann sighed as she looked at the face on her computer screen. 'Your report's just hit my email, but would you like to give me a quick summary?'

'I'll be quick because there isn't a lot in the report,' Scott retorted. 'The subject was a mixed-race male, white and Afro-Caribbean; he was aged in his thirties, I'd say, but I can't be any more definite. The head was removed roughly with what I surmise was a knife, rather than a sword. If you look at Caravaggio's depiction of the beheading of John the Baptist, that's all he thought necessary. This one probably had a clean, non-serrated edge, from the lack of marking on the spinal column.' He smiled. 'I'm sorry if that's too graphic for you, Sergeant Cotter,' he added, as if he had seen the DS blanch. 'The victim was in excellent physical health and shape,' the pathologist continued. 'His major organs were all clear and his musculature was very impressive. His last meal was a pizza, heavy on the pepperoni, last drink a small black coffee, possibly Colombian from the odour. There were no surgical scars on the body, but there was evidence of a couple of healed wounds, a slash on the left forearm that had been stitched and a jagged cut on the right calf muscle. Neither was recent. The only other distinguishing mark was a tattoo that looks like a military symbol or crest. My assistant thought it might be the Royal Marines, but she wasn't sure. She said she'd seen one like it, but she was vague, so I didn't press the point. I've attached a photograph.'

'All that's fine,' Mann said. 'What about time of death?'

'I can't be too precise,' Scott said, 'but I'm thinking Monday evening. Has this made the press yet?' he asked, suddenly. 'I heard nothing about it on the Radio Scotland news this morning.'

'In normal times they'd have been all over it, Graham,' the DCI told him. 'But lockdown conditions mean that the city centre's ghostlike just now. The pubs are shut and most folk that aren't furloughed are working from home. On top of that, I've been cracking down on anybody caught passing tips to the news desks, cops or civilian staff, or posting sensitive information on their social media accounts. We'll possibly make a public announcement this morning, but I've been waiting for you before briefing the press office.'

'How much are you going to tell them?'

'If we tell them anything at all, it'll be the least we can get away with. "A male body was found yesterday in a Glasgow city centre flat. Police are treating the death as suspicious and are asking for information about anything unusual seen in the Candleriggs area."'

'For example, somebody carrying a heavy weight in an Aldi bag with blood leaking out of it?'

'That would be helpful if it got us a good description. Otherwise, we're offering no more detail than that. The last thing I want are horror stories in the media, mainstream or social. I hope your assistant's aware of the need for secrecy.'

'Utterly. As for myself, I wonder what the *Sun* are paying for exclusives these days.'

'Not enough to make up for the pain that would ensue, I promise you. But Graham, one thing more. You're describing the victim as youngish, strong, possibly with a military background, and yet . . . You were in that flat too; there were absolutely no signs of a struggle. Can you explain how a man like that was overpowered? Were there any signs of restraint on the body? How many people would it have taken to hold him still while somebody else hacked his head off?'

The pathologist beamed. 'I was hoping you were going to ask me that, DCI Mann. The answer is none at all. However . . . I found traces of a circular burn on the neck, just below the point of decapitation. I have only seen something like that in a professional paper authored in Russia, where street crime takes all forms and is rarely constrained in its violence or its imagination. I believe that *Homo Candleriggs* was subdued by a taser, but not the kind the police carry. This one would require direct contact with the skin, and it would be a type of device that's absolutely illegal in this country. Lottie, this is as planned and professional a hit as I have ever seen. Whoever did it is special and really needs to be taken out of circulation as quickly as possible.'

Thirty-Four

Alex Skinner looked up as her door opened, her assistant's head appearing, one hand on the frame. 'There's a caller on the landline,' Clarice said. 'He's asking for you, but I'm wondering whether you want to take it or you'd rather be in court.'

'I am in court,' she replied, 'in under an hour. Who is it?'

'Sir Andrew Martin. That's not how he announced himself, mind,' the matronly secretary added. 'He simply said "It's Andy," as matter of fact as you like.'

Alex smiled. 'You know, Clarice, if Cerberus ever goes down with kennel cough, you'd do as a replacement.' Then she frowned. 'No further explanation?'

'None. It was as if the name itself was enough.'

She drew a deep breath. 'Tell him to fu—' She stopped in mid-instruction. 'No, some things shouldn't be delegated,' she murmured, as if to herself. 'I'll tell him myself. Put him through.'

Clarice withdrew; she knew her boss well enough to allow her thirty seconds for reflection, and Alex knew that she knew. She waited; when her phone rang she willed herself not to snatch it up, but counted off a further five.

'Sir Andrew,' she said, when, finally, she picked up. 'This is an unexpected . . .' she paused ' . . . moment. I'm sorry, but do you realise I'm not doing criminal defence work at the moment? I have an eighteen-month engagement as an Advocate Depute, so I can hardly appear on both sides of the court.'

'Something you said you would never do,' he drawled, 'when you packed in being a corporate lawyer to go on a crusade against injustice.'

She laughed, icily. 'There you go, same old same old. We can't even get past the pleasantries before you're having a pop at my professional choices. Why did I take this fucking call?'

'Sorry, sorry, sorry!' he exclaimed.

Her thumb was poised over the cut-off button but she heard enough contrition in his voice to hold it back.

'Well!' she snapped. 'At least you said it. When we were supposedly together and I made that decision, all I got was silent disapproval. It's a relief to hear what you really feel. Now, if that's all you called to say—'

'It's not what I feel,' he said, 'not anymore. Look, back then, no I didn't handle it well. I should have said that I was disturbed by the idea of the chief constable's girlfriend cross-examining his senior CID colleagues in a high-profile prosecution. I should have said it and we should have had it out.'

'You mean you should have talked me out of it.'

'No,' Martin sighed. 'I should have tried, that's all. I wouldn't have succeeded, that I knew, and that's why I didn't.'

'So instead, you took the huff.'

'I maintained a dignified silence,' he countered. 'That's how I prefer to look back at it.'

'And now,' Alex said, 'when you break that dignified silence you mock me for becoming an AD.'

'No, I don't. Please don't read that into it. You doing that, it doesn't surprise me at all. You're your father's daughter; prosecution's in your DNA. It was inevitable. I thought it might have taken a bit longer, that's all.'

'Something happened to push me in that direction,' she confessed. 'More than one thing in fact. An investigator I hired was murdered, and the people who did it came for me as well. It had an effect on me and then, on top of that, a guy I'd been seeing at that time, he was killed too. After all that I had a bit of a breakdown; I came out of it changed. I'd turned down the Crown Office before, but when they asked me again, I said yes.'

'Sorry, babe,' he said softly. 'I didn't know any of that.'

'Don't "babe" me, Andy. I'm not in need of consolation.'

'I didn't mean anything by it, honest. We've got a long history, you and me. If you're hurt so am I.'

'Do you say the same thing to Karen?'

'I would if it was necessary, but right now, I don't imagine that it is. I think she's doing fine for herself in the consolation department. She's dumped the kids on me for a few days.'

Alex laughed. 'That's a charming way of putting it.'

'I didn't mean it that way,' he protested. 'I love having them. It's just that there was no notice involved, no advance warning, just a phone call on Monday, saying pick them up from school and keep them until I get back.'

'When?' she asked, intrigued.

'A few days, that's all she said.'

'Could it be work? I know what she does now; Uncle Lowell told me.'

'It could be, but somehow I don't think that it is. There's a guy involved, I'm pretty sure.'

'She's a free woman, Andy, just like me.'

'That's what your dad said,' Martin admitted.

'And this is Karen we're talking about,' she added. 'I wasn't so young back then that I didn't hear the story about her shagging Sammy Pye . . . God bless and keep him . . . in the bike shed at Haddington nick.'

'It wasn't the bike shed,' he grunted.

'We've all got a past, Andy. Karen, you, me, and if every so often we feel like revisiting it . . . not that that's a suggestion by the way . . . it shouldn't be a surprise.'

'Maybe not.'

'How are the kids, anyway?' Alex asked.

'They're fine,' Martin replied. 'I do like having them at mine, honest. They're the main reason, maybe the only reason, why I didn't stay in America. I had serious offers from two different cities to become their police commissioner. Washington was one of them; the way it turned out, am I glad I didn't take that.'

'I'll bet.' She glanced at her wall clock. 'Andy, I have a trial this morning, and I need to be getting myself along there. Were you planning to tell me what this call is about?'

'What? Oh. Sure. You know I'm running for the Scottish Parliament?' he asked.

'Who doesn't?'

'In that case . . . I intend to be elected, Alex. I'm told I'm a certainty. The SNP will pull two seats from the top-up list, and I will be one of them. That means I'll be around Parliament from May onwards, and since you live next door, there's a good chance of us bumping into each other. That being the case I thought I should get any awkwardness out of the way now, clear the air, so to speak.'

'That's very thoughtful of you, Andy,' she said, adding cheerfully, 'but why are you confusing me with somebody who gives a toss?'

Thirty-Five

'It's a weird one, I'll grant you, DCI Mann,' Lowell Payne conceded, 'but there's been nothing on our radar pointing anywhere near that sort of terrorist outrage. You say Professor Scott reckons the killing took place on Monday. That's going on forty-eight hours ago. If it was the work of a terror group, I'd have expected them to have claimed it by now, maybe even released a video on the internet.'

'What if they tried, sir, and it was taken down by the platform?' John Cotter was the third person in the ACC's room in the Govan police office.

'We'd still know about it, Sergeant. The social media site involved would have made the intelligence community aware of it.' He glanced at Mann. 'Yes, Lottie, I will brief my surveillance people about it, but I can't do much more without specific information. It's an awkward one, I can see that.'

'Too right, sir,' she agreed. 'There's been no match for his DNA profile on any database, so far, and that was our best hope of identifying him. We need to recover the head to go any further, but no way am I going to tell the media that there's one missing.' She glanced at her watch. 'Head office is still considering whether we should release a statement in forty minutes. If we do, it'll be bland.'

'Isn't there a case for warning the public?' Payne asked.

'If there is, it's outweighed by the media hysteria that would follow. I've already had that discussion with Peregrine Allsop, the PR director. He took the opposite view and tried to countermand me, so I took it to DCC McGuire.'

The assistant chief smiled. 'Oh,' he murmured. 'Not our Perry's biggest fan.'

'It seems not. We had a three-way Zoom discussion and the boss backed me. Allsop demanded that he should let the chief decide. The DCC told him that Chief Constable McIlhenney was in the middle of a decision about the restructuring of Allsop's entire department. That shut him up.'

'I can imagine. I'm aware of that review, Lottie. The ice that Allsop's skating on is so thin he needs water-wings. Your call on how much information we release is absolutely the right one; he should have known that, but he's one of those guys who likes to have his stamp on everything.'

Mann frowned. 'Maybe Bob Skinner will give him a job on the *Saltire*.'

Payne pointed towards his office window. 'Look out there. There's as much chance of you seeing a green flag flying on Ibrox Stadium as there is of that happening!'

Thirty-Six

'Anything to get out of the office, Noele?' Sarah Grace suggested in jest as she entered the room where Inspector McClair was waiting. Both women were masked, and in uniform. The pathologist's was surgical; her hair was still damp from the shower that was part of her post-examination ritual.

'Witnessing a post-mortem is a shade extreme,' the police officer remarked, as her friend placed two takeaway coffees on the table and took a seat, 'but I've learned to take every opportunity that arises. I won't need to do that for much longer, though. I had a call from Sauce on the way here. I'm going back to CID, with effect from next Monday at the latest. He asked for me, and Mario McGuire's given it the thumbs-up. A year ago,' she added, 'if you'd told me this would happen I'd have laughed in your face.'

'If that's what you want I'm pleased for you. CID's more of a long-term condition than a job; once it's in your system it's there for good.'

McClair raised an eyebrow. 'So's genital herpes.'

'I hadn't thought of it that way,' Grace admitted. 'It's not an analogy I'll take too far, for Bob's a classic case. He questions everything in life, looking for motive, action and reaction. It's not just him. Maggie Steele's another case in point. He told me she's writing a crime novel. I said he should too, but his view is that one mystery author in our village is enough. He's very pally with Matthew Reid just now.'

'Bob led us here in a way,' the inspector said. 'It was him who kicked in Mrs Alexander's door, remember.'

'Matthew was involved too. He got Bob involved in the resilience group in the first place. If it hadn't been for that—'

'Someone else would have found her, and we'd still be here.'

'True.'

'So,' McClair continued, her voice slightly muffled by her mask, 'was everything as you expected during the examination?'

'A waste of public money,' Grace replied. 'Mrs Alexander died of heart failure, probably caused by the shock of her head hitting the corner of the kitchen table that I saw in the photographs of the scene. As Bob said to me, she had no business climbing those steps. She should have known better. Her medical records show that in addition to her arthritis she was subject to occasional attacks of vertigo, not an uncommon occurrence in someone of that age. She was like the late Mr Stevens in one respect; she shouldn't have been living at home, not without much more support than it seems she had. At least Michael had a carer.'

'And a traceable next of kin . . . pain in the arse although his is. I have my keen young constable looking through Mrs Alexander's recorded life, but she's having difficulty. I've sent her to Gullane to ask the neighbours whether she ever mentioned anyone to them.'

'Good luck with that.' The inspector saw Grace's eyes go somewhere else. 'That could have been me, you know,' she murmured, 'if my life had taken a different turning, if I'd never met Bob and died single and without a family. I have no relations that I know of. My dad was an only child, as am I; my mother was adopted and never knew who her natural parents were. Somewhere down the road that old lady lying dead on her kitchen floor could have been me.'

'But it won't be,' McClair declared. 'You'll be cared for by a regiment of kids and grandkids who won't let you climb up steps in your mid-eighties.'

'Jazz won't let me do that now,' Sarah laughed. 'Anyway, back to business. There will be nothing in my report that's remarkable in any way. The nervous fiscal will sign it off as an accidental death and that's how it will be recorded for all time. Nothing remarkable at all,' she hesitated, 'other than that fact itself.'

'What do you mean?'

'Apart from the injury that contributed to her death, the impact with the corner of the table, there were no other marks on the body. I was expecting to find bruising on other areas from the fall itself, and possibly even fractures given her fragility, but I didn't. However,' she added, 'given that death was pretty much instantaneous, it may be that there was simply no time for bruises to become visible before her circulation shut down.'

'Will you include that in your report?'

'Yes,' Grace told her, 'but I'll express it in exactly those terms, so don't expect the fiscal to overreact and for the file to land on your desk when you go back to CID.'

Thirty-Seven

A section of unpainted wood stood out brightly on Mrs Alexander's door frame. PC Tiggy Benjamin winced slightly as she saw it on her way past as she headed up the stairs to the attic flat. She was naturally optimistic, but even she thought that her mission was a waste of time. Yes, lockdown was in place, but as far as she could see, most people were interpreting the exercise provision fairly freely, particularly in Gullane where most of the population seemed to be dog owners.

The door of the lone apartment on the landing above was painted maroon. A Hearts supporter herself, she took it to be a sign of football allegiance. The man who opened the door appeared distinctly unathletic. He was shorter than her five feet seven, with thinning fair hair, but possessed of wide shoulders and with an ample belly; as she appraised him she had the feeling of looking at an enormous spinning top.

'Mr . . . ?' she ventured.

'Wilson, Mike Wilson,' he flashed her a toothy cheery smile. 'How can I help you, Constable?'

'Benjamin, PC Benjamin. Are you on furlough, Mr Wilson?'

'I wish,' he replied, the smile becoming a little rueful. 'I'm self-employed. I'm a personal trainer; all my stuff's one-on-one, in people's homes.' Mentally, Benjamin recategorised him, from spinning top to kettle bell. 'I can't work at all just now, and I'm struggling to get myself on to the Chancellor's payroll.'

'That's too bad,' she sighed, sympathetically. 'Maybe you could come to my garden.' *Where the hell did that come from?* she thought, as soon as the words had escaped, feeling her face flush.

'That would be nice, I'm sure,' he said. 'Where do you live?'

'Edinburgh,' she lied, covering her tracks. 'Of course, you can't leave East Lothian just now,' she added, extricating herself.

'Try telling that to half the people who cycle past my front window every day,' Wilson chuckled. 'It seems to be okay to leave your area if you're on a bike.'

'I will pass that thought on to my superiors, Mike,' she said, making a mental note to do no such thing, as his suggestion had already been put into practice. 'In the meantime, I'd like to ask you about your downstairs neighbour, Mrs Alexander.'

'Aye,' he nodded, 'is the old dear all right? I went out for a long walk yesterday, to North Berwick and back along the seashore and when I got home I saw that her door had been fixed. I never even knew it had been burst. What was that about?'

'I'm sorry to tell you that Mrs Alexander is dead. She had a fall in her kitchen.'

The trainer's cheery face fell. 'Aw, what a shame.' He sighed. 'No' a surprise though, I suppose. She was pretty shaky on her pins. We had this arrangement, she'd leave her rubbish bags from her kitchen bin at the front door and I'd put them in the green bin downstairs, then I'd take it out every fortnight. Same wi' the bags for the waste food caddy . . . no' that she wasted much. It took her a month to fill it.'

'When you spoke, Mike,' the constable asked, 'did she ever mention any family? We're having problems tracing her next of kin.'

'No' that I can remember.' His fair thin eyebrows rose. 'Come tae think of it she said to me once, after her cat died it was, that now she was completely alone on the world. She'd even left instructions wi' the minister for her funeral, for she had no family left to bury her. Poor old dear; I offered to get her another cat, but she said she didn't want to be leaving it behind her. I said I would take it if that happened. She was still thinking about it. I'd found her one, too; a mate of mine's having kittens . . . well, his cat is anyway.' He frowned, as a thought came to him. 'Her door was fixed, so who burst it?'

'Mr Skinner, Sir Robert that is,' she corrected herself, 'from the village resilience group. He called to drop something off for her.'

'I've got a key,' Wilson said. 'He could have asked me . . . but I wasn't in, was I?'

'In the moment I doubt that occurred to him, Mike.'

'Probably not.' He scratched the fair stubble on his chin. 'It rarely does. One of the benefits of living up a stair is that we don't get casual callers. The only person who rings my bell is the postie.' He paused. 'There was the kid, I suppose, but nobody else in a while.'

'What kid?'

'A young lad, secondary-school age maybe but not by much, longish fair hair, with a bit of cheek about him, wearing a padded jacket. He knocked on my door a couple of weeks ago and asked me if the grass at the back needed cutting. I told him

I took care of that. He told me he could do it cheap, but I told him he wouldn't be as cheap as me. He went downstairs, and I heard him ring Mrs Alexander's bell as well. I dinnae ken if she answered.' He paused. 'Come to think of it, he said he was part of the resilience group too.'

Something stirred in Tiggy Benjamin's memory banks. 'What colour was the jacket?' she asked.

'I think it was green.'

'Had you ever seen this boy before?'

'As a matter of fact, I had,' Wilson replied. 'A few times about the village. He cuts about on a bike. He goes all over the place, grass, pavements, you name it. Bloody wee nuisance he is.'

Thirty-Eight

Hector Sureda Roca's on-screen image froze for a second, then became animated once more. 'My God,' he said, 'here we are running a business that's entirely dependent on internet connections and we can't even have an office-to-office Zoom call without interruption.'

'Don't worry about it,' Skinner assured him. 'Girona's ahead of Edinburgh with its fibre network but when we catch up there will be no more glitches. We won't have a problem on Friday; the company aircraft is booked and the weather forecast's okay. I'll see you all at the same time as last week.'

'We will look forward to it. Goodbye, Senor Presidente.'

He smiled as the CEO of Intermedia vanished, recalling their first meeting, which had been unconventional to say the least, at the conclusion of a nationwide search with Xavi Aislado. Hector's parents, Simon and Pilar, had been important figures in what had been an ailing regional newspaper when Joe Aislado had bought it in the early days of democratic Spain. They had been constrained by the influence of associates of Franco, the old Caudillo, until Joe had swept them away, sanitising the company, as he had put it at the time. Released, they had helped him grow it into the multimedia empire that it had become before handing over their roles to their son, who was of the new era. Simon and Pilar had retired to their home in Begur, where they had ridden out the first wave of Covid in Spain, and were vaccinated against the second. If only Sheila had been jagged, Skinner mused.

There was a light knock on his door before it opened and Sylvia, the secretary he shared with June Crampsey, entered, carrying a tray. 'What's the canteen doing today?' he asked.

'Parmigiana,' she announced. 'It looks like lasagne but it's veggie.'

'I can barely wait,' he murmured, glancing at the plate with a degree of suspicion.

He was lifting his fork when his mobile sounded, in the holder on his desk where he left it on charge. The screen told him 'Number withheld'. That was an irritation, always, to a man who had known too many surprises in his life, but he suppressed his annoyance as he picked it up.

'Bob,' a mature female voice said, and he understood the precaution at once. The head of MI5 was not about to have her phone number in the public domain. There was a legend from decades in the past that the direct line of one of her predecessors had been engraved in the centre of a vinyl album by a punk band. It had sold millions of copies and had landed the record company and perpetrator in very hot water indeed.

'Dame Amanda,' he replied. 'Where's the crisis?' The two had been friends for many years, but rarely called each other on a casual basis. 'Or are you coming to Scotland and inviting me to dinner?'

'I couldn't, could I, with all the restaurants being closed.'

'I could entertain you here at the *Saltire*,' he offered, chuckling. 'Our canteen's still in business, as you'd see if we were on video. I could get them to knock out some bubble and squeak if that's still your favourite.'

'With gravy?'

'If you insist.'

'Let's keep that offer in reserve. So,' she continued, 'you're still a media tycoon, Bob. I wondered how long your enthusiasm would last.'

'It'll last as long as their enthusiasm for me,' he laughed. 'So far there's no sign of that being curbed.'

'I know. Chairman of the board, no less. Brexit hasn't got in your way.'

'You're on the ball.'

'We have automatic alerts set; your name popped up and it was reported to me. You know how it works.'

'I do,' Skinner agreed. 'What did I have for breakfast this morning?'

'Cereal and coffee.'

'How the fu—'

'A lucky guess,' Dennis said quickly. 'Well, the cereal was. As for the coffee, how long have we known each other?'

'Point taken. So, Director General, a pleasure though it is, why the call? I read some speculation that you were looking at retirement. Are you calling to offer me your job? If you are, given my recent step up at Intermedia, I doubt that the Home Secretary could afford me . . . even if I could overcome my distaste for the present incumbent.'

'I gave up trying to lure you to London a long time ago,' she admitted. 'As for the speculation, don't believe everything you read in the *Daily Mail* . . . indeed don't believe anything unless it's a football result and you've watched the game. I'm calling . . .' Her tone changed; it switched instantly from banter to business. '. . . because I have a question that needs answering. Why are your former colleagues asking questions about one of my safe houses?'

'How would I know?' Skinner retorted. 'I don't have access any longer, and they're not knocking my door down. I feel like an old stag who's been banished from the herd. Where is this safe house?'

'Glasgow, in the city centre. It's actually Clyde Houseman's place, but all the bills and tax payments are routed through one of our dummy accounts. A detective sergeant named Cotter has been poking his nose in, trying to find out who's behind it.'

'I know him; a Geordie lad. He's on the West of Scotland Serious Crimes team. I don't recall seeing any incidents reported in the *Saltire* this morning.'

'Maybe somewhere else?'

'If it was, we'd have picked up on it.' He frowned. 'Amanda, why are you asking me? Can't Houseman sort this out?'

'He could, if I could find him.'

'You what?' Skinner exclaimed. 'Are you telling me that the Director General of the Security Service can't find her point man in Scotland?'

'Even we have holiday entitlement, Bob. Clyde booked in for some time off, but he didn't tell HR where he was going.'

He felt the hair in the back of his neck prickle as the instincts of a lifetime kicked in. 'Leave it with me,' he said. 'I'm not due in Spain until Friday. I'll ask around.'

'Thank you,' Dennis said. 'I was hoping you'd say that. Discreetly mind, I don't want the security of the place to be blown.'

'Amanda! Please!'

Thirty-Nine

'Do you know who your replacement will be, ma'am?' PC Benjamin asked her inspector.

'Not a clue,' McClair admitted. 'They wouldn't tell me. You'll find out when the great wheel of command has turned. As it is, Sergeant Jackson will be in temporary charge from Monday, but it won't be him, unless the divisional commander decides to downgrade the post. Mind you, that wouldn't surprise me. I worked a hell of a lot harder as a DS than I've done here.'

'Will you be working harder still as a DI?' the young constable asked.

'As night follows day,' she laughed. 'I'm looking forward to it though. It'll be good to be reunited with Sauce.'

Puzzled, Benjamin frowned. 'Who?'

'Detective Chief Inspector Haddock. His real first name's Harold, but I've never ever heard him called that.'

'How did he get that name?'

McClair gazed at her. 'Where are you from, Tiggy?'

'I was born in Alberta, in Canada, like my mum, because she wanted that, but I was brought up in Oban. My dad's a teacher there. They met at university in Bristol.'

'Right. Consider this part of your cultural education that they obviously missed out on. DCI Haddock is called Sauce because people in the east of Scotland put brown sauce on their fish suppers. If he worked in Glasgow, I suppose they'd call him Vinegar, but it wouldn't have the same ring to it.'

'I suppose not.' The young PC hesitated. 'Ma'am,' she ventured. 'Is there any chance of me moving to CID with you?'

'Is that something you'd like to do?'

'I think so.'

'That's not quite enough. CID's not for everyone. It can be boring and mundane, run-of-the-mill robberies, it can be highly technical, fraud cases that take months, even years to wrap up and prosecute, and it can be brutal, racially motivated crimes, gangland killings and so on. Some people just aren't cut out for it.'

'I would be, I know it,' Benjamin insisted. 'I have an instinct for things, I just know it. There's the kid on the bike, for example.'

'What kid? What bike?'

'Remember when we were at Mr Stevens' house, when I went back to get the bolt cutter? A kid on a bike nearly knocked me over. Age twelve to fourteen, longish hair and wore a padded jacket?'

'I don't remember seeing him,' McClair admitted, 'but I was busy talking to the carer and assessing the situation. What about him?'

'Mike Wilson, Mrs Alexander's upstairs neighbour said that a kid chapped his door looking for work, and he thought he was going to try hers as well. From the way he described him it was the same lad.'

'So?'

'Isn't it a coincidence, him being near the scene of both incidents?'

The inspector nodded. 'Yes, if it was him, it's a coincidence. But Tiggy, Gullane has dozens of kids on bikes, my own son included. There's only an outside chance that it was the same boy. If it was, so what? These were two old people who died suddenly. Mrs Alexander was an accident and so was Mr Stevens. Even if the same kid was in the vicinity of both, that doesn't come close to justifying the opening of a criminal investigation.' She smiled, kindly. 'Going back to your question, no, I don't see any chance of your coming to CID with me. That's not the way it works. I'm going to a high-profile department, Serious Crimes, staffed by people with years of experience. I don't mind recommending you for a transfer when the time is right. By that I mean once you've gathered more experience as a community officer and put a few miles on your career clock. For now, be patient. But,' she concluded, 'don't stop looking out for the unusual, even if it is only a reckless kid on a bicycle.'

Forty

Chief Constable Neil McIlhenney moved from behind his impressive desk and bumped elbows with his visitor. 'Do we still call this the Wuhan handshake?' he asked.

'I doubt it,' Bob Skinner replied, as the two sat at a conference table. 'Definitely non-PC. There's bound to be a journalist or a blogger all too eager to label it as Sinophobia.'

'Aye, probably employed by you too.'

'Don't blame me, I'm only the chairman. Those decisions are made far away from me.'

McIlhenney stared at his friend. 'I am still getting my head round you at the head of any sort of a media organisation, least of all one of the biggest in Europe.'

'Ach, we're not that big.'

'Yes, you are. I googled you. Intermedia is the third biggest of its kind outside of America. It owns newspapers in Spain, Scotland, Italy, France and Germany, and its online editions are readable in all those languages plus Chinese, Arabic and Hindi. And you're not just the chairman, you're the executive chairman, which mean that the head honchos in all those countries report to you.'

Skinner smiled. 'Actually,' he said, 'they report to a bloke called Hector in Girona, and he reports to me. We touch base once a week.'

'Via Zoom?'

'Face to face. I fly there every Friday.'

The chief constable was puzzled. 'What airlines are still flying?'

'Air Intermedia. Company jet.'

'Fuck me,' McIlhenney gasped. 'Wait till I tell Louise that.' He gazed at Skinner. 'Are you such a high-flyer now that you think you can break the government's rules about travelling outside your local authority area? Okay, you needed to speak to me, you said, but we could have done it by video. I should hit you with a spot fine.' He grinned. 'In fact I think I will.'

'Fine, Chief,' Skinner laughed. 'You do that; I'll charge it to expenses. No, Neil,' he said, his tone changing, 'I'm not so locked in that I needed to see the sights of fucking Falkirk . . . sooner you move the HQ to Edinburgh or Glasgow the better by the way. I have something I need to discuss with you face to face, and probably Mario too, if he's in.'

'He is,' the chief confirmed. 'I'll get him through.' He moved back to his desk and pushed a button on a small console, then resumed his seat at the table.

A minute later the door was opened and Deputy Chief Constable Mario McGuire strode into the room. He stopped short as he saw Skinner. 'Bob?' he exclaimed. 'What the—?'

'And good afternoon to you too. Now you're here is some bugger going to get the coffee in, or do I have to go out to my car and fetch my cold takeaway?'

'Sorry, Bob,' McIlhenney sighed. 'I should have known.' He moved to a small sideboard on which stood a Nespresso machine.

When he returned, Skinner gazed at the cup that was handed to him, raised an eyebrow, and shook his head.

'I know, Bob, but I inherited it. Blame Maggie. You seen her, by the way?'

'Yes, she's blooming. But to business. I had a call from a lady I know with an office beside the Thames. She wants to know why you lot have been stomping over a flat in Glasgow, in Candleriggs.'

McGuire's eyes widened. 'Jesus Christ and his wee brother Joe!' he exclaimed. 'It's one of theirs. And we didn't know about it? I should have fucking guessed.'

'I thought you had,' Skinner retorted, 'since nobody on our Glasgow editorial staff picked up word of an incident there, not one that was worth reporting at any rate.'

'We decided not to make a public announcement. The city's quiet just now and the police presence went by unnoticed. It would have been a stick for our own backs, a real Singapore cane, in fact.'

'Why would that have been?' Skinner asked, quietly.

'There was a suspicious death,' the DCC replied. 'That's how we would have put it; actually, it was a lot more than that. A male victim; he was aged in his thirties, Graham Scott says, but there's no means of identification other than a tattoo.'

'There are no fingerprints or DNA on record?'

'None.'

'How about his teeth?'

'There was no fucking head, Bob. The victim was decapitated, and whoever did it took it away with him.'

'Bloody hell,' Skinner exclaimed; a fist seized his stomach and he felt his blood run cold. 'That sounds . . .'

'Islamic? Jihadi?' McIlhenney suggested. 'Yes it does, but nothing else fits that scenario. The whole point of terrorism is to create public alarm. If this was an Islamic State outrage they'd have been screaming about it. They'd have filmed the beheading and stuck it on YouTube.'

'Agreed. But it doesn't sound like a random killing either.' He paused. *'Bring me the head of Alfredo Garcia,'* he murmured.

Both officers stared at him. McGuire reacted first. 'Eh? Who the fuck is Alfredo Garcia? Are you telling me that's the victim's name?'

Skinner sighed. 'Oh dear,' he whispered sadly, shaking his head. 'It's a great, great Sam Peckinpah movie from before you guys were born. Alfredo Garcia had knocked up the daughter of a Mexican cartel boss and there's a million dollars on offer to the man who brings him his head. A cult classic; everyone gets killed in the end. So, was there a bounty on offer for this man's noggin? If so, who offered it and why?'

'That's a reasonable question,' McIlhenney agreed. 'But before we can begin to answer it we need to have a name for the victim. Since the property belongs to your friend's organisation, can you help us with that?'

He looked at the DCC. 'Mario, you mentioned a tattoo. Can you describe it?'

'I didn't see the body. Scott, the pathologist, told Lottie Mann about it. He said it was military.'

'What about the victim's ethnicity?'

'I confess that I don't know about that. I haven't seen the full post-mortem report; I only know what Mann told me.'

'Call her and ask her,' Skinner said, managing to alter his tone to make his words a suggestion rather than an instruction. He picked up his coffee and sipped it while McGuire took his phone to the window. His face wrinkled with distaste. 'Neil,' he murmured, 'this is pish.'

'Maybe,' the chief constable conceded, 'but there must be caffeine in it, for you're drinking it regardless.'

'Maybe you'll find my old coffee machine if you move your headquarters back to Edinburgh.'

'Is that what you would do?' McIlhenney asked.

'Now you want my input?' his friend murmured. 'I'd never have been here in the first place. I know it was decided by the Police Authority and they were following a hint dropped by the Justice Secretary, but if I'd been in your chair at the time, I'd have made my view clear, that the headquarters of a national force belong either in the capital city or the largest city, and that siting them somewhere in between is puerile.' He broke off as McGuire re-joined them.

'The victim was mixed race,' he announced. 'DNA analysis suggests that a grandparent was West African, Ghanaian or Nigerian.'

'Shit,' Skinner sighed. 'I was afraid you were going to say that.' His eyes moved from one to the other. 'Does the name Clyde Houseman mean anything to either of you guys?' he asked.

The DCC nodded. 'I know what he is,' he replied, 'although I've never met him. Lowell Payne might have, given that our counter-terrorism activity falls within the same broad network.' He looked at the chief constable. 'Clyde Houseman is the Security Service's specialist spook on Scotland . . . not the only one, but the only permanent presence . . .' He smiled and glanced at Skinner. '. . . apart from Sir Robert here, who's got discreet and informal links, since he and the Director General go back a long way.'

'I know about that,' McIlhenney said, nodding. 'He hauled me into an operation in London a couple of years ago, one that will never figure in anyone's memoirs.'

McGuire's dark eyes widened: he had believed he knew all of Skinner's secrets, even if Skinner did not know all of his. Masking his surprise, he moved on. 'There's contact between Houseman and our Special Branch team under Payne, but they don't operate together. He wouldn't overlap at all with Serious Crimes, Lottie's operation, so it's unremarkable that the idea of an MI5 link to the property didn't occur to her.'

The chief looked back at him. 'As it didn't to you, mate,' he murmured.

'Touché,' he conceded.

In the silence that followed, Skinner gazed at them, considering the wisdom of having friends as close as the Glimmer Twins in the top two positions of a national police service. He knew everything about them as police officers, and almost everything as men, including a secret so dark it could have ended the careers of everyone it touched, including his own for letting it stay buried. 'It's good to see you two challenging each other,' he said quietly. 'You have to, if this is going to work. If it doesn't, I might be looking for my old job back. There's no one else I'd trust in that chair over there.'

McIlhenney smiled and flexed his shoulders. 'That's comforting to hear, but I'm not too worried either way. If it doesn't, I can always go chasing a seat in the Scottish Parliament, now that the precedent's been set. Is your newspaper going to endorse Andy when the election comes along, Bob?'

'He's an SNP candidate,' his friend replied, 'and our newspaper isn't called the *Saltire* for nothing. But that's in the future. In the present, what am I going to tell Dame Amanda Dennis?'

'From the sound of things,' McGuire said, 'you're going to have to tell her to look for a new resident in Scotland.' He chuckled. 'Or will you take it on as another part-time job?'

'Cheeky bastard,' Skinner growled. 'There's something else she's going to want to know when I break the news about Houseman, and that is . . . what the hell are you bright boys doing to find out who killed him? And by the way, don't come to me for ideas. You need to be seen to stand on your own feet, remember.'

Forty-One

'I've got to tell you it'll be good to have you back, Noele,' DCI Sauce Haddock declared. 'I didn't fancy any of the DI candidates the DCC put before me. Every one of them was older than me for a start, and every one had more experience in the rank than I had before I was bumped up. I had feedback from a mate that one of them had been heard saying in the canteen that he didn't fancy taking orders from a fast-tracker with a degree. I sent word back to him to stop worrying about it because it wasn't going to happen, ever. I'm not a bloody fast-tracker,' he said indignantly. 'I joined the force as fast as I could after college, because it's what I always wanted to do. And I've only made DCI because Sammy went and died. If it would bring him back they could demote me to DC.'

'You don't have to justify yourself to me, Sauce,' McClair told him. 'I've worked with you, and I know you've made it on merit. Sammy was a high-flyer too, remember. If he hadn't contracted his illness, he'd have made detective super by now and you'd have been bumped up anyway.'

'Crawler,' Haddock chuckled.

'That'll be the day,' she retorted. 'It's true and you'll realise it if you think about it.'

'I suppose.' She saw him wink on her phone screen. 'There's no harm in having your ego boosted though.'

As she appraised him, it struck her that Haddock was no longer the young pup he had been when she had moved out of Serious Crimes a year earlier. He seemed older, with lines around his eyes that had not been there before, and perhaps with a slightly higher forehead. The burden that he had taken on, running a short-staffed unit because of Pye's absence on sick leave through his inevitably fatal disease, and her own departure seemed to have left its mark upon him. Or, she realised, there might be a simpler domestic explanation.

'How are the new Mrs Haddock and the even newer baby?' she asked.

'Samantha's good as gold, but she's voracious. Cheeky's knackered from feeding her, but you should see her, Noele. I don't think she's ever been happier. I'm not sure she'll go back to work once her maternity leave's over. Not with the firm anyway. Her grandpa's been on at her for a couple of years to work for him. She's starting to think about the flexibility it would give her.'

'How do you feel about that?'

'I'm easy about it. Cameron McCullough's a lot more open about his business activities these days. He's come out as a venture capitalist, with a knack of making everything he touches turn to gold. You should see him with the baby, him and Mia, I never thought of her as great-granny material, but she's a natural, although you call her that at your peril.'

'What about her granny, Cheeky's mum?'

'Inez? She's seen her, but the child will never spend a minute alone in that woman's company. Cheeky and I are agreed about that. My mother-in-law is an idiot and a sociopath.'

'I'm lucky then, my mum's great. She's practically bringing up Harry. She's his principal child-minder.'

'And how are you?' Haddock asked suddenly. 'Are you good now?'

'Am I over the loss of my sad ex-husband and my psychotic lover?' she said. 'I think so. It'll be a long time before I have another serious involvement, that I can promise you. I am sort of venturing out again; I thought about a Tinder account but decided very quickly that would be a bad idea, personally and professionally. I have had a few walks and garden coffees, with a much older man, a divorcee.' She grinned. 'I've thought about shagging him, but he does talk about some very nice restaurants that he'll take me to when they're open, and I wouldn't want to put that in jeopardy.'

'Why should it?'

'I wouldn't want to embarrass him,' Noele confessed. 'At his age he might not be up to the job.'

'You know, Inspector McClair, that sounds discriminatory to me. A touch of ageism.'

'That's true,' she conceded, 'and maybe an old dog could teach me some new tricks. He might not know himself until he sees the rabbit. Maybe I should park Harry with my mum and invite him for dinner at my place.'

'Have him for dinner, more like.'

'I'll have to give that some thought. For now I'll concentrate on next Monday. How's the team? Still the same?'

'Yes,' Haddock said. 'Tarvil Singh's still taking up as much space, and as you know, Jackie Wright finally passed her sergeant's exam and was promoted. That leaves us looking for a new DC. Any ideas?'

He saw her frown. 'I hadn't, because I poured cold water on

the kid's ambition earlier on, but I have a PC here who has stars in her eyes. She's only twenty-two, ears still dripping wet, but actually she's very good. She'd be a gamble, but she does show initiative.'

'Give me her name and I'll check her out.'

'Tiggy Benjamin. You should be able to access her file. She's full of ideas, and imagination. There were a couple of sudden deaths in Gullane, elderly people, one was misadventure, the other an accident, pure and simple, but she found a link between them and was ready to start a hunt for a serial killer.'

'I've heard more outlandish scenarios,' the DCI suggested.

'The link was a kid on a bike, early teens. Good thinking by her, but nothing in it. Sauce, I was at both scenes; trust me, both have been signed off by the fiscal and you do not want to be the person who asks for the files to be reopened.'

'Okay, I'll accept that; but I will take a look at PC Benjamin. I was a wet-eared twenty-two-year-old myself, not so long ago.'

Forty-Two

Lottie Mann gazed up at the deputy chief constable, but not by much. His summons to an early morning meeting in her Glasgow office had taken her by surprise, but its subject, when he finished revealing it, had astonished her. 'You're telling me that those premises are owned by MI bloody 5?'

Mario McGuire nodded. 'That's what I'm saying, but I repeat, that's not to be shared with anyone, not even DS Cotter. Chief Constable McIlhenney and I spoke with the Director General last night. She's adamant that nothing leaks. There's a vague awareness that Security Service operations can cross the border, and even that they can overlap with our own intelligence activities, but the fact that they maintain a permanent covert presence in Scotland, that would be dynamite.'

'Did you know?' the DCI asked, bluntly.

'I was aware that they had a staff member who took a particular interest,' he admitted. 'ACC Payne was aware too. Members of his team might even have met the individual to share intelligence they had gathered that might affect UK national security. But none of us actually knew officially that he had a flat in Candleriggs that was paid for by Millbank.'

'Why such secrecy? I can understand they might not want

the *Scottish Sun* publishing the address, but . . .'

'Because while it wouldn't come as a complete surprise to the First Minister, the Justice Minister, the Lord Advocate, and the rest of the Holyrood cabinet don't have a clue about it. Given that they belong to a party whose prime objective is to break away from the state whose integrity MI5 exists to protect, I'll let you work out how unhappy they'd be, and how big a political crisis there might be.'

'They'd think that MI5 was spying on the Scottish independence lobby? Is that what you're suggesting, sir?'

'Spot on.'

'So what do we do?'

'Treat it as an ordinary homicide, Lottie, and for everybody's peace of mind, keep the background suppressed and solve it as fast as you can.'

'It would help if we knew who the victim was,' Mann pointed out.

'Bob Skinner thinks it's a man named Clyde Houseman. Ex-Royal Marine, ex-special forces, now on the Security Service payroll and their man in Candleriggs.'

'Eh?' she exclaimed. 'How does Bob Skinner know?'

'Fuck's sake, Lottie, what doesn't Bob know?'

Forty-Three

'I can't imagine playing golf at your level, Anne,' Bob Skinner confessed. 'I'm a mid-handicap hacker these days.'

'No, you're not,' the old lady replied in a firm, strong voice. 'I've seen you play. I haven't forgotten being drawn against you and your daughter in the Hanky Panky competition a few years ago, when I was still playing a full round. You were off five, hit the ball a mile and rarely missed a green. Granted, you couldn't read a putt to save your life, but you could have been a scratch player if you'd devoted the time to it.'

'Thanks. I remember that match too. You didn't play a full round then either; you won four and three and to rub it in you and your partner were both in your eighties. Alex couldn't believe it, she's barely played since.'

'From what I've read of her, she's been far too busy. Like you, I suppose. You should play more, now you've retired.'

'Only from the police service,' Skinner protested. 'I'm busier than ever with my new job.'

'Indeed.' Mrs Eaglesham nodded. 'You're a media typhoon, according to the *Financial Times*.'

He smiled. 'You mean "tycoon".'

'That's what the *FT* said, but I choose my words carefully.

Can I invest in your company? Is it quoted in Spain, or anywhere else?'

'No, it's mostly family owned . . . not my family unfortunately.'

'Is there an heir?' she asked.

'Xavi, the majority shareholder, has a daughter. There's a stepson, but his copybook is pretty blotted. Paloma will inherit, eventually. In preparation her father is sending her to LSE; after that she's bound for Edinburgh to do a business administration masters.'

'No other family?'

'There are half-sisters, through his mother's second marriage. One of them is managing editor of the *Saltire*, but they're not in the line of succession and June isn't on the main board.'

'Your friend must be quite a man. I remember him too; I was a Hearts season ticket holder when he played for them. The man Draper was foolish to sell him to Merrytown. He was the best goalie we'd had in years and look what happened to him after he left. Injured his knee and never played again.'

'That's dealt with in his autobiography,' Skinner said.

'I didn't know there was one,' Mrs Eaglesham confessed. 'Is it still in print?'

'It never was, in the sense you mean. It was commissioned by Xavi himself, as a record of his life, but only ever given to people close to him. It's called *The Loner*. It was ghost-written by our friend Matthew Reid, although he used a pseudonym to avoid confusion with his detective series. I have a copy; if it ever was published it'd be a best-seller.'

'The ubiquitous Mr Reid. It was good of him to answer my cry for help.'

'Good of him?' Skinner exclaimed, leaning hard on the pronoun.

'Good of him, and even better of you,' she added. 'For you actually went to the store to fetch me the damn poultry food. I still can't believe I let myself run out.'

He reached out and touched the egg-box that lay on the garden table at which they sat. 'Your hens are still productive,' he said. 'Thank you very much, Anne. We'll have them for breakfast tomorrow, I promise. I had no idea you kept them.'

'Nor do many people in Gullane. The chicken run isn't overlooked by my neighbours, and I don't let them run free when I'm not there to keep an eye on them. Damn foxes!'

'Are they a problem?'

'Not if I see them. I shoot the buggers. And before you ask, yes, I do have a shotgun certificate.'

He laughed softly. 'That's not my business any longer. Mind you, I wouldn't tell too many people about it.'

'Why not? I shoot bloody magpies too,' she confessed. 'Wicked little buggers those are. Give them half a chance and all my eggs would be gone.'

'Maybe so, but I hate to think what some of the members of the Gullane Facebook News Group would make of it.'

'Make of it what they will,' she declared. 'This is my garden and I'll control the wild life as I choose.'

'I won't argue with that,' Skinner said, looking around. 'You know you really have a beautiful property, Anne. Can I visit you in spring and summer, when more things are in flower, not just the forsythia?'

'You may, Bob. Mind you, it's not always as tidy as this. That young fellow came back, the one I told you about, the one with the bike. He asked me for work once again and this time I relented. I give him my leaf blower and a rake and had him gather up all the fallen leaves. He filled the brown bin and three black sacks. He worked like a little Trojan, God bless him. I gave him thirty quid and a bottle of Lucozade; he wasn't so keen on that, but not many people are. I don't know why I buy the stuff. Habit, I suppose.'

'What was the kid's name? When you told me about him I asked my lads who he might be, but they said he didn't sound familiar.'

'I don't know, because I never asked. I did ask him to come back in a month. He said he'd try. I'll find out then.'

'You didn't let him in the house, did you?'

'I had to,' Mrs Eaglesham said. 'He wanted to use the bathroom. So can you if you need to,' she added. 'I could hardly let the child pee against a tree, could I? Don't worry, he left his jacket slung over his bicycle and his pockets weren't bulging when he left. Why are you so interested in him anyway, Bob?'

'I'm not,' Skinner replied, 'but he or someone very like him nearly ran over my toes on the pavement in the main street few days ago. I made a mental note to show him the error of his ways.'

'Bob, really, he's only a child. Anyway, you might not get a chance to show him anything. I don't think he's from Gullane. His accent was wrong; he didn't have the East Lothian twang that most kids do around here. Mind you, with all of these new houses that have gone up over the last couple of years, who's to know where anyone's from?'

Forty-Four

'In a couple of days this investigation will be a week old,' DCI Lottie Mann pointed out, addressing her team. 'Have we achieved anything that a naïve member of the public might interpret as progress?'

'We've got a possible grainy sighting of the victim heading for the crime scene last Sunday,' a keen young detective constable named McGuigan suggested.

'Very good, Barry,' she replied quietly. 'Given that the post-mortem told us that he was still alive on Sunday and that we know he made it to the crime scene because he was found dead there, I don't propose to make that a tick on the success column. Anything else?' She sighed, looking at DS Cotter. 'Never mind fucking progress. What do we know now, John, that we didn't know when the body was discovered?'

'You mean when most of it was,' an older constable grunted.

Mann's glare froze the smile on his lips. 'McDonnell, save it for the stand-up club. We're called Serious Crimes for a reason; we've got no room for would-be comedians.'

'We believe we know the identity of the victim,' Cotter said. 'Clyde Houseman, age thirty-six, born Edinburgh. He retired from the Royal Marines four years ago with the rank of captain.'

209

He paused then continued. 'We believe we know his identity, but,' he added, 'we can't confirm it. The Ministry of Defence should have his DNA profile and fingerprints on file, in case he was killed in action and they were needed, but they don't.'

'How could that happen?' DC McGuigan asked. 'I read a story about an ex-soldier in Inverness who set his house on fire. They needed DNA to identify him and they got it from the army.'

'I guess the Marines do it differently,' Cotter snapped. 'Bottom line, we can't prove it's Houseman in the morgue. We've tried to find family members, without success. His mother's dead, his father is a life-sentence prisoner who's currently in a secure mental hospital suffering from early onset dementia and his stepfather's a useless tool. DS Tarvil Singh from Edinburgh Serious Crimes tried to interview him but the guy's an alcoholic. He was so wasted on cheap wine that he couldn't even remember Houseman's given name. He claimed there was a younger sister and he always got them confused, but he couldn't remember her name either.'

'Could we find the sister through the Edinburgh education department?'

'Tarvil's colleague DS Wright tried that, Barry. There was only one Houseman on file and that was Clyde. Singh and Wright doubt that the sister even existed.'

DC McDonnell raised a hand. 'How about his old neighbours? Has anybody interviewed them?'

'Not yet,' Cotter admitted, 'but they'll be hard to trace. The housing scheme he grew up in, and ran away from, was demolished a couple of years after he left and the tenants were rehoused all over the city.'

'There's one thing I don't understand, Sarge,' McGuigan

said. 'With no evidence of terrorist involvement despite the brutality of the murder, this stinks of organised crime. We've got a headless corpse that's been unidentifiable so far, in a property with no marks of occupancy whose overhead costs are being met by an untraceable bank account, and yet we're going on the assumption that it's this man Houseman. How do we know that? Where did this suggested identity come from?'

'We have a source,' Mann declared.

'Are we allowed to know who that is?'

'No, Barry, you're not. All you need to know is what you're told, and that's all you need to do as well, all of you. Now, one positive is that Dorward's Crime Campus team have harvested various different DNA profiles from the scene. I need all of you to crack on with identifying as many of the owners as you can from the national database.'

'Where would we be without DNA?' McDonnell sighed, wearily.

'Even further up shit creek,' Mann shot back. 'Get on with the task. Even if we can't get a positive ID on the victim, find me some suspects.' As her team went back to their desks and computer terminals, she turned to Cotter.

'You know, boss, don't you?' he said quietly. 'You know who the source is.'

'Maybe I did,' she conceded, 'but for the purposes of the inquiry I've forgotten it already.' She paused, frowning. 'John, when you contacted the Ministry of Defence, did you ask them specifically for Captain Houseman's identification records? Did you ask for him by name?'

'Yes, boss, like you told me.'

'Maybe I was wrong. The one thing we know for sure about our victim is that he has a Royal Marine crest tattooed on his arm. Go back to the MoD, send them the profile that we hold and ask them to identify it. Maybe the source is wrong too. Maybe this is someone else's remains.'

Forty-Five

'I'm cursed by lethargic procrastination, Bob,' Matthew Reid confessed. 'I'm easily distracted. I determine that I will work from nine thirty every morning, then I open my email inbox and there's something that will lead me in another direction. I turn my attention back to the computer but before I get into my current novel, I decide to check Facebook, and I wind up debating the hot Gullane topic of the day with someone on the village news group. By that time, it's eleven so I get up from my desk to make myself a mug of tea. Then I decide I'd better check my bank accounts to see if my publishers have forwarded me any money. Not that that happens too often, but when it does I have to enter the details into the spreadsheet where I record my income for my accountant. That means opening Excel, and the software always needs updating so it can be a long time booting up. Then I remember I need to call or message someone about a resilience group task. They're not immediately available, so I finally get down to work, but I've barely got the document open when they call me back. Once we've agreed whatever has to be agreed the caller asks me if I've heard about such and such, and I haven't, so that's another ten or fifteen minutes written off. I hang up and then I notice that

I've got half a mug of cold tea on my coaster, so I get up again and I rinse out the mug before it gets so stained that it needs to go in the dishwasher, which I only run every three days, that being all you need when you live alone. Having done that I decide to make myself a coffee so I dry the mug and take a cup and stick a capsule in the Nespresso machine but before I switch it on I start to heat some milk in my frother, and time it so they're both ready together. Once the coffee's done I have to wash out the frother straight away before the residue burns into the surface. Once I've done that I am finally ready to work, but by that time it's gone midday and frankly I am no use after noon, unless I am right at the end of a book when I can see the whole story clear as a bell, at which point my creative mind takes over and the words just seem to pour on to the screen. I read once that Edgar Wallace claimed to have written a novel in a weekend just to show that he could do it. Maybe he did, but I will bet you it was no bloody good because the story-teller's mind shouldn't work like that. That said, once I'm at the stage I describe, when it becomes almost an involuntary act . . . I heard of a particularly vicious review once when a work was described as having been excreted rather than created – maybe that's why I never read reviews of my own work . . . anyway, once I'm at that stage I've known myself to get through fifteen thousand words in a weekend. When I'm not, as I said I'm mostly no use once the morning's over, so I head back into the house and make myself lunch, and maybe, if it's a nice day, phone a pal and invite them round for coffee in the garden in the afternoon, like I did with you today.'

Skinner laughed as his friend's monologue ended. They were seated in rattan armchairs at a glass-topped table, the furniture set in front of the author's office which stood apart from the rest of the house. Both wore disposable gloves, as a precaution against Covid. Even though Reid had received his first vaccine dose three weeks earlier he had cited an underlying health condition which he said would surely kill him if he contracted the virus.

'How long have you lived in the village, Matthew?' he asked.

'Small town,' Reid corrected him. 'We're a small town. According to the people who classify these things, Gullane is too big to be just a village. The upper population limit for a village is two and a half thousand. We have more than that on the electoral roll, even without the recent ridiculous over-development that the bloody council forced upon us. A nine-member planning committee and it was passed by four votes to three!' Real anger showed in the author's eyes but passed away as quickly as it had arisen. 'How long have I lived here?' he continued. 'It'll be fifty years soon. I'd been a golf club member for a few years when you arrived and before that I'd been a while on the waiting list.'

'I know you were,' Skinner acknowledged. 'You seconded my application form when I joined the list. Mind you, I didn't have all that long to wait.'

'No, Bob, you didn't,' Reid said. 'You were moved up after your first wife was killed in that car accident. You were given the first five-day vacancy that arose, out of sympathy.'

'I never knew that,' he confessed.

'Why should you? The committee didn't see the need to tell you, or anyone else for that matter. It was done, and that was that.'

'I didn't know you were ever on the committee.'

'I wasn't, but I knew people who were. I was quite involved with the club back in the day.'

'And yet you're never seen on the course nowadays.'

The writer shrugged. 'The truth is I never took pleasure from the game, mainly because I was never any good at it. I have too violent a nature, I suspect. I want to crush the ball, rather than encourage it to move forward. I keep a five-day membership just in case, but I don't think I'll ever play again. The price of golf balls these days,' he moaned, 'they were cheaper back then.'

Skinner winced. 'Back then,' he murmured. 'Not the best time in my life. You know, Matthew, aspects of Myra's accident are still a bit of a blur to me.'

His friend nodded. 'That's hardly surprising. Post-traumatic memory loss, they call it.'

'I couldn't even remember the make of car she was driving.'

'It was a Mini.'

Skinner looked at him in surprise. 'You know that?'

'Obviously it was reported at the time, and that detail must have stuck with me. I have that sort of memory, possibly because of the job I did.'

'What were you, before you became an author? I've always wanted to ask you, but Friday night in the pub wasn't the place to do it.'

Reid frowned. 'What was I? I suppose you might have called me "A Spokesman". I started my working life as a very bad journalist, very bad because I wasn't a social enough animal to build up the network of trusted contacts that you need to be a success as a reporter. As soon as I could I escaped into a job in the press office of a government department. The civil servants used to call us "Failed journalists" behind our backs. In all honesty they were probably right. I did that job for nine years. Some of it I enjoyed, but the writing side of it wore me down.

We churned out press releases that were meant to tell the press what the government was doing without ever crossing into politics.' He smiled. 'Basically, that meant we weren't allowed to use adjectives. Eventually I began to rebel; I was passed over for a promotion and finally it dawned on me that the long-term security and the cushy non-contributory retire-at-sixty pension just wasn't a high enough price to accept for my newly creative soul.'

'Does that imply that the civil service is the devil?'

'No way, it lacks the imagination for that. The guys I worked with at ground level, and they were all guys in those days, bar one, they were all good. So were most of the people at the top, but one or two of them were arrogant bullying wankers with post-graduate degrees in self-importance, and that was the culture that prevailed.'

It was Skinner's turn to smile. 'Not bitter, then,' he murmured, gripping his warm mug in his right hand and taking a sip of Reid's acceptable Colombian coffee.

'I might be now if I'd stayed there to the end, but an opportunity arose to use adjectives in hyperdrive, and I took it. I crossed the barrier and went to work for the party of government. That was liberation, and great fun. I made a lot of friends. I made a couple of enemies too, untrustworthy bastards who still made it to high office, but I gave up giving a shit about them a long time ago. Five years was enough of that, though. Finally, I privatised myself and went into business with a couple of people I'd met during that time. They were into corporate communications, and I was supposed to be the public relations arm. The problem was that my skills were in media relations.'

'What's the difference?' Skinner asked.

'There's less money in media relations, unless you're a

financial specialist. We did okay for a while, then the economy took a dive and so did we. However, when it was good we did well enough for me to have the time to start writing crime novels. The rest, as they say, is geography.'

'Do you enjoy it?'

'Yes. It began as a challenge, but it's become the main purpose of my life. Now I can create a mystery that not even you could solve. Guys like you need guys like me to keep your hand in. Did you enjoy policing?' the author countered, abruptly.

He considered the question. 'In CID,' he began, 'I enjoyed the satisfaction I got once the job was completely done and the perpetrator was sentenced. Then I made it to the top and found that some aspects of being a chief constable bored me rigid.'

'When you had to pull the trigger, Bob, how did that feel?'

Skinner frowned. 'Who says I did?'

'Come on. I know you did. I hear things in my line of work.'

'Then you shouldn't,' he said, firmly. 'You tell your sources, Matthew, that leaks that affect state security are taken very seriously.'

'Noted,' Reid conceded. 'Let's be hypothetical. What would someone in that position feel? I'm interested professionally.'

'In the moment, nothing. An armed police officer is trained to take that decision dispassionately. There might only be a second to assess the situation and make a judgement on the risk to the public, and the personal risk.'

'If they get it wrong?'

'Somebody dies. In theory, they could face prosecution for homicide, or be dead themselves. In practice, they don't get it wrong, because the threat is always clear and obvious.'

'Obvious or not, it must have been difficult for a compassionate person like you.'

Skinner beamed. 'Compassionate? Me?'

Reid smiled back. 'Yeah, you,' he repeated. 'I know you have this image as Britain's toughest cop, but that's a perception. It's a media shout line, like my publisher used on the jackets of my early Septimus Armour novels, to pull in readers like a fairground barker pulled in the punters. I don't see you as that man. I see you as someone who, suppose he was deep-sea fishing, strapped into a chair and hooked on to something big, would fight with it for an hour until all its strength was gone, then when it was ready to be brought on board and turned into a trophy, he'd cut the line.'

Skinner stared at him. 'Have you been talking to Sarah?' he asked. His host had described, in detail, an encounter that he had had several years before in the Gulf of Mexico, with a giant marlin that he hoped was still swimming around there.

'No, Bob, I haven't, I swear it. It's my impression of you, that's all. Christ man, if I thought you lived up to your reputation do you think I'd have asked you to go calling on vulnerable old ladies?'

'I'll tell Anne Eaglesham you said she was vulnerable,' he warned. 'She'd pull the trigger on you without a first thought, let alone a second.' He laid his mug back on the table and pulled off his disposable gloves. 'Matthew, that was a pleasant break. It seems that you know more about me than I do.' As he rose, his phone sounded. He took it from his pocket and read 'Hector Sureda' on the screen. 'I have to take this,' he said, heading for the garden gate. 'I'll be in touch.'

Forty-Six

DC Barry McGuigan had a low boredom threshold, but he was careful to disguise it. He had worked hard to become a member of DCI Mann's team and he had no wish to put that in jeopardy. Nevertheless, the tedious task of trawling through national databases for the owners of fingerprints and DNA profiles was one that he would have passed on happily to his worst enemy.

It was clear to him that the Candleriggs flat had not seen many callers, unless the SOCOs had missed as many of them as they had found. It was clear also so far that those who had visited were law-abiding citizens, for with all of the fingerprint samples checked through all the accessible collections, national, European and global, he had come up with as many positives as the UK entry in the Eurovision Song Contest usually gathered votes.

'Nil points,' he muttered as another DNA profile produced no matches. Moving on to the next, labelled C7, he pushed the send button and turned to his phone and his Facebook page as he waited. He was a member of three news groups, but rarely posted in any of them. His profile did not mention the fact that he was a police officer, but he was acutely aware that if anything he put up was politically incorrect, even accidentally, there could be professional consequences. His attention was caught by a warning about bomb disposal officers on an Ayrshire beach that was a favourite spot for both him and his boyfriend. He followed it through, smiling when the potential unexploded bomb was proven to be nothing more harmful than an old boiler. 'I had a date with one of them before I met Angus,' he whispered. He was still smiling when a corner of his eye registered a change on his computer screen. He laid down his phone and turned to give it his full attention.

His face froze as he scanned the information displayed; it was a DNA match, one hundred per cent, from the Scottish national database. His mind registered two things, astonishment and the need to pass the buck as quickly as possible. Grasping his mouse, he sent the entry to the printer, and was ready to retrieve it before it slid on to the tray. He grabbed the single sheet and headed along the corridor to the chief inspector's office. Happily, Mann was there.

She frowned at him as he burst into the room without waiting for a response to his knock, but stayed silent, possibly only because she was halfway through a Mars bar.

'Sorry, boss,' he said urgently, 'but you need to see this. It's a positive match for the Candleriggs flat.' He laid the print-out on her desk.

She stared at it. McGuigan found her reaction almost comical, realising that it matched his own.

'Are you sure about this?' she asked, quietly.

'It's what I got back, boss. There's no room for error, unless there's a fuck-up in the PNC.'

'Go and run it again,' she ordered.

She leaned back in her chair and waited, quietly munching

her Mars bar and considering the implications of the print-out that lay before her. She had just crumpled the wrapper and tossed it into her waste bucket when McGuigan returned, once again entering unbidden.

'No mistake, boss,' he exclaimed.

She whistled. 'Okay, Barry,' she said. 'Leave it with me. Carry on with the sample checks, and do not breathe a word about this to anyone, not even DS Cotter.'

As soon as the door had closed behind him, Mann picked up her mobile and found the DCC's number, realising that she was doing exactly as the DC had done, in moving a problem upstream. The call went straight to voicemail; rather than leave a message, she phoned the chief constable's direct line, which all senior CID officers had for emergency use. That also went unanswered. Finally, she called the executive officers' main switchboard and was connected to the chief's secretary, Claudia, a woman who famously saw herself as a human shield around her boss.

'They're in conference,' she told the DCI. 'All the command team are. Not to be disturbed.'

'They are now,' Mann replied, quietly, but with an edge to her voice that precluded debate. 'I need to speak to DCC McGuire, so go in there and haul him out.'

'What will I tell him?' Claudia asked.

'One word. Candleriggs.' She repeated it, slowly. 'You got that?'

'I have. If he agrees to leave the meeting, I'll call you back.'

'He will. I'll hold on.'

She waited, battling against the urge to reach for a second Mars bar: she had a history of sugar intake under stress. She kept her eyes on the wall clock, watching the second hand sweeping in a silent circle. It was halfway through a second revolution when McGuire came on-line. 'Lottie,' he said briskly, 'we've adjourned the meeting, you're on speaker and the Chief's with me. There's nobody else in the room. Now what's the crisis?'

'The DNA sample check, sir. It's established the presence of an individual at the crime scene. Obviously there's no time frame, but the DNA sample recovered is definite.'

'What do you need from us, DCI Mann?' McIlhenney asked.

'Authority, sir,' she replied. 'Because of who this is I need instructions from the highest level on how to proceed.'

'Lottie,' McGuire growled, 'you might not think that an arse being covered has a sound, but it does, and a very distinctive one at that. I can hear it right now. You're a senior CID officer in charge of a specialist unit. You proceed exactly as your experience tells you and this office will back you all the way. Now, who is this hot fucking potato?'

'Sir Andrew Martin: the first chief constable of the national force, and a candidate for the Scottish Parliament in the May elections. My only doubt is, sir, do I go to him, or do I ask him to come to me?'

'What's your thinking?' McIlhenney asked again.

'That if he's a suspect who or what he is doesn't matter. He should be interviewed under caution, with a lawyer present if he chooses. As for the venue, I can't cede any aspect of control of the situation. That means he comes to me, under arrest if that's what it takes.'

'Agreed,' McGuire said.

'Do either or both of you want to be there?'

'Mario and I have known Andy for years,' the chief constable replied. 'We worked with him, and he was our senior officer all of that time. We can't be in the room or even in the building when he's interviewed. You're fully in command of this one, DCI Mann. Proceed in any way you feel necessary without further reference to either of us or anyone else until you feel the need.'

Forty-Seven

Bob Skinner felt guilty on more than one level. His Covid isolation and virtual lockdown had brought it home to him that although he had lived in what Matthew Reid insisted was the small town of Gullane for more than half of his life, even allowing for a brief sojourn in Edinburgh during his first marriage to Sarah, his personal contribution to the community had been minimal.

Also, he had let Anne Eaglesham down. As they had parted at the end of his garden visit, she had asked him to retrieve her golf clubs from her locker in the clubhouse.

'With these hands I couldn't hit the ball out of my garden these days, Bob,' she had confessed, 'so I might as well knock a few balls around within its confines.'

She had given him her locker key and he had picked them up next day, but they still lay in his hallway, a fine set of Ping GLEs that could have been no more than three years old. They would stay there no longer, he determined, picking them up in their fine white bag, with the name 'Mrs Anne Eaglesham' embossed upon it.

He was grinning as he arrived at The Eyrie, imagining the old lady threading a drive between her trees, with no likelihood of hitting them. The broad entrance was closed as always, but a brown recycling box stood outside. He lifted its lid and glanced inside; it was crammed full of leaves. He assumed that the kid must have been back; *bright lad,* he thought, for Anne Eaglesham would always be a good payer. He stepped through the side gate and into the driveway, a smile still on his face in anticipation of the good deed he was about to complete. It faded when he saw the first of the feathers. They lay on the ground at the side of the house moving gently on the breeze. He picked up his pace and, as he drew closer, he saw that they were everywhere, on the drive, on the lawns and even among the trees. Laying the golf clubs on the ground he ran round to the back of the house. The door of the henhouse lay open, but there was no one home. He had no idea how many chickens Anne Eaglesham had kept but there were no survivors. The scene was one of carnage, blood, guts and feathers everywhere, with a few heads, wings and feet among them. He looked at the latch of the enclosure; the padlock that had secured it was unfastened, and the door had been left open. The slaughter had involved more than one fox, that was for sure, but a human had let the hens loose. Not Anne, so who? He thought of the likely candidates for such an act of sabotage; in the wider world of the politically correct there were people, no doubt about it, who disapproved of any form of poultry enclosure, but none that he knew of in Gullane. Even if there were, who knew that Anne Eaglesham had a hen coop? She was a figure of mystery to most; visitors to The Eyrie were few and far between. But there had been one recently, apart from himself.

The kid on the bike.

'Little bastard,' Skinner hissed, moving the boy instantly to the top of a very short list of persons of interest. 'You and I are going to be having a chat.'

But . . .

As his red-hot anger faded and relative calmness returned, another thought came with it. Poultry did not go quietly to the slaughter; there must have been a hideous noise as the foxes feasted, more than loud enough to rouse Anne Eaglesham and bring her out with her shotgun. And yet it had not.

There were three doors at the rear of the house, two of them in an L-shaped single storey section with a sloping roof. He surmised that the one on the left would have been the coal shed when the house was built. He opened it to check his theory; the walls were still blackened, but it contained only garden equipment, spades, hoes, rakes and trowels, with weedkiller, fertiliser and other products stacked on a high shelving unit. He left it and went straight to what he assumed was the back door of the house. It had two locks, one an old-fashioned mortice with a large keyhole, the other circular, not a Yale, but one he recognised as the work of a specialist locksmith company in Edinburgh that had been out of business for many years. He tried the handle and to his surprise the door opened.

He stepped inside, into a large kitchen. Glancing around, he surmised that the fittings were as old as the house itself. The cupboards and shelving units were the work of skilled carpenters, and the work surfaces were granite. There was a deep double sink beneath the window, with brass taps above, and a table in the centre of the room with four chairs around it. The only items that spoke of modernity were the electrics, the switches and plugs, and an Aga cooker. He knew the model because he and Sarah had considered it only to rule it out because its induction hob would have been at odds with his cardiac pacemaker.

'Anne,' he called out loudly, moving into the house. It was as much of a museum as the kitchen had been, with a wide hand-carved staircase rising from the hall and several doors off it. He checked the ground-floor rooms one by one, continuing to call the owner's name, even though he knew that she would have replied by that time, had she been capable. He went upstairs and checked each of the seven bedrooms; two of them were en-suite. The larger, obviously Anne's room from the items on the dressing table, had a circular shower enclosure of a type he had seen once before in his life, in a public school where he had gone to play an away game of rugby as a fifteen-year-old schoolboy. His rugby career had been brief and had ended that day. An opposition forward had grabbed him by the testicles. Skinner had broken his nose and fractured his eye-socket. The incident had been hushed up by the host school, but he had been suspended indefinitely by his own.

Layers of dust on the wooden furniture and windowsills on the first floor and attic rooms told him that all but the owner's had been unopened since the first lockdown a year earlier and possibly for longer than that. Later he would realise that, in spite of the importance and essential nature of his task, a part of him fell in love with the house as he searched it, but in the moment, he ran back downstairs as soon as he had looked behind every door, including the second en-suite and two family bathrooms.

Back in the kitchen he paused for thought, retracing his movements in his mind. There was only one door that he had not opened, one place that he had not explored. He stepped back outside and turned to his right, to the middle of the three rear doors, alongside which there was a small window with a white muslin curtain. There was a key in the lock; he swore softly at himself for not noticing it earlier as he twisted it anticlockwise, confirming that it was not engaged, then turned the handle, swung it open and stepped inside.

The architect who designed Eagle's Nest, before it became The Eyrie, had probably described the room as 'The Laundry'. It was spacious, with painted walls and an uncarpeted wooden floor, another original feature. A drying rail, the type for which a contemporary interior designer would pay a fortune, hung from the ceiling, restrained by a double cord attached to the wall. As in the kitchen there was a double Belfast sink, this with scrubbing boards on either side, one basin with the drainage tube of an ancient washing-machine hung over the side. Skinner thought of his grandmother's house; he could remember very little of her, but her Hoovermatic twin tub was fresh in his mind.

He thought of her again as he saw Anne Eaglesham slumped over the machine, one arm plunged into the washing compartment, wondering what the difference had been between their ages. He knew they had been born in the same century but that was all. He stepped towards her; he was about to check her for a pulse when he was stopped by the instinct for self-preservation that had served him well throughout his life. For a reason too obscure to pursue, The Laundry had not been re-wired with the rest of the house. Its power sockets were old style, round pin, fifteen amp, and the light switches were round and made of brass like the taps above the sink.

He looked for the fuse box and saw it, beside the window, within easy reach as he moved to pull the lever that shut off the electricity that had killed the old lady. Once that was done, he took out his phone. From the doorway he shot twenty seconds of video. Moving forward, he took still photographs from three different angles and one close-up of a section of the floor beside the machine. Only once he was satisfied that he had enough, did he remove the body from its unnatural pose and lay it down, gently.

He took a deep breath and stepped outside, reaching once again for his phone. He searched his contact list for 'S' and pressed the call button, listening to it ring out, once, twice.

'Gaffer,' Sauce Haddock said. 'What can you do for me?'

Skinner ignored the joke. 'You, son,' he replied, 'can help me break a bad habit I've developed lately.'

'What's that?'

'Finding old ladies dead in their homes. The first one fooled me, but this one doesn't. This is more than suspicious. This is homicide; I'm sure of it.'

'Where are you?' the young DCI asked, all business.

'I'm at a house called The Eyrie, in Gullane, not far from my place. The victim's name is Anne Eaglesham. Google her, adding the word "golf", and you'll find her in a second.'

'I'll be there on the double, with a full team.'

'The SOCOs need to process one other address, maybe two. Bring as many as you can get.'

'Will do, gaffer. Are you going to tell me who did it as well?'

'Definitely no, but as it stands, you're looking for a kid around fourteen years old, whose intelligence must be off the fucking scale.'

Forty-Eight

Sir Andrew Martin's eyes were green, but they were ablaze with anger as he walked into the interview room where DCI Lottie Mann and DS John Cotter waited. He was alone.

'Is your solicitor travelling separately, sir?' Mann asked, forcing herself not to make her voice sound deferential in any way, although she felt a level of nervousness that was new to her.

'I don't need a lawyer,' the former chief constable snapped. 'I have no idea what this is about. All I was told by your DC McGuigan was that it would be a formal interview, but that was all. My assumption is that it relates to my former service. If that's the case, Detective Inspector, I'm comfortable that it was as exemplary as it was brief.'

'Detective Chief Inspector,' Cotter corrected him. 'I thought you'd have known that.' He managed not to wince as Mann kicked him under the table, hard.

Martin's eyes turned from fire to ice. 'And you are?'

'John Cotter, sir. Detective Sergeant. We've met; you paid a brief visit to Aberdeen not long before you resigned.'

'You must have been at the back of the room. Or standing behind someone.'

Mann bridled at the slight and made no attempt to hide it. Cotter might be a short-arse but he was her short-arse. 'Please take a seat, Sir Andrew,' she said, curtly. She switched on the sound and video recorders and identified the three people in the room. 'You are not under arrest, Sir Andrew, but as DC McGuigan said this is a formal interview and is on the record for the purposes of any future court proceedings. If at any point you feel you would benefit from legal advice, we will stop to allow that. However, I need you to confirm for the record that you are happy to proceed without it.'

'I'm familiar with the Cadder ruling by the Supreme Court, and I do confirm it,' Martin declared. 'Now, also for the record, I want to warn you that if I have the slightest suspicion at any point that this summons to a police station has anything to do with my political ambitions, the interview will also stop, and the consequences will reach far beyond the chief constable's office.'

'Was that a threat, sir?' Cotter asked.

'No, Sergeant, it was a very clear warning. Now, let's get on with it. I'm looking after my kids just now and I've had to make special arrangements for them with a family member.'

The DS had neither forgotten nor forgiven the height slight. 'Would you like to tell us who that is, sir,' he murmured, 'should this interview get to the point where we need to safe-guard them?'

Martin looked Mann in the eye. 'What would you and this idiot do if I got up and walked out of here, right now?'

'We'd arrest you,' she replied.

'On what grounds?'

'That we have reason to believe that you have committed an indictable offence and that your detention is necessary for the furtherance of our enquiries and to protect the public.'

'What?' A laugh exploded from him. 'You are surely taking the piss. Is this Mario McGuire pulling my chain?' Mann gazed back at him, emotionless. 'Okay,' he said, 'let's hear it. What am I supposed to have done? Bought my house with crypto-currency that went belly up before the ink was dry on the deeds?'

'Did you?' Cotter growled.

Both Mann and Martin ignored him. 'Does the name Clyde Houseman mean anything to you?' the DCI asked.

The former chief constable frowned, accentuating the lines on his forehead. 'Off the top of my head, no it doesn't,' he replied. 'Should it?'

'We're told that you met, a long time ago in Edinburgh. You were a young CID officer then, with Sir Robert Skinner's Major Crimes team. Houseman was an even younger gang leader in a housing scheme that you and Sir Robert visited in the course of a murder investigation.'

'Mia Watson's brother's killing? That one?'

'I don't know the specifics,' Mann confessed.

'That would be it,' Martin continued. 'We went to interview the victim's mother, a brute of a woman who wound up dead herself. In the street outside a bunch of kids tried to hustle Bob. The usual, give us a fiver to mind your motor or it won't have wheels when you get back. I remember now, Bob showed him the error of his ways. He told him that if the real neighbourhood heavies saw him taking money from a pair of CID officers, it didn't matter how tough he thought he was, it would have an adverse effect on his life expectancy. From what you say that would be the boy. Okay, I met him but I never heard his name, so it couldn't have meant anything to me.'

'Does that mean you deny visiting Clyde Houseman recently, in a flat in Candleriggs, in the Merchant City in Glasgow?'

'I think I can deny ever having been in Candleriggs. I grew up in Glasgow but it wasn't somewhere I hung out in. I misspent most of my youth in rugby pubs and clubhouses.'

'In that case,' the DCI said, 'we have a problem. If you don't know Houseman, and you deny having a meeting with him, social or business, can you account for your genetic material being found on those premises, where a body that we believe to be his was also discovered?'

Martin's eyes locked on hers. Cotter moved and opened his mouth as if to emphasise or endorse the question, but his senior stopped him with the slightest movement of her hand.

'No,' their erstwhile commander replied. 'No, I cannot. But I want the name of the scene of crime technician who found the alleged sample of my genetic material and I want to see proof of its authenticity. You said that you believe the body to be his? But you don't know?'

'We don't, not for certain. The corpse wasn't identifiable, but Houseman lived at that address and the remains match his ethnic origins. As for giving you the name of a SOCO, you know better than that, Sir Andrew.'

'Maybe I do,' Martin conceded, 'but I can be fairly certain of one thing. Mine wasn't the only DNA recovered on the premises. How many others have you got?'

'Including the woman who found the body,' Cotter replied, 'and the cops who contaminated the scene, we have half a dozen so far. Others are still being processed.'

'Okay. I think I can work this out too. Houseman's details aren't on a database either, or you'd know for sure your body was him. Plus, your stiff has either never been to a dentist or the killer messed with his mouth to prevent identification through his records. Detective Chief Inspector,' he looked back at Mann, 'how many of your half dozen profiles have been identified?'

'Only yours, sir,' she admitted.

'So you have another five potential suspects. Why hit on me?'

'Come on!' she exclaimed. 'That's bloody obvious. Your presence there is incongruous to say the least, and there's a connection, however tenuous, between you and the suspected victim. If we'd swept it under the carpet and someone at Gartcosh had leaked it—'

'If someone at Gartcosh leaks this,' Martin spoke quietly, but looked up at the camera and made direct eye contact, 'it'll be the same person who took my profile from the database and planted it among the crime scene samples that were returned to you.'

'No,' Mann said, 'I've excluded that possibility. I asked Arthur Dorward about the source of the DNA that he found. You have very distinctive hair, sir; his team found two of them, stuck in the victim's blood.'

He looked back at her, considering what she had said. 'In that case, there's only one possible explanation for their presence. Someone planted them at the crime scene looking to incriminate me.'

'Is that right?' Cotter guffawed. 'Are the Tories so scared of you becoming an MSP they'd do that?'

In his years of working with Bob Skinner, Andy Martin had been in many interview rooms with him, and had witnessed his ability to extract the truth from suspects with nothing more than an ice-cold, unblinking stare. He turned his own version on the little detective, and it had a similar effect. 'Son,' he murmured, 'when this mess is cleared up, I am going to make it my business to bring your career to a grinding, painful halt. If you think that's an empty threat, you really don't know who you're dealing with. This is a formal interview, so I'm entitled to a copy of the recording. Imagine the rest.'

He stood up, abruptly. 'We're done, DCI Mann. You have a hair sample, but you can't prove my presence in those premises by any other means. You have my historic meeting with Houseman . . . I know who and what he is, by the way. As chief constable I had to know what the Security Service was up to on my patch . . . but you can't even prove that he's your dead man. Now, I'm going to pick up my kids. If you try to stop me, I will indeed call a lawyer. She might be an Advocate Depute just now, but I'm pretty sure she'd help me out. Tell the Glimmer Twins that Andy Martin said hello.'

Mann rose also. She stared after him as he left the room, but she made no move to stop him.

Forty-Nine

'I'll give you a formal statement as soon as I get home, Sauce,' Skinner promised, 'but basically this is what happened. I had picked up Anne's clubs from the clubhouse as she asked me to and called in to drop them off. As soon as I saw the feathers, I knew it wasn't good.'

'I googled her like you said,' Haddock told him. 'A very impressive record: I feel guilty, never having heard of her, me being a golfer and all.'

'You shouldn't feel too bad; Anne Eaglesham was even before my time. Her generation of amateur golfers is largely forgotten. Most folk these days think that the game only began when TaylorMade invented metal woods.' He grinned, wistfully. 'If you check her bag, you'll find that she used Pings. She moved with the times . . . on the golf course, and even in her eighties she was far too good for the likes of you and me. I reckon that a twenty-year-old version of Anne today would be world class . . . that's if she turned pro. If I had to compare her with any golfer it would be Bobby Jones, and he never did.'

The young DCI surveyed the scene in the garden. 'You reckon that the kid you spoke about did this?'

'He's my number-one suspect; he's the only person I know

to have been in the garden recently. Last time I was here that brown bin wasn't at the gate, full of leaves. He's been back since. Anne wouldn't have done it herself, and she didn't use any of the local gardeners. She employed a couple of green-keepers from the golf club in the spring and summer months, but in the winter the place took care of itself.'

'Could she have owed them money?'

'No chance,' Skinner declared. 'Anne was a generous lady. She donated to every fundraiser in the village whether she knew the organiser or not. The guys would never have been allowed to leave here unpaid.'

'Is it possible,' Haddock asked, 'that the kid turned up, did the work, then couldn't get an answer when he went to get paid? So he took it out on the chickens?'

'Yes, it's possible, I'll grant you. I am struggling to convince myself that the kid actually killed her, and yet he's a common factor, a link between three recent, sudden and apparently accidental deaths.'

'You said it, gaffer; accidental. I'm struggling to convince myself that anyone killed her at all. I've been in that laundry room. I've seen the old three-pin plug after Dorward's son took it apart. The earth wire's completely separated and the washing machine's resting on a nail, as you demonstrated on the photos you took before you lifted the victim out . . . which you should not have done, by the way. The thing was live, and as soon as she stuck her hand in . . . kaboom. I look at that and what I'm seeing is a tragic accident. Death by electrocution; that's what the autopsy report will say, and you know it.'

'Yes, I do, he conceded. 'Then I look at Mrs Alexander, another of my resilience group clients. I found her too, dead on the kitchen floor having fallen off a stepladder and hit her head on the corner of the kitchen table, with the mark of the impact clearly visible. I looked at that and I saw a tragic accident. Then I look at one man finding two victims within a few days of each other, and my inherent disbelief in coincidences kicks in.' The sound of feet crunching on gravel distracted him. He looked round to see Noele McClair approaching.

'Welcome,' Haddock exclaimed. 'You don't start until tomorrow, officially, but it's good that you could come. The gaffer's calling this a murder scene and linking it to another, but I need convincing.'

'Christ, did I teach you nothing, Sauce?' Skinner cried out. 'Always disregard coincidence until the facts are established. Mrs Eaglesham, electrocuted, discovered by me. Mrs Alexander, heart failure after a fall, discovered by me. What does that say to you?'

The DCI smiled. 'It says that you're a person of interest, gaffer.'

'Fuck off! Sorry Noele. Add in the early-teens kid on the bike that Anne Eaglesham employed to tidy up her garden, whose description matches a lad who nearly ran over my toes outside Mrs Alexander's flat.'

'He did more than that,' McClair volunteered. 'A boy fitting that description knocked on the door of Mrs Alexander's upstairs neighbour looking for work. It's a fair bet he asked her as well. Not just that, when Tiggy Benjamin and I attended the sudden death of Mr Michael Stevens, she was almost knocked over . . . almost certainly by the same lad. What colour was the bike, Bob?'

'Black. The lad was wearing a puffer jacket, and his fair hair hung down to his collar.'

'That's him.'

'What was Mr Stevens' cause of death?' Haddock asked.

'Cerebral haemorrhage as a probable result of ingesting too much blood-thinning medication.'

'You didn't find his body, did you, gaffer?'

'No, Sauce, I didn't, but my wife did the post-mortem.'

'Only because the deceased's daughter insisted on it,' McClair volunteered. 'She said that her mother passed away in similar circumstances last year, and that it was unexplained. Mr Stevens was having his afternoon drink with his cronies at the time.'

'See?' Skinner said. 'She didn't believe in coincidence either.'

'Maybe not, but her father's death was still classified as non-suspicious by the fiscal.'

Haddock frowned. 'What about the mother? What's known about her death?'

'Nothing other than that the GP certified it as a heart attack. She was on the waiting list for an aortic valve replacement. The procedure was delayed by the pandemic; the hospital was catching up on the backlog, but too slowly for her. We can't revisit it, Sauce, if that's what you were thinking. She was cremated.'

'I wasn't going to propose it,' the DCI told her. 'I'm not going to open a triple murder investigation either,' he added. 'However, I will do as the gaffer suggests and ask Mr Dorward's team to do a full sweep of the other two sites, in the hope that they haven't been totally contaminated by now. Tomorrow morning, DI McClair, when you and DC Benjamin start officially in Serious Crimes, your priority task will be to find this mysterious and omni-present kid.'

Fifty

When she had been in private practice as a solicitor advocate, Alex Skinner had never allowed a phone to ring unanswered. Her availability might make the essential difference between a client's liberty or their detention, seven days a week.

As an Advocate Depute, she took a different view. The court worked on a weekday basis, unless there was a need for an urgent appearance by a newly charged accused, and so did she. The downside was that in her downtime she was subject to the same lockdown rules as everyone else, unable to entertain or be entertained, and unable to leave her local authority area to visit her family in East Lothian, other than in emergency situations, as she had done when her father and stepmother had been isolated.

Yes, there were other exceptions, but the fate of other public officials who had been caught out was a powerful disincentive to testing their limits.

'How are you doing?' Dominic Jackson asked her as she took his call.

'Much the same as you, I guess,' she confessed. 'Bored out of my tits.'

'I wouldn't quite put it that way, but I understand what you mean. I spent this morning working on the final draft of my book, but since then . . . there's a limit to the amount of Mozart I can take. I'm about to go for a walk but I thought I'd call you first, to see if you were thinking the same.'

'I went running this morning,' she told him. 'Round Holyrood Park . . . twice. This afternoon I'm at such a loose end I actually thought of going down to Portobello beach for a swim.'

'A bit parky for that.'

'In my wetsuit,' she added. 'Imagine my nipples showing through all that rubber.'

'Alex!' he laughed.

'Imagine, that's all. You do realise, Dominic, that if we were shagging, we'd actually be able to visit each other, in a sort of conjugal bubble.'

'Well, we're not, and we agreed a while back that would be a bad idea. Besides, I've been celibate for most of this century. If we did, I suspect it would last about two seconds.'

'I've never known a man who didn't come back for more.'

'Enough! I'm off out. You do the same or try some Wolfgang. He's good at soothing savage breasts.'

She smiled as the phone went dead. She knew that she and Dominic would never get it together, as it would put at risk the truest friendship that either of them had ever known, but she still fantasised about it from time to time. She had been celibate herself for over a year and was getting used to it as a fact of her life.

'Alexa,' she said, firmly, 'play music by Mozart.'

The device was in the process of obeying when, to her great surprise, her door buzzer sounded. 'Who the —?' she whispered as she moved to the video screen. She gasped in surprise as her curtailed question was answered.

'Andy,' she said. 'What the hell are you doing here?'

'Probably breaking the law,' he replied, 'but there's a situation. It's been doing my head in for a couple of days and I need to talk to you about it.'

'Personal or professional?'

'The latter.'

'In that case, you can come up.' She pushed the entry buzzer and held it for a few seconds after his image had disappeared from the screen.

She opened the door and waited, watching the numbers above the lift as they counted the floors during its ascent to her penthouse apartment. The Andy Martin who stepped out had aged more than the three or four years that had passed by since their last meeting. He seemed to have surrendered to being middle-aged; mid-forties, but no one would have been blamed for taking him for a fifty-year-old. To her surprise she felt sorry for him, something that she could never have imagined at the height of their relationship. But almost immediately she realised there might be another reason for his different demeanour. He paused, looking back into the lift. 'Come on,' he said sharply, 'before the doors close on you.' He extended a beckoning hand, and two young children jumped out to join him.

Alex had never met Andy and Karen Martin's children, Danielle and Robert. When she and their father had been involved, she had kept them at a distance, out of respect for their mother's feelings as much as anything else. Danielle was blonde, a mirror image of her father as far as a seven-year-old could be. Robert was dark-haired, a smaller version of his mother.

'I'm sorry,' Martin said. 'I had no choice but to bring them.'

'You did,' she pointed out. 'You could have called me on

FaceTime, or Zoom, or something similar.'

'That wouldn't have been secure enough. I might be under surveillance.'

'And this is secure? If you are being watched and it's being done properly, they've followed you right to my door.' She frowned. 'Why did I ever let you in? You're breaking the law by coming here, and you've made me complicit.'

'Robert needs to pee,' he said. 'He really does.'

'Then he better had.' She smiled at the child, who looked back at her with a level of suspicion that made her feel like Cruella de Vil. 'Go on, sweetie. Daddy will show you the way.' She looked at Martin. 'I'm sure he remembers.' She turned to Danielle, as father and son departed. 'Have you kids eaten?'

'Not since we left Motherwell. Dad said he'd get us sandwiches, but he hasn't, not yet.'

'Typical,' she sighed. 'Come with me and we'll fix that. I'm Alex, by the way.'

The child gave her an appraising look as he followed her to the kitchen. 'Mummy says you're a witch,' she announced, frankly, 'but you don't look like one.'

She gave Danielle her best Cruella smile. 'Check the hall cupboard that we just passed. You might find my broomstick.'

'I don't think so.'

'Well thank you, young lady. For what it's worth, I think your mum's a princess. What would you like to eat? I can do corned beef sandwiches, or pepperoni pizza from my freezer . . . although that'll take longer.'

'Robert loves corned beef,' Danielle said, as her brother appeared in the kitchen doorway. 'Can I have mustard in mine, the kind with seeds?'

Alex opened her fridge and looked inside. 'Yes, you're in

luck, you can. I have some left. Would you and Robert like to watch TV while I make them? I have a little sister about your age, so I have Sky Kids, and Disney Plus.'

'Wow!' Robert gazed up at her; she felt like Mary Poppins. She took the children into the living room and set them up with an episode of *Paw Patrol*. She sensed that Danielle would have preferred something a little more mature but had learned to settle for a quiet life.

When she returned to the kitchen she found Martin at work, making the promised sandwiches for the children. 'Make yourself at home, why don't you?' she said.

'It's the least I can do,' he replied. 'You want some yourself?'

'No, I have a pot of Singapore curry in the cupboard. That's my lunch plan. Actually, I have two if you fancy.'

'Suits me.'

She frowned in his direction. 'Right, now we've sorted out the menu, are you going to tell me what the fuck this is about? Professional not personal, you said, yet here I am feeding a family.'

'Have you heard any talk in your office,' he began, 'about a homicide in Glasgow last week, in a flat in Candleriggs? It would be very hushed talk, I should tell you, because the death occurred in a flat owned by MI5 and used as its presence in Glasgow.'

She shook her head. 'Not a whisper, but if it only happened last week, and no arrest's been made it wouldn't have got to my level yet. Who's the victim?'

'I don't know for sure, nor do the Glasgow Serious Crimes squad . . .'

'Lottie Mann's outfit?' she asked, cutting across him.

'Yes. You know her?'

'We've met. My dad asked me to sort out a custody problem she was having with her ex-cop ex-husband. Lottie's top talent. What's the problem with the victim ID?'

'They didn't tell me, but the thinking is—'

'Wait a minute,' she exclaimed interrupting once more. 'Why would they tell you? You're a civilian now, Andy.'

'I'm also a suspect, it seems. Traces of my DNA were recovered at the scene. Lottie and an insolent little twat of a detective sergeant hauled me in for a formal interview a couple of days ago.'

'Without legal representation?'

'I was invited to bring a lawyer. I chose not to because I had no idea what it was about. I've spent the last two days brooding about it, until this morning I decided I had to see you.'

'Andy, I couldn't represent you, not without resigning as an AD and I don't want to do that at this stage.'

'I know that, but if it came to it, you could find me a capable substitute, yes?'

'Yes, I could,' she said. 'While I'm doing my stint as a prosecutor, my associate Johanna DaCosta's fronting my office. She's excellent and I can put you together. But it won't come to that, will it?'

'I hope not, but I don't like the way the thing's heading. I told them I had no idea how my DNA got there, but the fact is, I do.'

She gasped. 'You lied to Lottie Mann?'

Martin shrugged. 'I wasn't under oath, Alex, but in any event, I didn't see how I could tell her the truth. Thing is, I have been in that flat. When I was chief, there was a situation. The Security Service had credible information that a terrorist cell had a dirty bomb and were planning to set it off on Pacific

Quay. Amanda Dennis, the Director General, contacted me directly and asked me for manpower. She flew up and I met her there, in that flat; just me, her and one other; no other officer was involved, not even your uncle, Lowell Payne, the counter-terrorism ACC. We met, assistance was promised and given and the threat was neutralised.'

'I don't remember that ever getting to court.'

'It didn't. Don't you go asking Payne about it either.'

'Couldn't you tell Lowell,' she suggested, 'to get Lottie off your back?'

'I'm not sure it would. Mann said that two of my hairs were found in the victim's blood. I don't doubt that because I know how good Dorward and his people are, but if I say that they've been there for four or five years, it's a flimsy defence.'

'Defence against what? That isn't nearly enough to charge you. It's nothing. Christ if they don't even know whose the body is . . .'

'They asked me about a man named Clyde Houseman. He's Dennis' spook in residence in Scotland. I denied all knowledge of him, but the fact is I have met him. He was the third person at the meeting I told you about. I assume it was him that neutralised the threat.'

'Even so, if it is him, it's still possible that your five-year-old hair sample got mixed in with his blood. They don't have enough, Andy, not enough.'

He winced, as he cut the children's sandwiches into quarters pointing at their backs through an open hatch. 'There might be, with the icing on the cake. I'm pretty sure that Houseman's sleeping with their mother.'

Fifty-One

Detective Constable Tiggy Benjamin gazed around the Serious Crimes squad room, failing to disguise her excitement at being there. She knew none of her new colleagues other than DI McClair but guessed that at twenty-two she was the youngest person in the room by at least five years. Further, she surmised that there were not too many younger than the boss.

The newly minted DCI Haddock smiled at her from behind his desk as she and Noele McClair stepped into the former conference room that he had commandeered as his office. Its windows offered views of two schools, the architecturally bland Broughton High, which faced the building, and on a slope above, on the other side of Carrington Road, the independent Fettes College, a great baronial edifice with a dash of a French chateau in its design. A cold snap had hit the city overnight. Grey slush lay on the roads and pavements, and fine snowflakes fell lazily down to augment it.

'I was bricking it too on my first day in CID, DC Benjamin,' Haddock said, as they took seats. 'I wasn't much older than you either, and I wasn't sure I would survive, but I did, because my boss had faith in me, and because I was mentored by a great guy, Sammy Pye, who should be here today, in this chair but isn't. Pye and Haddock: they used to call us The Menu. Neither of us liked that much, but if I could have him back, they could call us anything they bloody liked and I'd take it happily. DI McClair will be your mentor. You're here on her recommendation, so it's only right that she looks after you. I'm hoping that it works out as well for you as it has for me.'

'Thank you, sir,' she responded, her voice almost a squeak. 'I'll do my best.'

'I know you will, because Noele won't accept anything less. One thing before we go any further. I don't like being called "sir" by anyone in this unit. "Boss" will be fine; once you've found your feet, you'll probably wind up calling me "Sauce",' he jerked a thumb towards the squad room, 'like most of those undisciplined bastards out there do.'

Benjamin nodded and turned to the DI. 'What do I call you, ma'am?'

'"Noele" will be fine, most of the time. You'll learn when it isn't; mostly that will be when we're on camera and audio with suspects and their lawyers. Recordings could wind up being played to a jury, so we have to be formal then.'

'Your first interview will possibly include an appropriate adult as well,' Haddock told her. 'Has Noele briefed you on our call-out yesterday to what appeared to be a fatal accident in Gullane?'

'Yes, she has. Was it really an accident, s— boss?'

'Officially it is until it's proved not to be.'

'If that's so,' she ventured, 'why is Serious Crimes involved? Why were you and Noele called to the scene?'

'Not so much why,' the DCI replied. 'More a case of who called us. Sir Robert Skinner has my mobile number. He's part of a coronavirus resilience group in Gullane. The victim was one of his clients, as was another accident fatality, Mrs Wendy Alexander. You were present at that scene, I believe.'

'I was, boss, but it seemed pretty straightforward.' She glanced at McClair for support. 'Didn't it, Noele? The old lady fell and hit her head on the corner of her kitchen table. You could see the mark.' She touched her left temple.

'That's how it seemed,' the DI confirmed. 'As far as I'm concerned it's still the likely explanation, but there is something that needs to be investigated, the link to the boy with the bike.'

'The kid who knocked on Mike Wilson's door?' She glanced at Haddock. 'Mrs Alexander's upstairs neighbour,' she explained.

'Yeah, I know,' Haddock said. 'It appears the boy was working for Mrs Eaglesham, yesterday's victim.'

'And he was outside Mr Stevens' place,' Benjamin added.

'Exactly. So, as I told Noele yesterday, your first task as a CID officer is to find him. It won't be easy without a photograph, but I suggest that you go back to Mr Wilson and get the best description he can give you, then take it to the head teachers at North Berwick High and the local primary schools.'

'Can I do something else first, boss?' she asked.

'What?'

'I know a bit about bikes, so I'm pretty sure I know the kind the lad was riding. It was a VooDoo Canzo, a top spec full-suspension men's mountain bike, and it looked fairly new. They don't come cheap; they cost over four figures, so you don't see them every day. Can I check with the specialist cycle shops and see if I can put together a list of buyers of that model in the last year or so? Even if they're bought online, they're still shipped out of stores.'

'Absolutely, Tiggy,' Haddock exclaimed, 'get right on it.' He grinned as he looked at McClair. 'I think you were right about this one, Noele.'

Fifty-Two

Sir Andrew Martin and Johanna DaCosta had never met before she arrived at his home to take him to the police office in Govan, but he was instantly impressed by his new lawyer.

'Before we do anything else,' she said, in his hallway, 'and before we leave here, are you sure you're happy with the arrangements you've made for your children?'

'I'm good,' he replied. 'She's a professional child-minder Karen's used for a while. I've arranged for her to pick them up from school and nursery . . . their mum's classed as a key worker . . . and take them to her place until I come for them.'

'Okay. If you weren't, I'd be telling DCI Mann either to reschedule the interview or come to you.'

'I'm not sure she'd do either of those things.'

'She'd have to,' DaCosta declared, 'or be prepared to arrest you and risk a big public fuss. My sense, based on what Alex told me, is that they don't want that. Whether the reasons are political, personal, or something else, that I don't know. Maybe we'll find out today. Let's go and find out.'

The solicitor advocate's car was a Ford Fiesta that had seen better days. She made room for her client by tossing a selection of confectionery wrappers, a dog lead and a rubber ball with toothmarks into the back seat. 'This is more Alby's car than mine,' she confessed. Martin thought that Alby might welcome an upgrade but said nothing.

The Fiesta was sportier than it looked. She accessed the motorway not far from Martin's home and drove westward, fast and confidently. 'How much did Alex tell you?' he asked.

'She told me that you withheld information at your first interview.'

'Did she tell you why?'

'No, she said you'd explain.'

'I didn't tell the police that I'd been there before because that visit involved a national security matter that's still secret. I would trust Lottie Mann with the truth, but her DS is a sarky wee twerp who'd be stationed at the Celtic end in a blue suit if I was still chief. He's definitely not on any need-to-know list.'

'Who is?'

'ACC Payne. He's your boss's uncle.'

'Alex isn't my boss,' DaCosta pointed out. 'I'm her associate. It's her name over the door, but we aren't a partnership.'

'Neither were we, ultimately.' He spoke quietly but she heard him and smiled.

'*Que sera, sera,*' she said. 'Yes, she has mentioned ACC Payne, and I know what his role is. I'll tell DCI Mann that you're prepared to expand on your original statement but only if he's in the room, and the sarky wee twerp isn't.'

The second invitation to the Glasgow Serious Crimes office had come in a telephone call from Mann herself, the afternoon before. She had told him that she spoke with the full authority of the chief constable, the clear implication being that a declination was not an option. She had given him twenty-four hours' grace, to make arrangements for his children, 'and to engage a lawyer, which I strongly advise you to do this time, sir.'

'What are the cities like?' Martin asked as they exited the motorway, and their destination came within sight. 'Apart from my professional visit to Alex on Sunday, I haven't been in one since lockdown began.'

'Not quite as ghostly as last year,' DaCosta told him, 'but it's eerie just the same. Most of the traffic is delivery vans. I do my supermarket shopping online too. In a way it makes me feel good, because I know I'm creating job opportunities.'

'Are you single too?'

'Apart from Alby, yes. He's my regular exercise.'

'Mine's a run round Strathclyde Park when I don't have the kids. Maybe I should get a dog too.'

'Who's going to walk it when you're an MSP?'

'Or when I'm in Barlinnie,' he countered gloomily.

She looked at him as she switched off the Fiesta's engine. 'Before we go in there,' she asked, 'is there anything else you need to tell me?'

'I didn't kill Clyde Houseman.'

'Did you want to?'

'No. If shagging my wife was grounds for homicide, there would be bodies all around.'

'She isn't your wife, Sir Andrew,' DaCosta pointed out.

'No, but I still think of her that way . . . which is why,' he added, 'Alex and I didn't stay the course. Karen's the mother of my kids and as long as she's alive, that'll always be special with me, always.'

Mann was waiting for them behind the security screen in the police office. She was wearing a mask, as they were obliged to but hers was no sort of a disguise. 'I saw you arrive,' she said, 'so I came down myself.'

'You didn't send Smeagol?' Martin grunted.

Lines around her eyes indicated a smile behind the mask. 'That's a new one. Usually he gets Frodo, or Bilbo. Arthur Dorward called him Tyrion last week; that was pretty good. John's not so bad,' she added. 'I had Dan Provan at my side all my career. When he retired, his successor couldn't be just any plod. Geordie midget he might be, but he's a solid detective. Dan approves of him; he's met him a few times.'

Martin was seized with a sense of his own inadequacy as a chief constable. He knew that DS Dan Provan had been a legend in Glasgow policing circles, but they had never met.

'However,' Mann continued, 'he won't be with us this time. He's on other duties; a more senior colleague will be sitting in. You'll know ACC Lowell Payne, I assume, Sir Andrew.'

'Of course,' he replied. 'Not well, but we met; I oversaw his department from a distance so our paths only crossed when necessary, which wasn't very often. I'm glad he'll be joining us, for reasons I will explain. Lead on.'

'Let's take the stairs,' the DCI said. 'The maximum capacity of the lift is two people; we'd have to do it in relays.'

ACC Payne was waiting for them at the door of the interview room. He nodded, unsmiling, as they approached from the stairway doors. 'Sir Andrew,' he murmured. Martin surmised that even if a handshake had been permissible, it would not have been offered.

'Lowell.' He nodded, curtly. 'This is Ms DaCosta, my solicitor; she's here as a witness as much as an adviser. I thought we had dealt with this business last week, so I'm not best pleased to have been summoned here again.'

'We take no pleasure from it either,' the ACC replied, 'but this is a serious situation. Let's go.'

Mann led the quartet into the room. It was not the one used in the first interview, but the layout was the same; windowless, with four seats at a table. There was a sound recorder, and another camera, mounted so that each person at the table was identifiable.

'Who's taking the lead?' Martin asked.

'DCI Mann,' Payne replied. 'She's the SIO; I'm here as an observer in deference to your former rank.'

The former chief constable surprised him by smiling. 'That's garbage, Lowell, and we both know it. You're here in case this interview goes in a direction that's above her pay grade. Ms DaCosta is here,' he turned to her '. . . with all due respect, Johanna . . . because your niece can't be, on account of her Crown Office role. But I have spoken to Alex, and she's spoken to her dad, so I know everything that McIlhenney and McGuire know and that you do, that's assuming they've shared it all with you. I'm going to spell it out, so you can decide who stays in the room, before the recording equipment gets switched on.'

The ACC leaned back in his chair, eyeing Martin and drawing a deep breath. 'If what you're suggesting is that sensitive,' he asked, 'is it within Ms DaCosta's pay grade?'

'It is if we're on the record.'

Payne sighed. 'Okay. Let's have a private chat, you and me, off the record, up to a point. When we get to that point, I call Lottie and Ms DaCosta in, and we go formal. Deal?'

'Deal.' He turned to his lawyer once more. 'Johanna, if you and DCI Mann will excuse us; I know this isn't conventional but it's probably best if you do.'

'Are you sure about this, sir?' Mann asked.

'There'll be no harm done,' the ACC said. 'I'm not going to sell your investigation down the river, that I promise you.'

'If you say so,' she replied. 'We'll be in my office. Come on, Ms DaCosta, let's you and I get a cup of tea.'

The two women left the room, replacing their masks for the short walk to Mann's room. As the door closed behind them, Martin leaned forward, elbows on the desk. 'You know what the Candleriggs place is, yes?'

'I've been told,' Payne said. 'It's owned, effectively, by the Security Service. When the body was discovered and we began our investigation, alarm bells went off in London. My bosses called me in and told me to keep a very close eye on the investigation, because of the political sensitivity as much as anything else. That fucking ball's burst now, of course, with you in the SNP camp.'

'The ball's still intact, Lowell. I might be an SNP candidate, but I'm not going to share UK national security information that I gathered in a previous life with Clive Graham or anyone else. That's why I could say very little to Lottie Mann in the interview last week. Do you know how the Twins found out about it? Did they tell you that?'

'No. All they said was that it was an MI5 safe house and that the dead man was probably a spook. They didn't say where their information came from but from what you said earlier, I can guess.'

'That's right. Bob Skinner has links to the Security Service that go way back, and he still has. The Director General called him and asked him to intervene.'

Payne nodded. 'Okay, Andy, that's understood, but what about your position? Your DNA was found on the premises; Mann can't ignore that, and neither can I. Fuck's sake, neither can Alex, if you think about it. She's one of the Lord Advocate's deputies. We all report to her boss.'

'You're right,' Martin conceded, 'and I didn't think about that. I should have.'

'And so should she, so let's leave that to one side. You told Mann you had no idea how your genetic material got there. Is that true?'

'No. I know how it could have happened. I was in that flat, as chief constable, a few years ago, for a reason I'm not going to disclose to you or anyone else even now. Once, for an hour, and that was all. I told nobody at the time, not even McGuire, because nobody needed to know, and they still don't. We don't have all that many real state secrets, but that discussion was one of them. All I will tell you is that Amanda Dennis was present and with her, I now recognise, was Clyde Houseman, although she didn't introduce him. It's possible that I shed a couple of hairs at that meeting, and it's possible they were still there after all that time. That said, what are the odds against them being found stuck in the victim's blood? That also said, if I was going to kill Houseman, do you think I'd have been that careless?'

'We don't know that it is Houseman,' the ACC volunteered. 'You've probably guessed by now that his head was removed.' Martin nodded. 'And that he's not on any database, fingerprint or genetic. That said, we believe it is him. What I do know, from information received through DCC McGuire, is that he's missing. He doesn't report into Millbank on a regular basis, but when the DG's office tried to contact him, they got no response from his phone, and they couldn't track it because it was switched off.'

'It wasn't in the flat?'

'No. But that probably means that the killer took it with

him.' He paused. 'And that's as far as we can go, Andy. It has to be formal from now on and Mann has to take over.' He took out his phone; Martin saw his right index finger move, awkwardly, as he composed and sent a text.

Mann and Johanna DaCosta returned within a minute. 'You may start the interview now, Chief Inspector,' Payne said, once the recording devices were active. 'Sir Andrew has updated his statement from last week. He now admits having been in the premises on police business some years ago, but not recently.'

'And I deny killing anyone,' Martin added.

'When did you last see Detective Chief Inspector Neville, your former wife?' Mann asked abruptly.

DaCosta raised a hand. 'What's the relevance of that question?'

'I'll get there.'

'The Sunday before last,' Martin replied. 'She turned up at my place, without warning, while the kids were at a party, and told me that I was having them for a fortnight. She told me to pick them up from school next day.'

'Did she tell you why?'

'Yes, she did. Karen and I have been talking around the idea of getting back together, for their sake. She said that she needed to get away for a while to think that through, before making a final decision.'

'I see,' Mann murmured. 'Did you know that she was in a relationship with Clyde Houseman, the suspected murder victim?'

'Why should—?'

She cut him off before he could continue. 'DCI Neville is on the database, and testing has shown her presence in the

Candleriggs apartment, all over the place, including in the bed.'

'I didn't know for sure, but I suspected,' Martin conceded. 'Two or three weeks ago I dropped off the kids at her house; I was a minute or two early and I saw a man leaving. I didn't have a clear view but now I believe it was him.'

'I thought you said you didn't know him, that you only heard of him recently and that your only actual meeting was when he was a teenager.'

'We've been there, DCI Mann,' Payne said, quietly. 'Sir Andrew acknowledges a meeting more recently than that.'

'Very good,' DaCosta exclaimed, 'but what's the issue?'

'The issue,' the detective replied, quietly, 'is that Karen Neville has disappeared. Her car's still in its garage, but she isn't at home, and her phone's switched off, same as Houseman's. There's no trace of her anywhere. And that leads me in only one direction. Sir Andrew has just told us that he wanted to renew his relationship with his ex-wife only to discover that she was having an affair. Now she's vanished off the face of the earth, and the headless body of a man we all believe to be her lover has been found in a secure apartment. We have Sir Andrew's admitted presence on the premises, and his hair in the dead man's blood. We only have his word for DCI Neville's possible whereabouts, and nobody has a clue about Houseman's. Our position is that Sir Andrew killed them both; that's what the evidence suggests.'

'And our answer,' the solicitor snapped, 'is that you are fantasising.'

'We haven't finished our enquiries,' Mann told her. 'I intend to seek permission to interview Sir Andrew's children.'

Martin leaned across the table facing her, his broad

shoulders hunched. 'You try that, and I will fight you, in court. While Danielle and Robert's identities will be protected whatever happens, I promise you that I'll make sure, with one phone call to a journalist I know, that this investigation comes out of the shadows and into the full blazing light of day. We'll see how much your bosses like that, Lottie.'

'Let's all just take a breath,' ACC Lowell Payne declared.

Fifty-Three

The newly minted detective constable looked up as a shadow was cast across her desk, created by the massive figure of Detective Sergeant Tarvil Singh. 'You okay, DC Benjamin?' he asked, amiably. 'It looks as if Sauce has your nose to the grindstone already.'

'I'm fine, thanks,' she replied. Haddock had introduced her generally to her colleagues, but he was the first to come over. 'I'm trying to trace a suspect.'

'Suspect in what?'

'A series of deaths in Gullane of old people living alone. On the face of it they're all accidental and unconnected, but there's a possible link between them that I'm trying to find.'

'Noele lives out that way, doesn't she?' Singh murmured, lowering himself on to a chair beside her desk. 'It was handy for the Haddington station, where Maggie Steele hid her away to get over the thing that happened. I've got to say it's good she's back, even if she did jump ahead of me on the ladder.'

Benjamin looked up at him. 'What was that thing? I know her ex was murdered, but nobody talked about it in Haddington.'

'It wasn't just her ex. There were two victims in the shooting, Terry Coats, Noele's ex . . . he was a DI in the old Strathclyde force until he resigned rather than take a posting to the wilderness . . . and one of ours, a uniformed inspector called Griff Montell. He and Noele were connected, but that had nothing to do with the killings. Griff was an innocent bystander, almost, in the wrong place at the wrong time.'

'I didn't know about him only about Coats. She's never talked about it with me. But why should she?'

'Indeed, which means I've probably said too much, so don't mention it.'

'I won't, Sarge, don't worry.' She paused, still looking up at him. 'Can I ask you something?' she ventured.

He smiled. 'Within limits, sure.'

'Your name's Singh, which means you're a Sikh. Is that right?'

'It's a reasonable guess.'

'Why don't you wear a turban?'

The DS scratched his shaggy grey-flecked hair. 'I'm sort of lapsed,' he replied. 'Besides,' he added, 'I've got a head the size of a Volkswagen as it is without adding to it. I'd struggle to find enough cloth. In return,' he went on, 'I'll ask you something. What's Tiggy short for?'

Her face flushed slightly. 'Nothing,' she admitted. 'That's what's on my birth certificate, and my driving licence, and my passport, and my warrant card. When my mum was expecting me, she and my dad were out for a walk one day in a park and heard a woman calling her dog Tiggy. They thought it was a nice name and so they stuck it on me. If you're wondering, it was a spaniel. Yes, I'm named after a bloody spaniel.'

'Your secret is safe with me,' Singh promised, standing. 'You'd better get on with your search. Usually you'll be working with me, as Jackie Wright's just got her stripes and prefers working alone anyway. Any problems, just ask.' As he walked away, she was sure she heard a gentle 'woof'.

She was smiling as she turned back to her computer terminal and to the list of cycle shops in central Scotland that might have sold a VooDoo Canzo mountain bike. She had been naïve in her assumption that it would be an easy task. The cycle was American made, and its website indicated that Halfords appeared to be the sole UK concessionaire. The chain had been helpful but unable to find any sales in Scotland, and it had warned her that there was a strong resale market for the model, online and in specialist stores. She had found one offered, used for sale, on eBay, but the vendor was located in Lancashire. A search on Amazon produced no results, and none of the other three online sellers that she found had taken her any further. That had left her with the long and tedious task of calling local shops. She saw it as her last hope before going back to Halfords and asking for details of every sale of the model in Britain, then tracking them down one by one. Even if it was only a few dozen, that could take for ever. She had begun, fingers crossed, with the shop closest to Gullane, in North Berwick. Fingers uncrossed, she had begun to work her way through the list, radiating outward, as she worked. She had gone through a dozen 'No, sorry' replies when Singh had interrupted her, and had made a further fourteen calls after resuming, before her luck turned. It was a shop in Whitburn, in West Lothian, owned by an enthusiastic woman with a young person's voice. Her name was Dale Rogers and she had a prodigious memory for detail.

'Yes, I sold one of those last September,' she replied at once. 'I advertised it as new, and they arrived on morning one.'

'They?'

'A father and son, but the dad was only there to do the driving. The lad knew exactly what he wanted, and he asked all the right questions. I think he must have been a competition rider although I didn't follow that up by looking for him. First thing he asked,' she continued, 'was whether the bike really was new. By which he really meant, if it was, what was it doing in a wee shop like mine. Not quite asking me if it was knock-off but that's what he meant. I really should have been offended but I wasn't. The story was that the bike had been bought from Halfords by a football manager for his son, as a surprise, but a day before it arrived the lad was out on his old bike and had an accident. He came off it and broke his leg, so badly that he wound up in Edinburgh Royal in a cast. When the new bike arrived and his mother saw it she went totally effing mental and said the kid would never have it. So the dad, the football manager, brought it along to me. He had all the proper receipts, shipping details and everything else, so I bought it off him for twenty percent less than he paid for it and put it on my shop's Facebook page as brand new, which it was. I wasn't cheating, really, was I?'

'Frankly,' Benjamin told her, 'I don't care. I'm CID, not trading standards, and I'm only interested in the name and address of the person who bought it, or his father's name if that's all you have.'

'That's not a problem,' Rogers said, with evident relief in her voice. 'I gave him a full receipt and registered him as the legal owner for warranty purposes. It was in the boy's name not the dad's, because it was the boy who paid for it. The VooDoo has an eighteen-inch frame; he was just about big enough to handle it with plenty of growth room left. He said he had just turned fourteen.'

'Can you give me a description?'

'He was just a boy; longish fair hair, and that was about it. Unexceptional. He wore a green puffer jacket.'

The young detective's eyebrows rose. 'And he paid for the bike himself? Are you saying he had his own bank account?' she asked.

'That's right. Starling Bank, it was. He paid for it using his phone.'

'Have you got a copy of the receipt and the registration with his name and address on it?'

'Sure. I'm looking it up on my computer as we speak; here it is now. His name is Rory Graham . . . same as Rag'n'Bone Man, the singer . . . and the address is Seventeen Raglan Place, Edinburgh.'

Edinburgh? Benjamin thought. *In that case what's he doing tooling around Gullane on his very expensive bike, looking for work?*

'That's outstanding, Ms Rogers,' she said. 'I don't expect to have to bother you again.'

'No problem. What's he done, this Rory, that you're looking for him?'

'Hopefully nothing,' the DC replied. 'Hopefully nothing at all.'

Fifty-Four

'This is not the most discreet thing you guys have ever done,' Sir Robert Skinner observed, eyeing his surprise visitors across his conference table. 'Yes, you were able to be driven straight into the car park. Yes, you were able to take the lift directly to this floor but, Jesus Christ and General Jackson, this is a newspaper office! It's full of very good reporters, not least the managing editor in the office next door. Her dad's a retired police officer, so she'd recognise both of you in a heartbeat.'

Neil McIlhenney smiled, and shifted in his chair. 'We thought it was best, under the circumstances.'

'Both of you?' Skinner peered at Mario McGuire, then back at his senior colleague. 'I know you're joined at the hip, but you can't both be chief constable. Like it or not, things will arise that are for your eyes only, Neil. For example, the meeting that Andy Martin attended, where he left his genetic material in the Candleriggs flat.'

'So far, we only have Andy's word for that,' McIlhenney pointed out.

'No, you have mine too. Amanda Dennis told me at the time.' He laughed, softly. 'This is fucking ironic, is it not? A few

267

days ago you were telling me to stay retired and keep my distance. Now here you are, turning up in my office at an hour's notice, invisible caps in hand.'

'Take it as a compliment,' McGuire said. 'We have a situation here, Bob, where we need your advice. Have you heard from Andy in the last week?'

'Not directly, but he visited Alex on Sunday, and now she's professionally compromised.'

'So are we,' McIlhenney muttered, morosely.

'In what way?'

'We can place Andy Martin right in the middle of a crime scene,' the chief constable replied, 'in which the victim is believed to be his ex-wife's lover. We have Karen's presence all over the same premises, and she's disappeared. Andy said she landed the kids on him with little or no warning and said she was going off for a while to sort herself out, but there's no proof of that. She booked two weeks' leave with Lowell Payne, but it was in a text message. Since then, her phone's been off. Andy's been interviewed by Lottie Mann twice, the second time with Payne present. When Lottie said she planned to get court permission to talk to the kids, he went ballistic and threatened to leak the story to the tabloids. Bob, potentially we have enough evidence to charge Andy with two murders, but we can't even report the matter to the fiscal, because he works for the Lord Advocate and the Lord Advocate owes his job to the SNP First Minister, who may be aware that a Tory UK government is maintaining a Security Service presence in Scotland but can't tell anyone. You're the one who warned us of the political implications of that. I believe,' he glanced at McGuire, 'we believe, the only reason Andy hasn't told the Lord Advocate, Lennon, himself is because it wouldn't make the potential murder charge go away and that would scupper his political ambitions. So, help; what do we do?'

'Nothing,' Skinner replied, immediately and emphatically. 'You have evidence that points to Andy as the perpetrator, but you don't have enough. If that is Houseman's body you found, I can tell you that he did stuff in his military career that would make his head a prime trophy for more than one Islamic group. Until you can knock down Andy's account of Karen asking him to look after the children, you have nothing to link him with her disappearance.'

'What do we do with Mann's investigation?' McGuire asked. 'Are you saying we should shut it down?'

'Of course not, but tell her to use her common sense,' he insisted. 'Use your own too. All three of us know perfectly well that Andy didn't kill anyone. I'm not saying that Lottie should disregard the evidence she has against him, but she shouldn't focus on it. She should concentrate on tracing the owner of every DNA sample found in that flat. When she does that, she'll have found her killer.'

Fifty-Five

The tall young man who was ushered into Sauce Haddock's office by Noele McClair was wearing a mask, but his red hair was a giveaway. Even if the DCI had not been told that Arthur Dorward's son had joined the Gartcosh crime scene team, he would have guessed at a connection.

'DCI Haddock?' he ventured as he took a seat and laid a briefcase on the table. 'Paul Dorward.' He extended a hand, then withdrew it. 'No, the First Minister says we can't do that, doesn't he?'

'Consider it shaken.'

'My boss, my father, sends his apologies.'

'That's a first,' McClair chuckled. 'Arthur and apologies haven't been found in the same sentence until now.'

The young man smiled. 'Actually, he doesn't. I made that up because I feel as if he's thrown me in at the deep end.'

'This is not deep,' Haddock promised. 'Lottie Mann, through in Glasgow, she can go down a few fathoms, but this is a paddling pool by comparison. So, what did Arthur bottle out of telling us himself? Have you drawn a blank at the three locations we asked you to test? Or are you going to need more time?'

'Neither,' Dorward replied, as he opened the briefcase and took out a folder. 'I've finished all three locations. None of them were complicated. Mr Stevens' property was brand new when he moved in, and the builder must have cleaned it thoroughly before the handover. I feared there would be multiple samples from painters, carpet fitters et cetera, but there were very few. Mr Stevens himself, his carers, yourself, Inspector McClair, and your colleague, PC Benjamin. There was one familial sample among them. Did Mr Stevens have a daughter?' The DI nodded confirmation. 'I assumed as much. There was another familial pairing, two brothers, but not connected to Mr Stevens. This is guesswork on my part, but I'd say they were the removal contractors who helped him move in. The location of their samples were consistent with that. I expect you'll be able to confirm it fairly easily.'

'The daughter will be able to help us confirm hers, I'm sure,' Haddock said. 'What about the other scenes?'

'Two elderly ladies, each of whom had lived alone for many years. As you would expect, their traces were all over the shop, but there were very few others. The Eyrie was an interesting place. There were recent signs of one individual rampaging through it. Fortunately, I was able to identify him—'

'Sir Robert Skinner?' Haddock ventured.

'Spot on.'

'Had to be. The gaffer told me he tore through the place looking for her after he found the henhouse opened and the chickens all killed. I guess you identified him in Mrs Alexander's kitchen as well. He had to kick her door in.'

'I did,' the scientist confirmed. 'And in Mr Stevens' place, as he warned us we would. He said he called in on him just after he'd moved in, with a few people from the golf club. The club gave me a list of all their names and DNA samples are being obtained for elimination. That leaves me with two anomalies; DNA samples, so far unidentified, that were present in all the locations, one in all three, the other in Mr Stevens, and Mrs Alexander's only. Both are white males, and one is considerably younger than the other. The younger's the one that was present in every location. He has Scottish, English and Italian heritage. The older is Scottish with a dash of Irish. Neither of them is identifiable from any of the databases to which we have access.'

'Can you be precise about age?' McClair asked.

'We haven't really tried to pinpoint it but based on the limited analysis that I've done of the samples' epigenetic markings . . . think of tree rings if you're wondering what they are . . . the younger one's maybe somewhere between twelve and sixteen. The older one is over sixty for sure.' He closed the folder. 'Does that take you any further?' he asked.

'That depends,' Haddock answered. 'Does it tell us that these three deaths were anything other than a series of consecutive misfortunes in a tight location? No, it doesn't. But if we decide to regard them as suspicious, it does offer us a couple of suspects . . . and we may know who one of them is."

Fifty-Six

Noele McClair gazed at her host across the small table as he topped up her glass. 'You do realise that this is a big step for me?' she murmured. 'Your invitation came out of the blue, and it's the most like a proper date I've had in over a year. It's Harry's first sleepover with Granny in a while too.'

'It's just a home-delivery dinner with a friend, in his garden.' Matthew Reid smiled. 'Okay, we're in an office pod, warm and under cover, not sitting out in the winter chill, but that's one of the grey areas in the Blessed Clive's strictures. Is it a date? If that's what you want to call it, I'm flattered . . . very flattered, given that I'm at least twice your age.'

'How old are you, Matthew?'

'I'm seventeen in my heart,' he replied. 'That's what a friend of mine used to say when someone asked him that question.'

'Too young for me in that case,' she grinned. 'Do better.'

'Okay, I've had my first shot of the AstraZeneca vaccine. Is that better?'

'It'll do,' she conceded. 'You don't look it, I have to say. You're sort of ageless. That's the trouble with men; they can do that. How do you pull it off?'

'By investing the best part of four hundred quid in a very

good electric shaver,' he ran his right hand over his hairless head, 'to make sure that the grey is never seen. Not that there's much left. I'd look like a bloody monk if I let it grow in.'

'Where would your cell be if you were a monk?'

He looked around the pod. 'You're probably sitting in it. This space is the centre of my world. It's where I work, it's where I do my most creative thinking, it's where I spend most of my day, other than when I'm walking the dog.'

'Where is the dog, by the way?' McClair asked. 'I was expecting his usual lavish welcome.'

'Sunny's on his holidays,' Reid replied. 'I put him in a boarding kennel every so often to give us a break from each other, and to help him socialise with other dogs; he's still only a pup.'

She picked up her wine glass and rolled its stem in her fingers. 'This is nice.'

'The Albarino or the glass?'

'Both.'

'The wine is Martin Codax, and the container is Riedel. I prefer Spanish wines and I like to present them as they deserve.'

'You prefer them to what?'

'Almost everything. I'm no wine snob, Noele, I know what I like, and I don't need to know why. What's your preference?' he asked.

'I go for Sauvignon Blanc usually; I like New Zealand best.' She swirled her glass again. 'But I must admit I could get used to this.'

'I'll bear that in mind,' he said. 'For next time.'

'Next time's at my place.' The words escaped her lips without warning; she had simply spoken a thought. 'So, Mr

Mystery Writer,' she said, moving on quickly to forestall any discussion, 'what's your own mystery? You came to my mother's book group, and we've had a few walks and coffees, but I still don't know anything about you, beyond what's on the cover of your books. Your Wikipedia page tells me nothing.'

'That's because I edit it,' he laughed. 'What do you want to know?'

'I suppose I want to know, first and foremost, whether there's a Mrs Reid . . . or even a Mr Reid. You don't live here all the time; you could have a spouse tucked away somewhere.'

'Well, I don't . . . but if I did,' he added, 'she'd be female.'

'Where do you live when you're not here? Where's your other life?'

'In Spain. My two lives tend not to overlap. When I'm away I avoid the ex-pat groups like the coronavirus. As it happens, I live not far from Bob Skinner's place over there although he doesn't know that. I really meant what I said about separate lives.'

'I thought Sir Robert knew everything,' she said.

'Not quite. For all that we're friends he knows very little about me. On the other hand, I know a lot about him, even where some of the bodies are buried, so to speak.'

'I sense that's how you like it.'

'You sense correctly. I create mysteries for a living, and it suits me to be a bit of a mystery myself.'

'What do you know about me?' Noele challenged.

'I know that you're thirty-four, divorced rather than widowed, although your former husband, Harry's father, is deceased. You were educated at Whitehill Primary School, at Hamilton Grammar . . . which was Hamilton Academy in my youth . . . and at Glasgow Caledonian University. You were badly affected when Terry Coats was killed, not only by his death, but by that of the man who died with him: so badly that you were moved out of CID to keep you in the force. You're getting over that now, I think, as witness you're back in your old unit at Fettes.' He reached his glass across the table and tapped hers, producing a clear crystal sound, 'and you're here tonight.'

'How do you know all that?' she asked, suddenly defensive.

'Have I been stalking you?' he exclaimed, smiling. 'Not unless following you on Instagram makes me one of those. Calling yourself by your married name on social media isn't a very good way of disguising yourself, Noele Coats. I'm sorry if that upsets you. I'm a writer; information is one of my stocks in trade, plus I'm naturally curious. I know things, I hoard things; can't help it.'

'What else do you know? About people I know. Do my bosses have any secrets I could use against them?'

'None that I know of,' Reid admitted. 'The new chief, McIlhenney, he was a surprise appointment to some because he wasn't a shining light before he moved down to the Met, but he was involved in an undercover investigation in London that gave his reputation a big boost. Involved along with Bob Skinner in fact. Sir Robert has links with the security apparatus that persist.'

Noele gasped. She drank more of her white wine, almost draining the glass. 'I never knew that, Matthew. How come you do?'

'I have links too,' he replied, as he refilled her glass, finishing a second bottle. 'Some of them are on the political side, some in business, one very good one is in the police. The fact is, Noele, guys who do what I do develop informants all over the place, but some of mine go back to before I became a professional mysterian. They're all secure though; the one thing I've carried with me from my brief journalistic career is the first thing every new reporter is taught . . . never reveal your sources.'

'I know about that one,' she confirmed. 'We run up against it frequently in CID. This hoard of knowledge that you have,' she continued, 'does it make its way into your books?'

'Some of it does,' he acknowledged. 'Septimus Armour, my fictional pot of real gold, he isn't based on anyone, but things about him might sound familiar. For example, he's had a couple of wives and one of them was a politician.'

She winced, but with a twinkle in her eye. 'Ouch!' she chuckled. 'How did Bob Skinner take that?'

'With equanimity,' Reid replied, raising an eyebrow. 'Between you and me, I don't think Bob's ever read one of my books. He fakes it pretty well, but I'm pretty sure he hasn't.'

'Why wouldn't he read them?'

'Dunno for sure, but possibly because he doesn't want to put a friendship at risk.'

Noele nodded. 'I could see that.' She sipped more of the Martin Codax. 'How about me? Will I ever make it into a Septimus yarn? Or have I already, without knowing it?'

'I haven't known you long enough for that to be possible,' he told her. 'But I'll make you a promise here and now. You won't be, unless you really want to.'

'I'll defer a decision on that,' she said, 'until I get to know you a little better. Or doesn't that happen, Matthew? Do people ever get to know you at all? Really well, I mean?'

He gazed at her over his glass. 'Oh yes,' he replied. 'Some have done. None of them are left, though.'

She saw sadness in his eyes and fell silent for a while; she realised that she was waiting for him to make the next move but saw no sign of it coming.

'Are you working on a book just now?' she asked, eventually.

He beamed, suddenly. 'That is my second most-asked question,' he laughed.

'What's the most asked?' She was smiling too, knowing that she had not felt as relaxed in over a year and pleased that she could.

'"Who's going to play him in the TV series?"' he answered.

'There's never been one?'

He shook his head. 'No, although I did have a close call once. A production company optioned the series; it got to the point where they sent me a script. I read it and I went mental. It bore no relation to anything I'd ever written, and it was shit to boot . . . not that I ever boot shit, you understand. I would like to have sunk a size ten into the writer, though. Suppose the project had made it all the way, it wouldn't have gone beyond a second series. I'd have made a few quid but nothing spectacular, and the books would have been damned by association with the garbage I was shown. We were almost there too, almost at the stage where it was commissioned, when the station involved decided to go in another direction. I waved them happily off and kept the option money.'

'Who would have played Septimus?' Noele asked.

'Christ knows. They never got to casting.' Reid scowled, theatrically. 'Probably Kate Winslet, the way things were heading.'

She laughed. 'Who would you have cast?'

'Brendan Gleeson, no question.'

Noele nodded. 'Yes, I could see that,' she agreed. 'He's a

genius. But what about my other question?' she went on. 'Are you working on something just now?'

'Yes,' Reid admitted. 'I am.'

'Spoilers?'

He grinned. 'Really? You serious?"

'Go on,' she persisted.

'All I'll say,' he began with a show of reluctance, 'is that I'm trying to write the perfect mystery novel.'

'What's that?'

'It's one with no crime and no perpetrator. The mystery is . . . is there a mystery at all? What's real and what's . . . ? You know the song.'

'Eh?' She stared at him. 'How can that be?'

'You'll have to wait for the best part of a year to find that out.'

'I don't know if I can. I'm intrigued. My appetite is well whetted.'

'Tough,' Reid chuckled. 'You'll have to feed it something else.'

'Mmm,' she murmured. 'Will there be sex in it?' she asked.

'I don't know,' he replied. 'I haven't got that far yet. The grim truth is I doubt if I'd know how to go about making sex sound convincing. It's been a long time since I did any research. I don't even know if I'd be up to it.'

'Me neither,' she confessed. 'I have my issues. But this I do know,' she said slowly, her eyes holding him. 'I'm not driving home tonight. And I'm not ageist, in any way.'

He returned her gaze. 'Neither am I, within conventional limits. But I was serious, when I said I don't know whether I'm up to it these days.'

'I'm sure you are, with the right kind of encouragement.'

'It would mean us going into the house,' he pointed out. 'Is that within the current lockdown rules, officer?'

'I think it is,' Noele said. 'If not, I can always issue us with spot fines.'

Fifty-Seven

'A penny for your thoughts, boss,' Tiggy Benjamin said as she laid a mug on Noele McClair's desk. She was still unsure about being on first-name terms with senior officers. 'You looked miles way there.'

'My thoughts would cost you a hell of a lot more than that,' the DI replied, sincerely. 'Thanks for the coffee. It's needed. A bacon roll would have been nice too.'

'I could go to the canteen if you like.'

'Don't be daft, Tiggy,' she laughed. 'I was kidding. Besides, you and DS Singh need to track down Master Rory Graham. Kid gloves, mind, Tarvil,' she called out. 'He's a minor.'

McClair smiled softly as the two detectives headed for the door. In fact, she had been thinking that she had made an old man very happy, or a happy man very old, or possibly even both, at the same time. She had undressed in Matthew Reid's en-suite, emerging to find him beneath the duvet with the room lit by a single bedside lamp. It was evident as soon as she slipped in beside him that his doubts about his capabilities had been unwarranted. In a night of surprises, in retrospect one of the biggest was the fact that she had not thought once of Terry or Griff Montell. They had been careful with each other, making love twice, on either side of a few hours' sleep, and from her perspective the exchanges had been both very satisfying and guilt free. She had left the bungalow at seven fifteen, unobserved by any neighbours.

'Is this going to happen again?' he had asked, as she emerged from his bathroom once more, fully clothed.

She had smiled, experiencing a strange mix of happiness at having knocked down an invisible wall and satisfaction that she felt not a scrap of guilt or embarrassment. 'I told you last night. My place next time.'

Do I really want a next time? she asked herself as she relived the exchange. 'Yes,' she answered, in a whisper, loud enough to cause DS Jackie Wright to glance across the space between their workstations. 'Yes, I bloody do.'

She took out her phone and called his. When he answered she could hear background noise, the whistling of the wind, she thought. 'Are you busy?' she asked him.

'We're on the beach,' he replied. 'Sunny and me; I picked him up from the kennels at nine and brought him straight here. How about you?'

'I'm in the office. At the moment it feels as if I've exchanged one desk for another. Two of my colleagues have just headed out to track down and interview a kid who might be a witness, might even be something more. I'm stuck here reading up on open investigations. Truth, I would rather be with you. What's it like? The sun's shining here.'

'Same in Gullane. The tide's out so we can walk from one end of the beach to the other then back again. I walk, Sunny runs. It's a rather nice morning and I feel at peace with myself in a way I haven't for a while.'

'Me too, Matthew, me too. Mind you, I admire your

stamina,' she chuckled. 'I thought you'd be having a lie-in.'

'I have no choice in the matter. The boy's body clock is incredible; he knows what happens at given times of the day almost down to the minute, and if they don't, God help me. Besides, I probably had as much sleep as I get most nights, and I didn't burn myself out, thanks to your energy. One of the great things about an Apple watch is its heart-rate monitor. Mine was remarkably steady. But what about you? Is this where you tell me that there's no future in it so let's make it a one-off?'

'No, it's where I ask you what you're doing on Friday night.'

'Seriously?'

'Seriously. Matthew, I went through a whole marriage wondering what an orgasm was, but I had one last night . . . and another this morning.'

'That's good to hear.' She sensed his smile. 'I thought you were just being polite.'

'I don't do that any longer, I promise you. As for the future, to hell with long-term thinking. My place, as I promised. I'll even cook, and if you want to stay for breakfast that's good too. The only thing is, it's contingent on me fixing another sleepover for Harry. My mum has something on, but I think I know somewhere he could go.'

'I'll need to find lodgings for Sunny as well, but yes, that would be good. I should tell you I will be giving up the virtual pub night on Zoom that the Friday gang have been doing all through lockdown. If that's not commitment, I don't know what is.'

'I am truly humbled, sir. I'll call you tonight once I've made my arrangements for Harry.'

Fifty-Eight

Seventeen Raglan Place was not what either Singh or Benjamin had been expecting. Maps had shown them that the street was in Edinburgh's West End, not far from the Caledonian Hotel, where the buildings were elegant Georgian terraces. They had assumed that it would be a flat conversion or possibly even an entire house, depending on how well-heeled Rory Graham's parents were.

In the event when they reached the address, they found that it was an office. The brass plate at the door read 'Pottender Limited' but offered no more information. The DS pressed the buzzer above it.

'Aye?'

The voice was male, definitely Scottish, and its owner sounded suspicious, by nature suspicious.

'Police,' Singh growled.

'What do yis want?'

'You opening the door would be a good start,' he boomed.

'Aye, but what do yis want?'

'Nothing we're going to talk to you about on the doorstep. DS Singh and DC Benjamin, Edinburgh Serious Crimes. Don't make your day any worse.'

'Aye all right, but Mr Potter's no gonnae like it.'

'That may well be the case,' the DS said as a buzz told him the lock had been disabled, 'whoever the fuck he is,' he added quietly as he pushed the heavy door open and ushered Benjamin inside.

The doorkeeper was seated behind an oak desk in a badly lit but well-furnished room. The DC's initial thought, that he might have been Rory, was banished as soon as she saw him, in his early twenties with short bleach-blond hair and a ring through his right nostril. He wore a purple suit with an un-buttoned Nehru jacket, and an open-necked white shirt.

'What is this place?' Singh asked as he and his colleague displayed their credentials.

'Like it says on the door; Pottender Management. Haud on, I'll let Mr Potter ken you're here.'

'No need, Rupert,' a voice advised as a door opened on the officers' right and a tall man in his forties stepped into the room. 'There's a second speaker from the door-entry system in my office,' he explained. The accent was predominantly Scottish, but with a hint of something else. 'Come on through; whatever Rupert said, I'm always happy to assist the police. My name's Gerry Potter, and my business is talent management. I'm an agent, broadly based across the entertainment industry. I represent musicians, comedians, actors and film and television professionals on both sides of the camera. Don't mind Rupert, by the way. He's got a part coming up in *River City*, and I'm trying to get him into character. He's very good, actually. You'd never know he was a vicar's son from Salisbury.'

'You're right there,' Singh agreed as they stepped into a much larger room, with a window that offered a view of Coates Place. 'I was prepared to lift the cheeky bastard.'

A bizarre possibility was developing in Benjamin's mind. 'Mr Potter,' she began, 'do you have a client named Rory Graham, a teenage boy?'

He nodded. 'Yes, I do. Rory's one of ours, I'm pleased to say; he's doing very well for a boy of his age, but he's not getting ahead of himself. He's coached by his mother at the moment, but he's planning to go to drama school when he's old enough. In the meantime, he's landed quite a few small roles in TV dramas and independent films, and he's been in a couple of TV commercials. They pay very well, I should tell you. Why are you asking about him?'

The DC glanced up at her sergeant who nodded. 'We're trying to trace him,' she continued, 'in connection with an investigation.'

'What's its nature?' Potter asked, immediately more serious.

'There have been a series of deaths in Gullane, in East Lothian, involving old people. On the face of it they're all accidental, but we're looking into them just in case they aren't. The only concrete link between them is the presence of a teenage boy on a bike, and we have information that it might be Rory.'

'Shit,' he murmured. 'You're not joking, are you?'

'Not in the slightest,' Singh said. 'We need to trace him, Mr Potter. We need you to give us his home address . . . and don't try to fob us off with client confidentiality. You're not a lawyer.'

'I wasn't going to; Rory's upstairs, in our apartment, home-schooling with Constanza, my wife. His full name is Rory Graham Potter and he's my son. He doesn't use his family name on his Equity card. With me doing what I do it wouldn't look so good. There might be accusations of me favouring him

286

over other young clients, although that's something I absolutely do not do.'

'May we speak to him . . . with you or his mother present, of course.'

'Yes, you may,' the father said, 'but first let me explain the background. Sit down, please.'

The room was furnished with a desk, a table and four chairs, and a three-piece suite facing a wall-mounted television above a fireplace. It felt like a den as much as an office. Singh chose the sofa, as if he doubted that the armchairs could accommodate his bulk.

'Yes,' Potter admitted, 'Rory was in Gullane. But it was a job, a professional engagement.'

'To do what?' the DS asked.

'Film work. I was approached by a man who said he was a docu-maker, planning a fly-on-the-wall film about village life in lockdown and beyond, with Gullane as the subject. But before he committed to it, he wanted to see if it would work in practice. He wanted to hire a young actor to work to a script, insinuating himself into post-Covid village life, meeting people, helping people and all the time being discreetly filmed. He said he wanted to prove to himself that the project was viable and had merit before taking it to the villagers and asking for their cooperation, with sample footage to win them over. He told me that he had development funding from Amazon with a commitment to bankroll a full-scale production. I was convinced, and Rory fitted the bill exactly, so I put him forward.'

'What was his name? Louis Theroux?'

'Not quite,' Potter said. 'He introduced himself as Alan Campbell. I asked him if he had a showreel. He said no, but he described himself as an emerging talent straight out of film school and said more or less that if he had Amazon behind him who the fuck was I to question his credentials.'

'Can you give us contact details?' Benjamin asked.

'Only an email address I'm afraid. That's how he contacted me.'

'How about a description?'

Potter frowned and looked away. 'We've never actually met,' he admitted.

Singh leaned forward, his eyebrows in a hard line. 'Has he paid you yet? Have you got bank details?'

'Cash. A package containing five grand was dropped off by a bicycle courier the day after I agreed to the project. It was fifty per cent up front.'

'That didn't strike you as iffy, Mr Potter?'

'This business is not always conventional, Detective Sergeant.'

'So let me get this right. You took the money, and you sent your son out to do the bidding of a man you'd never met, with no credentials other than an email address and a wadge of cash?'

Potter recoiled from his gaze. 'It doesn't sound good, does it?, when you look at it dispassionately.'

'Without the lure of a brown envelope full of washable banknotes? No, it doesn't. Can we see Rory now?'

'Yes, of course, I'll go and get him.'

Singh rose to his feet. 'I'll come with you, if you don't mind.'

'Sergeant, my wife's there,' Potter protested. 'She doesn't know about this. How can I explain your presence?'

'You can tell her I'm Harvey fucking Weinstein for all I care.'

Benjamin waited as the two men left the room, wondering

whether Potter was naïve, or greedy, an out-and-out liar or simply a man trying to do the best for his son. She knew that ten thousand would pay for more than half a year's school fees at George Heriot's College and if it was tax free, as cash payments often were, so much the better.

Armed with her knowledge of his background, she recognised Rory Graham Potter as soon as he walked into the room, between his father and Singh, not as the kid who had all but knocked her over outside Michael Stevens' flat, but as a mouthy young patient in an episode of *Holby City*, the BBC medical soap.

Singh grinned at her as he closed the door. 'He told his wife that I work for a film casting company,' he said. 'It makes a change from being taken for a bouncer. Actually, I was a bouncer, once upon a time.' He turned to the boy, who appeared more curious than concerned as he sprawled on the sofa. His hair was longer than Benjamin remembered it, but that could be said of most people since hairdressers were closed by Covid. He wore a Ralph Lauren sweatshirt with a bear on the front and white cotton trousers, rather than the puffer jacket and jeans that she had seen before.

'This is no more than an informal chat, Rory,' the DS began, once all four were seated. He took out a pocket recorder and placed it on the coffee table. 'For everyone's protection, I'm going to record it, and I suggest that your dad does the same.' Potter senior nodded agreement and turned on his phone's voice-memo facility. 'I don't want you to feel threatened by us in any way,' Singh continued. 'Your father's here to make sure of that.'

'I'm cool,' the boy said. 'It's better than doing maths with Mum. What's it about?'

'I'm going to put three names to you,' Singh told him, 'and I want you to tell me what they mean to you. Mr Michael Stevens, Mrs Wendy Alexander and Mrs Anne Eaglesham.'

'They were on the list,' Rory replied, 'the list of people I was given.'

'By Mr Campbell?'

'That's right.'

'What were your instructions?'

'It was a brief, rather than instructions. I had a role, as if it was an unscripted drama in which everybody was a character, including the people on the list, although they weren't supposed to know it.'

Benjamin intervened. 'That was the project?'

'That's right. The storyline was that I was a kid on a mission to help old folks that were sheltering during the lockdown, doing stuff they couldn't manage themselves. I was given the list and told where to be on specific dates. Mr Campbell said that I would be filmed, although I wouldn't see him with the camera or know where he was. I did what I was told, visited all three addresses . . . although I got one wrong. There was an attic flat above Mrs Alexander's, and I went there by mistake. Mr Campbell must have had some good gear. I never saw any cameras; I don't know how he hid them in the staircases, but I suppose he did.'

'You just knocked on their doors and asked if they needed help? Was that the instruction?'

Rory frowned as he looked across at the detective constable. 'Have I met you before?' he asked.

'In a manner of speaking,' she replied. 'You nearly knocked me over on your bike, outside Mr Stevens' flat. I was in uniform then.'

'Sorry about that. I got a bit of a shock when you and the other officer turned up in your patrol car. I'd been told to be there at nine o'clock, for some general footage of me knocking around on the bike. I wasn't expecting you, so I ad-libbed and got out of there. I really am sorry about nearly knocking you over. It was you turning to go back for something; I didn't expect that.'

'Apology accepted, Rory, now back to my question about the extent of your brief. Was it just door-knocking and offering to help?'

The boy shook his head. 'No, I was supposed to get into all three houses. I wasn't sure about that, with coronavirus and everything, but Mr Campbell said I was minimal risk because I'm a kid, so it was okay.'

'What was the point of that? How could he have filmed indoors?'

'I wore a bodycam,' he told her. 'He sent it to me here and told me to keep it charged and wear it all the time I was in Gullane. He told me it transmitted, and he would have everything it shot recorded on a hard disk.'

'That's right,' his father confirmed. 'That was dropped off by a bike courier too, like the cash. I can get it if you like.'

'Not right now.'

'Any chance of tracing the courier, Sarge?' Benjamin asked the DS.

'In the city, Tiggy? With people working from home and material being biked all over the place? Two chances, like Muhammad Ali said,' Singh sighed. 'Slim and none, and Slim's left town.' He turned to the boy. 'Did you manage to get into the houses, Rory?'

'All three. Mr Stevens asked me to get him a newspaper, a

pack of bog rolls, and a loaf, so I went to the Co-op. When I got back, I put the loaf in his kitchen and the bog rolls in his en-suite. He let me keep the change,' he added. 'Nice old bloke, even though he already had a loaf in his breadbin and half a dozen toilet rolls in his main bathroom that I saw when he let me go there for a pee. Mrs Alexander asked me to come in and get something off her top shelf in the kitchen. She said she had trouble getting up there, because her steps were shaky. She was right, I used them and nearly fell off myself. Somebody needs to get her a new set. Mrs Eaglesham, her house was massive, but she told me she only lives in a couple of rooms.' Rory grinned. 'She drinks Irn-Bru,' he said, 'an old lady like her. She told me to get a can from her fridge, so yes, I was in her kitchen.'

'Anywhere else in the house?'

'The toilet, and she has this laundry room at the back. That's where she keeps the lawn rake that I used for the leaves. She's the nicest of all of them. First time I went up there she said she had nothing for me, but when I went back, she'd changed her mind, and asked me to tidy her leaves. I did, and I went back another time after that to put her recycling bin out for the truck. She paid me; I wasn't going to take any money because that wasn't in the brief, but she insisted. She gave me a box of eggs too,' he added. 'She keeps hens, about a dozen of them. They're in a wire henhouse with a wooden floor . . . to stop ferrets and the like from burrowing in, she says . . . but not all the time. She says she lets them out every so often, when she collects the eggs, and they go back in when she tells them. I didn't believe her, but she showed me, and they did.'

'Are there any other names on Mr Campbell's list?' Singh asked.

'No, just those three for now. We're not done, though. Mr Campbell said he's analysing the footage before he decides on the next subjects. He has to report back to Amazon too. He said I'd hear from him in a week or so. He said he might even use some of my footage in the final product and give me a credit as a production assistant.'

'Sounds good. Rory, we're going to need to speak with Mr Campbell as well, but we don't have his address or contact details.'

'I don't either,' the boy replied. 'I've never met him face to face, and I don't know where he lives. When he was in touch with me it was always by text.'

'Sergeant,' Gerry Potter intervened, quietly, 'earlier you said you're investigating a series of deaths, linked by Rory's presence.' His son sat up, staring at him. 'Are you telling us that . . . ?'

'Yes,' Benjamin said, 'I'm afraid that we are.'

Fifty-Nine

'Did you believe the boy and his father?' Haddock asked as the recording ended.

'I did, Sauce,' Tarvil Singh replied. 'Rory was genuinely shocked when he learned that the three people he'd visited were all dead.'

'And so did I, boss,' Tiggy Benjamin added. 'Now that I think about it, he did look a bit startled when we had our close encounter outside Mr Stevens' flat. Everything fits.'

'It does,' the DCI agreed, 'but it is very, very weird. The car's on its way to Gartcosh now with the boy's DNA sample, but I think we know already that it's going to confirm his presence in all three locations. You said his mother's called Constanza?'

'Yes,' the DS confirmed. 'Second generation Italian, which fits with the profile.'

'And the mysterious Mr Campbell? Any joy yet in identifying him?'

'Negative on that,' Noele McClair said. 'I was able to check with Amazon Studios while Tarvil and Tiggy were on their way back. They've never heard of him; plus, they wouldn't be interested in that type of documentary. As for speculative funding, not a chance.'

'Rory has his mobile number on his phone,' Singh volunteered. 'He showed us all the texts and attachments he's had from him, and they back up his story all the way. I ran a check on the number. It's a pay-as-you-go, and it's no longer responding.'

'Can we trace its location?'

'I doubt it, we can be fairly sure it's in a bin by now. Historically? No, because there's never been a call made from it. He only ever used it to send texts.'

'You're saying "he", Tarvil, but we don't even know that,' Haddock pointed out. 'If all the communications with the Potters, father and son, were by text through that SIM card, we don't even know Alan Campbell's gender for sure. In fact, we know absolutely nothing. Here we are, a supposedly elite Serious Crime unit and we can't even prove that a single crime has been committed. We've even had an explanation for what happened to Anne Eaglesham's hens. Rory says she would let them loose for a while when she collected the eggs, and there was a tray of eggs in the laundry when she died. So, she gave her chickens their playtime as usual, went to transfer the laundry from the tub to the spin drier in her antediluvian washing machine, and was electrocuted. That's the only logical explanation for what happened to her and her poor bloody hens, and thanks to Rory, we know it.'

'Just as we know that Mrs Alexander had a shoogly step-ladder,' Benjamin added.

The DCI nodded. 'And that Michael Stevens was very absent-minded. However,' he added, 'thanks to Rory's body camera, which is working and transmitting according to Jackie Wright, who's just examined it, friend Campbell knows it too. And that, ladies and gentleman, is the only reason why I am not closing the book on this crazy situation. Pull out all the stops, people, and find me Alan Campbell, whoever he, she or it may be!'

Sixty

The male voice took Noele by surprise, because he answered her call by quoting the landline number. 'Bob?' she asked.

'No, it's Mark. I'm sorry, my dad isn't in. Is that Ms McClair?'

'Yes, it is. I'm sorry too, Mark. I should have realised, but you do sound like him.'

'That's what people say all the time, but it shouldn't be a surprise. He's brought me up since I was seven; I can't remember my real dad's voice. My mum's in.'

'Thanks. That's who I wanted.'

She waited, listening to voices in the background as Mark passed the handset to his mother. 'Hi, Noele,' Sarah said as she took the call. 'What's up that you're calling this number?'

'My mobile's on charge, and I've only got your landline programmed into mine.'

'Give it ten years and we won't have landlines, any of us,' Sarah forecast. 'So how are you?' she asked. 'Happier for being back in CID?'

'Much. Happier all round actually.'

'I thought there was a spring in your voice. Harry messaged Seonaid today saying that he stayed at his gran's last night. Could the two be connected, I ask myself? Hell, woman, I'm

297

asking you! Have you been getting it on? Don't worry,' she added, 'Mark's gone back to his programming, or hacking or whatever the hell he does, Jazz is running on the treadmill and Seonaid's introducing Dawn to the world of *Frozen*. You may speak freely.'

'I'm saying nothing, Sarah,' Noele laughed.

'You don't have to. I know the sound of a returning mojo. Don't bother to deny it. Who's the guy?'

'All right, I won't deny it; I had sex last night for the first time in over a year. And again this morning, if you really want to know. But no way am I going to tell you who the man was, no fucking way. It will probably be a short-term thing, and for the sake of future co-existence his identity should stay secret, until it isn't a short-term thing.'

'That serious?'

'Honestly, I don't know. It's complicated,' she added.

'Everything that involves interacting genitalia gets complicated sooner or later. I can tell you that personally and professionally. Now, if you're not going into the sticky details, how can I help you out?'

'Can Harry stay with you on Friday?' Noele asked. 'It's allowed under the lockdown rules. My mum will have him through the day as usual, but nine o'clock Saturday morning's her on-line tai chi class and nothing gets in the way of that.'

'Of course he can,' Sarah told her. 'Friday's Bob's Girona day and there's never a guarantee he'll be back that night. Actually, there's a panic in Spain right now that needs the chairman's attention. Ask your mum to drop him off here with an overnight bag, and I'll bring him home on Saturday whenever you've got your breath back.'

'It's not like that, honest,' she protested. 'It's very

comforting . . . a strange word for shagging, but it is . . . and very satisfying.'

'I'm intrigued. I still think of sex as something of a rodeo. I'll see you on Saturday.'

Noele hung up, giggling at her friend's analogy, and checked her mobile. It showed sixty per cent, enough for her to unplug the charger cable, find Matthew's number and call him.

It rang three times and went to voicemail. 'Hi, this is Matthew Reid. I'm sorry, I can't take your call at the moment. Please leave a message and, if I know you, I'll call you back. If, on the other hand, you're a hapless kid calling to discuss the blameless car accident that I never had, hang up now and get yourself a better job.'

'My name's Britney,' she began, 'and I'm from Sue, Grabbit and Run, solicitors.' She paused for a moment. 'But really it's Noele, calling to confirm Friday night. I guess you may be working just now, unless Sunny's body clock has insisted on an evening walk. If you want to talk when you're done, about anything or nothing, give me a call back.'

She was smiling as she hung up, musing over the complications of interacting genitalia. As far as she was concerned, they were worth it.

Sixty-One

'That prick Martin,' John Cotter drawled. 'Was he as big a bastard when he was chief constable?'

'Honestly, John,' Lottie Mann replied, 'I couldn't tell you. I never saw him when he was in the job, or even came close. Dan says that was his problem, he thought he could do the job remotely. He came from running a specialist agency and being deputy chief in Dundee. In each of those he could have thrown a blanket over his staff more or less. When he took over the national force, it was on an entirely different scale, and he just couldn't get his head round it. That's what Dan says.'

'Fine, but it doesn't necessarily make you a bastard.'

'He didn't think you were a special person either, John,' the DCI retorted. 'Look, I wasn't going to bollock you in front of him, but you were well out of order in there. Like it or not, he's a former chief constable, not your average person of interest in an investigation. He was entitled to more respect than you showed him. If you didn't like the way he reacted to you, learn from the fucking experience or I'll pull a couple of strings and have you posted to Shetland.'

'Could you do that, Lottie? I like it up there.'

She frowned at him. 'DS Cotter, I'm willing to bet that your experience of our most northerly islands doesn't extend beyond the TV series. That tends to miss out the part where the sun rises after breakfast and sets not long after lunch. Then there's the wind.'

He whistled. 'It's like that? I'd sooner you sent me to Sunderland.'

'That's not within our jurisdiction, but it could possibly be arranged. The message is, John, behave yourself.'

'Does that mean I'm back on the Candleriggs investigation?' he asked.

'You were never really off it, truth be told. Certain aspects of it are sensitive, even beyond Sir Andrew Martin's involvement, and need to be handled pretty much at executive level. I'm lucky I got into the second interview with Martin myself.'

'What's the deal, boss? I don't get it. We've got Martin's hair in the victim's blood. He can't deny he was there.'

'He doesn't, not any longer. But he is denying it was within the time frame of our homicide.'

'Can he prove that?'

'He doesn't have to. We have to show beyond reasonable doubt that he was.'

'What will that take?'

'Corroborating forensic evidence. Basically, something that takes the investigation beyond the confines of the flat.'

'What about his wife's involvement?' the DS argued. 'Isn't that corroboration of sorts?'

'Ex, John. Ex-wife. He has a very smart young lawyer, who would laugh that one right out of court.'

Cotter bowed his head and clasped his hands together.

'What are you doing now?' Mann asked, wearily.

'I'm praying,' he replied. 'Praying for evidence that's strong enough to let me slam a cell door on the sod.'

Mann shook her head and turned to her computer, just as a click advised her of an incoming email. Her hand was on her mouse when the door opened and DC Barry McGuigan strode into the room.

'I'm sorry to interrupt, boss,' he said, 'but I've just picked up an incident report from out in Lanarkshire. A human head's been fished out of the River Clyde in a plastic bag that's washed up on a bank. It's not in the best of condition after some time in the water, but indications are the skin tone might match our victim.'

'Do you have a location?' the DCI asked sharply.

'Yes, boss.' He showed her his phone. 'Apple maps puts it right there.'

For the first time that day Lottie Mann smiled. 'John, your prayer might have had a response. That's less than a mile from Sir Andrew Martin's house. Well done, Barry.'

'Thanks, boss,' he replied. 'But there's more. The Ministry of Defence has finally responded to DS Cotter's DNA request. We know who the victim is.'

Sixty-Two

'His name is Calder Bryant,' Mario McGuire said. 'When he was found and we learned what the flat was, the assumption was that he was Clyde Houseman. He lived there, the body matched his ethnic mix, and there was a Royal Marines tattoo on his arm. When we couldn't find his DNA on any existing database to confirm that assumption, Lottie Mann decided to go about it in reverse. Rather than look for Houseman specifically, she sent the profile to the Ministry of Defence. It took them a few days, but they got a result.'

'Who is he?' Neil McIlhenney asked. 'Who was he, rather?'

'A Marines sergeant, aged thirty-one, on leave from his unit after a two-year hitch with a United Nations peace-keeping force in Mali. He was single and lived in military accommodation; his CO said he was a good soldier, but a quiet bloke who kept himself to himself and had no close friends in his unit. According to his records, his next of kin is his father, William Bryant, of Bradford, Yorkshire, but when Lottie's DS, Cotter, tried to find him he discovered that he left this vale of tears last year, a victim of Covid-19.'

'The head found in the river—'

'—is with Graham Scott in the mortuary. He's still waiting

303

to match the genetic information to the rest of the body, but it's the missing piece, no doubt about it.'

'Does the Security Service know what Bryant was doing there?'

'The Director General is unavailable, would you believe,' McGuire replied. 'But her aide said that whatever he was doing there it wasn't on their business or with their approval. They've never heard of him, they say.'

The chief constable gazed at him. 'What do you make of the location where the head was found?'

'I was trying to make nothing of it, then I had a call from Arthur Dorward. He went to the scene personally as soon as the find was reported. The head was in a Sainsbury's bag, he said, but that wasn't the only thing he found in it. Stuck in a corner there was a receipt for eighty-seven quid's worth of groceries, paid for by a credit card.' McGuire paused, watching the colour leave his friend's face.

'Oh no,' McIlhenney whispered.

'Oh yes,' the DCC murmured. 'It was Andy Martin's.'

'Fuck me,' he whispered. 'Why would he kill a man when it seems he didn't even know him?'

'Simple. He thought it was Houseman. The scenario is, he followed Karen there, recognised the address and realised who she was having it off with, went back later, and killed him. Andy's still physically capable of it, no doubt about that.'

'What about Karen? She's missing too.'

'He had umpteen opportunities to kill her and make her disappear. We can put cadaver sniffer dogs in his car and see if they confirm it.'

'Jesus,' the chief constable exclaimed, 'I can't argue against any of that. We can't sweep this under the carpet, Mario. We need to bring him in again and be prepared to charge him.'

'If we do that,' the DCC said, 'we'll have to take it to the fiscal. Given who's involved, he'll run a mile and take it upstairs, to Steve Lennon, the Lord Advocate. That will let the MI5 cat out of the bag. We'll have the political scandal that Bob warned us about.'

'Not if we don't tell the fiscal who owns the crime scene. It's not relevant to the prosecution case.'

'Maybe not,' McGuire countered, 'but it will be to the defence. Andy's counsel's bound to reveal it to explain the presence of his genetic material. When that happens the Lord Advocate and the First Minister will be after our blood.'

'After my blood, mate. I'm the chief constable, not you. If a head has to roll over this, it'll be mine.'

'With all due respect, sir, I will not let you go to the guillotine on your own. We're in this together, like we always have been.'

McIlhenney sighed and leaned back in his chair, gazing across the table as he gathered his thoughts . . . and reached a conclusion. 'You know what, my dear friend?' he murmured. 'We've gone back on what we agreed a couple of weeks ago. We've let Bob Skinner back inside the tent, and worse than that, we've listened to him and his warning of political chaos. When he was our boss, in the old days, he disliked politicians almost to the point of hatred, remember? Then he bloody married one and he became a political animal overnight. His thinking changed, became much more complex, went beyond right and wrong to a space in between. But that space doesn't exist,' he declared, vehemently, 'not for us. If Whitehall has been keeping secrets from Holyrood, so what? If this invest-igation tilts the independence debate irreversibly in favour of the Yes vote, so what? Suppose it was your DNA in the murder victim's blood and your ID in that supermarket bag, so what? Suppose it was mine, so what? We're police officers, Mario,' he hesitated for a second, 'I was about to say, "first and foremost", but there is nothing else. That's all we are, not servants of the state but servants of the truth. There are no other considerations. There's only one thing that's stopping me from going to see the Lord Advocate myself, and the First Minister, giving them a full report of the investigation and then charging Andy Martin with murder.'

'What's that?'

'I flat out don't believe it.'

'So what?' McGuire said, quietly.

Sixty-Three

'Can we go and get him?' John Cotter asked. 'I'd just fucking love that.'

'That'll depend on what the bosses say,' Lottie Mann replied, 'but I'll tell you one thing. If it happens, you won't be in the party. I'm quite sure that if the chief gives the okay to arrest and book him, there will be an officer of command rank in charge of the raiding party, maybe ACC Payne, maybe ACC Stallings, maybe even DCC Mackie. I'll be lucky if I'm there myself.'

'Who's Mackie?'

'The number three man on the totem pole, DCC McGuire's deputy if you like. You really need to do your homework, John. We have fourteen executive officers, but I doubt that you could name more than four of them.'

'Why should I? There are a dozen teachers in my kid's school, but I'm only interested in the one that affects me, and that's his. In here I'm only interested in the person I report to and that's you. How many of the fourteen could you name?'

'All of them, although I admit I couldn't tell you what every one of them does.'

'Who's Stallings? Never heard of him.'

'You really don't know, do you?' she sighed. 'Becky Stallings is our immediate boss, yours and mine, the level between me and McGuire. She's shuttled back and forward between Scotland and London, a bit like McIlhenney, but she's here for good, I think, since her husband left the force and took a job in Edinburgh looking after the Scottish Government estate.'

'Is she all right?'

'You're going to find out for yourself, as soon as I can arrange it.'

'Can she get me on the team that lifts Martin?' Cotter asked.

'Nobody can do that. I'll—'

She broke off as her intercom buzzed. It was old technology, linking her office to the squad room, but it was rarely used in the era of texts and WhatsApp messages. She tugged the lever that opened the line. 'Boss, it's Barry. Sorry, I couldn't get a signal on my mobile. I'm doing a wide-ranging search for matches to the unidentified DNA samples from the Candleriggs crime scene, and I've come up with a bit of an anomaly. I think you're going to want to see it.'

'I'm on my way.' She turned to Cotter. 'You, stay here and spend some useful time on the force website, finding out about the people you work for.'

Sixty-Four

'**H**ave we been able to recover the recordings from the bodycam?' Sauce Haddock asked.

'Yes, that was easy,' DS Jackie Wright told him. 'It has an SD storage card in it as well as the transmitter. It's all there, exactly as the boy describes, including his exchanges with the three victims. That's why I'm here. I've transferred them on to my tablet, because there are a couple of things I want you to see.' She put the device on the table, supported by its folding case and angled so they could both see the display. 'It's really sad,' she said, 'seeing them there and knowing that they're all dead now.' She touched a green symbol, and the recording began to play. 'I haven't edited them, but I could fast forward if you like, to get to the significant bits.'

'No,' the DCI replied, 'let it run at normal speed.'

As they watched, the image moved towards a door. A buzzer was rung and more than a minute later, the door was opened, and an elderly man appeared in shot. 'Hello,' a young voice began, 'my friends and I have formed a group. We're visiting older people in the village to see if there's anything we can do to help you. Is there anything you need doing? Cleaning? Making you a sandwich, anything like that?'

'How very kind of you,' Michael Stevens exclaimed. 'As it happens, there are things I need, but I can't go out and about. They say I'm locked up again. Or is it locked down? I can't tell the difference really.'

'I see what you mean,' Haddock murmured, as the scenes played on. 'It's a bit eerie, isn't it?'

'Yes, but it bears out Rory's story.'

They watched as the boy noted the old man's requests. As he left the apartment, the screen went black, but sprang back into life a second later, as Rory returned with a loaf, a newspaper and a four-pack of toilet tissue, distributing them around the house as he had described on Singh's voice recording. 'Look,' Wright said, pointing as the camera showed the en-suite bathroom. She froze the image. 'The cabinet's open and you can see his medication quite clearly. The blue and white boxes, they're the blood thinners. I verified that with the Gullane pharmacy. They're called Pradaxa; it's a trade name for Dabigatran, the medication mentioned in the post-mortem report.'

'And the mysterious Mr Campbell will have seen that?'

'For sure . . . and will have been able to find out what they're for, quite easily, from the internet.'

The images on screen continued to play and the narrative moved on, resuming as Rory knocked on a second door. Another man appeared, much younger than Mr Stevens. 'That's the upstairs neighbour,' Wright explained. 'Tiggy confirmed it; she's met him. And now,' she said as the scene ended and moved on to the next, 'this takes us to the next interesting point.'

It began with the bird-like Mrs Alexander opening her door and Rory making his pitch. 'You've timed it well, son,' she chirped. 'I need to get a big box of tea bags off ma top shelf, but ma steps are awful shaky.'

'No problem,' they heard the boy reply, 'where are they?'

They saw the old lady lead him inside and show him the small folding ladder. They saw him climb on to the second rung and fetch a large box of Scottish Blend from the high second shelf. They saw him fold and replace the steps in the corner where they stood.

'You're right about those being shaky,' they heard him say.

'I ken, son. I don't use them myself now. It's only the tea that I need from up there, and a big box'll last me four or five month. The rest's stuff I never use anymore.'

'So what was she doing falling off them?' Haddock asked, as Wright froze the image.

'Exactly.' The DS pointed to the screen. 'Now look at that.'

He leaned forward peering at the image, at an object that lay on the work surface. 'It's a pack of wooden shelving, isn't it?'

'Exactly, from B&Q according to the label. Noele says that there's a handyman in Gullane that a lot of people use. His name's Sam. I called him and he told me that he'd arranged to go in and put them up for her, within her reach, once he's allowed by the lockdown rules.'

Sauce Haddock's eyes narrowed; he smiled. 'Talk us through it, Jackie.'

'When Mrs Alexander was found by Sir Robert Skinner, the immediate conclusion was that she'd fallen off her shaky steps and hit her head on the corner of the kitchen table, with fatal consequences. That's never been questioned, yet here we are with the lady . . . the victim . . . saying that she never used them, and with an object in the room that would have done the same sort of damage.'

'The gaffer would never have overlooked that; he was a detective for thirty years. It's in his blood still. He'd have clocked everything in that room and registered every possibility. Can we . . . ?'

'I have done, Sauce. I'm ahead of you. When the Gartcosh forensic team went in, they photographed and videoed the entire scene. I've checked them and on their footage the shelves are nowhere to be seen.'

'She could have put them in a cupboard, out of sight,' the DCI suggested. 'They wouldn't have been going up any time soon. Arrange to get the keys from whoever has them, get yourself out to Gullane and search that flat. Take Tiggy with you to help you look and to verify anything you find.'

'Will do, boss, but do you want to see the rest of the camera footage?'

'What does it show?'

'Mrs Eaglesham's laundry room, complete with old-style wiring, and ancient washing machine. There's also a shot of her collecting eggs and leaving the door open to let the hens have a run about. It's all there, Sauce, all the way through; a potential plan for three murders and a ready-made suspect, Alan Campbell.'

'Two suspects,' Haddock corrected her. 'We've seen nothing that rules out Rory Graham as a person of interest, regardless of his youth. Equally, we've got nothing to say categorically that the three deaths weren't exactly what we took them for at first sight, tragic accidents. Go on, get out to Gullane and look for those shelves.'

His mobile sounded. He checked the screen and frowned.

'DCI Mann,' he grunted. 'I wonder what she wants.'

He took the call as Wright exited. 'Hi Lottie, what's up in Glasgow?'

'First,' she said, 'congrats on the promotion, sorry about the circumstances. Your old boss was one of the best.'

'Thanks, appreciated on both counts. What's second?'

'An anomaly,' Mann replied. 'My team are involved in a very low-profile investigation, so low that I can't share too many details. As part of the process one of my DCs has been trying to identify all the genetic traces that we found at the scene. As he's worked, he's thrown his parameters wider and wider, until . . . one of them's found a match. The problem is that its twin is also unidentified, having been found at two locations in an open investigation that Gartcosh tells us is being run by your team. I asked Dorward for details, and he told me to talk to you. For once, he wasn't being an obstructive smartarse. He said it was a complex investigation and that you were best placed to discuss it. How much can you share?'

'Everything,' he replied, immediately, 'because I'm not sure I have anything at all. Mine's low profile too, but only because we don't know what we're looking at. The person you're talking about is a mature Scottish adult male with Irish ancestry, yes?'

'That's him.'

'I have him, at some point, on separate premises where two old people suffered ostensibly accidental deaths.'

'Can you tell me where?'

'Gullane, in East Lothian.'

'That's Skinner territory, isn't it?'

'Not just that, he found one of them. And a third,' he added. 'He's part of a group that have been offering help to the vulnerable. We're also looking at that third accident location, but the mystery DNA is definitely not there. Where it can be placed, each of the victims was vulnerable and had carers and helpers coming in, as well as the gaffer's lot. It's been impossible to identify all of those people, but one assumption, maybe the best, is that's why mystery man was there. How about yours? What can you share, if anything?'

'Very little. I'd need McIlhenney's authority to tell you the whole story, and I doubt that he'd give it. But I am certainly dealing with a homicide, and I have a prime suspect. Or I had, until a man who's been at the scene of two fatalities in East Lothian suddenly showed up in a bloodstained flat in the middle of fucking Glasgow.'

Sixty-Five

Bob Skinner frowned at his mobile's screen as his ringtone sounded. 'Number withheld' was the message and he did not like those. Nevertheless, in the world of international business of which he found himself a citizen, he felt that the luxury of rejection was no longer open to him. With an ill grace he touched the green symbol and put the phone to his ear.

'Bob?' Even in a single, whispered word, the caller sounded stressed and anxious.

'Yes,' he snapped. 'Who's this?'

'It's Clyde, Clyde Houseman.'

Skinner felt his eyes widen, as he suppressed a gasp, turning his back on his companions and putting distance between them. 'Where the hell are you?' he muttered.

'I'm in Glasgow, outside my flat,' Houseman said. 'I've been away for a few days. I needed to take myself off the grid for a while, to deal with a personal thing. I just got back, and there's a car outside. I spotted it as soon as I turned the corner. I made the passenger as one of Lowell Payne's counter-terrorism people and the driver as one of ours. Has Amanda pushed the panic button? If she has . . . man, she told me that if I ever needed space it would be okay just to take it. Is that it?

Am I in the shit, or has something big gone down?'

'Why are you calling me, son?' he asked.

'Because you'd know. If she had a crisis in Scotland, you'd be the first person she'd contact.'

'As it happens, I was,' he said. 'Clyde, when you went off on your break, did you leave anyone in your flat?'

'Yes, Calder, my half-brother. My mum was a Glaswegian,' he explained. 'She called her sons after the rivers that run through the city. He turned up out of the blue, the day before I went off; I said he could stay there as long as he liked, and we'd catch up when I got back.'

Skinner frowned. 'Then I'm sorry to tell you that your brother's dead.'

He heard a guttural sound, possibly a choked-off sob, followed by a hoarse question. 'How?'

'He was murdered, Clyde. It hasn't hit the media because the assumption was that he was you. That and other reasons, like politics.'

'Do they know who did it?'

'Not that I've heard. They have a suspect, but it wasn't him.'

'Who?' Houseman growled.

'I'm not fucking telling you. I don't know who did it, but I know who didn't, and I don't want you making any fatal errors. You want some advice? Get in touch with your Director General, then with Chief Constable McIlhenney.'

'Fuck that, Bob. Before I do any of that, I'm going to find the man who killed my brother. I might even know where to start looking.'

'Clyde!' Skinner shouted, forgetful of his companions, but the line was dead.

Sixty-Six

'This isn't exactly conventional, Mr McGuire,' Johanna DaCosta observed. 'If Sir Andrew is still a person of interest, I'd expect him to be interviewed in a police office as before, yet here we all are in his home with Detective Sergeant Cotter looking after the children, even. Is this an interview, or are you and DCI Mann here to apologise?'

'Neither,' the DCC replied. 'It's an update, that's all. Yes, we could have hauled you back to Govan, but this is more discreet. If I'd shown up there it would have signalled to everybody outside the loop that something serious was going on.'

'Why are you here, Mario?' Martin asked. 'I understood you and your pal keeping your distance before. What's happened to change that?'

'A couple of things. First, the man you were suspected of killing has turned up alive. The chief had a call from Bob Skinner, advising that Houseman had phoned him, from outside the crime scene. He spotted the surveillance car that was posted there and wanted to know what was up. When Bob told him what had happened, he went apeshit. The body and the recovered head are those of a serving Royal Marine, Calder

Bryant. He's Houseman's half-brother. It appears that he was raised by his father in Yorkshire but followed Clyde into the Marines. Clyde hung up on Bob and nobody's heard from him since. He thinks he knows who the killer is and he's gone after him. If he thinks it's you, Andy, that's a big problem.'

'For him if he comes anywhere near my kids,' Martin murmured, green eyes icy.

'He won't get near them or you,' McGuire promised. 'As soon as we became aware of this, I posted armed officers in every approach to this cul-de-sac. You're as safe as we can make you.'

'You said "a couple of things", Mr McGuire,' DaCosta reminded him. 'What's the other?'

'I'll let DCI Mann deal with that,' he replied. 'I'm here to advise you of the Houseman situation. It's still her investigation, and Andy, you are still a person of interest. Mistaking Bryant for Houseman, that would be quite easy to do given that you only met him twice, one of those times being twenty years ago, and that they each had Marines tattoos on their arms. Add to that, the fact that Karen is still missing. The chief is considering sending a report to the Crown Office and leaving a decision about charging to them. He may still be forced to do that but, Lottie, carry on please.'

Lawyer and client looked at Mann. 'We've established an anomalous presence at the crime scene. We don't know when it was left there, and we don't know whose it is, but the same DNA has shown up in an investigation that my opposite number in Edinburgh's carrying out in Gullane, in East Lothian.'

'Where?' Martin asked.

'Gullane,' she repeated. 'I know, Sir Robert Skinner lives there, but his DNA's on record and this isn't it.'

'What does it tell you about its owner?'

'It belongs to a mature adult male, predominantly Scottish, with Irish influences. Does that mean anything to you, Sir Andrew?'

He frowned, eyes narrowing. 'It m—'

He was interrupted by the sound of the front door opening, then being closed again, firmly. 'Andy,' a female voice called out, 'what are those bloody cars doing in your driveway? I could hardly get parked, and it's pissing down outside.'

Karen Neville walked into the living room, to find four people staring at her, one of them with undisguised relief and a love whose existence he had forgotten until that moment.

Sixty-Seven

Noele McClair hung her coat and scarf on their hook on the wall of the DI's room. Its last occupant had been Sauce Haddock, until he had commandeered the unit's virtually unused conference room as the DCI's office. The cubicle had been redecorated in a general refurbishment, but it had not been enlarged. She found it constricting and spent most of her working day at a workstation in the open-plan space outside, but before heading there she took out her phone and rang Matthew Reid. She frowned as her call went straight to voicemail. 'That's the most walked dog in Gullane,' she muttered as the announcement played again in her ear. 'Matthew,' she said, after a beep told her when to begin, 'this is just to confirm tonight. I expect to be home by six; I'll be an hour or so in the kitchen so any time after seven will be fine. Unless,' she added, 'you've chucked me already. Either way, let me know, there's a love.' She bit her lip as she ended the message, hoping that she had not sounded unsure of her ground with him, and wondering about that last word. *That's the trouble with voicemail*, she thought. *Once it's out there, you can't call it back.*

She had reached her desk when she saw Haddock, beckoning

to her from his room. Dropping her handbag on to her chair, she went to join him. 'What's up, Sauce?' she asked.

'The balloon, possibly,' he replied. 'I had a call from Lottie Mann through in Glasgow. She has a murder scene that's so sensitive she couldn't tell me about it, a victim that she couldn't discuss, and a seemingly nailed-on suspect that she isn't allowed to name, even to me. She also has various DNA samples harvested from the scene that are still unidentified. Believe it or not, one of them connects to our non-investigation out in Gullane.'

'You're kidding,' McClair exclaimed. 'How?'

'God knows, but it's true. Remember the unidentified genetic material that was found in the Stevens and Alexander properties? It matches Lottie's trace, and Arthur Dorward is adamant that there is no possibility of a cock-up in his lab.'

'And identifying the owner's been dumped on us? Is that what you're saying?

Haddock nodded. 'Effectively yes, Lottie says she's at a dead end. To be honest, Noele, I don't even know where to begin. I have this feeling that both here and through there, we're looking at the perfect crime.'

Out of nowhere, a shiver ran through her.

Sixty-Eight

'Look, Karen,' Lottie Mann said, 'I appreciate this is a discussion you might prefer to have with Sir Andrew. Alongside that, as a divorcee myself, I could see your point if you say it has nothing to do with him and you'd rather he wasn't here. It's a discussion that has to take place; you'll realise that as a cop, but we can do it on your terms.'

'I don't have a problem either way,' Neville replied. 'My kids are fine; they seem happy with that quaint wee sergeant of yours. The fact is I came here to have this discussion, as you put it, with Andy. If you and the DCC have to be witnesses, so be it. As for Ms DaCosta, I'd rather not have her here given her professional connection, but if you say it's necessary, I'll put up with that too.'

'I think I still need her,' Martin said. 'Sorry, but I do.'

She nodded grudging approval.

'We'll need to record it,' Mann warned her. 'You okay with that?'

'Of course. I'd be doing the same.'

Mann, McGuire, and DaCosta all put recording devices on a central table and switched them on. Neville thought for a moment, then took out her phone and activated Voice Memo.

'Might as well,' she murmured. 'Not that I don't trust everybody here.'

'I don't know if I do,' Martin muttered. McGuire shot him a hard look but said nothing.

'Karen,' her fellow DCI began, 'where have you been for the last few days?'

'I've been away,' she said. 'In a cottage near Fort William.' She looked at Martin. 'I told you, Andy, I needed to do that, to get away to think about how I want the rest of my life to be.'

He nodded. 'That's what I've been telling them. Thanks for confirming it.'

'Did you go on your own?' Mann continued.

'Of course not, I went with a friend, within the lockdown regulations as we read them. His name's Clyde: I don't really think you need to know any more than that about him. He's part of the intelligence community; he and I have been having a relationship for a few weeks.' She gazed at Martin once again. 'Not in a relationship, having a relationship; there's a difference.'

'Friends with benefits?' DaCosta suggested.

'That's the phrase; a throwback to my young, free and childless days. Anyway, Clyde and I went off to his old CO's place, to which he has a key, and which not even his boss knows about, had bracing walks and decent sex, and I came to a decision.' She turned to McGuire. 'That's between Andy and me,' she added, shifting awkwardly in her chair, 'but this furniture has to go.'

Mann allowed herself a small smile.

'And now,' Neville continued. 'I've been very patient with you, but it's time for someone to tell me what the fuck is going on here. Why are two senior police officers and a very expensive lawyer in my ex-husband's house! And why is there an unmarked car at the entrance to the street and another round the corner?'

'I'll explain that,' McGuire said, 'but this is where Ms DaCosta goes and makes herself a coffee or joins Cotter and the kids. I promise you, Johanna,' he added, 'nothing's going to happen that'll be prejudicial to your client.'

'It's okay, Johanna,' Martin told her, and she left.

As the door closed, the DCC switched off all of the recording devices and updated Neville on everything that had happened in her absence, looking at her throughout, watching the colour leave her face.

'Calder's dead?' she whispered, as he finished. 'He was a lovely guy, with a background nearly as tough as Clyde's that he escaped from in the same way. Who would do that to him? And why?'

'We believe that he was mistaken for Clyde,' Mann told her. 'All the evidence that we had points to Sir Andrew. Most of it still does,' she added.

'Have you all had your common-sense glands removed?' she laughed, wide-eyed with astonishment.

'Fortunately, we haven't,' McGuire replied, 'or Sir Andrew would have been charged by now and in the remand wing in Edinburgh. If it had been anybody else . . .' he let the rest of the sentence hang in the air.

'What are you doing to find the real killer?'

'Everything we can,' Mann assured her. 'Can you help us?'

'Any way I can,' Neville promised, 'but shouldn't Clyde be in on this too?'

'We believe he is already, but in a freelance capacity. He hasn't been contactable since he resurfaced in Glasgow, spotted officers watching his flat and called Bob Skinner. Why him, I'm wondering?'

'Because Bob's the man he respects more than any other. If he can't call Clyde in, that means trouble.'

'Then let's try to head that off,' McGuire declared. 'Karen, we know that you had visited Clyde's flat where the killing happened. Did you know that MI5 owned it and that his permanent presence in Scotland was never disclosed to the Scottish Government, formally or otherwise?'

'No, I didn't. Clyde's always vague about what he does, even with me. Yes, I know he's a spook of sorts, but I thought he was a security consultant. That's how he describes himself. I thought that maybe he was an agent for mercenaries, possibly even one himself.'

'Did you ever discuss your relationship with him with anyone? I know that you didn't share with ACC Payne, but did you confide in anyone else?'

She chewed her lip and looked at the floor. 'I mentioned it to my Uncle Matt at the start of the fling. I told him I was seeing a guy and that he had a love nest in Candleriggs. He had a laugh about that. He told me where the name came from; he said it was where candlemakers worked, a safe distance from the tenements, so they didn't start any fires. He's not my real uncle, by the way,' she added. 'He was my dad's best mate, and we've been close since I was a child.'

'What does he do, your Uncle Matt?' Mann asked.

Neville blushed. 'He writes mystery novels; he's reasonably well known. He visits me a lot. When he does, he's always asking me for ideas. I've given him some, but when we get talking about it, it's obvious he doesn't really need my help, or anyone else's. He's brilliant; his imagination is . . . it's transcendent. I'd love him to be an influence on the kids, but that can't be.'

'Why not?'

'Uncle Matt has a very big down on Andy. He never really liked him, but when he left us and went back to the Skinner woman he really was incandescent. As fond as I am of him, I can't risk him passing that on to Andy's children. It's my fault, I'm afraid. He saw how angry I was over the witch, and I passed it on to him.'

'It sounds as if your Uncle Matt isn't a man to cross,' Mann observed. 'Do you happen to know how old he is?'

'I couldn't really tell you, but my dad would have been sixty-seven. He'll be around that I imagine.'

McGuire leaned forward, catching her eye. 'What's his full name, Karen?'

It was Martin who replied. 'His name is Matthew Reid, and he lives in Gullane. I was on the point of telling you that when Karen arrived.'

'Sir,' Mann said, quietly. 'We need to bring Sauce Haddock into this. We may have identified our overlapping DNA.'

Sixty-Nine

'Noele,' Sauce Haddock said, looking at the DI. 'You live in Gullane, so does Matthew Reid. Do you know him?'

'We've met,' she replied. 'He spoke at my mum's book group, and I was there. I've seen him a few times since then.' Every word was true.

'What did you think of him?'

'I thought he was funny and far more comfortable in front of an audience than I would have been.' Again, not a word of a lie.

'What do you know about him, beyond the fact that he has about fifty crime novels in publication?'

She paused, considering the question. 'I know he's in his sixties but possibly older. I know he lives alone, with only a year-old Labrador for company. I know that every Friday he drank in the Mallard Hotel, before it closed, with Bob Skinner and a few others.' *I know that he made me come twice, as if it was second nature to him.* The last sentence was spoken only in her mind. 'Why?' she asked. 'What do you know about him?'

'Absolutely nothing,' Haddock replied. 'To all intents and purposes, Matthew Reid doesn't exist, not the version who lives in Gullane. Jackie's checked him out and got nowhere. He doesn't seem to have a National Insurance number, or an NHS number, or a passport. He isn't a patient of the local medical practice, although he's a paying customer of the dentist, and he isn't drawing a state pension. His car's registered to an offshore company and his publisher's finance department says that all his royalties and advance payments go there too, paid to him directly because he doesn't have an agent. We've even looked for him through his grandmother. Jackie looked at press interviews, and articles about him. He's said on public platforms that his granny's maiden name was Armour, the youngest of a family of seven, and that's where he took his cop character's name from. It turns out that was a fiction too; the Registrar General's office couldn't find anyone close to fitting that description. Noele, the Matthew Reid that you've met,' Haddock sighed, 'he could be described as a figment of his own imagination.'

McClair felt as if a lump of ice had formed in the pit of her stomach. 'I believe he has a place in Spain,' she volunteered. 'Have you tried looking there?'

'No, but thanks, we will.'

'Have you spoken to Bob Skinner? He knows him better than most.'

'I've tried, but for once the gaffer's uncontactable.' He paused, looking at her. 'The one advantage that we have over Reid,' he continued, 'is that he doesn't know we have an interest in him. It'll be interesting to see how he reacts when we pick him up, as we will as soon as Lottie Mann and DS Cotter get here. Be ready to go, Noele. Both investigations need to be equally represented, Lottie's and ours.'

She took a deep breath and gazed at him. 'If Cotter's coming you should probably take a DS rather than a DI to make it truly equal. To be honest, Sauce, I'd rather sit this one out.'

He stared back at her. 'Why, FFS? This could be big. I thought you'd be keen for a piece of it.'

'I know,' McClair conceded. 'It's just that having met him, I wouldn't feel comfortable with it. Take Jackie instead. She spends too much time in the office.'

Haddock frowned, then shrugged. 'Okay, Noele,' he said. 'If that's how you feel.' He grinned. 'If you want to miss out on a celebrity arrest, that's up to you.'

Seventy

'I meant it about the furniture,' Karen said, firmly but with a smile.

'It's no big deal,' Martin replied. 'I walked into a furniture warehouse and bought it off the floor; I told them I wasn't about to wait three months for delivery. They were remarkably compliant; even gave me a twenty-five per cent discount.'

'You called yourself "Sir Andrew", didn't you?'

'Of course.' He winked. 'One of the hidden benefits of a knighthood is the negotiating power it brings you.'

'But does it earn you the money to take advantage?'

'Oh yes. I was paid top dollar in the US and could have made more if I'd stayed. The cable news networks are always on the lookout for expert input to their rolling coverage, and I was starting to make an impact there . . . the Capitol riots, for example. I was on CBS then; the knighthood was worth a fair few extra bucks to them. It gets attention on the captions, the producer said. Egalitarian society my arse!' he laughed. 'I could go back to America, you know. We could, all four of us, as a family. I have a couple of offers on the table that'll be there for another few months. For example, I could be Dean of the Criminology Faculty in a university in Philadelphia.'

'I thought your heart was set on politics now?'

'This might sound corny,' he replied, 'but my heart is set on you and the kids, and on putting us back together as a family unit.'

'Even though I've just come back from a few days in the north with another man?'

'Even though,' he repeated. 'It means nothing to me.'

'And Alexis Skinner? Does she mean nothing to you?'

'Alex will always be a friend, but that's it. I should never have gone back to her. Not that I ever really did; even after you and I were divorced, she and I never lived together.'

'You didn't make it work with her second time around,' Karen observed. 'Are you confident that we can?'

'I'm certain. I've had a lot of time to think about myself. I know what I am: an introspective, broody, grumpy, impatient son of a bitch, intolerant of other people's views—'

'You'll make a great MSP, that's for sure,' she said.

He laughed, out loud, realising it was something he had not done in months, even years. 'Self-improvement starts with self-awareness,' he replied, 'that's the truth.'

'Do you love me?'

'I love the mother of my children, that's all I can tell you. I'm a displaced middle-aged man who needs to base his life on a solid foundation and that is family. Do you love me?'

She smiled, and nodded. 'I always did, you boring old fart.'

'What about Clyde Houseman?'

'He has no part in you and me; that was entirely physical, and we both knew it. I told him when we left to come home what I was planning to do and he's fine with that.'

'Even if he now thinks I killed his brother?' Martin asked.

'I don't believe he does, but I will call him, to talk him into coming in if I can. I don't see him as a threat, though. Clyde's not a murderer, Andy; yes, he and his special forces unit left a trail of dead behind them, but he insists that they were all legitimate military targets.'

'And your Uncle Matt, what about him? Is he a killer?'

'The Uncle Matt I know, no he isn't. But consider what he does, the stories he weaves. If he decided to bring one of them to life . . . He really does hate you, Andy, that I know for sure.'

'Part of the case against me involves two hairs found in Calder Bryant's dried blood. Could he have come by them?'

Karen frowned, considering the question. 'The night you came to mine and we started to discuss getting back together: when you stayed over because you'd had a drink and we slept in the same bed without actually shagging or anything?'

He grinned. 'Because you'd had even more than me and went to sleep as soon as your head hit the pillow? Yes, I remember that.'

'Next morning, when you used my bathroom, did you use my hairbrush as well?'

Martin nodded. 'Yes, I think I did.' He tugged at his hair, which was lockdown length. 'In fact, I'm sure of it, I remember it. Sorry.'

'Forgiven. Well, Uncle Matt visited me a couple of days later. I told him all about me being involved with Clyde, but I said that I wouldn't let it get in the way of you and me getting back together, and I told him what had happened with us. I didn't say it had been platonic, though. He told me I was off my fucking head to be thinking that way, that I was laying myself open to being kicked in the guts again. But then he cooled down. He was fine again by the time he left, but he did go upstairs before then, to say goodnight to the kids, he said. If you left hairs on my brush, he could have got them then.'

'Is he strong enough, do you think to have done what was done to Bryant? After all, he's an old guy.'

'He's an old guy who works out in the gym, three days a week,' Karen pointed out. 'Look, face to face, against a young fit marine, he'd have no chance at all, but if he was able to overpower him in some way, he'd be strong enough to do the rest.'

'The Sainsbury's bag,' Martin exclaimed, his eyes widening. 'What?'

'They told me that Bryant's head was found in a Sainsbury's bag along with a receipt for my credit card. A while back, I thought that someone had been going through my recycling boxes. At the time, I put it down to squirrels. Now . . .'

She stared at him. 'Uncle Matt? Is that what you're suggesting?'

'Could be, if it was him.' He sighed. 'Fuck it, I don't know. Let's leave it to the professionals, and you make that call to Clyde.'

Seventy-One

'Where is the place?' Lottie Mann wondered aloud, as Haddock cruised quietly along the narrow road. Bare trees overhung them on either side and, as they crested a rise, the sea came into view.

'This is the address that Jackie Wright found on the electoral roll,' her colleague replied, 'the only public listing where we could find any trace of Matthew Reid. The houses have names, not numbers; Reid's is called "L'Altre". Jackie said it's Catalan for "The Other".'

'That's it!' Mann exclaimed.

Haddock's eyes followed her right-pointing finger, until they settled on a name board affixed to a tree, one of two on either side of a gap in a boundary wall. It was an entrance, but not obviously so; there was no property visible from the street. 'Jesus,' he whispered. 'It's as if the guy's house doesn't exist either.' He eased the vehicle between the two trees onto a narrow, curving red ash drive, with a high beech hedge on the left. There was no dwelling to be seen until they reached its end and made a sharp right turn.

'Are you sure we're going in here with legal authority?' Mann asked. 'We don't want to be screwing this up.'

'You've got reason to believe a crime has been committed,' Haddock replied, 'and DCI Neville's information points to Reid as a possible subject. That is right, isn't it?'

'Yes, that's right.'

'Then we have all the authority we need. If he refuses to cooperate, we can lift him. If he refuses to give us a DNA sample, Dorward's team can take it by force, when they get here.'

He drew to a halt; Cotter and Wright, who had been following in another vehicle, parked alongside him. Reid's home was modest, a single-storey dwelling with bay windows on either side of a covered vestibule, but the plot was extensive. To the right they saw a separate building, a glass-fronted unit with a flat, sloping roof. It faced west and would have caught the sun had the mid-afternoon sky not been leaden, with clouds bearing the promise of heavy rain. Inside, a computer sat on a fitted unit, and in the centre of the space there was a small table, with two chairs.

Haddock led the quartet to the bungalow's front door. When he reached out and pressed the bell set in the centre, to his surprise it swung open. 'Mr Reid,' he called out, his voice echoing, 'it's the police, we need to talk to you.'

They waited, for more than a minute. Haddock repeated his call, again with no response.

'Fuck this, Sauce,' Mann muttered. She pulled on sterile overshoes and gloves and strode past him, indoors. He and the sergeants followed suit and joined her.

The house was open plan, a single living space, much larger than the frontage had indicated. The kitchen and dining area was to the right; the rest was dominated by three large armchairs, facing a vast wall-mounted television set. The floor was wooden, without carpets or rugs, and everything was shining.

'Jackie, John,' Haddock murmured, 'get back outside. One of you look out for the Gartcosh team. They can't be far away. One of the main reasons we're here is to get a sample of Reid's DNA; we don't want to be doing anything that compromises it.'

'True,' Mann agreed. 'There's something very off here, Sauce. The place smells of something. I can't put my finger on it.'

'It smells of clean,' he replied. 'It's shining, everything's spotless. Do you want to take a look?'

She shook her head, her greater experience giving her an authority that he recognised. 'No,' she said, 'you were right. We should wait for the SOCOs. Reid's not here to be found. Did you see a car outside?'

'No,' he admitted, shaking his head.

'No,' she repeated. 'Something's spooked him. I can only hope it wasn't Karen Neville calling him to warn him. Whatever, he's gone.'

'Agreed,' Haddock murmured. 'Was he ever really here? It seems that our mysterious author's a work of fiction too. So, who the hell is he?'

Seventy-Two

'DCI Neville,' Lowell Payne said, wearily. 'You work in counter-terrorism and intelligence-gathering. I know you signed off on leave, and I know that you needed a clear head to sort out your personal life, but the first rule of the turf for officers in our department is to be contactable at all times. That means never switching off your mobile.'

'I'm sorry, sir,' she replied, contritely. 'I know that, and I shouldn't have, but things have been quiet lately, so I took a chance. It wasn't the office I was thinking about; I didn't want Andy contacting me at that time. My head was a mess.'

'At least you've still got a head,' the ACC grunted, 'unlike Clyde Houseman's brother. What about Houseman?' he added. 'Do we have a problem there?'

'No. I called him and told him that Andy's no longer a suspect. It took a wee while, but eventually he believed me. I've heard from him since. He's been in touch with his boss, and she's told him to contact the SIO in the case and cooperate, without any mention of the Security Service. As far as Lottie Mann's report is concerned, he'll be an ordinary civilian.'

'Is there really no chance at all,' Payne wondered, 'of this being a terrorist incident, given what Houseman used to do in his special forces days?'

'I did ask him that,' Neville said. 'He says no. When they went on a mission they never left anyone behind to identify any of them, and they wore no ID themselves, not even dog tags, in case of capture. I can barely believe it, but the only suspect, so far,' she added, hoping to be contradicted but knowing that would not happen, 'is Uncle Matt.'

'In that case,' Payne said, 'it's probably best that you continue your leave.'

'I was planning to anyway,' she told him. 'Andy and I have stuff to sort out. We're getting married again.'

'Jesus,' he laughed. 'DCI Lady Martin. How's that going to look on your warrant card? If that's the case, it's all the more important that Lottie and Haddock catch Matthew Reid before he finds out.'

Seventy-Three

'The early indications are,' Arthur Dorward said, 'that the place is pristine.'

'All of it?' Lottie Mann exclaimed. 'The whole property?'

'Yup. It's been sterilised, everything has been wiped, probably room by room over a period of a few days. Everything that could have yielded a fingerprint or any bodily fluid or secretion, or hair.'

'According to the photo on his book covers Reid's stone bald,' John Cotter pointed out.

Dorward glowered at him. 'Only if he shaves his crotch, his chest, and his oxters,' he barked.

'What about his clothing? His underwear?' Sauce Haddock asked.

'There's none here. It's all gone. There are very few signs that anyone ever lived here.'

'Crockery, cutlery?'

'Every plate, cup, saucer, knife and fork is in the dishwasher, having been through a high temperature wash programme. He's left not a trace behind,' he paused, 'except . . . we found his dog, locked in a puppy crate in a conservatory to the side of the house. My excellent technician Paola reckons she might have lifted a viable partial print from that. We don't have Reid's on record, obviously, but if it gives us DNA as well, we can compare that with the site in Glasgow and the two in Gullane where we have the same unidentified genetic material.'

'The computer,' Mann said. 'Even if that and the keyboard are clean, there may be helpful material in there. I'll have that back in Glasgow.'

'Or I'll have it in Edinburgh,' Haddock countered.

'You might as well take half each,' Dorward chuckled, 'because there's no hard disk in it.'

The DCIs looked at each other. Mann sighed. 'There's nothing at all? No physical evidence?'

'Well, there's this.'

Dorward brought his left hand round from behind his back and held up an evidence bag, containing a large, bladed object. 'It's a kukri,' he announced, 'a type of machete made famous by the Gurkha soldiers. It was wall-mounted in his office, and it's sheathed. That of itself is interesting, because there was another empty mount below it. I'm thinking that used to hold the sheath, separately. Legend has it that the blade couldn't be re-sheathed until it had drawn blood. Are you a betting woman, DCI Mann?'

'The Candleriggs murder weapon,' she said, anticipating what was coming next.

He nodded. 'It's sharp enough to do the job, that is for sure.'

The sound of Haddock's ringtone cut into the silence that followed. His colleagues watched him as he took the call, taking in his reaction to the message he was being given, waiting until it finished.

'Reid's car's been found,' he said, 'beside the Whiteadder

reservoir, up beyond Garvald. There's no sign of him, though. Arthur, you need to get people there, now.'

The veteran scientist frowned at him. 'Tell me something I don't know, boy.'

Seventy-Four

'I appreciate you coming here, officers,' Paul Dorward said as he walked into the meeting room at Gartcosh Crime Complex. 'My dad meant to meet you himself, but he's working in the lab, double-checking everything. What I'm going to tell you is subject to confirmation, but I don't have any doubt that it'll stand up.'

Mann and Haddock gazed back at him. Their respective partners had each given them a degree of grief over their early start, on a weekend, but they knew that the forensic team had been working through the night and so they simply nodded understanding.

'The Candleriggs murder,' the younger Dorward began. 'This is going to be incredibly frustrating for you, DCI Mann, but we can't say categorically that Matthew Reid's kukri killed Calder Bryant. The handle is absolutely clean; there are no traces of the user, none at all, on either the weapon or the sheath. We even looked inside the sheath hoping for deposits there, but we found nothing. As for the blade, we hoped, maybe even expected, that we would find microscopic traces of blood, skin, flesh or bone, possibly all four, but we couldn't. The knife has been subjected to the same cleaning process as Reid's

342

house was. Without his DNA for comparison, we can't put him in Glasgow for you, nor can we prove that his knife was ever in that flat.' He turned to Haddock; the younger DCI saw him frown and found it ominous. 'I have more for you, Chief Inspector, but you are not going to like it.'

'I haven't liked a single thing about this investigation so far,' Haddock replied. 'Why should that change?' His baby's favourite toy was Winnie the Pooh's dolorous donkey friend, Eeyore; he felt a sudden kinship.

Paul Dorward smiled, but only briefly. 'Matthew Reid's car,' he continued. 'Mercedes C Class, Night Edition, a lovely piece of kit. That had been super-cleaned as well, like the house and office, but we did lift identifiable prints from the steering wheel. They were a match for the partial print that Paola lifted from one of the bolts of the puppy crate where we found Reid's dog . . . which is now in police kennels,' he added, 'in case either of you were wondering.'

Mann was no dog lover. 'I wasn't,' she growled.

The young scientist blinked, then returned his gaze to Haddock, more than a little nervously. 'We've identified those fingerprints,' he continued, hesitantly, as if he was delaying the moment, 'although this is the part that my dad is double-checking. They belong to Sir Robert Skinner.'

Seventy-Five

'What the f . . . have we got to do here?' Mario McGuire pondered aloud.

Lottie Mann had headed home from Gartcosh, frustrated, deflated, and sworn to keep the secret even from Dan Provan. Sauce Haddock, on the other hand had called his immediate boss, ACC Becky Stallings, who had considered the situation for less than ten seconds before instructing him to call the DCC.

They sat at McGuire's kitchen table, hands clasped round mugs of coffee, with ciabatta stuffed with Italian sausage on a plate between them.

'We can't ignore it, sir,' Haddock said, regretting his words immediately under the weight of the deputy chief's heavy black eyebrows.

'Of course not,' he murmured. 'Those are Bob's prints, no question, and we have his DNA on the scene of all three deaths that you're looking at. We've got to question him, as Lottie did with Andy Martin, but without the less-than-helpful input of a twat like Cotter. We'll need to do it formally too, if it comes to that.'

'If?'

'If we can't sort it out informally.' McGuire picked his phone up from the table and opened WhatsApp. As Haddock watched, he went through his list until he found 'Bob', clicked the audio symbol, and put the device on speaker.

There was a delay of a few seconds, but eventually they heard a tone. A few seconds later, they heard an answer. 'Mario,' Skinner said. 'What's up on WhatsApp?' Neither McGuire nor Haddock reacted to the pun.

'We have a problem, Bob,' the DCC said.

They heard a laugh. 'As in Apollo Thirteen? Houston? You sound like Tom Hanks.'

'I wish this was a film, Bob, but it's not.'

'How can I help?'

'Matthew Reid, the author, you know him, yes?'

'Yes, I know him. He's a friend and a near neighbour. We've been working together in the village resilience group. What's wrong with him? He hasn't died, has he? We've had too many seniors passing away lately, and he is definitely in that age group.'

'How much do you know about him, gaffer?' Haddock asked.

'Are you there too, Sauce? This must be really serious.' Skinner still sounded amused. 'As it happens, I know less about Matthew than I thought I did.'

'Have you ever had a problem with him?'

'Only when he forgot to get his round in at the Mallard one Friday. Otherwise, never. Why?'

'Because he's disappeared,' McGuire said. 'He's gone and all traces of him have been wiped from his house. All traces of everything in fact, apart from fingerprints on his dog crate.'

'What about the dog?' Skinner asked, suddenly engaged in the discussion.

'He's okay. However,' the DCC continued, 'his car was gone too, but it turned up, also clean as a whistle apart from the same prints on the steering wheel. And Bob, they're—'

'Are you going to tell me they're mine?' Skinner asked.

'How did you know?'

'Never play poker, Mario; you offer every fucking card in your hand, every time, even on audio. A blind man could read you.'

'Bob, do you need to make a statement?'

'No, I need to ask a question. When's all this supposed to have happened?'

'Within the last couple of days.'

'I see.' They heard a deep breath. 'Mario, put me on video.'

'Okay. I'll switch you to my tablet as well.' He opened the app on his iPad, then pressed the camera icon. A few seconds later, Skinner appeared on screen. The background was unfamiliar to either detective, but clearly it was an office. 'Hold on,' he said. As they watched they saw him pick up another phone, from a desk, and say a few words. 'Now wait.'

They did as they were told, listening to a door opening in the background and to a brief conversation in a language neither understood fully, although the DCC's Italian back-ground offered him fragments.

Skinner pointed his phone at the newcomer, a man in his mid-thirties. 'Tell them who you are, Hector.'

'Certainly,' the man said, in accented English. 'My name is Hector Sureda, and I am the CEO of the Intermedia communications group. I report to Senor Robert.'

'Where are we, Hector, you and I?'

'We are in the group headquarters, in Girona, in Catalunya.'

'Why am I here and when did I arrive?'

'We are negotiating the takeover of a media group in Florida, and you are involved as Presidente of our company. You have been here for four days, and we are still not done. Almost, but not quite.'

'Thanks, Hector, I think that's all my friends will need.'

Skinner came back on camera. 'Somebody's been playing games, boys. It's up to you to prove who it is.'

'Have you ever driven Reid's car, gaffer?' Haddock asked.

'No, never. I've never even sat behind the wheel. Nor have I ever touched his puppy crate.'

'Then how did your prints get on them both?'

'That's a very good question,' Skinner conceded, as a slow smile spread across his face. 'I think I know the answer, but I'll let you two work it out for yourselves. That, as they say, is why they pay you the big bucks.'

Seventy-Six

'I'm sorry to call you in at the weekend,' Sauce Haddock said to the colleagues seated around his table, 'but I thought you'd all want to be involved given the amount of effort you've put in. Jackie's excused,' he added, 'as she promised to look after her wee nephew today.'

'It feels like the end of a Poirot novel,' Tarvil Singh remarked, 'only there's no cast of suspects. Did you ever consider a waxed moustache, Sauce?'

'Fuck off, Sergeant.' He laughed, in spite of his gloom. 'Your analogy's a good one, though. We've all worked our arses off here, you, Noele, Tiggy . . . especially you Tiggy, brand new in the door . . . and what do we have to show for it? Sweet Fanny Adams as my grandpa used to say whenever my granny was near enough to hear him . . . what he said when she wasn't you can all guess.'

'We've been played, haven't we?' McClair sighed. *Me more than anyone*, she thought, *and yet maybe I wasn't*, as her denial gene kicked in. *Maybe it was just two single people having a fuck, and nothing to do with the rest.*

'We don't even know that for certain,' the DCI replied. 'If anyone has, it's the gaffer. He was at the scene of all three sudden deaths at one time or another and he even found two of them. Plus his prints were planted in Reid's house and car.'

His eyes narrowed. 'What can we prove, Noele? Not a fucking thing. It's still entirely possible that all those three deaths were what we assumed them to be. Equally it's possible that Mr Stevens' blood-thinning drugs were doctored, and he was fed an overdose in a whisky – although if he was, we'll never know whether it killed him; it's possible that Mrs Alexander was hit with the shelving that's gone missing; and it's possible that Mrs Eaglesham was tasered to subdue her like we know the Glasgow victim was, before having her arm plunged into that machine, earthed through a nail that had been raised for the purpose.

'With the involvement of young Rory and his camera footage showing how all these things could be done you might even say it's overwhelmingly likely, but nothing is overwhelming if you cannot fucking prove it beyond a reasonable doubt and, Goddammit,' he snapped, 'we can't!' Haddock was furious in his frustration, a side of him that neither McClair nor Singh had ever seen in the years they had worked together.

'We can't find Rory's Alan Campbell,' he continued, 'and we have no physical description of him, meaning we can't prove either, that he and Matthew Reid are one and the same ... that's if they are. To put the tin helmet on it, in the absence of proof of Reid's role in the deaths, and with his total disappearance, maybe we're wrong in our assumptions and he's now a victim himself. Maybe he and all his clothing really are lying weighed down on the bottom of the Whiteadder Reservoir, as the evidence suggests, too deep for any angler ever to snag his line on. We can't rule anything out, not even that.'

'Have we tried everything, Sauce?' Tiggy Benjamin

ventured. 'Does nobody know anything about the man?'

'There is one last shot,' Haddock replied. 'Reid's an author, with a publisher. It's called Portador Mystery and within that outfit, he'll have an editor. I've reached out to him and I'm waiting, no, I'm hoping for a call. If I don't hear from him in ten minutes, I'm ordering pizza takeaways because that's as near as I can get to taking everybody out to lunch in this bloody lockdown and wrapping up this investigation.'

'Has it got to be pizzas?' Singh moaned.

'Yes, but you can have two, you fat bastard.'

'Then why wait for a call that's not going to happen?' the DS asked. 'We might as well order them now.'

'True,' the DCI conceded. 'Get on line and everyone can make a cho—' His ringtone stopped him in mid-sentence.

He snatched his mobile from his pocket. The number displayed meant nothing to him, but he hoped for the best and took the call, on speaker. 'DCI Haddock,' he called out, 'with three others.'

'How intriguing,' a young male voice exclaimed. 'I'm Freddie Hagen, Matthew Reid's editor at Portador Mystery. What's the problem? Has he crossed a line in one of his novels? I do hope not.'

'No,' Haddock replied. 'We're trying to contact him, that's all. So far we've been unable to find him and I'm wondering if you know where he is.'

'I've been trying to contact him too,' Hagen said, 'with as little success as you. I've just finished reading the manuscript of his latest book. He sent it to me two days ago, and I want to tell him it's brilliant. It's the perfect mystery novel. I've never read anything like it; a crime story without a crime and without a perpetrator.'

As he spoke, Noele McClair heard his words in her mind as she had heard them before, trying without success to suppress a shudder, although no one saw it. *He really did*, she thought, *and he lived it. We all did. Jesus we're all bloody characters. I'll bet he even shags one of the cops.*

'Is it first person?' she asked.

'No, but he's built it around himself, obviously.'

'Using his own name?'

'No, in the book he calls himself Alan Campbell.'

'Fuck!' Haddock hoped that his whisper had been inaudible. 'Can I ask you something, Mr Hagen?' he continued, quickly. 'Does any of the story take place in Glasgow?'

'No, it's all set in his home village. Why do you need to speak to him?' the editor asked.

'Nothing important,' he replied. 'It's just something that's happened at his house, only he's not around. Given that we're in lockdown conditions here in Scotland, we're surprised by that.'

'Really?' The first note of concern sounded in Hagen's voice. Haddock wondered if he had described scenes in the novel.

'It's nothing,' he said. 'It involves his dog, that's all. '

'Sunny? Oh dear, what a shame. As for getting in touch with him,' he continued, 'I don't know that I'm going to be able to help. I'm his editor, but I haven't been with Portador for long. We've never managed to meet face to face and the only contact I've had with him is by email. Ours is a very basic relationship. He sends us a book every year and we send him money rather more often than that; probably less than they're worth, truth be told, especially this one. The best I can do, Mr Haddock, is to ask him to call you if he gets in touch with me.'

'Please do that, Mr Hagen,' the DCI said, ending the call and looking around the table, at three stunned expressions.

'Mine's a calzone,' Singh whispered. 'Double.'

Seventy-Seven

'He really has done us, Noele,' Haddock sighed, gazing at the discarded pizza boxes. Singh and Benjamin had gone home, leaving their senior officers to clear up. 'Every step of the fucking way, never giving us anything we could pin down. But leaving no DNA trail behind him, nothing tucked away anywhere. Imagine that; it's bloody genius.'

'Maybe not quite,' Noele McClair murmured. As they had eaten, in silence, she had been thinking, analysing, wondering. Haddock had called Hagen back and persuaded him to send them a copy of Reid's manuscript. Would she be in it, in a thinly disguised form? Would their relationship be exposed or had that been something really private?

'Glasgow was different,' Haddock continued, unaware of her observation. 'The real life, real death, story he created in Gullane, the three murders that we can never prove, the red herring of the gaffer's prints in his car . . . all of that was a game, an intellectual exercise, an ego trip by a minor author trying to prove that he really is the best, before disappearing off into the shadows. Glasgow though, that was different; that was vicious, malicious, rage-fuelled. I believe that was the real man, and he's a fucking monster.'

She nodded. 'He surely is.'

As she had devoured half of her four-cheese special, as much as she could manage, Noele's mind had wandered, until it had taken her to her earliest days in CID, when she had been a detective constable on a rape unit in Glasgow. What had she been taught? A viable sample could be recovered from a victim for up to five days; she counted back on her fingers, one at a time . . . without reaching her thumb.

But nobody's perfect, she thought. *He didn't use a condom.*

'Yes, he's really done us,' Haddock sighed.

'Maybe not quite,' she repeated.

She looked at him directly, eye to eye. 'Sauce,' she said, 'there's something I need to tell you.'